PENGUIN BOOKS

WARS

Angus Calder read English Literature at Cambridge and produced a doctoral thesis, on Second World War politics in Britain, at the University of Sussex. After *The People's War: Britain 1939–1945*, published in 1969, his next large-scale work was *Revolutionary Empire* (1981, new edition 1998), a survey of the rise of the English-speaking empires from the fifteenth century to the American War of Independence. Meanwhile, in 1979, he became Staff Tutor in Arts with the Open University in Scotland, retiring early in 1993 with the title Reader in Cultural Studies. *The Myth of the Blitz* appeared in 1991, and a collection of essays, *Revolving Culture: Notes from the Scottish Republic*, in 1994. He co-edited, with Paul Addison, *Time to Kill: The Soldier's Experience of War in the West 1939–1945* (1997).

He has lectured in literature at several African universities and published extensively on nineteenth-century Russian fiction, on African literature, and on English and Scottish literature. For some years he co-edited the *Journal of Commonwealth Literature*. For Penguin, he has edited novels by Dickens, Scott and Waugh, and poetry by Burns and R. L. Stevenson. He has latterly collaborated on a comprehensive edition of the hitherto uncollected prose of Hugh MacDiarmid. He has published verse here and there all his life, won a Gregory Award in 1967, and brought out his first volume of poems, *Waking in Waikato*, in 1997.

Since 1971, he has lived in or around Edinburgh, where he was the first Convener of the Scottish Poetry Library, founded in 1984.

WARS

Edited by
ANGUS CALDER

PENGUIN BOOKS

PENGUIN BOOKS

Published by the Penguin Group
Penguin Books Ltd, 27 Wrights Lane, London W8 5TZ, England
Penguin Putnam Inc., 375 Hudson Street, New York, New York 10014, USA
Penguin Books Australia Ltd, Ringwood, Victoria, Australia
Penguin Books Canada Ltd, 10 Alcorn Avenue, Toronto, Ontario, Canada M4V 3B2
Penguin Books (NZ) Ltd, Private Bag 102902, NSMC, Auckland, New Zealand

Penguin Books Ltd, Registered Offices: Harmondsworth, Middlesex, England

Published in Penguin Books 1999
10 9 8 7 6 5 4 3 2 1

Set in 9.5/12.5 pt PostScript Adobe New Caledonia
Typeset by Rowland Phototypesetting Ltd, Bury St Edmunds, Suffolk
Printed in England by Clays Ltd, St Ives plc

Contents

Acknowledgements

For permission to publish copyright material in this book grateful acknowledgement is made to the following:

ANNA AKHMATOVA: 'To the Victors' and 'And you, my friends', translated by Judith Hemschemeyer, from *The Complete Poems of Anna Akhmatova*, edited by Roberta Reeder (Zephyr Press/Canongate Books, 1992), © 1992 by Judith Hemschemeyer, by permission of Zephyr Press: GUILLAUME APOLLINAIRE: 'Fête' translated by Patrick Creagh (Open University Press, 1975), by permission of the publisher; LOUIS ARAGON: 'Stanzas in Memory,' translated by John Manson, from *Chapman Magazine*, 89–90 (1998), by permission of John Manson; W. H. AUDEN: 'The Shield of Achilles' from *Collected Poems*, edited by Edward Mendelson (Faber & Faber, 1991), by permission of the publisher, ISAAC BABEL: from *Lyubka the Cossack and Other Stories*, translated by Andrew R. MacAndrew (Signet Books, 1963), by permission of Marie-Christine MacAndrew; OMER BARTOV: from *Hitler's Army: Soldiers, Nazis, and War in the Third Reich* (Oxford University Press, 1992), © 1992 by Oxford University Press Inc., by permission of the publisher; from *Murder in Our Midst: The Holocaust, Industrial Killing, and Representation* (Oxford University Press, 1996), © 1996 by Oxford University Press Inc., by permission of the publisher; ALEKSANDR BLOK: 'The Twelve', translated by Jon Stallworthy and Peter France, from *Selected Poems*, translated by Jon Sallworthy and Peter France (Penguin Books, 1974), by permission of the publisher; HEINRICH BOLL: from *Children Are Civilians Too*, translated by Leila Vennewitz (Penguin Books, 1976), by permission of Writer's House Inc., on behalf of the estate of the author; JACQUES BREL: 'Au Suivant' (Next') from *Oeuvre Integrale* (Editions Robert Laffont, 1986), 'Next', version by Mort Shuman and Eric Blau from *Souvenir Album: Jacques Brel is Alive and Living in Paris* (Hill and Range Songs Inc., 1968), © Editions Musicales Pouchenel, Bruxelles, 1964, by permission of Editions Musicales et Cinematographiques SPRL;

VERA BRITTAIN: from *Testament of Youth* (Virago Press, 1978), by permission of Mark Bostridge and Rebecca Williams, her literary executors, and Victor Gollancz, publisher; LUIS BUÑUEL: from *My last Sigh*, translated by Abigail Israel (Jonathan Cape, 1984), by permission of Random House UK Ltd; ITALO CALVINO: from *Adam, One Afternoon*, translated by Archibald Colqhuoun and Peggy Wright (Picador, 1984), by permission of Random House UK Ltd; PAUL CELAN: 'Death Fugue', translated by Michael Hamburger, from *Selected Poems* (Penguin Books, 1966), by permission of Michael Hamburger; LOUIS-FERDINAND CÉLINE: from *Journey to the End of the Night*, translated by Ralph Manheim (John Calder, 1988), by permission of the Calder Educational Trust; KEITH DOUGLAS: 'Sportsman' from *The Complete Poems*, edited by Desmond Graham (Oxford University Press, 1978), by permission of the publisher; MARGUERITE DURAS: from *La Douleur*, translated by Barbara Gray (Collins, 1986), by permission of HarperCollins Publishers; MARTIN GILBERT: from *A History of the Twentieth Century, Volume 1: 1900–1933* (HarperCollins, 1997), by permission of the publisher; DAVID GILMOUR: from *Curzon* (John Murray, 1994), by permission of the publisher; ROBERT GRAVES: from *Goodbye to All That* (Penguin Books, 1960), by permission of Carcanet Press; VASILY GROSSMAN: from *Life and Fate*, translated by Robert Chandler (Flamingo, 1986), by permission of HarperCollins Publishers; SEAMUS HEANEY: 'Summer 1969' from *North* (Faber & Faber, 1975), by permission of the publisher; MOIRA HEDGES: from *War Diary*, © the Trustees of the Mass-Observation Archive at the University of Sussex, by permission of Curtis Brown Ltd., London; JOSEPH HELLER: from *Catch-22* (Vintage, 1994), © Joseph Heller, 1955, by permission of A. M. Heath & Co Ltd. on behalf of Joseph Heller and Random House UK Ltd; RICHARD HOLMES: from *Firing Line* (Jonathan Cape, 1985), by permission of Random House UK Ltd; RUDOLPH HÖSS: from *Commandant of Auschwitz*, translated by Constantine Fitzgibbon, excerpted in *The Bloody Game: An Anthology of Modern War*, edited by Paul Fussell (Scribner's, 1991), by permission of Paul Fussell; RANDALL JARRELL: 'The Death of the Ball Turret Gunner' and 'Losses' from *The Complete Poems of Randall Jarrell* (Faber & Faber, 1969), by permission of the publisher; JOHN KEEGAN: from *The Face of Battle: A Study of Agincourt, Waterloo and the Somme* (Vintage, 1977), by permission of the author and Sheil

Land Associates; RUDYARD KIPLING: 'Epitaphs of War' from *Rudyard Kipling's Verse: Definitive Edition* (Hodder & Stoughton, 1940), by permission of A. P. Watt Ltd on behalf of The National Trust for Places of Historic Interest or Natural Beauty; DANILO KIŠ: from *The Encyclopedia of the Dead*, translated by Michael Henry Heim (Farrar, Straus & Giroux, 1989), translation © 1989, Farrar, Straus & Giroux Inc., by permission of the publisher; T. E. LAWRENCE: from *Seven Pillars of Wisdom* (Jonathan Cape, 1973), by permission of the Trustees of the Seven Pillars of Wisdom Trust; 'Lili Marlene' (Words by Hans Leip, Tommie Connor and Jimmy Phillips; Music by Norbert Schultze), © 1944 Peter Maurice Music Co Ltd/EMI Music Publishing London, London, WC2H 0EA, by permission of International Music Publications Ltd; PRIMO LEVI: from *If This Is A Man* (Abacus, 1987), by permission of Random House UK Ltd; CECIL LEWIS: from *Sagittarius Rising* (Peter Davies, 1966), by permission of Greenhill Books; ALFRED LICHTENSTEIN: 'Prophecy', translated by Christopher Middleton, from *Modern German Poetry 1910–1960*, edited by Michael Hamburger and Christopher Middleton (MacGibbon & Kee, 1962), translation © Christopher Middleton, by permission of Christopher Middleton; SORLEY MACLEAN: 'Death Valley' and 'Heroes' from *From Wood to Ridge: Collected Poems in Gaelic and English* (Carcanet Press, 1989), by permission of the publisher; LOUIS MACNEICE: 'Brother Fire' from *Collected Poems* (Faber & Faber, 1979), by permission of David Higham Associates; HARRY MULISCH: from *The Assault*, translated by Calire Nicolas White (Pantheon, 1985), © 1985 by Random House Inc., by permission of Pantheon Books, a division of Random House Inc; SEAN O'CASEY: from *Juno and the Paycock* from Plays: Volume 1 (Faber & Faber, 1998), by permission of the publisher; GEORGE ORWELL: from *Homage to Catalonia*, in *The Penguin Complete Longer Non-Fiction of George Orwell* (Penguin Books, 1983), © George Orwell, 1938, by permission of Mark Hamilton as the Literary Executor of the Estate of the Late Sonia Brownell Orwell and Martin Secker & Warburg Ltd; MIKLÓS RADNÓTI: 'Forced March' and 'Postcards' from *Forced March: Selected Poems of Miklós Radnóti*, translated by Clive Wilmer and George Gömöri (Carcanet Press, 1979), by permission of Clive Wilmer; ERIK HAZELHOFF ROELFZEMA: from *Soldier of Orange* (Sphere Books, 1982), by permission of Little, Brown UK Ltd; TADEUSZ RÓŻEWICZ: 'Pigtail' and 'Massacre of the Boys' from *They Came to*

See a Poet, translated by Adam Czerniawski (Anvil Press Poetry, 1991), by permission of Adam Czerniawski; NEILLIE SACHS: 'O the Chimneys', translated by Michael Roloff, and 'You Onlookers', translated by Ruth and Matthew Meade, from *Selected Poems* (Jonathan Cape, 1968), © Suhrkamp Verlag Frankfurt am Main 1961, by permission of Suhrkamp Verlag; JORGE SEMPRUN: from *Literature of Life*, translated by Linda Coverdale (Viking, 1997), translation © 1997 by Penguin Books USA; original text © 1994 by Editions Gallimard, by permission of Penguin, a division of Penguin Putnam Inc; VINCENT SHEEAN: from *Between the Thunder and the Sun* (Macmillan, 1943), by permission of The Peters Fraser & Dunlop Group Ltd; WILLIAM SHIRER: from *The Rise and Fall of the Third Reich* (Simon & Schuster, 1960), © The William L. Shirer Literary Trust, by permission of Noel Rae, Trustee; CLAUDE SIMON: from *The Flanders Road*, translated by Richard Howard (John Calder, 1985), by permission of the Calder Educational Trust; BORIS SLUTSKY: 'Clerks', translated by J. R. Rowland, from *Twentieth Century Russian Poetry* by Yevgeny Yevtushenko (Fourth Estate, 1993), © Doubleday, a division of Bantam Doubleday Dell Publishing Group Inc., by permission of Doubleday, a division of Random House Inc.; PETER STRONGMAN: from *Wartime Diary* (previously unpublished), by permission of the author; GEORG TRAKL: 'Lament' and 'Grodek', translated by Michael Hamburger, from *Selected Poems*, edited by Christopher Middleton (Jonathan Cape, 1968), by permission of the Michael Hamburger; LEON TROTSKY: from *The History of the Russian Revolution*, translated by Max Eastman (Pluto Press, 1977), by permission of the pulblisher; KURT VONNEGUT: from *Slaughterhouse 5* (Vintage, 1991), by permission of Random House UK Ltd; EVELYN WAUGH: from *The Diaries of Evelyn Waugh*, edited by Michael Davie (Penguin Books, 1979), by permission of The Peters Fraser & Dunlop Group Ltd; JONATHAN WILLIAMS: from *Mahler* (Cape Goliard Press, 1969), by permission of Random House UK Ltd; W. B. YEATS: 'Easter 1916', 'The Rose Tree', 'An Irish Airman Forsees His Death', and lines from 'Meditations in Time of Civil War' from *Colledted Poems* (Macmillan, 1950), by permission of A. P. Watt Ltd on behalf of Michael B. Yeats.

Every effort has been made to trace or contact all copyright holders. The publishers would be pleased to rectify any omissions brought to their notice, at the earliest opportunity.

Other Sources

Bobrowski, Joannes, *Selected Poems*, translated by Ruth and Matthew Mead (Penguin Books, 1971).

Brecht, Bertolt, *Mother Courage and Her Children*, translated by Eric Bentley, *Plays, Volume II* (Methuen, 1962).

Brooke, Rupert, *The Complete Poems* (Sidgwick & Jackson, 1932).

Conrad, Joseph, *Heart of Darkness* (Oxford University Press, 1990).

Deighton, Len, *Fighter: The True Story of the Battle of Britain* (Triad/ Panther, 1979). D'Este, Carlo, *Decision in Normandy* (Harper Perennial, 1991).

Ellis, John, *The Sharp End of War: The Fighting Man in World War II* (David & Charles, 1980).

Hašek, Jaroslav, *The Good Soldier Švejk*, translated by Cecil Parrott (Penguin Books, 1973).

Henderson, Hamish, '"Puir Bluidy Squaddies Are Weary": Sicily, 1943; in *Time to Kill: The Soldier's Experience of War in the West, 1939–1945*, edited by Paul Addison and Angus Calder (Pimlico, 1997).

Heym, Georg, 'War', in *Twentieth-Century German Verse*, translated by Angus Calder, edited by Patrick Bridgwater (Penguin Books, 1968).

Holub, Mairoslav, 'Five Minutes after the Air Raid', translated by George Theiner, in *Poems Before & After: Collected English Translations*, translated by Ian & Jarmila Milner, Ewald Osers and George Theiner (Bloodaxe Books, 1990).

Ledwidge, Francis, *Selected Poems*, edited by Dermot Bolger, introduced by Seamus Heaney (New Island Books, 1992).

Maclean, Fitzroy, *Eastern Approaches* (Penguin Books, 1991).

Malraux, André, *Days of Hope*, translated by Stuart Gilbert and Alastair MacDonald (Penguin Books, 1970).

Middlebrook, Martin and Everitt, Chris (eds.), *The Bomber Comand War Diaries: An Operational Reference Book* (Viking, 1985).

Miłosz, Czesław, *The Captive Mind*, translated by Jane Zielonko (Penguin Books, 1980); *The Collected Poems, 1931–1987* (Viking, 1988); *Native Realm: A Search for Self-Definition*, translated by Catherine S. Leach (University of California Press, 1981).

Owen, Wilfred, *Collected Poems*, edited by C. Day Lewis (Chatto & Windus, 1963).

Pennington, Reina, 'Offensive Women: Women in Combat in the Red Army', in *Time to Kill: The Soldier's Experience of War in the West, 1939–1945*, edited by Paul Addison and Angus Calder (Pimlico, 1997).

Quasimodo, Salvatore, *Selected Poems*, translated by Jack Bevan (Penguin Books, 1965).

Remarque, Erich Maria, *All Quiet on the Western Front*, translated by A. W. Wheen (Putnam, 1980).

Richards, Frank, *Old Soldiers Never Die* (Faber & Faber, 1933).

Rosenberg, Isaac, *Collected Works*, edited by Gordon Bottomley and Denis Harding (Chatto & Windul, 1937).

Schmidt, Heinz Werner, *With Rommel in the Desert* (Constable, 1997).

Simpson, Louis, 'Carentan O Carentan', in *The Bloody Game: An Anthology of Modern War*, edited by Paul Fussell (Scribners, 1991).

Ungaretti, Giuseppe, *Selected Poems*, translated by Patrick Creagh (Penguin Books, 1971).

US Airman, *Diary of an Unknown Aviator*, in *The Crowded Sky: An Anthology of Flight*, edited by Nevil Duke and Edward Lanchebery (Corgi, 1964).

Yevtushenko, Yevgeny, *Selected Poems*, translated by Robin Milner-Gulland and Peter Levi (Penguin Books, 1962).

Introduction

This book collects together writings of various kinds about wars in the European theatre (which includes the Near East and North Africa) during the first half of the twentieth century. Retrospective writing from the second half of the century broods, meditates and agonizes over the wars of the first. Though the selection embraces American writers who came to Europe, and American historians, it excludes European writing about colonial wars or the 1941–45 war in the Far East. It leaves out almost entirely the wars at sea, about which there seems to be no writing available in English of strength to compare with Wolfgang Petersen's film masterpiece *Das Boot* (1982). Even so, only a tiny fraction of the writers and topics that might have been included will be found here. My aim has been to find items and extracts with which to 'through-compose', as it were, each section in turn, and provide links between sections. Anthologies are books we drop into and pick'n'mix from – but I have imagined an ideal reader who would read this one right through in sequence.

Poetry has sometimes flourished on the battlefield itself. Most worthwhile war fiction (with the amazing exception of Malraux's *Days of Hope*) has evolved through memory and research years after. A high proportion of the most powerful writing from Europe and America in both these genres has dealt directly with international and civil wars. Countless memoirs and diaries exist in which professional and private writers have recorded their experiences. Penetrating journalists have reported on the battlefronts and explored the aftermaths of these traumas. Recently, the 'New Military History' has explored carnage with unprecedented sophistication.

Selection here from so much material concentrates upon what John Ellis calls 'the sharp end of war'. Queues for tomatoes and GI romances are amply anthologized elsewhere. This book is about killing and being killed. Its cartography is not one of commerce, but of slaughter.

I flick through a cheap atlas of the kind which my household, like most, contains. Dresden is there, but not Auschwitz. Étaples is there, but, amazingly, not Ypres (or 'Wypers' as First World War British Tommies called it). El Alamein features, and Cassino, but not Passchendaele, nor the Jarama River, nor the airfields in East Anglia whence RAF and USAAF bombers flew to pound German cities through storms of flak. I knew one man fairly well who flew in Bomber Command. After forty years he made a start on coming to terms with that experience. In the East, Stalingrad is now Volgograd. The villages through which the Hungarian Jew Miklós Radnóti passed on his forced march in 1944 are of course not visible, though the town of Brody, where Isaak Babel rode for the Red Cavalry against the Poles, is noted, and I think of my fictional neighbour in Edinburgh, Miss Jean, forever purporting to mourn her fiancé Hugh, Flower of the Forest fallen in Flanders, and of my friend's real-life mother, possessed by Alzheimer's in her eighties, still mourning her own true love dead in Sicily.

Most of Europe now appears to be at peace with national neighbours, except in and around football matches. The appalling return to the 'Former Yugoslavia' in the 1990s of certain scenarios of atrocity does not feature directly in this book, since I do not think we have focused yet on what this atavism portends in a time when TV cameras create the illusion that we know 'what it must be like' to be there. (Probably, scenes witnessed this way tell us more about television than about war, just as most war-shots by the formidable Robert Capo prompt us, primarily, to consider the problematics of photography.) I acknowledge the present-day Balkans in this anthology with a concluding extract from a story by a great Serbo-Croat writer, Danilo Kiš, who died before the eruption of 'ethnic cleansing'. It speaks for all the forgotten and anonymous dead.

Maybe they grew fruit, maybe flowers. Maybe they fished at weekends. They probably loved their mothers. Into the innocence of Christmas shopping, of evening strolls and plans for marriage or retirement, entered, in the era of industrialized murder and 'total war', monstrous evil. As H. G. Wells, who prophesied this evil in his *War in the Air* (1908), conceived matters, the problem was that most people lacked imagination to see it as evil. 'The horror, the horror' – the words given to the dying imperialist Kurtz by another prophet Joseph Conrad in his *Heart of Darkness* represent the feebleness of the discourse of 'European Civilization' in the face of imperialistic greed, atavistic cruelty and the miraculous new technology at the disposal of these forces.

The late distinguished actor Robert Urquhart went to war in 1939. He was not a published, let alone a professional, writer, and perhaps his verses speak more directly because of that:

> How joyously we heard the call
> Of bugle, fife and drum
> And carelessly we set aside
> The silly questions deep inside
> Until one morning after death
> We looked around and caught our breath
> Is this gray havoc which we see
> All that we did?
> Oh God forbid that you who follow us
> Disguise the horror of our deed . . .

It is precisely because Kurtz can utter the horror at last that Conrad's narrator can admire him.

It may be easy to explain the evil which makes nonsense of high-sounding ideals and perverts the use of brilliant inventions. Christians in the past had no difficulty with the idea that we are all born into sin as a consequence of Adam's Fall, and post-Darwinian natural history could readily persuade us that aggression and cruelty are innate in all human beings. In which case, there is no 'problem of evil'. The difficult questions ask: how can there be what we call 'good' and, related to that, how do societies cohere at all? A grim answer to these would be that 'good' is simply whatever Humpty Dumpty chooses to call it and that societies cohere by perceiving and coping with external threats from 'evil' embodied in people with different beliefs or differently shaded faces. Comradeship depends on scapegoating and exclusion of non-comrades.

Such an answer would not satisfy the finest writers represented here. It is because the imagination insists on them that not-evil and good can have serious, meaningful existence. 'For this world we live in', as a Brecht song puts it, 'none of us is bad enough'. Writing itself, 'exploding silences' (I borrow this phrase from the Ugandan poet Okello Oculi), reveals both horror and that which is not horror. Imagination inhabits the multi-ethnic plum-treed vastnesses of Joannes Bobrowski's 'Sarmatia', a Roman name, which he revived, for the debatable flatlands of Eastern Europe. It perceives with Kurt Vonnegut the ironic yet inspirational significance of a welcome given to American POWs by a blind German innkeeper after Dresden has been incinerated. It insists with Primo Levi that humanity can survive the death camps. When George Orwell asserted, in verses prompted by his service in the Spanish Civil War, that 'No bomb that ever burst / Shatters the crystal spirit', his utterance, which has no scientific or philosophical validity whatsoever, came to us from the arena where the imagination, through literature, forms its necessary truths.

Heart of Darkness is regarded as an important early manifestation of that 'Modernism' in the arts which strove to come to terms with a 'modern' Europe playing with new technological marvels. The motor car gained ascendancy, aeroplanes first flew, wireless and movies emerged as powerful new forces in the period – say, 1900–1930 – when Modernist experiment had its heyday.

If the US Civil War of 1861–65 might be seen as the first 'modern' war in its application of new technology and its 'total' character, it was in the twentieth century that the 'death factory' emerged as a central feature of 'modernity'. While many millions of Europeans died, some made vast profits out of manufacturing war materials. The colossal carnage of 1914–18, rendered possible by new technology, prefigured, Omer Bartov argues, Auschwitz.

Lenin's overall analysis was flawed, but his phrase 'imperialist war' sticks. The old territorial imperatives were mixed up with the drive for resources and markets of a blindly insatiable capitalism attempting to take over every inch of the world. In the First World War six empires contended in Europe and the Middle East, then the rising-imperial USA joined in. The Turkish Empire finally collapsed and the overweening challenge of imperial Germany was temporarily checked. The victors – Britain, her Dominions and France – acquired by League of Nations mandate control over former German colonies and Turkish provinces. The new Soviet Union failed to retain the western provinces of the Tsarist Empire. The freedom of Poland irked both Hitler and Stalin, and the Second World War began with the division of that country by their armies. However, the 'imperialist' character of the Second World War was never quite so clear-cut. Britain and France could be seen as contending for 'democracy' against Nazism, and the Soviet Union, while still in effect a vast multi-territorial empire, was not a capitalist-imperialist country. If the USA's second intervention in Europe emphasized its position as superpower and gave it hegemonic status over

Western Europeans and their colonies, no one in their senses could argue that Nazi domination was an acceptable alternative. Many people in Britain, as the left-wing poet C. Day Lewis put it, fought to 'defend the bad against the worse'. The noble aim of self-determination for all peoples set out by Britain and America in the Atlantic Charter of 1941 preceded bloody post-war conflicts in Africa and south-east Asia as whites tried unsuccessfully to hold on to privilege in their colonies. But the settled growing affluence of large areas of Europe made loss of direct overseas rule tolerable, and Europeans shared in the profits made by multinational corporations from what came to be called 'developing countries'.

Yet the subconscious of affluent Europe is still haunted, not only by accusing ghosts of Jews, but by the spectres of dead infantrymen. Convincing figures for casualties have never been assembled, but we can venture that the First World War killed up to ten million in battle and millions more from war-related causes. The Second World War was much more lethal: six and a half million Germans died, twenty-five million or many more in the Soviet Union. More than four million Poles died and Yugoslavia lost a tenth of its population. Deaths in concentration camps ran to eight figures. The bombing of cities became routine, so that carnage spread far from the battlefronts.

John Keegan in his Reith Lectures of 1998 argued that 'the worst of war is now behind us'. Much as I respect a pioneer of the New Military History who has influenced two generations of scholars enormously, I cannot share his optimism. Violent evil still moves in and around us, as we learn from reports of well-heeled football hooligans, of outwardly respectable connoisseurs of snuff videos, of rich wife-beaters and collectors of Nazi memorabilia.

Leaving the licentious soldiery out of 'social history', as British writers at least have tended to do, has involved gross distortion by omission. For many millions of Europeans in the twentieth century 'service' in armed forces has been a formative experience. Returning soldiers nursed physical wounds, great and small. They were commonly unable to talk to their wives and to civilian contemporaries about their experiences – the half-centenaries of D-Day in 1994 and VE Day in 1995 released an alarming flood of long-suppressed reminiscence. Trauma does not handle survivors lightly. It will never be possible to quantify the effects of war on men returning to civilian life, as expressed in depression, alcoholism, wife-beating and child-abuse. The football hooligans of the

1990s may have been giving vent to the secret brutalities of their grandfathers and great-grandfathers, passed down in a genealogy of rage. It is clear enough that massacres and counter-massacres among the southern Slavs in the same decade related to the atrocities committed by the Croatian Ustasa, given puppet power by the Nazis in 1941, and the reciprocal ferocity of Serbs and Bosnians. 'Those to whom evil is done', as W. H. Auden writes, 'do evil in return.'

The writings considered for this book have ranged from Derek Walcott's evocation of the Desert War in his Caribbean epic *Omeros*, through the soldierly memoirs of the New Zealand commander Kippenberger, to the casualty lists on the war memorial in a little Scottish Highland port, Lochinver. Variety of genres and modes was an end in itself. In the end, choice was determined by a quest for continuities. Granted that either the writing itself or the content of the writing was stark and striking, how would it fit in to my kind of story?

I begin with Conrad's prophecy, mentioned above, and two German Expressionist poets likewise prophetic. Prophecy came true, but why did men fight? My second section deals category by category with motivations impelling men to fight, those suggested by the New Military History, through examples chosen from several wars. Chronology then takes over, with the apocalyptic carnage of the First World War – exceeded later, but still definitive, the yardstick of all subsequent horrors, as when we say that Cassino was 'as bad as' the Somme (though nothing, I think, was ever as 'bad' as the Eastern Front from 1941 to 1945). Chronologically, again, the Russian Revolution, Irish independence and the Spanish Civil War, with, at the centre of the book, the death of one private citizen, the poet Lorca.

Where to place the Holocaust was always a problem. The Final Solution emerged in the middle of the Second World War. However, the idea of waging war against allegedly demonic enemies by extermination of passive populations was embodied in the *Einsatzgruppen* (mobile killing squads) first deployed by the Nazis in Austria in March 1938. They then followed the Wehrmacht into Poland in 1939. Their targets included the Polish élite and, later, Soviet commissars. But war against Jews, few of these armed or in uniform, became their major task. This was more than latent in 1930s Nazism. Indeed, it was latent in the use of poison gas by both sides on the Western Front in 1914–18 and in German bombing raids during that war, and it was akin to the logic of area bombing as the British followed it from 1941. In Total War, while the complete extermination of an opposing army would be useful, civilians also are seen as legitimate targets. In war against presumed demons, to settle matters 'for once and for all', the Final Solution is to kill mothers, children and women who might bear children. Paradoxically, however, the Nazis needed slave labour to service their economy. So under the smoke from the death-camp chimneys 'sub-human' Jews and Slavs endured the degradations of forced labour.

The term 'Blitzkrieg' became slippery, and I exploit the slip to move from the first application of the term to the Nazi advances in Poland and northern Europe in 1939–40, through the prolonged British experience of aerial bombardment nicknamed 'the Blitz', to the Allied bombardment of Germany. The two following sections refer to the battlefronts of 1941–45.

Grief and its consort guilt have been latent, sometimes apparent, throughout a book of which so much has been written retrospectively. But they need, and get here, a separate chapter, before the final 'Reckonings'. I use these last items and extracts to affirm my faith that very good writing can expand our imaginations, can create conscience, and can direct conscience. It will not 'save the world'. But it can help us stop things getting worse.

This last point was modified in my mind on Armistice Day, 11 November 1998, as a media orgy of lamentation and celebration connected with the eightieth anniversary of the end of the 'Great War' drew to a climactic close. In Flanders, centenarian veterans from Britain were present at a ceremony at the Menin Gate in Ypres where the names of 55,000 of the British Empire personnel killed in battles in the area in 1914–18 who have no known graves are listed. Queen Elizabeth II, who attended, had been kept very busy before this. With President Chirac of France she had been at the Arc de Triomphe to honour the dead at the Tomb of the Unknown Soldier, had joined him in unveiling a statue, in Paris, of Winston Churchill and then with the Irish President Mary McAleese had unveiled a 'peace tower' in the Belgian village of Messine, a few miles from Ypres. Protestant and Catholic Irish volunteers had erected this, in memory of those compatriots who fell in a local battle and as token of political reconciliation between North and South.

For days beforehand, documentary footage of the Great War (not all of it faked for propaganda purposes) had been seen on British TV, in this new era of '24-Hour News', literally morning, noon and night. It should have been clear to all watchers of any channel that horror, grief and anger still dominated the memories of very old men, conscripted now as 'talking heads', who had lost friends, and in some cases themselves suffered grievous wounds, more than eight decades before.

But the question which was rarely asked, if at all, was why the 'war to end all wars' had been followed in 1939 by a longer and (though not for Britain) still bloodier war? What forces in human nature and society have propelled us towards repetition of such horrors – in Vietnam, in the Gulf War? Next . . . ?

I was convinced on the evening of the 11th that an anthology such as this one, centred on killing, killing, killing, might be especially useful when I attended a reading in Edinburgh given by Gary Geddes, a redoubtable Canadian poet, new to most of the twenty-odd people who came to hear him. His imaginative, compassionate and painful sequence about the fate of the Canadian troops in the small Hong Kong garrison which was briskly overwhelmed by the Japanese in December 1941 was known to me already, so that I listened to understand it more fully. Two friends in the audience who had dedicated their lives to poetry – four or five decades in both cases – told me independently that they found these poems, on first encounter with them, almost unbearably horrible – too much. Having just exposed myself, for the purpose of making this anthology, to the colossally greater horrors of the 1941–45 Eastern Front and the attendant Holocaust, I suddenly had a feeling akin, however mildly, to those of Graves, Owen and Sassoon back in Britain from the still-raging Great War: 'These civilians – they *don't understand*.' Yet my friends had certainly absorbed these major writers, the 'war poets', probably starting as I did, aged round fifteen, at school. And that was the problem – they *had* absorbed them. These writers had become 'classic' and even 'beautiful', as remote as the *Iliad* and the *Henry IV* plays well known to civilian acquaintances of the 'war poets'.

I hope that this book, positioning Graves beside Céline, Owen in relation to Trakl, de-anaesthetizes such readers, and younger ones, so as to restore vivid, immediate meaning to bleeding. In my experience, lecturing in public where they have been present, veterans don't object to my suggestions that killing is horrible in all cases and that the British, too, have committed 'atrocities'. I have sensed that they may be relieved when a view of war centred on its immediate objective – killing – is presented, carefully, by someone in possession of truthful information.

Owen insisted that it was not 'sweet and decorous to die for your country', yet, absorbed into the cultural mainstream, he was quoted on and before 11 November 1998 by people committed to suggesting that, somehow or other, it had been.

While picking my somewhat random way through bookshops and libraries, I have been grateful for conversations, suggestions – not always taken, sorry – review copies and other help, to various people, including Chris Agee, Peter Arnott, Liz Calder, Michael Glenday, Rosemary Goring, Alasdair Gray, Catherine Lockerbie, Annalena McAfee, Celia Nazir, Ronan O'Donnell, Ana Pinto, Mario Relich, Kenneth Richards, Dorothy Sheridan, Zara Steiner, Jean Urquhart (thanks for Robert's poem) and the indefatigably generous Eric Wishart. My friendly-neighbourhood-booksellers Sally Evans and Ian William King of Old Grindle's have been subjected to my neuroses almost daily. I owe my serious introduction to military history to transactions with the Department of History at Edinburgh University, and in particular to Paul Addison and Jeremy Crang who now direct the Centre for Second World War Studies there. Paul Keegan of Penguin Books, as always, has been a great source of erudition and ideas. Much-felt thanks also to Penguin's Anna South, and Monica Schmoller.

I feel just now that I should dedicate this book to the memory of my children's Great Uncle Harry, from Aberdeen, dead in the 1914–18 Royal Flying Corps, and to those unknown relatives of theirs on the other side of their mother's family who once lived in the Vilnius Ghetto. But I should extend dedication also to my living friend and mentor Hamish Henderson, soldier, scholar, poet and singer.

January 1999
Edinburgh

1

Prelude: Voices Prophesying War

At the turn of the twentieth century the symptoms of imperialist war were becoming plain. Britain and France sparred in Africa, then made it up. The Russians took on the just-modernized Japanese and were humiliated. The USA hounded Spain out of Cuba and the Philippines. A naval arms race developed between the most obvious rivals, Britain and Germany. German industry was more advanced and its products had knocked the British out of numerous markets. But Britain had many colonial possessions, Germany relatively few.

A sense that European war must come was shared by many intellectuals across the continent. Much popular fiction traded in fantasies of future war. It is not easy to say whether certain ideological tendencies should be classed as causes or as symptoms of war fever. There was the pseudo-Darwinian idea that among human races 'the fittest' must assert itself by conquest – Europeans over Asiatics and Africans, obviously, but Teutons, perhaps, over Latins and Slavs. There was the morbidity of the Wagnerian ethos allied to the cult of Norse Gods, and the Celtic Twilight of Arthurian, Ossianic and Fenian heroes – while the mild Irish poet Yeats merely dreamed of violence, some of his fellow-countrymen were beginning to think again of armed revolt, in a long tradition. Nationalism pervaded the utterance of large countries and smaller repressed ethnicities. Socialists, syndicalists, communists and anarchists cherished their various conceptions of 'class war' and social revolution, some of them specifying or implying violence. There was the anti-Christian philosophy of Nietzsche. One might add to all these the energies of artistic Modernism, directed in violent assault upon bourgeois sensibilities and representing the frustration of young people with their easy-living elders.

Meanwhile, technological advances were providing future warmakers with unprecedented opportunities. Petrol-driven vehicles were now a common sight. The first motor-bicycle arrived in 1901, the year in which Marconi successfully sent a 'wireless' message across the Atlantic. In December 1903 Orville and Wilbur Wright made the first successful flight in an aeroplane with a petrol engine. Italians were the first to practise aerial bombardment, against Turks in Tripoli in 1911–12.

Heart of Darkness

Joseph Conrad (born to Polish parents in the Ukraine in 1857 and baptized Jozef Teodor Konrad Korzeniowski) first published Heart of Darkness *in 1899 as a serial in* Blackwood's Magazine. *It appeared in book form in 1902, and became one of the most widely influential literary texts of the twentieth century, affecting writers as different as T. S. Eliot, V. S. Naipaul and, recently (for instance), Caryl Phillips, as well as informing the conception of Francis Ford Coppola's Vietnam War movie* Apocalypse Now *(1979).*

Its context is the notably vicious European exploitation of the Congo region, most of which King Leopold of the Belgians had acquired as a personal possession from the late 1870s. A conference of Western powers partitioning Africa in Berlin in 1885 recognized his 'Congo Free State' on the understanding that its trade would be open to all Europeans. It was formally annexed by Belgium only in 1908. Conrad worked on the great river in 1890 as a seaman in the employ of the Société Anonyme Belge pour le Commerce du Haut-Congo. Though Heart of Darkness *is marked by racist touches typical of its period, Conrad was a vehement critic of imperialism, and the novella exposes powerfully the rapacity and intrigues of the Société. Marlow, the seaman who tells this 'yarn' to a group of amateur sailors gathered on the Thames, takes a paddle steamer up river to relieve Kurtz, a charismatic employee of the Société who has acquired fabulous quantities of ivory by allying himself with Africans and 'going native'. On the way Marlow's black helmsman is killed by an arrow shot from the river bank. 'The pilgrims' is Marlow's ironic way of referring to Kurtz's colleagues who envy him and want him out of their way. Why include Kurtz in this anthology? Conrad uses him to illustrate what became, in the age of Freud and Jung, a truism for many intellectuals – that under the superstructure of 'liberal civilization', the ideology by which high-minded Europeans justified their subjugation of non-white peoples 'for their own good', lurked unaccommodated man, a bare forked animal prone to bestial appetites and savage excesses. The horrors of 1914–18 could be interpreted in the light of this. In so far as the 'great' wars of the twentieth century have been basically imperialist in motivation, Conrad's critique of the exalted professions which mask cynical self-interest, but convince* bien-pensant *middle-class persons that their nation has a just and noble cause, seems relevant to everything which follows in this book.*

There was a pause of profound stillness, then a match flared, and Marlow's lean face appeared, worn, hollow, with downward folds and dropped eyelids, with an aspect of concentrated attention; and as he took vigorous draws at his pipe, it seemed to retreat and advance out of the night in the regular flicker of the tiny flame. The match went out.

'Absurd!' he cried. 'This is the worst of trying to tell . . . Here you all are, each moored with two good addresses, like a hulk with two anchors, a butcher round one corner, a policeman round another, excellent appetites, and temperature normal – you hear – normal from year's end to year's end. And you say, Absurd! Absurd be – exploded! Absurd! My dear boys, what can you expect from a man who out of sheer nervousness had just flung overboard a pair of new shoes! Now I think of it, it is amazing I did not shed tears. I am, upon the whole, proud of my fortitude. I was cut to the quick at the idea of having lost the inestimable privilege of listening to the gifted Kurtz. Of course I was wrong. The privilege was waiting for me. Oh, yes, I heard more than enough. And I was right too. A voice. He was very little more than a voice. And I heard – him – it – this voice – other voices – all of them were so little more than voices – and the memory of that time itself lingers around me, impalpable, like a dying vibration of one immense jabber, silly, atrocious, sordid, savage, or simply mean, without any kind of sense. Voices, voices – even the girl herself – now –'

He was silent for a long time.

'I laid the ghost of his gifts at last with a lie,' he began, suddenly. 'Girl! What? Did I mention a girl? Oh, she is out of it – completely. They – the women I mean – are out of it – should be out of it. We must help them to stay in that beautiful world of their own, lest ours gets worse. Oh, she had to be out of it. You should have heard the disinterred body of Mr Kurtz saying, "My Intended." You would have perceived directly then how completely she was out of it. And the lofty frontal bone of Mr Kurtz! They say the hair goes on growing sometimes, but this – ah – specimen, was impressively bald. The wilderness had patted him on the head, and, behold, it was like a ball – an ivory ball; it had caressed him, and – lo! – he had withered; it had taken him, loved him, embraced him, got into his veins, consumed his flesh, and sealed his soul to its own by the inconceivable ceremonies of some devilish initiation. He was its spoiled and pampered favourite. Ivory? I should think so. Heaps of it, stacks of it. The old mud shanty was bursting with it. You would think there was not a single tusk left either above or below the ground in the whole country. "Mostly fossil," the manager had remarked, disparagingly. It was no more fossil than I am; but they call it fossil when it is dug up. It appears these niggers do bury the tusks sometimes – but evidently they couldn't bury this parcel deep enough to save the gifted Mr Kurtz from his fate. We filled the steamboat with it, and had to pile a lot on the deck. Thus he could see and enjoy as long as he could see, because the appreciation of this favour had remained with him to the last. You should have heard him say, "My ivory." Oh yes. I heard him. "My Intended, my ivory, my station, my river, my –" everything belonged to him. It made me hold my breath in expectation of hearing the wilderness burst into a prodigious peal of laughter that would shake the fixed stars in their places. Everything belonged to him – but that was a trifle. The thing was to know what he belonged to, how many powers of darkness claimed him for their own. That was the reflection that made you creepy all over. It was impossible – it was not good for one either – trying to imagine. He had taken a high seat amongst the devils of the land – I mean literally. You can't understand. How could you? – with solid pavement under your feet, surrounded by kind neighbours ready to cheer you or to fall on you, stepping delicately between the butcher and the policeman, in the holy terror of scandal and gallows and lunatic asylums – how can you imagine what particular region of the first ages a man's untrammelled feet may take him into by the way of solitude – utter solitude without a policeman – by the way of silence – utter silence, where no warning voice of a kind neighbour can be heard whispering of public opinion? These little things make all the great difference. When they are gone you must fall back upon your own innate strength, upon your own capacity for faithfulness. Of course you may be too much of a fool to go wrong – too dull even to know you are being assaulted by the powers of darkness. I take it, no fool ever made a bargain for his soul with the devil: the fool is too much of a fool, or the devil too much of a devil – I don't know which. Or you may be such a thunderingly exalted creature as to be altogether deaf and blind to anything but heavenly sights and sounds. Then the earth for you is only a standing place – and whether to be like this is your loss or your gain I won't pretend to say. But most of us are neither one nor the other. The earth for us is a place to live in, where we must put up with sights, with sounds, with smells, too, by Jove! – breathe dead hippo, so to speak, and not be contaminated. And there, don't you see? your strength comes in, the faith in your ability for the digging of unostentatious holes to bury the stuff in – your power of devotion, not to yourself, but to an obscure, back-breaking business. And that's difficult enough. Mind, I am not trying to excuse or even explain – I am trying to account to myself for – for – Mr Kurtz – for the shade of Mr Kurtz. This initiated wraith from the back of Nowhere honoured me with its amazing confidence before it vanished altogether. This was because it could speak English to me. The original Kurtz had been educated partly in England, and – as he was good enough to say himself – his sympathies were in the right place. His mother was half-English, his father was half-French. All Europe contributed to the making of Kurtz; and by-and-by I learned that, most appropriately, the International Society for the Suppression of Savage Customs had intrusted him with the making of a report, for its future guidance. And he had written it, too. I've seen it. I've read it. It was eloquent, vibrating with eloquence, but too high-strung, I think. Seventeen pages of close writing he had found time for! But this must have been before his – let us say – nerves, went wrong, and caused him to preside at certain midnight dances ending with unspeakable rites, which – as far as I reluctantly gathered from what I heard at various times – were offered up to him – do you understand? – to Mr Kurtz himself. But it was a beautiful piece of writing. The opening paragraph, however, in the light of later information, strikes me now as ominous. He began with the argument that we whites, from the point of development we had arrived at, "must necessarily appear to them [savages] in the nature of supernatural beings – we approach them with the might as of a deity," and so on, and so on. "By the simple exercise of our will we can exert a power for good practically unbounded," etc. etc. From that point he soared and took me with him. The peroration was magnificent, though difficult to remember, you know. It gave me the notion of an exotic Immensity ruled by an august Benevolence. It made me tingle with enthusiasm. This was the unbounded power of eloquence – of words – of burning noble words. There were no practical hints to interrupt the magic current of phrases, unless a kind of note at the foot of the last page, scrawled evidently much later, in an unsteady hand, may be regarded as the exposition of a method. It was very simple, and at the end of that moving appeal to every altruistic sentiment it blazed at you, luminous and terrifying, like a flash of lightning in a serene sky: "Exterminate all the brutes!" The curious part was that he had apparently forgotten all about that valuable postscriptum, because, later on, when he in a sense came to himself, he repeatedly entreated me to take good care of "my pamphlet" (he called it), as it was sure to have in the future a good influence upon his career. I had full information about all these things, and, besides, as it turned out, I was to have the care of his memory. I've done enough for it to give me the indisputable right to lay it, if I choose, for an everlasting rest in the dust-bin of progress, amongst all the sweepings and, figuratively speaking, all the dead cats of civilization. But then, you see, I can't choose. He won't be forgotten. Whatever he was, he was not common. He had the power to charm or frighten rudimentary souls into an aggravated witch-dance in his honour; he could also fill the small souls of the pilgrims with bitter misgivings: he had one devoted friend at least, and he had conquered one soul in the world that was neither rudimentary nor tainted with self-seeking. No; I can't forget him, though I am not prepared to affirm the fellow was exactly worth the life we lost in getting to him. I missed my late helmsman awfully, – I missed him even while his body was still lying in the pilot-house. Perhaps you will think it passing strange, this regret for a savage who was no more account than a grain of sand in a black Sahara. Well, don't you see, he had done something, he had steered; for months I had him at my back – a help – an instrument. It was a kind of partnership. He steered for me – I had to look after him, I worried about his deficiencies, and thus a subtle bond had been created, of which I only became aware when it was suddenly broken. And the intimate profundity of that look he gave me when he received his hurt remains to this day in my memory – like a claim of distant kinship affirmed in a supreme moment.'

. . .

'The brown current ran swiftly out of the heart of darkness, bearing us down towards the sea with twice the speed of our upward progress; and Kurtz's life was running swiftly, too, ebbing, ebbing out of his heart into the sea of inexorable time. The manager was very placid, he had no vital anxieties now, he took us both in with a comprehensive and satisfied glance: the "affair" had come off as well as could be wished. I saw the time approaching when I would be left alone of the party of "unsound method". The pilgrims looked upon me with disfavour. I was, so to speak, numbered with the dead. It is strange how I accepted this unforeseen partnership, this choice of nightmares forced upon me in the tenebrous land invaded by these mean and greedy phantoms.

'Kurtz discoursed. A voice! a voice! It rang deep to the very last. It survived his strength to hide in the magnificent folds of eloquence the barren darkness of his heart. Oh, he struggled! he struggled! The wastes of his weary brain were haunted by shadowy images now – images of wealth and fame revolving obsequiously round his unextinguishable gift of noble and lofty expression. My Intended, my station, my career, my ideas – these were the subjects for the occasional utterances of elevated sentiments. The shade of the original Kurtz frequented the bedside of the hollow sham, whose fate it was to be buried presently in the mould of primeval earth. But both the diabolic love and the unearthly hate of the mysteries it had penetrated fought for the possession of that soul satiated with primitive emotions, avid of lying fame, of sham distinction, of all the appearances of success and power.

'Sometimes he was contemptibly childish. He desired to have kings meet him at railway-stations on his return from some ghastly Nowhere, where he intended to accomplish great things. "You show them you have in you something that is really profitable, and then there will be no limits to the recognition of your ability," he would say. "Of course you must take care of the motives – right motives – always." The long reaches that were like one and the same reach, monotonous bends that were exactly alike, slipped past the steamer with their multitude of secular trees looking patiently after this grimy fragment of another world, the forerunner of change, of conquest, of trade, of massacres, of blessings. I looked ahead – piloting. "Close the shutter," said Kurtz suddenly one day; "I can't bear to look at this." I did so. There was a silence. "Oh, but I will wring your heart yet!" he cried at the invisible wilderness.

'We broke down – as I had expected – and had to lie up for repairs at the head of an island. This delay was the first thing that shook Kurtz's confidence. One morning he gave me a packet of papers and a photograph – the lot tied together with a shoe-string. "Keep this for me," he said. "This noxious fool" (meaning the manager) "is capable of prying into my boxes when I am not looking." In the afternoon I saw him. He was lying on his back with closed eyes, and I withdrew quietly, but I heard him mutter, "Live rightly, die, die . . ." I listened. There was nothing more. Was he rehearsing some speech in his sleep, or was it a fragment of a phrase from some newspaper article? He had been writing for the papers and meant to do so again, "for the furthering of my ideas. It's a duty."

'His was an impenetrable darkness. I looked at him as you peer down at a man who is lying at the bottom of a precipice where the sun never shines. But I had not much time to give him, because I was helping the engine-driver to take to pieces the leaky cylinders, to straighten a bent connecting-rod, and in other such matters. I lived in an infernal mess of rust, filings, nuts, bolts, spanners, hammers, ratchet-drills – things I abominate, because I don't get on with them. I tended the little forge we fortunately had aboard; I toiled wearily in a wretched scrap-heap – unless I had the shakes too bad to stand.

'One evening coming in with a candle I was startled to hear him say a little tremulously, "I am lying here in the dark waiting for death." The light was within a foot of his eyes. I forced myself to murmur, "Oh, nonsense!" and stood over him as if transfixed.

'Anything approaching the change that came over his features I have never seen before, and hope never to see again. Oh, I wasn't touched. I was fascinated. It was as though a veil had been rent. I saw on that ivory face the expression of sombre pride, of ruthless power, of craven terror – of an intense and hopeless despair. Did he live his life again in every detail of desire, temptation, and surrender during that supreme moment of complete knowledge? He cried in a whisper at some image, at some vision – he cried out twice, a cry that was no more than a breath –

'"The horror! The horror!"

'I blew the candle out and left the cabin. The pilgrims were dining in the mess-room, and I took my place opposite the manager, who lifted his eyes to give me a questioning glance, which I successfully ignored. He leaned back, serene, with that peculiar smile of his sealing the unexpressed depths of his meanness. A continuous shower of small flies streamed upon the lamp, up on the cloth, upon our hands and faces. Suddenly the manager's boy put his insolent black head in the doorway, and said in a tone of scathing contempt –

'"Mistah Kurtz – he dead."'

Der Krieg

Georg Heym, born in Silesia in 1887, was a leader in Berlin of the Expressionist movement in German poetry at the time of his death in 1912, drowned trying to rescue a friend in a skating accident. 'Der Krieg' was written in 1911.

WAR

He has arisen who was long asleep,
Arisen from a subterranean deep.
Now vast, uncanny, in the dusk he stands
To crush the moon in his immense black hand.

There fall from far on cities' nightfall noises
The frost and shadow of an eerie darkness.
The whirlpools of the markets clench as ice.
No noise. They look around, are none the wiser.

On shoulders, in the streets, a touch, light.
Question. No answer. And a face turns white.
The distant trembling peal of bells rings thin
And beards tremble round their pointed chins.

Upon the mountains he begins to dance.
He bellows, All you warriors – advance!
He tosses his black head. There is an echo.
A thousand skulls are strung on his crude necklace.

As the day flees, he blots out like a tower
The last glow over rivers flushed with gore.
Already, countless corpses in the reeds
Are covered white with death's strong birds.

Into the night, crosscountry, he drives fire,
Red hound, with yelling of wild mouths of ire.

From darkness leaps up the black world of night,
Fringed by volcanoes, their horrendous light.

Tall and sharptipped a thousand bonnets strew
The darkling plains and flicker in the view.
What flees upon the roads in swarms, he casts
Into flameforests and their roaring blast.

Forest after forest is devoured by blaze
While yellow bats claw, jagged, at the leaves,
While, like a charcoal burner, at fire's core,
He thrusts his poker to adjust the roar.

Foundered in yellow smoke, all mute, a city
Pitched itself into the abyss's belly.
But now he towers over glowing ruins,
Stabs his torch three times at the wild heavens,

Past the mirroring clouds storm tore to tatters,
Into the cold wastelands of dead darkness,
To dry up distant night with his brand's roar,
Pour drenching fire and brimstone on Gomorrha.

'Expressionism' is a loose term covering the work of a wide range of gifted young poets in pre-1914 Germany who had close associations with Expressionist painters. Alfred Lichtenstein, born in 1889, killed on the Western Front in September 1914, had time to develop an ironic mode very distant from Heym's apocalyptic tones. 'Prophecy' dates from 1913.

PROPHECY

Soon there'll come – the signs are fair –
A death-storm from the distant north.
Stink of corpses everywhere,
Mass assassins marching forth.

The clump of sky in dark eclipse,
Storm-death lifts his clawpaws first.
All the scallywags collapse.
Mimics split and virgins burst.

With a crash a stable falls.
Insects vainly duck their heads.
Handsome homosexuals
Tumble rolling from their beds.

Walls in houses crack and bend.
Fishes rot in every burn.
All things reach a sticky end.
Buses, screeching, overturn.

2

'Swimmers into Cleanness Leaping'?

Why do men fight? And fight on?

For the cheering hordes of Europeans who rushed to enlist in August 1914, why they should fight was no mystery. Their nation needed them. With the encouragement of mothers, girlfriends, mates at work, they were prepared to be heroes and die glorious deaths if necessary. The primary motivation of patriotism should not be sneered at. It did not necessarily involve chauvinism or jingoism. As at a football match, one might simply prefer one's own team to win. One might be deeply committed to the idea, or feeling, that one's own culture – English literature, the 'Russian word', German music, French republicanism – represented something uniquely valuable which must not be defeated and overridden. One might be a Jock or a Cossack, fiercely proud of a special military tradition. But there is abundant evidence that grandiose patriotic verbiage did not impress men 'at the sharp end', on the front line. Nor did broader ideological gestures.

For regular soldiers fighting was a job. As in mining or deep-sea fishing you accepted risks and got paid for taking them. But what kept conscripts going as the First World War in the West developed the character of disgusting attrition? Through the horrors of Stalingrad and Alamein, the D-Day beaches and the Normandy bocages? What kept civilians going on their front line, as bombers smashed and burnt cities night after night? Germany and the Soviet Union in 1941–45 are special cases, to be considered later in this book. In both, the sanctions of discipline were exceptionally ferocious. The Wehrmacht may have digested Nazi ideology; just possibly, quite a lot of Soviet citizens found Communism inspirational, and Russian patriotism was certainly intense, irrespective of Stalin. But simple fear of being shot for desertion was clearly a major reason for endurance. In Britain and the USA, by that time, deserters were merely treated for shell-shock.

For writers and, more generally, men with literary and aesthetic proclivities, inquisitive detachment may have assisted adaptation. To be there *. . . To see* that *. . . What one saw might at times be men who seemed to love fighting – 'war heroes'. Some would be decorated and celebrated. Others, whether quixotic officers or private drunks and nutters, provided, uncelebrated, as 'battle posts', to use Sorley Maclean's expression from the Gaelic, inspiration for more timorous creatures.*

The new art of flying provided such models – like Albert Ball VC of the Royal Flying Corps who refused to take normal precautions over the trenches and paid the price after shooting down a couple of score of German planes. But 'a lonely impulse of delight' might inspire the most prudent of men after he took to the air: flying was addictive.

So, to be candid, was strong drink. How much wine supplied by friendly villagers had those New Zealanders drunk when they made their famous counter-attack against the inexorably advancing German paratroops at Galatas on Crete in May 1941? Was vodka swigged by Soviet troops, the Wehrmacht's most deadly foe on the snowy plains of Russia?

At bottom though it seems that most men kept going simply because their mates kept going.

Patriotism and Pleasure

If I Should Die

Rupert Brooke, identified by many as the most promising young English poet of his generation, died a volunteer soldier on a hospital ship in the Aegean in 1915, before he had seen active service. He had not been a conventional jingoist. He was a member of the Fabian Society, and receptive towards experimental verse. But his reputation was fixed by a group of sonnets in eminently traditional style written after the outbreak of war. Even those who have sneered at them as naïve have never been able to forget them.

PEACE

Now, God be thanked Who has matched us with His hour,
And caught our youth, and wakened us from sleeping,
With hand made sure, clear eye, and sharpened power,
To turn, as swimmers into cleanness leaping,
Glad from a world grown old and cold and weary,
Leave the sick hearts that honour could not move,
And half-men, and their dirty songs and dreary,
And all the little emptiness of love!

Oh! we, who have known shame, we have found release there,
Where there's no ill, no grief, but sleep has mending,
Naught broken save this body, lost but breath;
Nothing to shake the laughing heart's long peace there
But only agony, and that has ending;
And the worst friend and enemy is but Death.

THE DEAD

Blow out, you bugles, over the rich Dead!
There's none of these so lonely and poor of old,
But, dying, has made us rarer gifts than gold.
These laid the world away; poured out the red
Sweet wine of youth; gave up the tears to be
Of work and joy, and that unhoped serene,
That men call age; and those who would have been,
Their sons, they gave, their immortality.

Blow, bugles, blow! They brought us, for our dearth,
Holiness, lacked so long, and Love, and Pain.
Honour has come back, as a king, to earth,
And paid his subjects with a royal wage;
And Nobleness walks in our ways again;
And we have come into our heritage.

THE SOLDIER

If I should die, think only this of me:
That there's some corner of a foreign field
That is for ever England. There shall be
In that rich earth a richer dust concealed;
A dust whom England bore, shaped, made aware,
Gave, once, her flowers to love, her ways to roam,
A body of England's, breathing English air,
Washed by the rivers, blest by suns of home.

And think, this heart, all evil shed away,
A pulse in the eternal mind, no less
Gives somewhere back the thoughts by England given;
Her sights and sounds; dreams happy as her day;
And laughter, learnt of friends; and gentleness,
In hearts at peace, under an English heaven.

Akhmatova's Courage

Those contemptuous of Brooke's patriotism might ponder the case of one of the century's indubitably major poets, Anna Akhmatova. Since the Revolution she had seen other great Russian poets – Esenin, Mayakovsky, Tsvetaeva – commit suicide, and Osip Mandelstam hounded to death by Stalin. From 1925 to 1940 there was an unofficial ban on the publication of her own poetry. Her son and her partner were arrested in 1935, and she began to write her unpublishable sequence Requiem *as a tribute to the victims of Stalin's purges and the women who waited outside the prisons for word of them. Yet when the Nazis invaded her country in 1941 her patriotism was instantly and completely engaged against them. Her publishable poem 'Courage' was recited all over Russia, and during the siege of Leningrad she broadcast in honour of the women of that city at the request of Stalin's government. Her vast new popularity did not save her from further persecution after the war.*

TO THE VICTORS

The Narvsky Gates were behind,
Ahead there was only death . . .
Thus the Soviet infantry marched
Straight into Big Bertha's blazing barrels.
They will write books about you:
'You laid down your life for your friends,'
Unpretentious lads –
Vankas, Vaskas, Alyoshkas, Grishkas –
Grandsons, brothers, sons!

29 February 1944
Tashkent

'AND YOU, MY FRIENDS . . .'

And you, my friends from the latest call-up!
My life has been spared to mourn for you.
Not to freeze over your memory as a weeping willow,
But to shout all your names to the whole wide world!
But never mind names!
None of that matters – You are with us!
Everyone down on your knees!
A crimson light pours!
And the Leningraders come through the smoke in even rows –
The living and the dead: for glory never dies.

August 1942
Dyurmen

Apollinaire's Festival

For that matter, the ebullient French Modernist Guillaume Apollinaire had been an unabashed French patriot, who volunteered in 1914 and rose to be an artillery officer. He was badly wounded, was awarded the Croix de Guerre and returned to civilian life to die, ironically, of Spanish influenza in the month of victory, November 1918. He wrote about the front with ambivalence, but with exuberance.

FÊTE

Display of steel-hard pyrotechnics
How charming of this light to mix
A little grace with bravery
It's one of those artificer's tricks

Two shells go off
Pink burst a pair
Of breasts one suddenly lays bare
Offering their tips immodestly
HE SURE COULD LOVE
    some epitaph

A poet in the landscape
Watches with indifference
    His pistol with the catch on safe
As the roses die of hope

He dreams of the roses of Saadi
And suddenly his head droops
Because a rose reminds him of
The soft curve of a woman's hips

The air is full of terrible alcohol
Filtered through the half-closed stars
While the shells caress the dull
Perfume of night where you repose
    O gangrene of the rose

Ungaretti's Golden Front Line

Giuseppe Ungaretti, a young Italian, became a friend of Apollinaire in pre-war Paris. He had barely glimpsed Italy having spent his first twenty-four years in Alexandria, Egypt, where his parents had emigrated. When war broke out he went to Milan. As soon as Italy entered the war in 1915 he enlisted as a private in the infantry. His first book of poems (1916) was written in the trenches, but as his translator Patrick Creagh puts it: 'Ungaretti's war poems . . . have in them less bitterness and more love of life than most poets could manage if they were basking at ease in Eden, instead of under gunfire.'

'Cima Quattro' was 'Hill Four', on the front line.

WATCH

Cima Quattro, 23 December 1915

A whole night through
thrown down beside
a butchered comrade
with his clenched teeth
turned to the full moon
and the clutching
of his hands
thrust
into my silence
I have written
letters full of love

Never have I
clung
so fast to life

Fire and MacNeice

The wry Irish poet Louis MacNeice, while fully committed to war against the Nazis, was prepared to admit, even as early as November 1942 with the big 'Blitz' only a year and a half behind, to fascination with the spectacular effects of air raids which had been one factor in the heroic fortitude of Londoners.

MacNeice's reference to 'topless towers', echoing Marlowe's Faustus, *assimilates the city with Homer's Troy.*

BROTHER FIRE

When our brother Fire was having his dog's day
Jumping the London streets with millions of tin cans
Clanking at his tail, we heard some shadow say
'Give the dog a bone' – and so we gave him ours;
Night after night we watched him slaver and crunch away
The beams of human life, the tops of topless towers.

Which gluttony of his for us was Lenten fare
Who mother-naked, suckled with sparks, were chill
Though cotted in a grille of sizzling air
Striped like a convict – black, yellow and red;
Thus were we weaned to knowledge of the Will
That wills the natural world but wills us dead.

O delicate walker, babbler, dialectician Fire,
O enemy and image of ourselves,
Did we not on those mornings after the All Clear,
When you were looting shops in elemental joy
And singing as you swarmed up city block and spire,
Echo your thoughts in ours? 'Destroy! Destroy!'

November 1942

Huntsmen in Tanks: Keith Douglas

Traditions of cavalry warfare proved to be drastically unfitted for twentieth-century circumstances. In 1914–15 British guards, lancers and hussars rode gallantly to be slaughtered. Samuel Hynes, in The Soldier's Tale: Bearing Witness to Modern War *(Allen Lane, 1997), observes that 'The officers of these regiments were soldiers in the tradition of the European officer caste, sons of the aristocracy and gentry, for whom the army was a career, a vocation, and often the ultimate field sport'. Hynes draws attention to the principles on which such officers were selected, which are made clear in a standard textbook, published in 1912, Major-General M. F. Rimington's* Our Cavalry*: 'We all know the type of officer required . . . a man who combines an addiction to, and some knowledge of, field sports, involving horses, with sufficient intelligence to pass into Sandhurst . . . We particularly want the hunting breed of man because he goes into danger for the love of it.'*

Keith Douglas served in North Africa in 1942–43 in a tank regiment which had cavalry traditions. Officers, as he saw it, behaved accordingly.

SPORTSMEN

'I think I am becoming a God'

The noble horse with courage in his eye,
clean in the bone, looks up at a shellburst:
away fly the images of the shires
but he puts the pipe back in his mouth.

Peter was unfortunately killed by an 88;
it took his leg off; he died in the ambulance.
When I saw him crawling, he said:
It's most unfair, they've shot my foot off.

How then can I live among this gentle
obsolescent breed of heroes, and not weep?
Unicorns, almost,
for they are falling into two legends

in which their stupidity and chivalry
are celebrated. Each, fool and hero, will be an immortal.

These plains were a cricket pitch
and in the hills the tremendous drop fences
brought down some of the runners, who
under these stones and earth lounge still
in famous attitudes of unconcern. Listen
against the bullet cries the simple horn.

Tunisia [May–June] 1943

Heroes

Lawrence of Arabia

The 1914–18 war threw up perhaps two, and only two, definitive 'heroes' – men whose behaviour convinced others that gas and tanks and brutal artillery had not wholly superseded the modes of epic and chivalry. One was the 'Red Baron' Von Richthofen, the German assassin of the air, buried with full military honours by the British when he died behind their lines. The other was T. E. Lawrence 'of Arabia', who 'led' Bedouin clansmen in a successful 'Arab Revolt' against Turkish rule. This was not a picturesque sideshow, as some have supposed. The Suez Canal was of such vital strategic significance to the British Empire, on the route between Britain and India, that at one point the War Cabinet seriously contemplated abandoning their French allies on the Western Front and committing all effort to the Middle East. Lawrence, an official British agent, bribing his allies with British gold, assisted General Allenby's more orthodox push from Egypt through Palestine. Lawrence's magnificent account of his war, Seven Pillars of Wisdom *(1926), reflects his deviousness and his profound inconsistencies. But many passages in it enforce the idea of a clean war, full of movement, in clean desert air, with allies cast in an antique heroic mould. In the passage which follows, supported by Nasir, the Sherif of Medina, and the brave and mercenary clan chief Auda, he is leading his irregulars to capture the port of Akaba on the Red Sea in 1917.*

After dusk, when our departure could not be seen, we rode five miles westward of the line, to cover. There we made fires and baked bread. Our meal, however, was not cooked before three horsemen cantered up to report that a long column of new troops – infantry and guns – had just appeared at Aba el Lissan from Maan. The Dhumani-yeh, disorganized with victory, had had to abandon their ground without fighting. They were at Bara waiting for us. We had lost Aba el Lissan, the blockhouse, the pass, the command of the Akaba road: without a shot being fired.

We learned afterwards that this unwelcome and unwanted vigour on the part of the Turks was accident. A relief battalion had reached Maan that very day. The news of an Arab demonstration against Fuweilah arrived simultaneously; and the battalion, which happened to be formed up ready with its transport in the station yard, to march to barracks, was hurriedly strengthened by a section of pack artillery and some mounted men, and moved straight out as a punitive column to rescue the supposedly besieged post.

They had left Maan in mid-morning and marched gently along the motor road, the men sweating in the heat of this south country after their native Caucasian snows, and drinking thirstily of every spring. From Aba el Lissan they climbed uphill towards the old blockhouse, which was deserted except for the silent vultures flying above its walls in slow uneasy rings. The battalion commander feared lest the sight be too much for his young troops, and led them back to the roadside spring of Aba el Lissan, in its serpentine narrow valley, where they camped all night in peace about the water.

Such news shook us into quick life. We threw our baggage across our camels on the instant and set out over the rolling downs of this end of the tableland of Syria. Our hot bread was in our hands, and, as we ate, there mingled with it the taste of the dust of our large force crossing the valley bottoms, and some taint of the strange keen smell of the wormwood which overgrew the slopes. In the breathless air of these evenings in the hills, after the long days of summer, everything struck very acutely on the senses: and when marching in a great column, as we were, the front camels kicked up the aromatic dust-laden branches of the shrubs, whose scent-particles rose into the air and hung in a long mist, making fragrant the road of those behind.

The slopes were clean with the sharpness of wormwood, and the hollows oppressive with the richness of their stronger, more luxuriant growths. Our night-passage might have been through a planted garden, and these varieties part of the unseen beauty of successive banks of flowers. The noises too were very clear. Auda broke out singing, away in front, and the men joined in from time to time, with the greatness, the catch at heart, of an army moving into battle.

We rode all night, and when dawn came were dismounting on the crest of the hills between Batra and Aba el Lissan, with a wonderful view westwards over the green and gold Guweira plain, and beyond it to the ruddy mountains hiding Akaba and the sea. Gasim abu Dumeik, head of the Dhumaniyeh, was waiting anxiously for us, surrounded by his hard-bitten tribesmen, their grey strained faces flecked with the blood of the fighting yesterday. There was a deep greeting for Auda and Nasir. We made hurried plans, and scattered to the work, knowing we could not go forward to Akaba with this battalion in possession of the pass. Unless we dislodged it, our two months' hazard and effort would fail before yielding even first-fruits.

Fortunately the poor handling of the enemy gave us an unearned advantage. They slept on, in the valley, while we crowned the hills in wide circle about them unobserved. We began to snipe them steadily in their positions under the slopes and rock-faces by the water, hoping to provoke them out and up the hill in a charge against us. Meanwhile, Zaal rode away with our horsemen and cut the Maan telegraph and telephone in the plain.

This went on all day. It was terribly hot – hotter than ever before I had felt it in Arabia – and the anxiety and constant moving made it hard for us. Some even of the tough tribesmen broke down under the cruelty of the sun, and crawled or had to be thrown under rocks to recover in their shade. We ran up and down to supply our lack of numbers by mobility, ever looking over the long ranges of hill for a new spot from which to counter this or that Turkish effort. The hill-sides were steep, and exhausted our breath, and the grasses twined like little hands about our ankles as we ran, and plucked us back. The sharp reefs of limestone which cropped out over the ridges tore our feet, and long before evening the more energetic men were leaving a rusty print upon the ground with every stride.

Our rifles grew so hot with sun and shooting that they seared our hands; and we had to be grudging of our rounds, considering every shot and spending great pains to make it sure. The rocks on which we flung ourselves for aim were burning, so that they scorched our breasts and arms, from which later the skin drew off in ragged sheets. The present smart made us thirst. Yet even water was rare with us; we could not afford to fetch enough from Batra, and if all could not drink, it was better that none should.

We consoled ourselves with knowledge that the enemy's enclosed valley would be hotter than our open hills: also that they were Turks, men of white meat, little apt for warm weather. So we clung to them, and did not let them move or mass or sortie out against us cheaply.

They could do nothing valid in return. We were no targets for their rifles, since we moved with speed, eccentrically. Also we were able to laugh at the little mountain guns which they fired up at us. The shells passed over our heads, to burst behind us in the air; and yet, of course, for all that they could see from their hollow place, fairly amongst us above the hostile summits of the hill.

Just after noon I had a heat-stroke, or so pretended, for I was dead weary of it all, and cared no longer how it went. So I crept into a hollow where there was a trickle of thick water in a muddy cup of the hills, to suck some moisture off its dirt through the filter of my sleeve. Nasir joined me, panting like a winded animal, with his cracked and bleeding lips shrunk apart in his distress: and old Auda appeared, striding powerfully, his eyes bloodshot and staring, his knotty face working with excitement.

He grinned with malice when he saw us lying there, spread out to find coolness under the bank, and croaked at me harshly, 'Well, how is it with the Howeitat? All talk and no work?' 'By God, indeed,' spat I back again, for I was angry with everyone and with myself, 'they shoot a lot and hit a little.' Auda, almost pale with rage, and trembling, tore his head-cloth off and threw it on the ground beside me. Then he ran back up the hill like a madman, shouting to the men in his dreadful strained and rustling voice.

They came together to him, and after a moment scattered away downhill. I feared things were going wrong, and struggled to where he stood alone on the hill-top, glaring at the enemy: but all he would say to me was, 'Get your camel if you want to see the old man's work.' Nasir called for his camel and we mounted.

The Arabs passed before us into a little sunken place, which rose to a low crest; and we knew that the hill beyond went down in a facile slope to the main valley of Aba el Lissan, somewhat below the spring. All our four hundred camel men were here tightly collected, just out of sight of the enemy. We rode to their head, and asked the Shimt what it was and where the horsemen had gone.

He pointed over the ridge to the next valley above us, and said, 'With Auda there': and as he spoke yells and shots poured up in a sudden torrent from beyond the crest. We kicked our camels furiously to the edge, to see our fifty horsemen coming down the last slope into the main valley like a run-away, at full gallop, shooting from the saddle. As we watched, two or three went down, but the rest thundered forward at marvellous speed, and the Turkish infantry, huddled together under the cliff ready to cut their desperate way out towards Maan, in the first dusk began to sway in and out, and finally broke before the rush, adding their flight to Auda's charge.

Nasir screamed at me, 'Come on', with his bloody mouth; and we plunged our camels madly over the hill, and down towards the head of the fleeing enemy. The slope was not too steep for a camel-gallop, but steep enough to make their pace terrific, and their course uncontrollable: yet the Arabs were able to extend to right and left and to shoot into the Turkish brown. The Turks had been too bound up in the terror of Auda's furious charge against their rear to notice us as we came over the eastward slope: so we also took them by surprise and in the flank; and a charge of ridden camels going nearly thirty miles an hour was irresistible.

My camel, the Sherari racer, Naama, stretched herself out, and hurled downhill with such might that we soon out-distanced the others. The Turks fired a few shots, but mostly only shrieked and turned to run: the bullets they did send at us were not very harmful, for it took much to bring a charging camel down in a dead heap.

I had got among the first of them, and was shooting, with a pistol of course, for only an expert could use a rifle from such plunging beasts; when suddenly my camel tripped and went down emptily upon her face, as though pole-axed. I was torn completely from the saddle, sailed grandly through the air for a great distance, and landed with a crash which seemed to drive all the power and feeling out of me. I lay there, passively waiting for the Turks to kill me, continuing to hum over the verses of a half-forgotten poem, whose rhythm something, perhaps the prolonged stride of the camel, had brought back to my memory as we leaped down the hill-side:

> For Lord I was free of all Thy flowers, but I chose the world's sad roses,
> And that is why my feet are torn and mine eyes are blind with sweat.

While another part of my mind thought what a squashed thing I should look when all that cataract of men and camels had poured over.

After a long time I finished my poem, and no Turks came, and no camel trod on me: a curtain seemed taken from my ears: there was a great noise in front. I sat up and saw the battle over, and our men driving together and cutting down the last remnants of the enemy. My camel's body had laid behind me like a rock and divided the charge into two streams: and in the back of its skull was the heavy bullet of the fifth shot I fired.

Mohammed brought Obeyd, my spare camel, and Nasir came back leading the Turkish commander, whom he had rescued, wounded, from Mohammed el Dheilan's wrath. The silly man had refused to surrender, and was trying to restore the day for his side with a pocket pistol. The Howeitat were very fierce, for the slaughter of their women on the day before had been a new and horrible side of warfare suddenly revealed to them. So there were only a hundred and sixty prisoners, many of them wounded; and three hundred dead and dying were scattered over the open valleys.

A few of the enemy got away, the gunners on their teams, and some mounted men and officers with their Jazi guides. Mohammed el Dheilan chased them for three miles into Mriegha, hurling insults as he rode, that they might know him and keep out of his way. The feud of Auda and his cousins had never applied to Mohammed, the political-minded, who showed friendship to all men of his tribe when he was alone to do so. Among the fugitives was Dhaif-Allah, who had done us the good turn about the King's Well at Jefer.

Auda came swinging up on foot, his eyes glazed over with the rapture of battle, and the words bubbling with incoherent speed from his mouth. 'Work, work, where are words, work, bullets, Abu Tayi' . . . and he held up his shattered field-glasses, his pierced pistol-holster, and his leather sword-scabbard cut to ribbons. He had been the target of a volley which had killed his mare under him, but the six bullets through his clothes had left him scatheless.

He told me later, in strict confidence, that thirteen years before he had bought an amulet Koran for one hundred and twenty pounds and had not since been wounded. Indeed, Death had avoided his face, and gone scurvily about killing brothers, sons and followers. The book was a Glasgow reproduction, costing eighteen pence; but Auda's deadliness did not let people laugh at his superstition.

He was wildly pleased with the fight, most of all because he had confounded me and shown what his tribe could do. Mohammed was wroth with us for a pair of fools, calling me worse than Auda, since I had insulted him by words like flung stones to provoke the folly which had nearly killed us all: though it had killed only two of us, one Rueili and one Sherari.

It was, of course, a pity to lose any one of our men, but time was of importance to us, and so imperative was the need of dominating Maan, to shock the little Turkish garrisons between us and the sea into surrender, that I would have willingly lost much more than two. On occasions like this Death justified himself and was cheap.

Little Big Man

John Keegan, discussing the reasons why, against all reason, soldiers go on fighting, attributes much to the influence of 'big men'. These soldiers may or may not be big physically, but their courage inspires others round them. Sorley Maclean saw one such in the British army in North Africa in 1942. The translation from the original Gaelic is by Maclean himself.

HEROES

I did not see Lannes at Ratisbon
nor MacLennan at Auldearn
nor Gillies MacBain at Culloden,
but I saw an Englishman in Egypt.

A poor little chap with chubby cheeks
and knees grinding each other,
pimply unattractive face –
garment of the bravest spirit.

He was not a hit 'in the pub
in the time of the fists being closed,'
but a lion against the breast of battle,
in the morose wounding showers.

His hour came with the shells,
with the notched iron splinters,
in the smoke and flame,
in the shaking and terror of the battlefield.

Word came to him in the bullet shower
that he should be a hero briskly,
and he was that while he lasted
but it wasn't much time he got.

He kept his guns to the tanks,
bucking with tearing crashing screech,
until he himself got, about the stomach,
that biff that put him to the ground,
mouth down in sand and gravel,
without a chirp from his ugly high-pitched voice.

No cross or medal was put to his
chest or to his name or to his family;
there were not many of his troop alive,
and if there were their word would not be strong.
And at any rate, if a battle post stands
many are knocked down because of him,
not expecting fame, not wanting a medal
or any froth from the mouth of the field of slaughter.

I saw a great warrior of England,
a poor mannikin on whom no eye would rest;
no Alasdair of Glen Garry;
and he took a little weeping to my eyes.

The Desert Fox

The twentieth century was not a good one for Generals in Europe. Pétain died the disgraced leader of a pro-Nazi government. Haig's success in 1918 did not outweigh colossal losses inflicted by his strategies earlier. Eisenhower achieved supreme success, but as a bureaucrat, not as a fighting soldier. Montgomery and Patton had charisma, but personal vanity flawed their reputations. Zhukov had the misfortune to be the official hero of a vile state. Von Runstedt's break-out in the Ardennes in late 1944 was a gesture too late to affect the war's outcome. Even Erwin Rommel (1891–1944) is not highly regarded by German historians. But his British opponents were not ashamed to admire him, led by Churchill himself, who acclaimed him as 'a great general'. He commanded one of the Panzer divisions which routed the French in 1940. Promoted to Major-General, he was put in charge of the Afrika Korps in the Western Desert, where the British had swept Hitler's Italian allies before them. He disobeyed commands to remain on the defensive. From his arrival in February 1941, he drove forward. Though he was nominally under Italian command, the prestige was his when Tobruk fell to his forces in June 1942, and he was promoted Germany's youngest field marshal. He was starved of supplies, and was forced into retreat at the Battle of El Alamein in November 1942, but he made life very difficult for his pursuers. Eventually, in 1944, he assumed control of all forces in France waiting to repel the expected Allied invasion. Implicated in the unsuccessful July bomb plot to kill Hitler, he was offered the options of trial or suicide with a field marshal's funeral. He chose suicide.

Heinz Werner Schmidt, a twenty-five-year-old student raised to lieutenant, was posted to Rommel's staff in Africa in March 1941 and became his right-hand man. His book With Rommel in the Desert, *published in English in 1951, is very vivid and far from uncritical. Here he describes an unsuccessful attack on Tobruk in 1941.*

We went for the little fort in the Desert, and the British positions round it, from three directions. The engagement was sharp but lasted only a couple of hours. We took the British commander,

Major-General Gambier-Parry, in his tent. The haul of prisoners numbered almost 3000. We had a further spectacular success. A mobile force of motor-cyclists caught up with a British column moving eastward across the Desert below the Jebel Akhdar near by, and to their astonishment held up the two heroes of the British advance to Benghazi: Lieutenant-General Sir Richard O'Connor, who had just been knighted for his successes against the Italians, and Lieutenant-General Sir Philip Neame, VC. So we had three generals in the bag.

Mechili landing-ground was littered with destroyed planes. British machines swooped down to attack it afresh at short intervals. At the height of one assault, 'my' Fiesler Storch dropped in out of the sky. Out stepped Rommel, smiling buoyantly, fresh from a personal reconnaissance of the Desert scene.

The command trucks of the captured British generals stood on a slight rise. They were large, angular vehicles on caterpillar tracks, equipped inside with wireless and facilities for 'paper' work. We christened them 'Mammoths' then, but I did not realize that these useful trucks would be used by Rommel and his staff and commanders right through the long struggle that was now beginning in the Desert.

Rommel inspected the vehicles with absorbed interest after a brief interview with the captured British generals. He watched them emptied of their British gear. Among the stuff turned out he spotted a pair of large sun-and-sand goggles. He took a fancy to them. He grinned, and said, 'Booty – permissible, I take it, even for a General.' He adjusted the goggles over the gold-braided rim of his cap peak.

Those goggles for ever after were to be the distinguishing insignia of the 'Desert Fox'.

Rommel led the onward march against Tobruk before daybreak. The night before the German Afrika Korps staff had come up to Mechili. I avoided any meeting with Major Eblert. Rommel allocated one of the Mammoths to General Streich of the 5th Light, and kept two for himself and his personal staff. He had the German cross painted on them all. We had taken a fair number of enemy vehicles, and I was allotted an open staff car similar to the one that Rommel generally used.

Aldinger, who was about to leave in the leading car with Rommel, gave me instructions. 'Herr Schmidt, from now on you will always travel immediately behind the General's car. You are to be entirely at his disposal.'

*

These were dramatic days. On March 27 King Peter had taken over control of Yugoslavia after the 'Palace Revolution' at two in the morning. On the 28th our Italian allies had been trounced by the Royal Navy in the battle of Cape Matapan. The following day, with the arrival of the 1st South African Brigade in Dire-dawa, in Abyssinia, it became clear that the fate of Addis Ababa was sealed. Asmara was to fall two days later. Rommel's move at El Agheila began hesitantly on the 30th. By April 2 we had forced the British out of Mersa Brega on the coast and also out of Agedabia, and the next day they evacuated Benghazi, always a difficult city to hold. Simultaneously a pro-Axis *coup d'état* was achieved in Iraq by Rashid Ali, and Wavell had another problem to think about. Foreign Minister Eden and General Sir John Dill, the British Chief of the Imperial General Staff, had both just been in Athens in answer to an appeal by the Greeks for military aid. Wavell had to undertake to send troops from the Middle East to Greece, which Germany invaded on the morning of April 6, at the same time entering Yugoslavia.

By April 7 we had taken Derna. Addis Ababa had fallen, and my old haunt, Massawa, was on the eve of surrender; but in the Desert Rommel was on top.

During a brief halt Rommel received a wireless signal from Behrendt: 'Derna reached.' Oberleutnant Behrendt, assistant to the I c, had been placed by Rommel in command of a mixed group of troops with a few anti-tank guns, temporarily formed into a combat group, and had been ordered to make for Derna. He had outpaced the Italian forces moving along the coast road and had taken a number of prisoners.

The Luftwaffe for some days past had been flying companies of reinforcements for the 15th Panzer Division across the Mediterranean. The Divisional Commander, General von Prittwitz, was the first of the new men to set foot in Africa. Rommel had the briefest of interviews with him, and then von Prittwitz led the advance on Tobruk. He ran straight into the forward defences and was killed – the first German general to fall at the head of his troops in Africa.

At nightfall Rommel and the rest of us on his staff reached a white-washed home – in peace-time a road engineer's residence – west of Tobruk. An Australian had artistically employed the outer walls of the square building to extol the qualities of his favourite beverage, and had decorated them also with lively horse-racing scenes. Telegraph poles were spaced across the Desert between this building and the fort at Acroma. Close to this building we buried von Prittwitz and the other Germans who had fallen with him.

Staff headquarters was set up in a wadi south-west of the White House. Eblert appropriated one of the Mammoth's ACVs (Armoured Command Vehicles) as Operations Office. The other was reserved for Rommel himself.

Next morning Rommel set out for Acroma. His car was escorted only by my own and a light armoured vehicle. We ploughed along the dusty Acroma track, which was to be a familiar and trying line of communications for a long time until the Axis by-pass road was built, to the primitive Desert fort. From Acroma Rommel headed south-east in the direction of El Adem. Artillery fire from Tobruk was suddenly laid down around us, and startled gazelles plunged among our three vehicles. The shells followed us, well registered, for some distance.

When we had driven for half an hour we came across companies of German infantry who were taking up positions on the high ground short of El Adem. Rommel stopped for a brief talk with their officers who had been there just a few hours. Among them I met Lieutenant Schmidt, my comrade of the Marada–Jab expedition. While the General talked, a salvo of enemy shells fell among us. A young lieutenant was killed, and my friend Schmidt lost an arm.

Two miles farther east we found General Streich with a Mammoth and his staff lying in isolation in a wide wadi. The Tobruk batteries had ceased firing now, and Rommel remarked to Streich with a twinkle: 'It is perhaps better for the English to spare their ammunition. They may yet need all they have.'

As if to belie this, we heard the howling shriek of a fresh salvo, which burst near by and was obviously meant for us. But we were quick to note that these shells had come not from Tobruk but from the south. We gazed through glasses at a ridge of high ground surmounted by a long, low building and a row of telegraph poles. 'El Adem,' says Rommel softly, glancing swiftly at his map, surveying the area again through his binoculars.

He spotted a lone armoured car, which must, we concluded, contain the enemy artillery observation officer. We were still trying to arrange counter-measures when, after a quarter of an hour, the car went away, and with it the shell-fire.

Meanwhile the Generals discussed the tactical situation. Before we drove away, Rommel reiterated to the Divisional Commander: 'We must attack Tobruk with everything we have, immediately your Panzers have taken up their positions, and before Tommy has time to dig in.'

At sunrise we left the bivouac west of the White House and again drove through the thick dust to Acroma. Columns from the opposite direction and vehicles ahead all churned up such clouds that we could only establish the approximate direction of the track by means of the telegraph poles along it. Again there were just the three vehicles – Rommel's, mine, and the light armoured car.

At Acroma Oberleutnant Wahl with four Panzers snapped to attention as the General arrived. I had a chat with Wahl, an engaging fellow full of fun and high spirits, while Rommel intently scanned the Tobruk strong-points in the east through his field-glasses. He was silent, as though fascinated. His compact torso was erect above his straddled legs, his elbows crooked as he held the Zeiss glasses to his eyes. His chin was thrust out. The Mechili goggles were there on his cap peak.

'Herr Leutnant, we're off!' Rommel snaps suddenly. 'Tell that officer to follow with his Panzers.' He leaps into his car and drives ahead. I pass on his orders. The Panzer officer calls up his tanks with a signal – several upward thrusts of the arm. Wahl climbs aboard his own Panzer and grins: 'Off to Tobruk!'

We drive east for some miles. Now and again bursts of shell-fire erupt about us. In a wadi we pass an Italian battery which is feverishly replying to fire from King's Cross in Tobruk.

Rommel halts and studies his map. I turn round and notice that the Panzers have been unable to keep up our pace. Away back, their dust clouds are flurrying forward. The General beckons, and I run to his side. An energetic finger thrusts at a section of the map: I recognize the western flank of the line.

'The battery is positioned correctly, but where is the Bersaglieri battalion? It should be in position on the high ground immediately ahead.'

He glances at the map again, then adds angrily: 'The Italian Command evidently indicated the wrong position.' Then: 'The Italian commander is apparently not yet with his men.'

At that moment the Panzers come up behind us. The whole wadi is suddenly plastered with shell-bursts. A salvo explodes almost on top of us. 'Drive back and order the Panzers to stay where they are until they get further instructions,' Rommel barks at me. 'I am going forward to the rise.'

It is no pleasure to drive back through the wadi towards the Panzers, where the fire is hottest. I am relieved when I have passed on the order and can instruct my driver to turn and make rapidly for the front again. I leave the car at the bottom of the rise and trot up the slope. I find Rommel lying on the ground with shells exploding right and left. He is all alone, for he has even left Aldinger behind to-day – to attend to arrears of correspondence.

I watch Rommel as he lies on his belly, intently studying the ground ahead through his glasses. His firm mouth is tight-lipped now; his prominent cheek-bones stand out white. His cap is perched on the back of his head.

'Fort Pilastrino!' he mutters. I glance quickly at his map before I crouch down behind a heap of stones and also survey the terrain ahead. The ground slopes down ahead of us, and then slopes upward again equally gradually. On the crest is a triangular-shaped ruin of stones surmounted by a close network of barbed wire. Considerably further back is a higher mound of stones. I surmise that this is Pilastrino and an enemy OP.

Rommel is looking for the first time at the actual defences of Tobruk, but we have no means of gauging their strength. Now we both see a few forms moving along the perimeter of the ruins. The huntsman's urge seems to take possession of Rommel. 'Leutnant!' he commands. 'Orders to the Panzers! Attack the stone ruins ahead – two Panzers through the northern wadi, two through the southern wadi close to the ruins.'

'*Jawohl, Herr General.*' I repeat the order. I have earlier observed that there is a deeper wadi not far from the southern wadi, and rashly venture to suggest, 'Shouldn't the Panzers advance along the deeper wadi, Herr General?'

Rommel's eyes flash, and his face reddens. 'Herr Leutnant, I am not nearly as stupid as you think!'

I salute, and hurry off to carry out my instructions, mortified at my brashness. For a while the bursting of shells around me seem of little consequence.

Reaching the Panzers, I explain the orders to the lieutenant and briefly describe the ground ahead. He relays the orders of the other tank commanders through the microphone of his radio-telephone. He smiles calmly and waves to me before he closes the hatch and roars off with the other Panzers at his heels.

We watch the charge of the Panzers. They obey orders and get close to their objective – the ruins. Then an unexpected and murderous fire falls round them. A few moments later the fire of several batteries is directed at our own observation post. We race for shelter along the slope. But the shell-fire grows still fiercer. Shells drop among the battery of Italian artillery. One gun and its crew are wiped out by a direct hit. All hell is let loose until sun-down, when the shell-fire ceases. We drive back to Advanced Headquarters near the White House. The Panzers do not return. Weeks later a group of combat engineers attacking at Ras Medawwa came on the torn body of the Panzer lieutenant hanging across the barbed-wire defences in front of the ruins.

. . .

For some days Rommel used his Mammoth for visiting the line. It afforded admirable protection against dive-bombers, aerial strafing, and shrapnel, and we had plenty of this during our daily tours. But Rommel usually sat high up on the roof of his Mammoth, dangling his legs through the open doorway. Aldinger, who had been with him in the First World War too, was almost always with him.

The General inspired all ranks with enthusiasm and energy wherever he appeared. He could not tolerate subordinates who were not as enthusiastic and active as himself, and he was merciless in his treatment of anybody who displayed lack of initiative. *Out!* Back to Germany they went at once.

Our front-line tours began early in the morning and frequently lasted until after nightfall. Rommel often took over the wheel from his tired driver. His sense of direction was remarkable, and he had an almost uncanny ability to orient himself by the stars at night.

Aviators

Major Gregory foresees his Death

The new art of flying conveyed to those who had discovered it a mysterious authority. They literally saw the world and its battles as other men could not. The risks they took, in war, from 1914 onwards, were exceptionally high, yet they did not endure the mud of the trenches or hump their packs on long routes of march.

With Lady Augusta Gregory W. B. Yeats had laboured to create a new national theatre for Ireland. Her son Robert died on active service for the British Empire which Irish nationalists rejected, killed as an airman in the Royal Flying Corps on the North Italian Front in January 1918.

AN IRISH AIRMAN FORESEES HIS DEATH

I know that I shall meet my fate
Somewhere among the clouds above;
Those that I fight I do not hate,
Those that I guard I do not love;
My country is Kiltartan Cross,
My countrymen Kiltartan's poor,
No likely end could bring them loss
Or leave them happier than before.
Nor law, nor duty bade me fight,
Nor public men, nor cheering crowds,
A lonely impulse of delight
Drove to this tumult in the clouds;
I balanced all, brought all to mind,
The years to come seemed waste of breath,
A waste of breath the years behind
In balance with this life, this death.

Sagittarius Rising

Cecil Lewis volunteered for the Royal Flying Corps in 1915 as a sixteen-year-old schoolboy, and by the end of the war was a twenty-year-old senior Flight Commander with a Military Cross. His memoir Sagittarius Rising *appeared in 1936, by when he was convinced, like H. G. Wells, that a World State was needed to end wars. The book conveys the immense excitement which flying inspired in his own generation, when it was almost new.*

In retrospect it seems to have been lightly decided. Actually I suppose it was the last link in a long subconscious chain of wish fulfilment. For, now I come to think of it, I hardly remember a time when I was not air-minded. At prep school I was already making gliders out of half-sheets of paper, curving the plane surfaces, improvising rudders and ailerons, and spending hours launching them across the room from chairs and tables. I devoured the pages of *Flight* and *The Aero*. I could tell all the types of machines – Latham's Antoinette, Blériot's monoplane, the little Demoiselle. I followed the exploits of the Wright brothers in America and Cody on Laffan's Plain. I remember well my disappointment when Latham set off to fly the Channel only to fall into the sea a mile from the Folkestone Cliffs. I remember my annoyance when Blériot actually did it, for to my youthful aesthetic sense Blériot's stubby little machine was not to be compared with Latham's lovely bird . . .

But, in spite of this passion for 'aeronautics' – as they were then called – it never occurred to me that I might be actively concerned in them. That I myself might fly a real full-sized aeroplane was beyond the bounds of the wildest possibility. Then came the War. Warneford brought down a Zeppelin. The importance of the air began to be realized. An immense impetus was given to aircraft design and manufacture. The opportunity opened, and the onlooker became participant.

[*Training at St Omer in France enhanced Lewis's love of planes and flying.*]

Follow-my-leader with Patrick gave me my first taste of aerial fighting, getting your nose and your guns on the enemy's tail and sitting there till you brought him down. It was a year later before I actually did any; but, from the first, the light fast single-seater scout was my ambition. To be alone, to have your life in your own hands, to use your own skill, single-handed, against the enemy. It was like the lists of the Middle Ages, the only sphere in modern warfare where a man saw his adversary and faced him in mortal combat, the only sphere where there was still chivalry and honour. If you won, it was your own bravery and skill; if you lost, it was because you had met a better man.

You did not sit in a muddy trench while someone who had no personal enmity against you loosed off a gun, five miles away, and blew you to smithereens – and did not know he had done it! That was not fighting; it was murder. Senseless, brutal, ignoble. We were spared that.

As long as man has limbs and passions he will fight. Sport, after all, is only sublimated fighting, and in such fighting, if you don't 'love' your enemy in the conventional sense of the term, you honour and respect him. Besides, there is, as everybody who has fought knows, a strong magnetic attraction between two men who are matched against one another. I have felt this magnetism, engaging an enemy scout three miles above the earth. I have wheeled and circled, watching how he flew, taking in the power and speed of his machine, seen him, fifty yards away, eyeing me, calculating, watching for an opening, each of us wary, keyed up to the last pitch of skill and endeavour. And if at last he went down, a falling rocket of smoke and flame, what a glorious and heroic death! What a brave man! It might just as well have been me. For what have I been spared? To die, diseased, in a bed! Sometimes it seems a pity.

So, if the world must fight to settle its differences, back to Hector and Achilles! Back to the lists! Let the enemy match a squadron of fighters against ours. And let the world look on! It is not as fanciful as you suppose. We may yet live to see it over London.

[*Lewis somehow survived the Battle of the Somme where he flew as an observer of the enemy. He was disgusted by the mud and carnage. But even there, flying could bring mystery, delight and magic.*]

Six months' continuous flying low over the trenches had affected my eyes. I had long ago given up goggles because they fogged in the oil fumes from the engine. Besides, leaning out of the cockpit to scan the ground carefully – for you dared not make a mistake as to the identity of the men in the trenches when the guns bombarded the place on the strength of your report – was almost impossible with goggles on. Now it was getting colder; acute conjunctivitis set in. I had to stop flying, and went home for another fortnight's sick leave. Secretly I hoped for a longer rest; for I was utterly tired of it all. But, after a fortnight, with eyes cured, I returned to the squadron.

. . .

Now a sort of desperation was in the air. The battle had failed. The summer was over. The best men had gone. Well, you had to carry on. Harvey Kelly, the Major, had gone too, and I didn't like the new man. I went off to the lines and wandered round at any old height, two hundred, three hundred feet, asking for trouble. My good luck must be over. Why should I remain when those chaps were gone? It seemed unfair. What I needed was a direct hit. That would wind up the show in style.

They gave me a new machine, faster, prettier, more comfortable than the other, the latest thing, and mine the first in the squadron. But even that didn't cheer me. I could only write epitaphs for the old one: 'This was my last trip on old 5133. I had her when I arrived at the squadron and I've flown her ever since. Two or three half-axles and one Vee-piece were the only things ever replaced. She always flew well. She never let me down. On her I got an MC and did the best work I shall ever do in this war. She's held jolly gallant men in the back seat. The best one is dead. I flew her over to be broken up. She looked a bit decrepit standing there beside the new one – all spit and polish. But she's seen me through – so far. She might have lasted me out. God, how sick I am of this war!'

. . .

Magnificent days of blue and crystal, when to be in the air made everything worthwhile, were over. Damp hangars, muddy roads, cold quarters, clouds and rain – these were to be our lot from now on.

One dreary grey morning I went up alone on patrol. The clouds were at two hundred feet, but they might break farther east over the lines. I rose into the cloud-bank – a featureless obscurity, a white dark, as you might say – and started climbing.

A pilot flies by his horizon. He keeps his machine on an even keel, or indeed in any position, by reference to it. Take away the horizon and he doesn't know where he is. This is the reason for gyroscopic controls, false horizon indicators, and all the modern gadgets (to say nothing of beam wireless) which enable a man to fly 'blind', and a commercial pilot to bring his thirty-eight passengers on to Croydon aerodrome in a pea-soup fog without too much anxiety. But in 1916 a chap had an air-speed indicator and a lateral bubble (which was supposed to tell him if he was on an even keel), and the rest was the luck of the game and his native 'nouse'.

In a cloud there is no horizon, nothing above, below, in front, behind, but thick white mist. It's apt to make you panic after a while, and many a man has fallen out of the clouds in a spin through losing his head and, without knowing it, standing his machine on its ear. Usually low cloud-banks aren't so very deep, so if you go carefully and watch the controls closely you get up through them all right; but on this particular morning there seemed to be no top to them. I climbed and climbed, looking up all the time, hoping to see that thinning of the mist and the halo of the sun above which means you're almost through. But it wasn't until I reached two thousand feet that I saw the welcome sheen of gold overhead. It thinned. Mist wraiths drew back and showed blue. They curled away. I was out.

But what in heaven had happened to this cloud-bank? It wasn't level. It was tilted as steeply as the side of a house. The machine was all right – airspeed constant, bubble central – and yet here were the clouds defying all natural laws! I suppose it took me a second to realize that I was tilted, bubble or no bubble, that I had been flying for the best part of fifteen minutes at an angle of thirty degrees to the horizon – *and had never noticed it*! If I had tried to fly this way on purpose, it would have seemed impossible, at the best most unpleasant. The machine would have shuddered and slipped. I should have been in a dither after half a minute. If you'd told me anyone could fly like it quite happily for ten minutes, I should just have laughed. It shows what a little ignorance can do.

I put the machine level and gazed around in wonder. Here it was still summer. Below, life was dying back into the earth. Gold plumes fluttering from the poplars. The mournful voice of the October wind.

But here! As far as the eye could reach, to the four horizons, a level plain of radiant whiteness, sparkling in the sun. The light seemed not to come from a single source, but to pervade and permeate every atom of air – a dazzling, perfect, empty basin of blue.

A hundred miles, north, south, east, west. Thirty thousand square miles of unbroken cloud-plains! No traveller in the desert, no pioneer to the poles had ever seen such an expanse of sand or snow. Only the lonely threshers of the sky, hidden from the earth, had gazed on it. Only we who went up into the high places under the shadow of wings!

I sailed on for a time, alone in the wonderful skies, as happy as I have ever been or ever shall be, I suppose, in this life . . .

I shut off, turned east, and came down. The white floor, several thousand feet below, rose up towards me, turned at last from a pavement of pearl to just a plain bank of fog. I plunged into it. I might be going back from paradise to purgatory, so grey and cold and comfortless it was. And as I sank through it, listening to the singing of the wires, I was thinking how some day men might no longer hug the earth, but dwell in heaven, draw power and sustenance from the skies, whirl at their will among the stars, and only seek the ground as men go down to the dark mysteries of the sea-floor, glad to return, sun-worshippers, up to the stainless heaven.

The melancholy landscape of stubble fields and bare trees appeared. I picked up a road, got my bearings, and swept off home at a hundred feet.

'Did you see anything?' said another pilot, strolling up to the machine.

'Nothing. It's completely dud.'

Dutchman over Berlin

It was even possible for a man to remember flying on an RAF raid over Berlin with nostalgia, for all the appalling Bomber Command casualty rates (q.v.) which indicate how dangerous the job was.

Erik Hazelhoff Roelfzema was a Dutchman from a well-to-do family, a law student at Leyden University when the Germans occupied his country in 1940. After much trial and error he managed to escape to England where he worked on liaison with the Dutch resistance, and was enmeshed in the intrigues in and about the Dutch Government in exile and the exiled Queen Wilhelmina. Eventually, he joined the RAF and saw active service at last after training as a pilot. He describes a typical raid in his war memoir, Soldier of Orange *(1982).*

From a throwaway remark we learn that he survived an astonishing number of sorties.

Ben is late. He's always late, but never too late. How many times now have we been over Germany together? Fifty-eight? Sixty? Still, every time he's late, I worry. Actually, it's more a case of my being early. He's a cool one, old Ben; he likes to fiddle around until the very last moment with his maps, his pencils and dividers, his wind directions, bombing runs and ETAs, talking to the little computer strapped to his thigh as if the bloody thing were alive. I myself prefer to sit in the cockpit of our Mozzie for a while before takeoff, nice and quiet. It's so small, even for a crew of just two, that you've got to get used to it every time all over again.

I adjust the harness straps across my chest, tight but not too tight; wiggle back and forth on my parachute, which forms the seat in the metal chair, until it feels as if my tail will survive some five hours of continuous contact; reach out to various knobs and levers, first with open eyes, then blindly, until I can find my way by touch in the confusion around me; then I just sit, staring ahead. After a few minutes I begin to feel better, less awkward. It's very important to me, especially when the weather is bad. The weather is always bad.

Outside, the winter evening smothers Upwood. Drizzle spots the windshield, distorting everything. Hangars look like battleships; runway and perimeter lights fuse into a muddled mess. The De Havilland Mosquito: Rolls-Royce engines, revolutionary construction, the latest in electronics, but simple wind-shield wipers – forget it. Typical RAF. The most sophisticated aircraft of World War II, I swear by it, but we never leave the ground without an ample supply of rubber bands and chewing gum for essential small repairs in the cockpit.

Darkness reaches down from the sky. It's cold, you can be sure there's ice up there. Cloud-base below three hundred feet when we get back, five hours from now, I'll bet on it. Bloody Met blokes and their forecasts. Nightfighters, flak, rockets, I'll take them all in exchange for some decent weather. But I guess we'll manage. Survive the first five missions and you'll be all right, they say. After my very first one, to Hamburg some six months ago with Flying Officer Ray Snelling DFC, I never thought I'd make it.

Of course, as a Pathfinder flying a Mosquito you have to get used to some odd ideas; mainly, that your plane is made of wood and carries no guns whatsoever. The wood is pressed and strong, but operating unarmed we are supposed to survive by being smarter and luckier as well as fast. To help us do so, we have a gadget in the cockpit called the Boozer. It's secret. It starts to glow when the Jerries pick us up in their radar: red when they track us, bright red when they lock us into the aiming mechanism of their heavy guns, yellow when we have a nightfighter on our tail.

From the moment Ray and I crossed the Dutch coast the Boozer glowed. Every time it jumped to bright I threw our Mozzie wildly off course, and once when the yellow came on I yanked her into such a steep diving turn that I almost lost control. All this in solid cloud, pitch black, hour after hour. It was a miracle that we ever found Hamburg, or even England on the way home. We reported no sign of the enemy, but the following morning Q – Queenie was under repair, with seventeen fist-size holes in her wooden fuselage.

After four operations with Ray Snelling I ran into Ben Hein in the Blue Boar in Cambridge. He patted me approvingly on the chest, where underneath the Williams Order my brand-new Pathfinder's wings gleamed.

'Hazelsnout,' he declared over a pint of Watney's, 'with you I'll fly. We may fall flat on our arses, but we won't turn back when the going gets sticky. There's more of that in this war than you might think.'

My desire to fly with Ben was based on less heroic considerations. As a lieutenant in the Netherlands Navy Air Service he was bound to be a superior navigator. Also, we had been to high school together, in The Hague, which should make for a happy team. He requested and obtained a transfer to Upwood.

. . .

Here he is, jumping down from the crew van, I can tell from here that he's all set to go, looking for action, ready to clobber them. Ben likes big, fat targets, and tonight it's a juicy one. Navigation board under his arm, chin stuck out, he strides pugnaciously across the dispersal, around Mosquitos that stand silently in groups of three and four, slender as wasps. He stops at T–Tommy and says something to Dave Groom and 'Rosie' O'Grady, who are about to climb the little ladder to the hatch in the nose. They move like bears in their parachutes and Mae Wests. They laugh, jab Ben in the ribs, and hoist themselves up the steps and through the hole. The ground crew slams the hatch cover and locks it. Now they're no longer Dave and Rosie, only T–Tommy.

'Hello, Hazelsnout!' Ben's head sticks up through the floor of the cockpit, round and smooth in the leather helmet except for the earphones. Other pilots are addressed as captain or skipper; I have to make do with Hazelsnout. He squirms through the hole like a giant beetle, into his seat to the right of me. We both face forward, shoulder to shoulder in the mass of instruments. While he struggles into his harness, cursing contentedly, I switch on the wingtip lights. The ground sergeant holds up his thumb and shuts the hatch. He scurries off, wheel chocks in one hand, speedometer pilot head cover in the other. I look at my watch – from now until we have marked the target for the bomber fleets behind us, we live by the second-hand. Two minutes and twenty seconds till takeoff. It's almost dark now outside, all around glow the little red and green wingtip lights. Ben sits silently beside me; everybody and everything is waiting and it's very quiet everywhere, very quiet. . . .

. . .

We're approaching the heart of Germany. The weather has turned clear, right down to the ground. All around us lie the fat, juicy targets, legendary, awe-inspiring names that have bounced around in our subconsciousness ever since we put on Air Force blue. Now they're getting it, by day from the Americans, by night from the RAF. This morning it was the Flying Fortresses. To starboard the sky glows; below it rivers of fire run into four orange pools: Brunswick. Far to the north a trickle of amber sparks drips down, then more, hundreds, thousands, a rain of golden flares that quickly knit themselves into a brilliant canopy over the unfortunate city below: Hamburg. Elsewhere, also, the big boys are on the prowl, Lancasters and Halifaxes; in several places I see the lacework of heavy flak spattering delicately. Here and there near the ground climb the leisurely tracers of light anti-aircraft fire. Everybody's in the act tonight.

The Boozer flicks to bright. Now it's serious. This is Hanover and here they know their business.

'Have we time for evasive action?' I'll go by what Ben tells me.

'What kind?'

'Slalom.'

'Plenty time.' Had he answered in the negative, we would have ploughed straight on. It's as simple as that.

I wait for the initial shell burst; they rarely score first go. There it is, an innocent-looking little black cloud to the left of us, slightly high. Now the Jerries below start correcting the error. I know that it takes a shell about twenty seconds to reach us, so after fifteen seconds I change course five degrees to the left. If they are efficient down there the change will have occurred after they fired the next round, but before it gets to us. Poof! There it is, on schedule, to the right where it ought to be. Below they're correcting again. Meanwhile I change course to the right, ten degrees this time to make up for the previous deviation to the left. Poof! Very nice, to the left of us. Ten degrees to the left. Poof! To the right of us. And so on, occasionally combined with a gain and corresponding loss of a few hundred feet of altitude. In this way we maintain our original direction of flight while staying alive. But you need capable, reliable gunners below.

'Hey, Hazel, what time do you make it?' I almost jump out of my seat. I recognize the carefree, down-under accent of Rosie O'Grady, somewhere out there in the dark, but he sounds so close that I instinctively glance over my shoulders. We always maintain radio silence, except for emergencies and irrepressible Australians. I tell him the time, that's all. I'm acutely aware that hundreds of Germans are listening to these two enemy voices deep inside their country. They all know the game. It can't be long now. Ben is immersed in calculations.

'Last course into target.' Everything now revolves around Ben and his radar box, and the accuracy with which I follow his instructions. We know our job, we want to be the best.

'Course one four eight. First lose two and a half minutes. We're early.'

'Lose two and a half minutes. Course one four eight. Okay.' I put Queenie into a specific turn; exactly two and a half minutes later the circle is complete, we are at the same spot. 'One four eight . . . now!'

Ben, staring at his watch, grunts with satisfaction and shoots off a route marker. Before sticking his head back into the radar box, he pulls a stopwatch from his pocket and presets it with the duration of the bombing run. Since our radar will be useless over the actual target due to the angle, we have to fly the final, critical miles by dead reckoning; course, speed, height, time, all determined beforehand. Bombers weave into the target area and fly straight and level no longer than it takes to drop their loads accurately, but Pathfinders must maintain an absolutely steady bombing run for up to several minutes to produce the basic requirement of a successful attack: a valid aiming point. Sometimes I wonder if it's worth the little gold eagle.

I lower my seat and turn up the instrument lights. Whatever happens outside, from here on in there's little I can do about it. We have penetrated so far east, surely by now the Jerries know what it's all about . . . Ah, there they are, and they are ready for us. Dead ahead, wholly unreal but bristling with menace, hundreds of searchlights pierce the cloudless sky, rigid, motionless, like quills of a giant porcupine: Berlin.

'Come and get it,' they say. We're coming.

As soon as someone enters the frozen forest of searchlights, it comes alive. The blue-white beams begin to weave slowly, each in its own section, long, slim fingers feeling their way, touching the inside of the transparent black dome above, unhurried, hesitating, but always moving on, searching. Over to port I see a speck of solid matter in this rarefied world. On the ground they have seen it also – ten, fifteen beams whip over to it and cross each other where the Mosquito holds them together like a clasp. White lacework begins to spatter around her. Undaunted, the little ship ploughs on, straight as can be – one of ours, 139 Squadron.

Suddenly I find myself staring at some tiny cracks in the paint of our own port engine nacelle, which a second ago was invisible in the dark. As I look over the side an unblinking, glittering eye meets mine, bitterly hostile, so blinding that I quickly pull back. Wham-wham-wham-wham ... four more beams smack in on us, then half a dozen more. We're tightly coned; down below pools of violent light surround us. Even Ben looks up from his box. I can see every hair on his unshaven chin. 'This is what they pay us for,' he says soothingly.

'How much longer?' We're well into the bombing run.

'Ninety-six seconds ... ninety-five ... ninety-four ...'

I drop my seat all the way; only the top of my head sticks above the cockpit. Don't look, just keep going. We are droning along inside a light-ball of incredible intensity. Course, height, speed, everything steady, just the way Ben wants it: on rails. Next to me, parallel to Queenie and only a shade higher, five or six black puffs. I can't help seeing them out of the corner of my eye. Twenty seconds until the next salvo. No slalom this time, straight ahead, level and steady.

'Sixty seconds coming up.' Ben never takes his head out of the radar box; he wants this Christmas tree in the right place. 'Sixty seconds ... now. Fifty-nine ... fifty-eight ...' Poof! There they are, corrected for height, still to the left but close enough to hear the roar of the engines. Keep going. Crrrack! Very close, smack in front. We sail through the black clouds; I can smell the cordite. At the same moment a cluster of three yellow flares pops out of nowhere, right above us: German nightfighters. They are signaling to the gunners below: 'Hold your fire. We're here. This one is ours.'

'Thirty seconds. Open bomb doors.'

'Bomb doors open.'

Actually we're not carrying bombs tonight, only target indicators, reds and greens. I must remember to call them out to the main force, to offset the dummy TIs the Germans are shooting up from the ground. Final check: course – exact; speed – exact; height – exact. It should be a fine aiming point, if we make it. It's ominously quiet around us. Where is the flak? Then suddenly the yell in our earphones: 'Fighters! Look out! Fighters!'

'Steady ...' Ben has one eye on the radar, one on the stopwatch, and his thumb on the bomb release. Does he give a damn that we're lit up like a showcase, visible for miles, an unarmed sitting duck for every nightfighter around?

The yellow Boozer flashes on. Fighters, here they come! 'Steady ... steady as you go. It's moving in beautifully. Ten seconds to go. Steady. Five ... four ... three ... two ... one. TIs gone!'

'Q – Queenie, TIs gone! Reds and greens! Reds and greens!' Shouting my message to the main force, I yank the Mozzie into a vertical turn, dropping the nose steeply.

'Hit them, you peasants,' Ben growls to himself.

We are diving, twisting, turning, climbing. The Boozer goes out. One by one the searchlights lose us. Suddenly we're in darkness, safe. In a warm, exulting wave, life floods over me.

Dutch Courage

This excerpt from Richard Holmes's Firing Line *(1985) should be self-explanatory.*

RUM AND BLOOD

One of the many valuable elements in John Keegan's contribution to our understanding of what happens on the battlefield is his treatment of battlefield narcosis. Some of the French knights at Agincourt had been drinking heavily on the eve of the battle, Corporal Shaw of the Life Guards was fighting drunk when he hewed nine Frenchmen through steel and bone at Waterloo, and some of the soldiers who advanced on the morning of July 1916 were fortified by more than *esprit de corps* . . . Drink and drugs are time-honoured ways of palliating stress, and their use is infinitely more widespread than bland official histories might suggest. The very expression 'Dutch courage' has military origins, dating from the predisposition of English soldiers in the Low Countries to fortify themselves with a nip or two of *genever*.

There are four main aspects to the question of alcohol and drug use in armies. Firstly, both drugs and drink have an entirely legitimate function in helping overwrought men to sleep. Alcohol is more useful in this context than is often recognized . . . Major J. R. Phillips, a regimental medical officer in 1940, was short of drugs: 'there was, however, an ample supply of alcohol, an excellent sedative, which proved most effective'. Alan Hanbury-Sparrow, on the receiving end, was utterly frank. 'Certainly strong drink saved you,' he acknowledged. 'For the whole of your moral forces were exhausted. Sleep alone could restore them, and sleep, thanks to this blessed alcohol, you got.'

Secondly, soldiers in garrison in both peace and war tend to over-indulge in alcohol as a means of making an unbearable existence more tolerable. Brigadier Richard Simpkin declared: 'every army I know of – except the Swedish, Swiss and Israeli forces – conspires to make its conscripts' life so wretched that they are fully occupied in coming to terms with it or in using drink or drugs to distance themselves from it'.

Jean Morvan recounted the spirited performance of a First Empire officer who habitually drank two bottles of wine with his lunch. He then had a well-deserved nap, enjoyed another bottle in bed, had dinner, and then took a short walk and another drink before turning in. On a more serious note, drink and drugs play an important part in crime in most armies: one-third of law violations by Soviet military personnel are carried out in a state of drunkenness.

Communal drinking also assists in the small-group bonding process . . . Stuart Mawson noticed 'a subtle parade of manhood, an unconscious swagger in the manner of drinking' the night before the drop on Arnhem . . .

It is with the fourth aspect of alcohol and drug use – as a means of mitigating the stresses of battle – that we are most concerned. To a degree, at least, this use has been officially approved . . .

. . .

The function of alcohol as a morale booster in the British army of the First World War remains a matter of dispute. On the one hand there are those who argue that privately purchased alcohol was in relatively short supply, and that its officially issued cousin was not misused. Charles Carrington trenchantly observed that the cost of spirits put them out of the reach of many: 'Whisky – at seven and sixpence a bottle, a subaltern's daily pay – was a rarity which we husbanded.' And what of the issue rum, in its pottery jars marked SRD – Special Rations Department, but rumoured to mean Seldom Reaches Destination? General Jack pointed out that regulations clearly specified that it had to be drunk in the presence of an officer, and was 'in no sense a battle dope'.

On the other hand, there is abundant evidence that rum made an important contribution to battle morale, and both it, and privately obtained liquor, were deliberately used to help men stand the strain of battle. One of the medical officers who testified before the War Office's 1922 Shell Shock Committee said, 'had it not been for the rum ration I do not think we should have won the war'. In his battalion of the Black Watch, they always tried to give the men a good meal and a double ration of rum in coffee before they went over the top. Colonel W. N. Nicholson recognized that rum had two specific functions. It helped make trench life bearable: 'The private soldier's ration of rum', he wrote, 'saved thousands of lives.' He also considered that it stiffened the spirit before or after battle: 'It is an urgent devil to the Highlander before action; a solace to the East Anglian countryman after the fight.' The practice of issuing rum after battle, to help men unwind, was followed by the Australians. 'For the boys who wanted rum there was plenty,' remembered one, '– in the AIF the rule was, no rum before a fight; the rum was given afterwards when the boys were dead beat.'

Rum looms large in the personal accounts of front-line soldiers. An infantryman recalled that the air smelt of 'rum and blood' during a British attack. Norman Gladden admitted that he and his comrades had drunk some smuggled rum in the trenches. 'Rarely had I seen a party in such a woeful situation so joyfully carefree,' he wrote . . .

Rudolf Binding testifies that the need for alcohol was not confined to the British army. He observed that heavy bombardment produced a great desire for drink. 'They have a craving for brandy which can hardly be satisfied,' he wrote, 'and which shows how badly they yearn to lose the faculty for feeling.' A fierce desire to get hold of drink motivated many of the German soldiers involved in the March offensive. As Rudolf Hartmann revealed, about a quarter of his unit were keen because they hoped to loot food and drink. Many German soldiers succeeded in their self-imposed search-and-destroy missions. Binding lamented the fact that the cellars at Albert and Moreuil 'contained so much wine that the divisions, which ought properly to have marched through them, lay about unfit to fight in the rooms and cellars . . . The disorder of the troops at these two places . . . must have cost us a good fifty thousand men.' Stephen Westman bewailed the fact that the offensive was soon held up, 'not for lack of German fighting spirit, but on account of the abundance of Scottish drinking spirit'.

The British army persisted with its rum ration during the Second World War, with tots being issued when a medical officer was prepared to certify that the conditions warranted it. 'We simply kept going on rum,' admitted John Horsfall. 'Eventually it became unthinkable to go into action without it. Rum, and morphia to silence our wounded.' He described how one of his NCOs 'entered his penultimate battle reduced to the ranks, in close arrest and quite wonderfully drunk'. In his next battle this soldier was wounded and taken to the Regimental Aid Post, but, again fighting drunk, broke out and was later found dead in the German positions. 'He was a true Faugh with simple tastes,' reflected Horsfall, 'rum and the regiment.' . . . On the Eastern Front, both sides used whatever alcohol they could get their hands on to blur the horror. A wounded infantryman told Guy Sajer: 'There's as much vodka, schnapps and Terek liquor on the front as there are Paks [anti-tank guns] . . . It's the easiest way to make heroes. Vodka purges the brain and expands the strength.'

American soldiers, in an army which was, in theory, 'dry', were less fortunate. In practice, as Charles MacDonald tells us, officers received a monthly allowance, which they had to pay for. In the winter of 1944–5 this amounted to one quart of Scotch, one pint of gin, one or two bottles of cognac, a bottle of champagne and a bottle of Cointreau. An officer would usually share this around his platoon, and there was little chance of wholesale drunkenness ensuing . . . Two enterprising members of the Fort Garry Horse obliterated pre-battle tension on their voyage to Normandy by draining the alcohol from the compass in their tank, mixing it with powdered orange-juice, and drinking it. Plied with black coffee by their troop sergeant, they were sober by the time the regiment went ashore.

Bonding

Comradeship at the Sharp End

Drink may have assisted the process of bonding, but even without it bonding is the primary motor of war, as all military historians seem to agree. Men fight for the men they fight alongside. John Ellis tackled this topic in his pioneering work of New Military History, The Sharp End of War *(1980), which concentrates on 1939–45.*

ATTITUDES

A fierce sense of pride [existed] among front-line soldiers about their ability to hang on in conditions inconceivable to those further back. Out of this pride there arose a sense of exclusivity, of apartness, that in turn blossomed into a deep compassion for and loyalty towards other members of the same élite brotherhood. Pride was a shared emotion, in which *mutual* esteem, a sense of common suffering, dominated over any tendency to selfish individualism.

Yet there were hints of the latter, and these must be mentioned before concentrating upon the prevailing spirit of comradeship. A tendency towards a more personal pride, almost selfishness, was more overt in the American army, a reflection no doubt of the fact that the ethic of individualism and self-sufficiency is almost written into the Constitution. A veteran interviewed in hospital in 1944 summed it up admirably when he proclaimed: 'A real soldier is a guy – he'll drink and swear – but he relies on himself; a guy that can take care of himself.' James Jones brought out the selfish aspects of such an attitude when he explained how the veteran's experience and expertise forced him to try and blot out any thoughts of his fellows and concentrate purely on assessing and maximizing his own chances of survival:

> He knew by the sound of incoming shells whether they would land near enough to be dangerous. He knew by the arc of falling aerial bombs if they would land nearby or farther out. He had learned that when fire

> was being delivered, being thirty yards away could mean safety, and that fifty or a hundred yards could be pure heaven. He had learned that when the other guy was getting it a couple of hundred yards away, it had nothing to do with him; and that conversely when he was getting it, the other guy two hundred yards away wanted nothing to do with him, either.

The one group at the front who did sometimes suffer from these potentially callous attitudes were the replacements, especially those who had arrived in a unit only a few days or even hours before being thrown into combat. In such circumstances the novices from replacement centres, or 'repple depples' as the Americans called them, had no time in which to get to know their fellow soldiers in the platoons and squads, and this lack of personal contact, as well as the rookies' often infuriating ignorance, sometimes tempted the veterans and their officers to use them almost as cannon fodder. A survey of returning American veterans put forward the proposition, 'When a replacement comes into an outfit during combat, the veterans usually try to help him all they can,' and 88 per cent of the interviewees agreed. Other sources, however, are more honest. James Jones recalled a conversation with an American sergeant who had been at Anzio:

> One day . . . we got eight new replacements into my platoon. We were supposed to make a little feeling attack that same day. Well, by next day, all eight of them replacements were dead, buddy. But none of us old guys were. We weren't going to send our own guys out on point in a damnfool situation like that. We knew nothing would happen. We were sewed up tight. And we'd been together through Africa, and Sicily, and Salerno. We sent the replacements out ahead.

Another American was even more blunt, recalling a sense of contempt for the gaucheness of the hapless rookies, 'a contempt with which even the gentlest of us viewed these unqualified victims of tactical necessity. It was a contempt that was certainly mixed with pity, but I think there's always something disgusting about victims. You can't help it . . . We called them poor sons of bitches, and we almost smiled when we said it'.

In many cases, however, the fast turnover in replacements simply meant that no other troops had been available. In the later stages of the European and Pacific campaigns, casualties were so high that raw soldiers had to be sent out immediately on tough assignments because there was simply no one else to do the job. But their inexperience exacted a terrible toll . . . In a sample from four American divisions in Italy in April 1945 (line companies only), only 34 per cent of the men had been with their outfit when it landed in that country. All the rest were replacements, over 50 per cent of whom had gone into combat within two days of joining their unit, and a further 20 per cent within less than a week. In a typical chronically understrength Canadian regiment in north-west Europe, less than half of its 379 combat soldiers had more than three months' training, of any kind, while 174 of them had received only one month or less.

. . .

But rookies only remained such for a very short time. Either they were hit or they soon acquired the instinctive caution of the other veterans. Then they were absorbed into the fraternity of the front line and began increasingly to share the comradeship, the mutual respect and regard that typified the sharp end of battle. The tensions and antipathies that existed within the armies have been described at some length, for it would be poor homage to sentimentalize the experience of the fighting soldier. Nevertheless it cannot be emphasized too strongly that such animosity is in no way typical of army life at the most basic level, that of the squadron or the section. In the stress of battle there emerged a poignant combination of sympathy and respect to be found amongst men in hardly any other situation. As one American officer wrote: 'This sense of comradeship is an ecstacy . . . In most of us there is a genuine longing for community with our human species, and at the same time an awkwardness and helplessness about finding the way to achieve it. Some extreme experience – mortal danger or the threat of destruction – is necessary to bring us fully together with our comrades . . .' For those so exposed the presence of others was of crucial importance, both for their explicit attempts to comfort and reassure, and for their tacit proof that they were suffering as grievously as oneself and that they seemed to be able to take it. Military psychiatrists were not slow to recognize the importance of small-group solidarity in enabling soldiers to keep going . . .

A British doctor, Lieutenant Colonel T. F. Main, wrote: 'The sense of separation from home, from its security and comforting permanence and its familiar reassurance of one's personal status, is a permanent stress. A camaraderie is the only human recompense for a threatening sense of impotence in the face of death and the waywardness of elemental forces and the decisions of the mighty who use soldiers like pawns.' The Second Army psychiatrist, in Normandy, was even more to the point. In July 1944 he averred: 'The emotional ties among the men, and between the men and their officers . . . is the single most potent factor in preventing breakdown.' . . .

It was not only observers who commented on the vital importance of emotional ties among the men. Almost all participants' accounts mention it and often regret that this sense of comradeship had no real equivalent in peacetime. It operated at many levels. In the more far-flung theatres whole armies were bound together by shared sufferings and privations. Major Paddy Boden of the Rifle Brigade wrote of the desert war:

> A large body of men sharing a common experience over a period of months and even years, isolated from all contact with their home country, developed a set of customs, habits and even jargon of their own. We felt different from, and by reason of our longer experience and of the flattering accounts of our exploits which appeared in the press, superior to the [First Army] men of England, sometimes mockingly referred to as 'those bloody Inglese'.

For other soldiers the battalion was held to be the crucial unit, holding men together by a mixture of earned respect for the officers and regimental pride . . . However, as the war dragged on and the battalions were increasingly made up of heterogeneous collections of replacements, it ceased to be realistic to claim that loyalty to a mere organization was sufficient to keep men going. Bill Mauldin got to the heart of the matter in the following observation about American troops in Europe. He was referring to the large number of soldiers who went straight back into the line once they had been discharged from hospital, making no attempt to take convalescent leave. What motivated them was not loyalty to the unit as such. 'A lot of guys don't know the name of their regimental commander. They went back because their companies were very short-handed, and they were sure that if somebody else in their own squad or section were in their own shoes, and the situation were reversed, those friends would come back to make the load lighter on them.' Another American soldier, interviewed by army researchers, emphasized the fact that it was at squad level that the front-line soldier found most support from his fellows:

> The men in my squad were my special friends. My best friend was the sergeant of the squad. We bunked together, slept together, fought together, told each other where our money was pinned in our shirts. We write to each other now. Expect to get together when the war is over . . . If one man gets a letter from home over there, the whole company reads it. Whatever belongs to me belongs to the whole outfit.

But this is not to say that the troops were unconcerned with the sufferings of those in other units. An important component of their attitude towards the war was their sense of exclusivity, of being members of a unique brotherhood of the damned which embraced all front-line soldiers. The very term 'the sharp end' was their own, highlighting the absolute distinction between those who put their lives on the line and the vast majority who only catered to their needs . . .

On many fronts, this sense of apartness was compounded with a cynical, fatalistic, fey almost, pride in their utter isolation from the normal world . . . In the Middle East, particularly during the see-saw campaigns of 1941 and 1942, such affected bitterness was very much the order of the day. When the British found themselves fighting alone, in mid-1941, a popular catchphrase was that 'we're in the final now', the point being that everyone else had scratched rather than we who fought our way through the qualifiers. Some months later it was widely asserted that the letters MEF (Middle East Force) stood for 'Men England Forgot'. An American correspondent recalled these same soldiers singing a song about the folks back home that included the chorus

> Poor guys are dying
> For bastards like you.

Italy, too, from mid-1944 to the end of the war, seemed another forgotten theatre and the soldiers reacted in characteristic fashion. After D-Day had been trumpeted around the world, Eighth and Fifth Army men would ask each other with mock seriousness, 'Which D-Day? Sicily, Salerno, Anzio?' They picked gleefully upon a notably crass remark by Lady [Astor] who felt, in her infinite military wisdom, that the men in Italy were just sun-tanned malingerers or 'D-Day Dodgers' as she called them. A song was soon current:

We're the D-Day Dodgers out in Italy,
Always drinking vino and always on the spree.
Eighth Army shirkers and the Yanks,
We live in Rome and dodge the tanks –
We are the D-Day Dodgers,
The boys whom D-Day dodged.

If you look round the mountains and through mud and rain,
You'll see the rows of crosses, some which bear no name.
Heartbreak and toils and suffering gone,
The boys beneath they linger on –
They were some of the D-Day Dodgers
And they're still in Italy.

But even those on whom this D-Day spotlight was turned were not immune to similar feelings. In north-west Europe, a war correspondent with the Canadian troops noted a similar perverse pride amongst the front-line troops enduring the hardships of the appalling Dutch winter. He was driven to try and analyse the mood of the troops and ask himself why they carried on in conditions that almost beggared description. This mood he found

> profoundly interesting. How they put up with it – or don't put up with it. Why they put up with it. How they digest the horrors, assimilate sights and experiences for which all their upbringing, all the life they have known previously, has given them no experience . . . [In fact] the Canadians were not really unhappy, or if they were they had a curious pleasure in it, like men stubbing sore toes . . . A peculiar sense of isolation had been growing in them up from the Seine . . . They had felt that the main strength of the war had turned away, and that they were increasingly forgotten. They heard the triumphant echoes of the armoured thrusts, the tears, laughter, flowers and champagne of the liberations . . . Their own experiences had been in a lower key. They began to take a pride in that, a provincial pride, the pride of the unsung, the unappreciated, and with an underlying bitterness, a derision . . . The Canadians had become welded together, kindred, a tight community. The truth is that they wanted to feel alone, alone with the sustained and terrible experience which they had begun to clasp to themselves as something personal, and upon which no one had a right to intrude.

This last quote, however, comes near to implying self-pity and that would be a travesty of the truth. Certainly the troops at the front were often preoccupied with their role in the war, and the contrast between their day-to-day existence and that of the soldiers further back, but they never became preoccupied with their *personal* suffering, never immersed themselves in their *individual* anguish. Out of their sufferings there emerged a real sense of selflessness and equality and it is these that ultimately characterize this exclusive fraternity. An officer in north-west Europe recalled a visit to the front: 'It was a tonic to find oneself again in the free air of good comradeship, co-operation and good-humoured stoicism of the front line after months of jealousies and petty rivalries so rampant farther back.' A tankman made an interesting observation on front-line *mores* that show how a man's standing in the world back home was deemed irrelevant, how he was only to be judged in terms of his day-to-day behaviour within the unit. A new tank commander

> soon learned the unwritten rules: the abuse was kept within carefully understood limits – a man's honour, courage, honesty, truthfulness or morals could be torn to shreds with impunity, it was permissible to accuse another man of always avoiding work, to maintain that he would run like a rabbit at the sound of a pop-gun, to accuse him of lying, cheating or stealing and no offence would be taken; but nothing could be said that reflected upon his social status, his ability to pay his share, his personal cleanliness, or his family . . .

It is this egalitarianism, this sense of common identity that overrode any tendency to individual self-pity. At the front the troops nearly always tried to make the best of their situation and concentrated upon doing everything possible to help each other through. In every theatre and unit one finds repeated evidence of a loving concern and respect for one's fellows.

House 6/1

Vasily Grossman's epic novel centred on the Battle of Stalingrad, 1942–43, Life and Fate, *was banned by the Soviet censors when it was submitted in 1960, though the writer had formerly been acclaimed as a master war correspondent, then as a suitable novelist. All manuscripts were, apparently, seized from the author. Nevertheless, a copy on microfilm finally reached the West where the book was published more than twenty years after Grossman himself had died in 1964.*

Its panoramic view of Soviet society under Stalin presents the selfless courage and ardent comradeship of the front-line soldiers who eventually beat the Germans in opposition to the cold-blooded manoeuvring of the bureaucracies at their backs, in a situation where a malicious informer can destroy a man's career or have him sent to the Gulag. 'House 6/1' acquires symbolic significance in relation to this theme. An outpost well in advance of the Soviet lines, encircled by German forces, it is controlled by an officer, Grekov, who rejects paperwork and despises commissars. The latter sense in him the spirit of the Partisans who had fought as guerrillas against the Germans – deplorable from the Party's point of view because they operated outside its control, propelled by fierce patriotism and tight bonding. Krymov, the commissar who eventually reaches House 6/1, is an idealistic and decent Old Bolshevik: by the end of the novel he will be in prison himself, on the basis of false accusations, House 6/1 will have been obliterated with all its occupants in a big German offensive, and Grekov, safely dead, will have been hailed as an official war hero. Meanwhile, the Army put into House 6/1 a very young female radio operator. Compassionately, Grekov sends her to Regimental Headquarters with Seryozha, the very young soldier she loves, just before the Germans launch their fatal offensive.

On a cold clear evening, the day after Grekov's dismissal of Shaposhnikov and Vengrova, Krymov, accompanied by a soldier with a tommy-gun, left Regimental HQ on his way to the notorious encircled house.

As soon as he set foot in the asphalt yard of the Tractor Factory,

Krymov felt an extraordinarily acute sense of danger. At the same time he was conscious of an unaccustomed excitement and joy. The sudden message from Front Headquarters had confirmed his feeling that in Stalingrad everything was different, that the values and demands placed on people had changed. Krymov was no longer a cripple in a battalion of invalids; he was once again a Bolshevik, a fighting commissar. He wasn't in the least frightened by his difficult and dangerous task. It had been sweet indeed to read in the eyes of Pivovarov and the divisional commissar the same trust in his abilities that had once been displayed by all his comrades in the Party.

A dead soldier was lying on the ground between the remains of a mortar and some slabs of asphalt thrown up by a shell-burst. Now that Krymov was so full of hope and exaltation, he found this sight strangely upsetting. He had seen plenty of corpses in his time and had usually felt quite indifferent. This soldier, so full of his death, was lying there like a bird, quite defenceless, his legs tucked under him as though he were cold.

A political instructor in a grey mackintosh ran past, holding up a well-filled knapsack. Then a group of soldiers came past carrying some anti-tank shells on a tarpaulin, together with a few loaves of bread.

The corpse no longer needed bread or weapons; nor was he hoping for a letter from his faithful wife. His death had not made him strong – he was the weakest thing in the world, a dead sparrow that not even the moths and midges were afraid of.

Some soldiers were mounting their gun in a breach in the wall, arguing with the crew of a heavy machine-gun and cursing. From their gestures Krymov could more or less guess what they were saying.

'Do you realize how long our machine-gun's stood here? We were hard at it when you lot were still hanging about on the left bank!'

'Well, you are a bunch of cheeky buggers!'

There was a loud whine, and a shell burst in a corner of the workshop. Shrapnel rattled across the walls. Krymov's guide looked round to see if he was still there. He waited a moment and said:

'Don't worry, comrade Commissar, this isn't yet the front line. We're still way back in the rear.'

It wasn't long before Krymov realized the truth of this; the space by the wall was indeed relatively quiet.

They had to run forward, drop flat on the ground, run forward and drop to the ground again. They twice jumped into trenches occupied by the infantry. They ran through burnt-out buildings, where instead of people there was only the whine of metal . . . The soldier said comfortingly: 'At least there are no dive-bombers,' then added: 'Right, comrade Commissar, now we must make for that crater.'

Krymov slid down to the bottom of a bomb crater and looked up: the blue sky was still over his head and his head was still on his shoulders. It was very strange; the only sign of other human beings was the singing and screaming death that came flying over his head from both sides. It was equally strange to feel so protected in this crater that had been dug out by the spade of death.

Before Krymov had got his breath back, the soldier said, 'Follow me!' and crawled down a dark passage leading from the bottom of the crater. Krymov squeezed in after him. Soon the passage widened, the ceiling became higher and they were in a tunnel.

They could still hear the storm raging on the earth's surface; the ceiling shook and there were repeated peals of thunder. In one place, full of lead piping and cables as thick as a man's arm, someone had written on the wall in red: 'Makhov's donkey.' The soldier turned on his torch for a moment and whispered: 'Now the Germans are right above us.'

Soon they turned off into another narrow passage and began making their way towards a barely perceptible grey light. The light slowly grew brighter and clearer; at the same time the roar of explosions and the chatter of machine-guns became still more furious.

For a moment Krymov thought he was about to mount the scaffold. Then they reached the surface and the first thing he saw was human faces. They seemed divinely calm.

Krymov felt a sense of joy and relief. Even the raging war now seemed no more than a brief storm passing over the head of a young traveller who was full of vitality. He felt certain that he had reached an important turning-point, that his life would continue to change for the better. It was as though this still, clear daylight were a sign of his own future – once again he was to live fully, whole-heartedly, with all his will and intelligence, all his Bolshevik fervour.

This new sense of youth and confidence mingled with his regret for Yevgenia. Now, though, he no longer felt he had lost her for ever. She would return to him – just as his strength and his former life had returned to him. He was on her trail.

A fire was burning in the middle of the floor. An old man, his cap pushed forward, was standing over it, frying potato-cakes on some tin-plating. He turned them over with the point of a bayonet and stacked them in a tin hat when they were done. Spotting the soldier who had accompanied Krymov, he asked: 'Is Seryozha with you?'

'There's an officer present,' said the soldier sternly.

'How old are you, Dad?' Krymov asked.

'Sixty,' said the old man. 'I was transferred from the workers' militia.'

He turned to the soldier again. 'Is Seryozha with you?'

'No, he's not in our regiment. He must have ended up with our neighbours.'

'That's bad,' said the old man. 'God knows what will become of him there.'

Krymov greeted various people and looked round the different parts of the cellar with their half-dismantled wooden partitions. In one place there was a field-gun pointing out through a loophole cut in the wall.

'It's like a man-of-war,' said Krymov.

'Yes, except there's not much water,' said the gunner.

Further on, in niches and gaps in the wall, were the mortars. Their long-tailed bombs lay on the floor beside them. There was also an accordion lying on a tarpaulin.

'So house 6/1 is still holding out!' said Krymov, his voice ringing. 'It hasn't yielded to the Fascists. All over the world, millions of people are watching you and rejoicing.'

No one answered.

Old Polyakov walked up to him and held out the tin hat full of potato-cakes.

'Has anyone written about Polyakov's potato-cakes yet?' asked one soldier.

'Very funny,' said Polyakov. 'But our Seryozha's been thrown out.'

'Have they opened the Second Front yet?' asked another soldier. 'Have you heard anything?'

'No,' said Krymov. 'Not yet.'

'Once the heavy artillery on the left bank opened up on us,' said a soldier with his jacket unbuttoned. 'Kolomeitsev was knocked off his feet. When he got up he said: "Well, lads, there's the Second Front for you!"'

'Don't talk such rubbish,' said a young man with dark hair. 'We wouldn't be here at all if it wasn't for the artillery. The Germans would have eaten us up long ago.'

'Where's your commander?' asked Krymov.

'There he is – over there, right in the front line.'

Grekov was lying on top of a huge heap of bricks, looking at something through a pair of binoculars. When Krymov called out his name he turned his head very slowly, put his fingers to his lips and returned to his binoculars. After a few moments his shoulders started shaking; he was laughing. He crawled back down, smiled and said: 'It's worse than chess.'

Then he noticed the green bars and commissar's star on Krymov's tunic.

'Welcome to our hut, comrade Commissar! I'm Grekov, the house-manager. Did you come by the passage we just dug?'

Everything about him – the look in his eyes, his quick movements, his wide, flattened nostrils – was somehow insolent and provocative.

'Never mind,' thought Krymov. 'I'll show you.'

He started to question him. Grekov answered slowly and absent-mindedly, yawning and looking around as though these questions were distracting him from something of genuine importance.

'Would you like to be relieved?' asked Krymov.

'Don't bother,' said Grekov. 'But we could do with some cigarettes. And of course we need mortar-bombs, hand-grenades and – if you can spare it – some vodka and something to eat. You could drop it from a kukuruznik [light biplane].' As he spoke, Grekov counted the items off on his fingers.

'So you're not intending to quit?' said Krymov. In spite of his mounting anger at Grekov's insolence, he couldn't help but admire the man's ugly face.

For a brief moment both men were silent. Krymov managed, with difficulty, to overcome a sudden feeling that morally he was inferior to the men in the encircled building.

'Are you logging your operations?'

'I've got no paper,' answered Grekov. 'There's nothing to write on, no time, and there wouldn't be any point anyway.'

'At present you're under the command of the CO of the 176th Infantry Regiment,' said Krymov.

'Correct, comrade Battalion Commissar,' replied Grekov mockingly. 'But when the Germans cut off this entire sector, when I gathered men and weapons together in this building, when I repelled thirty enemy attacks and set eight tanks on fire, then I wasn't under anyone's command.'

'Do you know the precise number of soldiers under your command as of this morning? Do you keep a check?'

'A lot of use that would be. I don't write reports and I don't receive rations from any quartermaster. We've been living on rotten potatoes and foul water.'

'Are there any women in the building?'

'Tell me, comrade Commissar, is this an interrogation?'

'Have any men under your command been taken prisoner?'

'No.'

'Well, where is that radio-operator of yours?'

Grekov bit his lip, and his eyebrows came together in a frown.

'The girl turned out to be a German spy. She tried to recruit me. First I raped her, then I had her shot.'

He drew himself up to his full height and asked sarcastically: 'Is that the kind of answer you want from me? It's beginning to seem as though I'll end up in a penal battalion. Is that right, Sir?' Krymov looked at him for a moment in silence.

'Grekov, you're going too far. You've lost all sense of proportion. I've been in command of a surrounded unit myself. I was interrogated afterwards too.'

After another pause, he said very deliberately:

'My orders were that, if necessary, I should demote you and take command myself. Why force me along that path?'

Grekov thought for a moment, cocked his head and said:

'It's gone quiet. The Germans are calming down.'

'Good,' said Krymov. 'There are still a few questions to be settled. We can talk in private.'

'Why?' asked Grekov. 'My men and I fight together. We can settle whatever needs settling together.'

Although Grekov's audacity made Krymov furious, he had to admire it. He didn't want Grekov to think of him as just a bureaucrat. He wanted to tell him about his life before the war, about how his unit had been encircled in the Ukraine. But that would be an admission of weakness. And he was here to show his strength. He wasn't an official in the Political Section, but the commissar of a fighting unit.

'And don't worry,' he said to himself, 'the commissar knows what he's doing.'

Now that things were quiet, the men were stretching out on the floor or sitting down on heaps of bricks.

'Well, I don't think the Germans will cause any more trouble today,' said Grekov. He turned to Krymov. 'Why don't we have something to eat, comrade Commissar?'

Krymov sat down next to him.

'As I look at you all,' he said, 'I keep thinking of the old saying: "Russians always beat Prussians."'

'Precisely,' agreed a quiet, lazy voice.

This 'precisely', with its condescending irony towards such hackneyed formulae, caused a ripple of mirth. These men knew at least as much as Krymov about the strength of the Russians; they themselves were the expression of that strength. But they also knew that if the Prussians had now reached the Volga, it certainly wasn't because the Russians always beat them.

Krymov was feeling confused. He felt uncomfortable when political instructors praised Russian generals of past centuries. The way these generals were constantly mentioned in articles in *Red Star* grated on his revolutionary spirit. He couldn't see the point of introducing the Suvorov medal, the Kutuzov medal and the Bogdan Khmelnitsky medal. The Revolution was the Revolution; the only banner its army needed was the Red Flag. So why had he himself given way to this kind of thinking – just when he was once again breathing the air of Lenin's Revolution?

That mocking 'precisely' had been very wounding.

'Well, comrades, you don't need anyone to teach you about fighting. You can give lessons in that to anyone in the world. But why do you think our superior officers have considered it necessary to send me to you? What have I come here for?'

'Was it for a bowl of soup?' asked a voice, quietly and without malice.

This timid suggestion was greeted by a peal of laughter. Krymov looked at Grekov; he was laughing as much as anyone.

'Comrades!' said Krymov, red with anger. 'Let's be serious for a moment. I've been sent to you, comrades, by the Party.'

What was all this? Was it just a passing mood? A mutiny? Perhaps the reluctance of these men to listen to their commissar came from their sense of their own strength, of their own experience? Perhaps there was nothing subversive in all this merriment? Perhaps it sprang from the general sense of equality that was such a feature of Stalingrad.

Previously, Krymov had been delighted by this sense of equality. Why did it now make him so angry? Why did he want to suppress it?

If he had failed to make contact with these men, it was certainly not because they felt crushed, because they were in any way bewildered or frightened. These were men who knew their own strength. How was it that this very consciousness had weakened their bond with Krymov, giving rise only to mutual alienation and hostility?

'There's one thing I've been wanting to ask someone from the Party for ages,' said the old man who had been frying the potato-cakes. 'I've heard people say that under Communism everyone will receive according to his needs. But won't everyone just end up getting drunk? Especially if they receive according to their needs from the moment they get up.'

Turning to the old man, Krymov saw a look of genuine concern on his face. Grekov, though, was laughing. His eyes were laughing. His flared nostrils were laughing.

A sapper, a dirty, bloodstained bandage round his head, asked: 'And what about the *kolkhozes*, comrade Commissar? Couldn't we have them liquidated after the war?'

'Yes,' said Grekov. 'How about a lecture on that?'

'I'm not here to give lectures,' said Krymov. 'I'm a fighting commissar. I've come here to sort out certain unacceptable partisan attitudes that have taken root in this building.'

'Very good,' said Grekov. 'But who's going to sort out the Germans?'

'Don't you worry about that. We'll find someone. And I haven't come here, as I heard someone suggest, for a bowl of soup. I'm here to give you a taste of Bolshevism.'

'Good,' said Grekov. 'Let's have a taste of it.'

Half-joking, but also half-serious, Krymov continued:

'And if necessary, comrade Grekov, we'll eat you too.'

He now felt calm and sure of himself. Any doubts he had felt about the correct course of action had passed. Grekov had to be relieved of his command.

It was clear that he was an alien and hostile element. None of the heroism displayed in this building could alter that. Krymov knew he could deal with him.

When it was dark, Krymov went up to him again.

'Grekov, I want to talk seriously. What do you want?'

'Freedom. That's what I'm fighting for.'

'We all want freedom.'

'Tell us another! You just want to sort out the Germans.'

'That's enough, comrade Grekov!' barked Krymov. 'You'd do better to explain why you allow your soldiers to give expression to such naïve and erroneous political judgements. With your authority you could put a stop to that as quickly as any commissar. But I get the impression your men say their bit and then look at you for approval. Take the man who asked about *kolkhozes*. What made you support him? Let me be quite frank . . . If you're willing, we can sort this out together. But if you're not willing, it could end badly for you.'

'Why make such a fuss about the *kolkhozes*? It's true. People don't like them. You know that as well as I do.'

'So you think you can change the course of history, do you?'

'And you think you can put everything back just as it was before?'

'What do you mean – everything?'

'Just that. Everything. The general coercion.'

Grekov spoke very slowly, almost reluctantly, and with heavy irony. He suddenly sat up straight and said:

'Enough of all this, comrade Commissar! I was only teasing you. I'm as loyal a Soviet citizen as you are. I resent your mistrust.'

'All right, Grekov. But let's talk seriously then. We must stamp out the evil, anti-Soviet spirit that's taken hold here. You gave birth to it – you must help me destroy it. You'll still get your chance for glory.'

'I feel like going to bed. You need some rest too. Wait till you see what things are like in the morning.'

'Fine. We'll continue tomorrow. I'm in no hurry. I'm not going anywhere.'

'We'll find some way of coming to an agreement,' said Grekov, with a laugh.

'No,' thought Krymov, 'this is no time for homeopathy. I must work with a surgeon's knife. You need more than words to straighten out a political cripple.'

'There's something good in your eyes,' said Grekov unexpectedly. 'But you've suffered a lot.'

Krymov raised his hands in surprise but didn't reply. Taking this as a sign of agreement, Grekov went on:

'I've suffered too. But that's nothing. Just something personal. Not something for your report.'

That night, while he was asleep, Krymov was hit in the head by a stray bullet. The bullet tore the skin and grazed his skull. The wound wasn't dangerous, but he felt very dizzy and was unable to stand upright. He kept wanting to be sick.

At Grekov's orders, a stretcher was improvised and Krymov was carried out of the building just before dawn. His head was throbbing and spinning and there was a constant hammering at his temples. Grekov went with him as far as the mouth of the underground passage.

'You've had bad luck, comrade Commissar.'

A sudden thought flashed through Krymov's head. Maybe it was Grekov who had shot him?

Towards evening his headache got worse and he began to vomit. He was kept at the divisional first-aid post for two days and then taken to the left bank and transferred to the Army hospital.

3
The Great War

The 1914–18 war was called 'the Great War' after *the event. Though the World War of 1939–45 exceeded it in length, in casualties, in atavistic barbarity and in nightmarish application of new technology, 1914–18 remains the 'Great' modern war.*

Submarines and balloons had been used in the American Civil War of 1861–65. The Maxim Gun dated back to 1884, and the effect of 'mechanized' fire was already well known. But the Western Front of 1914–18 brought together in a terrifying new combination old inventions and new ones. Poison gas was used by both sides. So, from the outset, were aeroplanes. The first tanks – British – went into action in 1916. Radio began to hint at its military potential. Paradoxically, the medical facilities now available meant that for the first time the majority of war casualties were caused by enemy action, not disease. (In 1861–65 Lincoln's Union army had lost nearly twice as many men from disease as were killed in action.) Italy, which entered the war in 1915 on the side of the Western Allies, lost 615,000 men killed in action. British Empire dead numbered 947,000. The French lost 1,400,000 (with three times as many wounded). Austria–Hungary lost 1,300,000. Russian losses were 1,700,000. And 1,800,000 German soldiers were killed. After one adds lesser combatants – a third of a million Romanians, a similar number of Turks, 90,000 Bulgarians, 55,000 Serbs – and 48,909 men from the United States – the total number of deaths in action was certainly more than eight million – that is, more than the combined populations today of Scotland and Wales.

But this horrific blood-letting was compounded by the physical and psychological wounds which survivors carried into old age, and by the brutalization of many of the men who participated. The 'Black and Tan' veterans sent in by Britain to bully the Irish and the Freikorps *of post-war Germany are nasty and immediate examples, while the rise of*

Fascism in Italy and Nazism in Germany, and the routine murderousness of the new Soviet Union, must be related to the experience of mass slaughter which made nonsense of existing moralities and cheapened life exponentially.

For the British and Americans, French and Germans, the prototypical arena of the 'Great' nightmare was the trenches of the Western Front. There was nothing at all novel about trenches. Digging trenches was an obvious recourse for soldiers seeking protection from persistent enemy fire. But the trench culture which developed on a continuous line from the English Channel to Switzerland, from 1914, had no precedent. Men on both sides lived in muddy trenches and dirty dugouts which became their homes. Return from the trench-world on leave seemed like a transition from significant reality to frivolous phantasmagoria.

In the late 1920s and early 1930s still-shocked writers who had survived purged their feelings in notable books. The English 'war poets' – Graves, Blunden and Sassoon – wrote famous prose accounts of trench warfare. Remarque in Germany, Céline in France also published bestsellers. The impact of these books initially contributed to a tide of pacifist feeling, turned back as the menace of 'Fascism' – a term used rather too loosely to include Nazism – became fully apparent in the late 1930s. More enduringly, it meant that, while the German military developed tactics designed to avert trench stalemate, young Frenchmen and Britons believed when war came again in 1939 that a repetition of 1914–18 was what they were in for. While the Second World War was exhibiting new horrors even in arenas of rapid movement, young writers continued to believe that their predecessors of the Great War had said it all.

Journey to the End of the Night

Louis-Ferdinand Céline's Voyage au bout de la nuit *(1932) has a controverted position in the roster of twentieth-century 'classics' since its author (actual surname Destouches) became a virulent anti-Semite, supported the Nazi occupation of France and was lucky to suffer exile and imprisonment rather than execution after 1945. But this tour of the downside of modern life, a bestseller when it first appeared, retains unique freshness – satirical, grimly realistic, anarchistic, nihilistic, scatological.*

The protagonist and narrator Ferdinand Bardamu volunteers for the French army when war breaks out in August 1914. Within months, his nerves wrecked, he is in a psychiatric hospital. Paul Déroulède, to whom Céline refers here, was a writer and politician, founder of the League of Patriots – an extreme nationalist.

When you're in, you're in. They put us on horseback, and after we'd been on horseback for two months, they put us back on our feet. Maybe because of the expense. Anyway, one morning the colonel was looking for his horse, his orderly had made off with it, nobody knew where to, probably some quiet spot that bullets couldn't get to as easily as the middle of the road. Because that was exactly where the colonel and I had finally stationed ourselves, with me holding his orderly book while he wrote out his orders.

Down the road, away in the distance, as far as we could see, there were two black dots, plunk in the middle like us, but they were two Germans and they'd been busy shooting for the last fifteen or twenty minutes.

Maybe our colonel knew why they were shooting, maybe the Germans knew, but I, so help me, hadn't the vaguest idea. As far back as I could search my memory, I hadn't done a thing to the Germans, I'd always been polite and friendly with them. I knew the Germans pretty well, I'd even gone to school in their country when I was little, near Hanover. I'd spoken their language. A bunch of loud-mouthed little halfwits, that's what they were, with pale, furtive eyes like wolves; we'd go out to the woods together after school to feel the girls up, or we'd fire pop-guns or pistols you could buy for four marks. And we drank sugary beer together. But from that to shooting at us right in the middle of the road, without so much as a word of introduction, was a long way, a very long way. If you asked me, they were going too far.

This war, in fact, made no sense at all. It couldn't go on.

Had something weird got into these people? Something I didn't feel at all? I suppose I hadn't noticed it . . .

Anyway, my feelings toward them hadn't changed. In spite of everything. I'd have liked to understand their brutality, but what I wanted still more, enormously, with all my heart, was to get out of there, because suddenly the whole business looked to me like a great big mistake.

'In a mess like this,' I said to myself, 'there's nothing to be done, all you can do is clear out . . .'

Over our heads, two millimetres, maybe one millimetre from our temples, those long searching lines of steel that bullets make when they're out to kill you, were whistling through the hot summer air.

I'd never felt so useless as I did amidst all those bullets in the sunlight. A vast and universal mockery.

I was only twenty at the time. Deserted farms in the distance, empty wide-open churches, as if the peasants had gone out for the day to attend a fair at the other end of the district, leaving everything they owned with us for safe-keeping, their countryside, their carts with the shafts in the air, their fields, their barn yards, the road, the trees, even the cows, a chained dog, the works. Leaving us free to do as we pleased while they were gone. Nice of them, in a way. 'Still,' I said to myself, 'if they hadn't gone somewhere else, if there were still somebody here, I'm sure we wouldn't be behaving so badly! So disgustingly! We wouldn't dare in front of them!' But there wasn't a soul to watch us! Nobody but us, like newlyweds that get down to the dirty business when all the people have gone home.

And another thought I had (behind a tree) was that I wished Déroulède – the one I'd heard so much about – had been there to describe his reactions when a bullet tore open his guts.

Those Germans squatting on the road, shooting so obstinately, were rotten shots, but they seemed to have ammunition to burn, whole warehouses full or so it seemed to me. Nobody could say this war was over! I have to hand it to the colonel, his bravery was remarkable. He roamed around in the middle of the road, up and down and back and forth in the midst of the bullets as calmly as if he'd been waiting for a friend on a station platform, except just a tiny bit impatient.

One thing I'd better tell you right away, I'd never been able to stomach the country, I'd always found it dreary, those endless fields of mud, those houses where nobody's ever home, those roads that don't go anywhere. And if to all that you add a war, it's completely unbearable. A sudden wind had come up on both sides of the road, the clattering leaves of the poplars mingled with the little dry crackle aimed at us from down the road. Those unknown soldiers missed us every time, but they spun a thousand deaths around us, so close they seemed to clothe us. I was afraid to move.

That colonel, I could see, was a monster. Now I knew it for sure, he was worse than a dog, he couldn't conceive of his own death. At the same time I realized that there must be plenty of brave men like him in our army, and just as many no doubt in the army facing us. How many, I wondered. One or two million, say several millions in all? The thought turned my fear to panic. With such people this infernal lunacy could go on for ever . . . Why would they stop? Never had the world seemed so implacably doomed.

Could I, I thought, be the last coward on earth? How terrifying! . . . All alone with two million stark raving heroic madmen, armed to the eyeballs? With and without helmets, without horses, on motorcycles, bellowing, in cars, screeching, shooting, plotting, flying, kneeling, digging, taking cover, bounding over trails, bombarding, shut up on earth as if it were a loony bin, ready to demolish everything on it, Germany, France, whole continents, everything that breathes, destroy, destroy, madder than mad dogs, worshipping their madness (which dogs don't), a hundred, a thousand times madder than a thousand dogs, and a lot more vicious! A pretty mess we were in! No doubt about it, this crusade I'd let myself in for was the apocalypse!

You can be a virgin in horror the same as in sex. How, when I left the Place Clichy, could I have imagined such horror? Who could have suspected, before getting really into the war, all the ingredients that go to make up the rotten, heroic, good-for-nothing soul of man? And there I was, caught up in a mass flight into collective murder, into the fiery furnace . . . Something had come up from the depths, and it was happening now.

The colonel was still as cool as a cucumber, I watched him as he stood on the embankment, taking little messages sent by the general, reading them without haste as the bullets flew all around him, and tearing them into little pieces. Did none of those messages include an order to put an immediate stop to this abomination? Did no top brass tell him there had been a misunderstanding? A horrible mistake? A misdeal? That somebody's got it all wrong, that the plan had been for manoeuvres, a sham battle, not a massacre! Not at all! 'Keep it up, colonel! You're doing fine!' That's what General des Entrayes, the head of our division and commander over us all, must have written in those notes that were being brought every five minutes by a courier, who looked greener and more shitless each time. I could have palled up with that boy, we'd have been scared together. But we had no time to fraternize.

So there was no mistake? So there was no law against people shooting at people they couldn't even see! It was one of the things you could do without anybody reading you the riot act. In fact, it was recognized and probably encouraged by upstanding citizens, like the draft, or marriage, or hunting! . . . No two ways about it. I was suddenly on the most intimate terms with war. I'd lost my virginity. You've got to be pretty much alone with her as I was then to get a good look at her, the slut, full face and profile. A war had been switched on between us and the other side, and now it was burning! Like the current between the two carbons of an arc lamp! And this lamp was in no hurry to go out! It would get us all, the colonel and everyone else, he looked pretty spiffy now, but he wouldn't roast up any bigger than me when the current from the other side got him between the shoulders.

There are different ways of being condemned to death. Oh! What wouldn't I have given to be in prison instead of here! What a fool I'd been! If only I had had a little foresight and stolen something or other when it would have been so easy and there was still time. I never think of anything. You come out of prison alive, you don't out of a war! The rest is blarney.

If only I'd had time, but I didn't. There was nothing left to steal. How pleasant it would be in a cosy little cell, I said to myself, where the bullets couldn't get in. Where they never got in! I knew of one that was ready and waiting, all sunny and warm! I saw it in my dreams, the prison of Saint-Germain to be exact, right near the forest. I knew it well, I'd often passed that way. How a man changes! I was a child in those days, and that prison frightened me. Because I didn't know what men are like. Never again will I believe what they say or what they think. Men are the thing to be afraid of, always, men and nothing else.

How much longer would this madness have to go on before these monsters dropped with exhaustion? How long could a convulsion like this last? Months? Years? How many? Maybe till the whole world's dead, and all these madmen? Every last one of them? And seeing that events were taking such a desperate turn, I decided to stake everything on one throw, to make one last try, to see if I couldn't stop the war, just me, all by myself! At least in this one spot where I happened to be.

The colonel was only two steps away from me, pacing. I'd talk to him. Something I'd never done. This was a time for daring. The way things stood, there was practically nothing to lose. 'What is it?' he'd ask me, startled, I imagined, at my bold interruption. Then I'd explain the situation as I saw it, and we'd see what he thought. The essential is to talk things over. Two heads are better than one.

I was about to take the decisive step when, at that very moment, who should arrive at the double but a dismounted cavalryman (as we said in those days), exhausted, shaky in the joints, holding his helmet upside-down in one hand like Belisarius, trembling, all covered with mud, his face even greener than the courier I mentioned before. He stammered and gulped. You'd have thought he was struggling to climb out of a tomb, and it had made him sick to his stomach. Could it be that this spook didn't like bullets any more than I did? That he saw them coming like me?

'What is it?' Disturbed, brutally, the colonel stopped him short; flinging at him a glance that might have been steel.

It made our colonel very angry to see that wretched cavalryman so incorrectly clad and shitting in his pants with fright. The colonel had no use for fear, that was a sure thing. And especially that helmet held in the hand like a bowler was really too much in a combat regiment like ours that was just getting into the war. It was as if this dismounted cavalryman had seen the war and taken his hat off in greeting.

Under the colonel's withering look the wobbly messenger snapped to attention, pressing his little finger to the seam of his trousers as the occasion demanded. And so he stood on the embankment, stiff as a board, swaying, the sweat running down his chin strap; his jaws were trembling so hard that little abortive cries kept coming out of him, like a little dog dreaming. You couldn't make out whether he wanted to speak to us or whether he was crying.

Our Germans squatting at the end of the road had just changed weaponry. Now they were having their fun with a machine-gun, sputtering like handfuls of matches, and all around us flew swarms of angry bullets, as hostile as wasps.

The man finally managed to articulate a few words:

'Colonel, sir, Sergeant Barousse has been killed.'

'So what?'

'He was on his way to meet the bread wagon on the Etrapes road, sir.'

'So what?'

'He was blown up by a shell!'

'So what, dammit!'

'That's what, colonel, sir.'

'Is that all?'

'Yes, sir, that's all, colonel, sir.'

'What about the bread?' the colonel asked.

That was the end of the dialogue, because, I remember distinctly, he barely had time to say 'What about the bread?' That was all. After that there was nothing but flame and noise. But the kinds of noise you wouldn't have thought possible. Our eyes, ears, nose and mouth were so full of that noise that I thought it was all over and I'd turned into noise and flame myself.

After a while the flame went away, the noise stayed in my head, and my arms and legs trembled as if somebody were shaking me from behind. My limbs seemed to be leaving me, but then in the end they stayed on. The smoke stung my eyes for a long time, and the prickly smell of powder and sulphur hung on, strong enough to kill all the fleas and bedbugs in the whole world.

I thought of Sergeant Barousse, who had just gone up in smoke as the man had told us. That was good news. Great, I thought to myself. That makes one less stinker in the regiment! He wanted to have me court-martialled for a tin of meat. 'It's an ill wind,' I said to myself. In that respect, you can't deny it, the war seemed to serve a purpose now and then! I knew of three or four more in the regiment, real scum, that I'd have gladly helped to make the acquaintance of a shell, like Barousse.

As for the colonel, I didn't wish him any harm. But he was dead too. At first I didn't see him. The blast had carried him up an embankment and laid him down on his side, right in the arms of the dismounted cavalryman, the courier, who was finished too. They were embracing each other for the moment and for all eternity, but the cavalryman's head was gone, all he had was an opening at the top of the neck, with blood in it bubbling and glugging like jam in a pan. The colonel's belly was wide open and he was making a nasty face about it. It must have hurt when it happened. So much the worse for him! If he'd got out when the shooting started, it wouldn't have happened.

All that tangled meat was bleeding profusely.

Shells were still bursting to the right and left of the scene.

I'd had enough, I was glad to have such a good pretext for clearing out. I even hummed a tune, and reeled like when you've been rowing a long way and your legs are wobbly. 'Just one shell!' I said to myself. 'Amazing how quick just one shell can clean things up. Could you believe it?' I kept saying to myself. 'Could you believe it!'

There was nobody left at the end of the road. The Germans were gone. But that little episode had taught me a quick lesson to keep to the cover of the trees. I was in a hurry to get back to our command post, to see if anyone else in our regiment had been killed on reconnaissance. There must be some good dodges, I said to myself, for getting taken prisoner ... Here and there in the fields a few puffs of smoke still clung to the ground. 'Maybe they're all dead,' I thought. 'Seeing they refuse to understand anything whatsoever, the best solution would be for them all to get killed instantly ... The war would be over, and we'd go home ... Maybe we'd march across the Place Clichy in triumph ... Just one or two survivors ... In my dream ... Strapping good fellows marching behind the general, all the rest would be dead like the colonel ... Like Barousse ... like Vanaille (another bastard) ... etc. They'd shower us with decorations and flowers, we'd march through the Arc de Triomphe. We'd go to a restaurant, they'd serve us free of charge, we'd never pay for anything any more, never as long as we lived! We're heroes! we'd say when they brought the bill ... defenders of the *Patrie*! That would do it! ... We'd pay with little French flags! ... The lady at the cash desk would refuse to take money from heroes, she'd even give us some, with kisses thrown in, as we filed out. Life would be worth living.

As I was running, I noticed my arm was bleeding, just a little though, a far from satisfactory wound, a scratch. I'd have to start all over.

It was raining again, the fields of Flanders oozed with dirty water. For a long time I didn't meet a soul, only the wind and a little later the sun. From time to time, I couldn't tell from where, a bullet would come flying merrily through the air and sunshine, looking for me, intent on killing me, there in the wilderness. Why? Never again, not if I lived another hundred years, would I go walking in the country. A solemn oath.

Walking along, I remembered the ceremony of the day before. It had taken place in a meadow, at the foot of a hill; the colonel had harangued the regiment in his booming voice: 'Keep your courage up!' he had cried. 'Keep your courage up! and *Vive la France*!' When you have no imagination, dying is small beer; when you do have imagination, dying is too much. That's my opinion. My understanding had never taken in so many things at once.

The colonel had never had any imagination. That was the source of all his trouble, especially ours. Was I the only man in that regiment with an imagination about death? I preferred my own kind of death, the kind that comes late . . . in twenty years . . . thirty . . . maybe more . . . to this death they were trying to deal me right away . . . eating Flanders mud, my whole mouth full of it, fuller than full, split to the ears by a shell fragment. A man's entitled to an opinion about his own death. But which way, if that was the case, should I go? Straight ahead? My back to the enemy. If the MPs were to catch me roaming around I knew my goose was cooked. They'd give me a slapdash trial that same afternoon in some deserted cloakroom . . . There were lots of empty classrooms wherever we went. They'd play court martial with me the way kids play when the teacher isn't there. The noncoms seated on the platform, me standing in handcuffs in front of the little desks. In the morning they'd shoot me: twelve bullets plus one. So what was the answer?

And I thought of the colonel again, such a brave man with his breastplate and his helmet and his moustaches, if they had exhibited him in a music hall, walking as I saw him under the bullets and shellfire, he'd have filled the Alhambra, he'd have outshone Fragson, and he was a big star at the time I'm telling you about. Keep your courage down! That's what I was thinking.

Rats

Isaac Rosenberg, a Jew from the slums of East London, brought a notably fresh vision to the Western Front. He died in 1918.

BREAK OF DAY IN THE TRENCHES

The darkness crumbles away –
It is the same old druid Time as ever.
Only a live thing leaps my hand –
A queer sardonic rat –
As I pull the parapet's poppy
To stick behind my ear.
Droll rat, they would shoot you if they knew
Your cosmopolitan sympathies
(And God knows what antipathies).
Now you have touched this English hand
You will do the same to a German –
Soon, no doubt, if it be your pleasure
To cross the sleeping green between.
It seems you inwardly grin as you pass
Strong eyes, fine limbs, haughty athletes
Less chanced than you for life,
Bonds to the whims of murder,
Sprawled in the bowels of the earth,
The torn fields of France,
What do you see in our eyes
At the shrieking iron and flame
Hurled through still heavens?
What quaver – what heart aghast?
Poppies whose roots are in man's veins
Drop, and are ever dropping;
But mine in my ear is safe,
Just a little white with the dust.

Frank Richards published Old Soldiers Never Die *in 1933, after the impact of Western Front war memoirs by poets who had been young officers. In his book he mentions, and praises, both Robert Graves (see below) and Siegfried Sassoon as good officers – and Graves was not only instrumental in getting his book published, but also polished Richards' prose for him. However, his view of the war was utterly different from theirs. He had joined the Royal Welch Fusiliers in 1901 and served eight years as a regular soldier, nearly seven of them in India and Burma. Then he returned to civilian life, as a timberman's assistant in a Welsh coalmine. But he was still an army reservist. He was recalled to the Colours on the very first day of war in August 1914 and served continuously to the very end in November 1918, latterly as a front-line signalman. Though old comrades and new friends were killed and maimed around him, Richards' own worst legacy of the war was a bad case of haemorrhoids, not operated on until the war was long over. His survival clearly depended on luck, of which he mentions many instances, but also on long experience. He thought the conditions of this war were appalling and that the top brass were out of touch and incompetent. He had no animus against Germans and there is in his writing not the slightest trace of noisy patriotism. He often records, without censure, the British soldier's yearning for a 'Blighty' wound – one which would heal and would not maim, but would ensure transport back to hospital in 'Dear old Blighty'.*

He details with subdued merriment the British Tommy's less respectable traits – his swearing, his looting of French villages, his liaisons with willing mademoiselles *and his propensity to get as drunk as he possibly could whenever opportunity offered itself. He won the Distinguished Conduct Medal and the Military Medal, and could have become an NCO and worked his way up to a commission as other old regulars did, but he preferred to remain a private. His matter-of-fact manner makes his tale of Dann and the rat curiously convincing. It crops up in a particularly vivid passage about trench warfare in 1916.*

During one spell in the line at Hulloch, Dann and I came out of our little dug-out, which was about fifteen yards behind the front-line trench, to clean our rifles and bayonets. We were just about to begin when there appeared, on the back of the trench we were in, the largest rat that I ever saw in my life. It was jet black and was looking intently at Dann, who threw a clod of earth at it but missed, and it didn't even attempt to dodge it. I threw a clod at it then; it sprung out of the way, but not far, and began staring at Dann again. This got on Dann's nerves; he threw another clod but missed again, and it never even flinched. I had my bayonet fixed and made a lunge at it; it sprung out of the way for me all right, but had another intent look at Dann before it disappeared over the top. I would have shot it, for I had a round in the breech, but we were not allowed to fire over the top to the rear of us for fear of hitting men in the support trench; one or two men had been hit in this way by men shooting at rats, and orders were very strict regarding it. Dann had gone very pale; I asked him if he was ill. He said that he wasn't but the rat had made him feel queer. I burst out laughing. He said: 'It's all right, you laughing, but I know my number is up. You saw how that rat never even flinched when I threw at it, and I saw something besides that you didn't see or you wouldn't be laughing at me. Mark my words, when I do go West that rat will be close by.' I told him not to talk so wet and that we may be a hundred miles from this part of the front in a week's time. He said: 'That don't matter: if it's two hundred miles off or a thousand, that rat will be knocking around when I go West.' Dann was a very brave and cheery fellow, but from that day he was a changed man. He still did his work, the same as the rest of us, and never shirked a dangerous job, but all his former cheeriness had left him. Old soldiers who knew him well often asked me what was wrong with him. But I never told them; they might have chaffed him about it. Neither I nor Dann ever made any reference about the rat from that day on, and though we two had passed many hours together shooting at rats for sport in those trenches, especially along at Givenchy by the canal bank, he never went shooting them again . . .

. . .

We were relieved, and some days later we entrained for the Somme. We had a new colonel now, Colonel Crawshay, who proved to be the best we ever had. I had soldiered with him in the Channel Isles and abroad. He was universally liked by everyone, a stickler for discipline, and when in the line, no matter what the conditions were, was always visiting the front-line trenches and seeing things for himself. He had a cheery word for everyone and was as brave as they make them. Captain Stanway had left us to take command of a new service battalion. He and Fox had been the only two sergeant-majors of the Company that never pinched our rum.

It had been very noticeable during the last few months that all old hands were getting killed and youngsters who had only been out a few months were receiving lovely blighty wounds. This had happened so frequently of late that we old hands used to remark that when we did get hit it would either be a bullet through the pound or stop a five-point-nine all on our own. But we considered that men were very lucky who met their death in this way: they didn't know anything about it and it was the death we all wished for if death must come our way. It was much preferable than to be blinded for life or to be horribly wounded and disfigured by shell splinters and perhaps still survive it.

We arrived on the Somme by a six days march from the railhead, and early in the morning of the 14th July passed through Fricourt, where our First Battalion had broken through on 1st July, and arrived at the end of Mametz Wood which had been captured some days before by the 38th Welsh Division which included four of our new service battalions. The enemy had been sending over tear-gas and the valley was thick with it. It smelt like strong onions which made our eyes and noses run very badly; we were soon coughing, sneezing and cursing. We rested in shell holes, the ground all around us being thick with dead of the troops who had been attacking Mametz Wood. The fighting was going on about three-quarters of a mile ahead of us.

Dann, a young signaller named Thomas, and I, were posted to A Company. The three of us were dozing when Thomas gave a shout: a spent bullet with sufficient force to penetrate had hit him in the knee – our first casualty on the Somme. Dann said: 'I don't suppose it will be my luck to get hit with a spent bullet; it will be one at short range through the pound or a twelve-inch shell all on my own.' I replied, as usual, that he would be damned lucky if he stopped either, and that he wouldn't be able to grouse much afterwards. 'You're right enough about that, Dick,' he said. A few hours later the Battalion moved around the corner of the wood, the Company occupying a shallow trench which was only knee-deep. The first officer casualty on the Somme was the lieutenant who got the MC for shouting: 'We'll have to surrender. They've got behind us.' Hammer Lane was next to this officer, deepening the trench when a very small bit of shrapnel ricocheted off his shovel hit the officer in the foot. He began to holler like mad and the Colonel who was not far off rushed up and wanted to know if he was badly hit. Lane answered: 'No, sir. He's making a lot of bloody row over nothing at all.' The Colonel told Lane to shut up and never speak of an officer in that way again. Lane told me later in the day that if the officer had had his bloody belly ripped open he could not have made more row than what he did.

Dann and I were by ourselves in one part of this trench, the Company Commander being about ten yards below us. The majority of the Company were soon in the wood on the scrounge; we had been told that we were likely to stay where we were for a day or two. I told Dann that I was going in the wood on the scrounge and that I would try and get a couple of German topcoats and some food if I could find any. The topcoats would be very handy as we were in fighting order, and the nights were cold for July. Just inside the wood, which was a great tangle of broken trees and branches, was a German trench, and all around it our dead and theirs were lying. I was in luck's way: I got two tins of Maconochies and half a loaf of bread, also two topcoats. The bread was very stale and it was a wonder the rats hadn't got at it. Although gas destroyed large numbers of them there were always plenty of them left skipping about. I returned to Dann telling him how lucky I had been, and that we would have a feed. 'Righto,' he replied, 'but I think I'll write out a couple of quick-firers first.'

Enemy shells were now coming over and a lot of spent machine-gun bullets were zipping about. He sat on the back of the trench writing his quick-firers when – zip! – and he rolled over, clutching his neck. Then a terrified look came in his face as he pointed one hand behind me. I turned and just behind me on the back of the trench saw the huge black rat that we had seen in Hulloch. It was looking straight past me at Dann. I was paralysed myself for a moment, and without looking at me it turned and disappeared in a shell hole behind. I turned around and instantly flattened myself on the bottom of the trench, a fraction of a second before a shell burst behind me. I picked myself up amid a shower of dirt and clods and looked at Dann, but he was dead. The spent bullet had sufficient force to penetrate his neck and touch the spinal column. And there by his side, also dead, was the large rat: the explosion of the shell had blown it up and it had dropped by the side of him. I seized hold of its tail and swung it back in the shell hole it had been blown from. I was getting the creeps. Although Mametz Wood was, I daresay, over fifty miles as the crow flies from Hulloch I had no doubt in my own mind that it was the same rat what we had seen in the latter place. It was the only weird experience I had during the whole of the War. There was no one near us at the time and men on the right and left of us did not know Dann was killed until I told them. If I hadn't handled that rat and flung it away I should have thought that I had been seeing things, like the many of us who saw things on the Retirement.

The Face of Battle

John Keegan's book The Face of Battle *(1976) was a revelation to historians and may be seen as the essential pioneering work of the New Military History. Keegan demolished the conventions by which military historians had previously described combat. Making close and critical use of available documents and setting his narratives in social and cultural context, he rewrote the history of European warfare with very detailed accounts of three major battles – Agincourt (1415), Waterloo (1815) and the first day of the Battle of the Somme (1 July 1916). In the last account he uncovered the paradox that, with advances in military technology and telephone communication, commanders had less, not more, control of what happened, and historians would find it harder, not easier, to comprehend events. Overall, the first day on the Somme was indescribable.*

The plan of the French and British commanders was to attack in force on the Somme sector of the trenches near the Franco-Belgian border. An unprecedented week-long artillery barrage would destroy the German barbed wire and front lines and make advance straightforward – then the barrage would move up and troops would proceed to take the Germans' reserve trenches and make possible a drive towards Germany itself. But the massive allied barrage, for several technical reasons, did not soften up the German front sufficiently. In particular, it failed to stifle the German machine-guns which cut swathes of men down as they advanced. Even when German trenches were occupied, to proceed under the new barrage was beyond decimated and exhausted units. While the British force at the Somme included crack Regular army battalions, a high proportion were enthusiastic but inexperienced volunteers from Kitchener's 'New Army', raised since the onset of war. There were also Territorial Army soldiers who had trained part-time before the war. Keegan describes in detail the experience of one of the most famous Territorial battalions, the London Scottish, which, numbering 856 at dawn, had been reduced by death and wounds to 266 by dusk.

THE VIEW FROM ACROSS NO-MAN'S-LAND

Such was one result, duplicated at thirty or forty other points up and down the Somme battlefront on the evening of July 1st, of trusting in the power of contemporary artillery to destroy an enemy position and 'shoot the infantry through' its ruins. The . . . forms of failure just examined do not exhaust the list of mishaps consequent on such an undertaking. The Ulster Division failed to carry its final objective, after a very rapid advance to its first, because the British barrage actually held it up, so allowing the Germans time to man with reinforcements brought from the rear positions which the Ulstermen would otherwise have found empty. Understandably, therefore, the Ulster Division counted July 1st a victory and the date, which also happens to coincide with the anniversary of the Battle of the Boyne (Old Style), is observed by the Protestants of the province as one of their holy days. Again, some battalions' attacks failed because their supports could not or would not follow the trail they had blazed into the German positions, so leaving them cut off deep within the enemy lines. This seems to have been the fate of some of the 12th York and Lancasters, whose graves were found on November 13th, at the very end of the battle, when the village of Serre, one of the uncaptured first-day objectives, at last fell into British hands. Many battalions of the second wave failed to make their attacks work because, arriving in the German trenches, they became so intermingled with the survivors of a battalion which had gone over before them that they lost order and cohesion themselves. But some battalions, one should not forget, succeeded. The 7th Division took some, the 18th most, the 30th all its first objectives, and battalions of the 21st and 34th secured sizeable sections of the German trenches opposite their own. The French, better-trained, more experienced and with much more heavy artillery, had taken all their first-day objectives, and would have gone on if the plan had provided for unexpected success. The first day of the Somme had not been a complete military failure.

But it had been a human tragedy. The Germans, with about sixty battalions on the British Somme front, though about forty in the line, say about thirty-five thousand soldiers, had had killed or wounded about six thousand. Bad enough; but it was in the enormous disparity between their losses and the British that the weight of the tragedy lies: the

German 180th Regiment lost 280 men on July 1st out of about three thousand; attacking it, the British 8th Division lost 5,121 out of twelve thousand. In all the British had lost about sixty thousand, of whom twenty-one thousand had been killed, most in the first hour of the attack, perhaps the first minutes. 'The trenches', wrote Robert Kee fifty years later, 'were the concentration camps of the First World War'; and though the analogy is what an academic reviewer would call unhistorical, there is something Treblinka-like about almost all accounts of July 1st, about those long docile lines of young men, shoddily uniformed, heavily burdened, numbered about their necks, plodding forward across a featureless landscape to their own extermination inside the barbed wire. Accounts of the Somme produce in readers and audiences much the same range of emotions as do descriptions of the running of Auschwitz – guilty fascination, incredulity, horror, disgust, pity and anger – and not only from the pacific and tender-hearted; not only from the military historian, on whom, as he recounts the extinction of this brave effort or that, falls an awful lethargy, his typewriter keys tapping leadenly on the paper to drive the lines of print, like the waves of a Kitchener battalion failing to take its objective, more and more slowly towards the foot of the page; but also from professional soldiers. Anger is the response which the story of the Somme most commonly evokes among professionals. Why did the commanders not do something about it? Why did they let the attack go on? Why did they not stop one battalion following in the wake of another to join it in death?

Some battalions were stopped. On the northern face of the Gommecourt salient, where the 46th North Midland Division's attack had failed completely with heavy loss in the morning, one of the brigade commanders, Brigadier-General H. B. Williams, who had seen the 1/6th North Staffordshire and 1/6th South Staffordshire massacred shortly after zero, declined to send forward their sister battalions, the 1/5th North Staffords and the 1/5th South Staffords, later in the afternoon. The whole of the 10th and 12th Brigades, in 4th Division, were held back from a pointless renewal of the attack north of Beaumont Hamel about the same time, and in the evening General de Lisle, commanding the 29th Division, countermanded orders for the 1/4th and 1/5th King's Own Yorkshire Light Infantry, which had been brought forward from X Corps' reserve, to make a further attempt on the corpse-strewn slopes of Thiepval. There were other reprieves, but the majority of battalions scheduled to attack did so, no matter what had happened to those which had preceded them. There are a number of ways of explaining why this should have been so. Normal military sense of commitment to a plan was one reason, the spirit of contemporary generalship, schooled to believe in the inevitability of heavy casualties another, the mood of self-sacrifice which had the Kitchener armies in its grip a third. But most important of all was the simple ignorance of what was happening which prevailed almost everywhere on the British side of no-man's-land throughout most of the day.

Even sixty years later, it is very difficult to discover much that is precise, detailed and human about the fate of a great number of the battalions of the Fourth Army on July 1st. Many of the London Territorial regiments, with a strong and long-established sense of identity, a middle-class character, and personal connections with metropolitan journalism and publishing, produced after the war excellent regimental histories in which the official chronicle is supplemented and illuminated by a great deal of personal reminiscence from literate and articulate survivors. The regular battalions of the Guards and the regiments of the line added copiously to their existing histories. But, as we have seen, the Somme was predominantly a battle of humbler and more transient groups than these, over which the regular army had temporarily cast the cloak of its identity, but which at the peace vanished from public memory almost as quickly as they had been conjured into existence. It was not a deliberate act of obscuration. The regular regiments which had raised the greatest number of 'Service' battalions were often the least affluent (the rough rule of thumb in calculating the social status of an English regiment is that the farther from London its depot, the less fashionable will it be, and the less monied its officers) and the least able therefore to stand the expense of printing a really exhaustive history. There was moreover a difficulty about sources. The principal source of a unit's history is the War Diary, which the intelligence officer is supposed to write up daily. When he is an amateur its contents tend always to be sketchy, and when action is intense and casualties heavy it may run for days in arrears, later to be written up for form's sake from a single, sometimes second-hand memory of events. All these caveats apply to the War Diaries of July 1st. Consequent uncertainty about the experience of particular Kitchener battalions has added an extra poignancy to their collective story. The uncertainties might have remained forever undispersed. At the very last moment, however, a Lincolnshire farmer, Martin Middlebrook, in whom a chance visit to the war cemeteries of the Somme in the late nineteen-sixties aroused an obsessive curiosity about the nature and fate of the Kitchener armies, embarked on a quest to discover survivors of July 1st, and in a truly heroic effort of historical fieldwork, found and interviewed 546 of them, by then, with the exception of a few enlisted under age, men of seventy or over.

The book which he made from his interviews [*The First Day on the Somme*] is a remarkable achievement, comparable with Siborne's history of Waterloo, constructed on the same basis, and certainly fit to stand beside it, as well as being a great deal more readable. But whereas Siborne addressed his inquiries to all surviving officers, and from their replies was able to piece together a meaningful account of the battle, Middlebrook's answers came, of course, only from the junior ranks whose view was a very local one and which collectively depict almost indecipherable chaos . . . What Middlebrook's evidence emphasizes is the extent to which a hundred years of technological change had further reduced the range of effective vision on the battlefield, particularly in those not familiar with the realities of war. 'On my left,' wrote a private of the 1/8th Royal Warwicks, of the scene at zero hour, 'I could see large shell bursts as the West Yorks advanced and saw many men falling forward. I thought at first they were looking for nose-caps (a favourite souvenir) and it was some time before I realized they were hit.' On the far side of no-man's-land, 'I found the German wire well cut,' wrote a private of the 4th Tyneside Scottish, 'but only three of our company got past there. There was my lieutenant, a sergeant and myself. The rest seemed to have been hit in no man's-land . . . the officer said, "God, God, where's the rest of the boys?"' Private Tomlinson, of the 1/7th Sherwood Foresters, accompanied his commanding officer across no-man's-land, who had gone to find out for himself what was happening to his battalion. 'When we got to the German wire I was absolutely amazed to see it intact, after what we had been told. The colonel and I took cover behind a small bank but after a bit the colonel raised himself on his hands and knees to see better. Immediately he was hit on the forehead by a single bullet.'

With a view of events so hard and dangerous to come by at close quarters with the enemy, it is to be taken for granted that in the British lines a composite picture of the battle was even more difficult to piece together. Rowland Feilding, a Coldstream Guardsman who had come up to observe the battle from a point opposite Mametz, wrote to his wife, 'the sight was inspiring and magnificent. From right to left, but particularly opposite the French . . . the whole horizon seemed to be on fire, the bursting shells blending with smoke from the burning villages . . . this is a district of long views. Never was there a field better suited for watching military operations.' But Feilding was there as a sight-seer, seeking sensation, not precise information. A sight-seer with a more professionally inquisitive motive, J. F. C. Fuller, found on arrival 'an intense bombardment . . . in full swing, and so much dust and smoke [covering] the Gommecourt salient that it was difficult to see anything clearly. At five minutes to zero a somewhat scattered barrage was put down, then came the attack across no-man's-land. I cannot say that I saw it. All I can vouch for is that a little later on through my glasses I did see several groups of men, presumably of the 139 Brigade, moving towards Pigeon Wood.' A commanding officer on the Gommecourt sector, almost under Fuller's eyes, Colonel Dickens, of Queen Victoria's Rifles, saw even less than he did: 'For two hours after zero, no news whatsoever was received from the front,' (which was only about a thousand yards distant) 'all communications, visual and telephonic having failed. Beyond answering appeals from the Brigade' (next headquarters upward) 'for information, we had leisure to observe what was going on.' But he learnt nothing until, after nine o'clock, he was visited by 'two plucky runners who [had] returned to our line through the barrage'.

Why should he have had to depend on runners? The reason is simple to explain. The communication system in Fourth Army, resembling in essentials that installed up and down the Western Front and on both sides of no-man's-land, was a comprehensive one. It was based on the telephone and the telegraph, the latter replacing the former where amplification was difficult to ensure, and ran through an extremely elaborate network of 'land line' and 'air line'. Air lines ran from the major headquarters – GHQ at Montreuil and Fourth Army HQ at Querrieux, fifteen miles from the front – to Corps, and Division, with as much lateral branching as was necessary to make communication to a flank possible. Forward of Division, to Brigade and Battalion, the lines left their poles to descend earthward, becoming 'land lines', by this stage of the war no longer strung vulnerably along the walls of the communication trenches, but buried under the duckboards on the floor. The nearer it approached the front trench, the deeper was it buried, until in the forward zone it reached a depth of six feet. The installation of this 'six-foot bury' had been one of the most time-consuming preparations for the offensive, but was justified by the security of communication it provided even under the heaviest enemy shellfire. It had, however, one disabling short-coming: it stopped at the edge of no-man's-land. Once the troops left their trenches, as at 7.30 a.m. on July 1st, they passed beyond the carry of their signals system into the unknown. The army had provided them with some makeshifts to indicate their position: rockets, tin triangles sewn to the backs of their packs as air recognition symbols, lamps and flags, and some one-way signalling expedients, Morse shutters, semaphore flags and carrier pigeons; but none were to prove of real use on July 1st. Indeed, these items seem only to have further encumbered men already heavily laden, in a fashion more reminiscent of explorers setting off on an expedition than soldiers entering battle. The story of Scott's Last Expedition, news of which had magnetized the English-speaking world on the eve of the war, may have seemed, as it does in retrospect, of special significance to a reflective soldier of the Fourth Army as, bowed under the weight of rations and protective clothing, he prepared to leave base-camp for the dash to the final objective on the evening of June 30th; it has its parallels in the fate of the vanished party of the 12th York and Lancasters, whose bodies were discovered five months after the attack in the heart of the German position.

That a party could disappear so completely, not in the Antarctic wastes but at a point almost within visual range of their own lines, seems incomprehensible today, so attuned are we to thinking of wireless providing instant communication across the battlefield. But the cloud of unknowing which descended on a First World War battlefield at zero hour was accepted as one of its hazards by contemporary generals. Since the middle of the nineteenth century, the width of battlefields had been extending so rapidly that no general could hope to be present, as Wellington had made himself, at each successive point of crisis; since the end of the century the range and volume of small-arms fire had been increasing to such an extent that no general could hope to survey, as Wellington had done, the line of battle from the front rank. The main work of the general, it had been accepted, had now to be done in his office, before the battle began; and indeed one of the pieces of military literature most talked of in the British army before the First World War was a short story, *A Sense of Proportion*, by General Sir Edward Swinton, which had as its central character a general – obviously based on the great Moltke – who, having made his dispositions on the eve of battle, spends its hours casting flies for trout, serene in the assurance – which the story's conclusion vindicates – that he had done all he could.

No British general spent July 1st fishing. But the spirit which informs the plans laid by the Fourth Army, whether those of a formation like XIII Corps (equivalent in size to Wellington's Waterloo army) which ran to thirty-one pages (Wellington issued no written plan for Waterloo), or of a unit like Queen Victoria's Rifles, a force of under a thousand men, which run to twenty numbered paragraphs, is essentially Swintonian. It is a spirit not of providing for eventualities, but rather of attempting to preordain the future; a spirit borne out by the language of the orders: 'infantry and machine-guns will be pushed forward at once . . .'; 'the siege and heavy artillery will be advanced . . .' 'After the capture of their final objective the 30th Division will be relieved by the 9th Division . . .' Man's attempts at preordination are always risky and require as a minimum precondition for success the co-operation of all concerned. Upon that of the Germans the British could not of course count. Consequently, at every point where the future threatened to resist preordination, Haig and Rawlinson had reinsured themselves – by lengthening the duration of the bombardment, adding to the targets to be destroyed, increasing the ratio of troops to space.

The effect of these reinsurances was to complicate the plan. And the complication of a plan which would depend for its success on the smooth interaction of a very large number of mutually dependent elements invited its frustration. Interaction requires articulation, to adopt the language with which J. F. C. Fuller was fond of obscuring military truths; which means that if major operations are to be carried through in the teeth of enemy resistance, commanders must at all time be able to talk to their troops, troops to their supporting artillery and so on. Such conversations were easily arranged while everyone was on the same side of no-man's-land. But once the infantry departed on their journey, conversation stopped, to be carried on, if at all, through the medium of the battalion runners, upon whose messages Colonel Dickens, for example, had to rely for news, two hours old, of the progress of his fighting companies.

Discontinuities of this order in the receipt of information, particularly when the information concerned difficulties or failure, made the management of a battle, in the tactile and instantaneous fashion open to Wellington at Waterloo, impossible. Commanders could not discover where the soldiers were . . . Throughout the morning and afternoon,

Rawlinson, at Querrieux, and Haig, in his advanced headquarters at the Château de Beauquesne, ten miles to the north, attempted to follow the battle from scraps of imprecise information several hours old. Neither made real sense of it. Neither, very wisely, ordered any substantive changes of plan. Many of the gunners, whose fire, if properly directed, would have been so effective in saving British lives, also remained, though closer at hand, inactive spectators: 'On the whole', wrote Neil Fraser Tytler of a Lancashire Territorial Field Brigade, 'we had a very delightful day, with nothing to do except send numerous reports through to Head Quarters and observe the stupendous spectacle before us. There was nothing to do as regards controlling my battery's fire, as the barrage orders had all been prepared beforehand.' Throughout this period, the only group of soldiers with precise information to offer of the whereabouts and circumstances of their units were the battalion runners. It is ironic to reflect that the taunt thrown into the faces of so many highly trained German Great General Staff officers, excluded by official policy from service in the trenches, by Hitler, ex-runner of the 16th Bavarian Reserve Regiment – that he knew more about the realities of war than they – had after all a coarse grain of truth to it.

Owen's Spring Offensive

Wilfred Owen soon became, and has always remained, the most directly appealing of the English 'soldier-poets' of the Great War. His death in action just before the Armistice made him an emblematic martyr.

SPRING OFFENSIVE

Halted against the shade of a last hill,
They fed, and lying easy, were at ease
And, finding comfortable chests and knees,
Carelessly slept. But many there stood still
To face the stark, blank sky beyond the ridge,
Knowing their feet had come to the end of the world.

Marvelling they stood, and watched the long grass swirled
By the May breeze, murmurous with wasp and midge,
For though the summer oozed into their veins
Like an injected drug for their bodies' pains,
Sharp on their souls hung the imminent line of grass,
Fearfully flashed the sky's mysterious glass.

Hour after hour they ponder the warm field –
And the far valley behind, where the buttercup
Had blessed with gold their slow boots coming up,
Where even the little brambles would not yield,
But clutched and clung to them like sorrowing hands;
They breathe like trees unstirred.

Till like a cold gust thrills the little word
At which each body and its soul begird
And tighten them for battle. No alarms
Of bugles, no high flags, no clamorous haste –
Only a lift and flare of eyes that faced
The sun, like a friend with whom their love is done.

O larger shone that smile against the sun, –
Mightier than his whose bounty these have spurned.

So, soon they topped the hill, and raced together
Over an open stretch of herb and heather
Exposed. And instantly the whole sky burned
With fury against them; earth set sudden cups
In thousands for their blood; and the green slope
Chasmed and steepened sheer to infinite space.

Of them who running on that last high place
Leapt to swift unseen bullets, or went up
On the hot blast and fury of hell's upsurge,
Or plunged and fell away past this world's verge,
Some say God caught them even before they fell.

But what say such as from existence' brink
Ventured but drave too swift to sink,
The few who rushed in the body to enter hell,
And there out-fiending all its fiends and flames
With superhuman inhumanities,
Long-famous glories, immemorial shames –
And crawling slowly back, have by degrees
Regained cool peaceful air in wonder –
Why speak not they of comrades that went under?

Goodbye to All That

Robert Graves, marked out in his teens as an outstandingly promising poet, served as an officer, like his friend Sassoon, in the Royal Welch Fusiliers. The war traumatized him deeply, and he did not fully purge himself of it by publishing Goodbye to All That *(1929), a memoir which included pre-war and post-war life and managed to make wry, sub-satirical humour out of the trenches – though he went on to become one of the finest love poets in English, and a best-selling historical novelist. He was invalided home in 1916 after sustaining a serious injury to a lung in the Battle of the Somme. A premature obituary reference had appeared in* The Times *newspaper. His mother was German – Amalia von Ranke – hence his nickname 'Von Runicke'. He was sent home for good soon after the events described here.*

In December, I attended a medical board; they sounded my chest and asked how I was feeling. The president wanted to know whether I wanted a few months more home-service. I said: 'No, sir, I should be much obliged if you would pass me fit for service overseas.' In January I got my sailing orders.

I went back an old soldier, as my kit and baggage proved. I had reduced the original Christmas-tree to a pocket-torch with a fourteen-day battery, and a pair of insulated wire-cutters strong enough to cut German wire (the ordinary Army issue would cut only British wire). Instead of a haversack, I bought a pack like the ones carried by the men, but lighter and waterproof. I had lost my revolver when wounded and not bought another; a rifle and bayonet could always be got from the battalion. (Not carrying rifle and bayonet made officers conspicuous during an attack; in most divisions now they carried them; and also wore trousers rolled down over their puttees, like the men, instead of riding-breeches – because the Germans had learned to recognize officers by their thin knees.) The heavy blankets I had brought out before were now replaced by an eiderdown sleeping-bag in an oiled-silk cover. I also took a Shakespeare and a Bible, both printed on India paper, a Catullus and a Lucretius in Latin; and two light-weight folding canvas arm-chairs –

one as a present for Yates, the quartermaster, the other for myself. I wore a very thick whip-cord tunic, with a neat patch above the second button and another between the shoulders – my only salvage from the last time out, except for the reasonably waterproof pair of ski-ing boots, in which also I had been killed – my breeches had been cut off me in hospital.

I commanded a draft of ten young officers. Young officers, at this period, were expected, as someone has noted in his war-memoirs, to be roistering blades over wine and women. These ten did their best. Three of them got venereal disease at the Rouen Blue Lamp. They were strictly brought-up Welsh boys of the professional classes, had never hitherto visited a brothel, and knew nothing about prophylactics. One of them shared a hut with me. He came in very late and very drunk one night, from the *Drapeau Blanc*, woke me up and began telling me about his experiences. 'I never knew before,' he said, 'what a wonderful thing sex is!'

I said irritably, and in some disgust: 'The *Drapeau Blanc*? Then I hope to God you washed yourself.'

He was very Welsh, and on his dignity. 'What do you mean, captain? I did wass my fa-ace and ha-ands.'

There were no restraints in France; these boys had money to spend and knew that they stood a good chance of being killed within a few weeks anyhow. They did not want to die virgins. The *Drapeau Blanc* saved the life of scores by incapacitating them for future trench service. Base venereal hospitals were always crowded. The troops took a lewd delight in exaggerating the proportion of army chaplains to combatant officers treated there.

At the Bull Ring [training centre at Étaples], the instructors were full of bullet-and-bayonet enthusiasm, with which they tried to infect the drafts. The drafts consisted, for the most part, either of forcibly enlisted men, or wounded men returning; and at this dead season of the year could hardly be expected to feel enthusiastic on their arrival. The training principles had recently been revised. *Infantry Training, 1914* laid it down politely that the soldier's ultimate aim was to put out of action or render ineffective the armed forces of the enemy. The War Office no longer considered this statement direct enough for a war of attrition. Troops learned instead that they must HATE the Germans, and KILL as many of them as possible. In bayonet-practice, the men had to make horrible grimaces and utter blood-curdling yells as they charged. The instructors' faces were set in a permanent ghastly grin. 'Hurt him, now! In at the belly! Tear his guts out!' they would scream, as the men charged the dummies. 'Now that upper swing at his privates with the butt. Ruin his chances for life! No more little Fritzes! . . . Naaoh! Anyone would think that you *loved* the bloody swine, patting and stroking 'em like that! BITE HIM, I SAY! STICK YOUR TEETH IN HIM AND WORRY HIM! EAT HIS HEART OUT!'

Once more I felt glad to be sent up to the trenches.

I found the Second Battalion near Bouchavesnes on the Somme, but a very different Second Battalion. No riding-school, no battalion mess, no Quetta manners, no regular officers, except for a couple of newly arrived Sandhurst boys. I was more warmly welcomed this time; my supposed spying activities had been forgotten. But the day before I reported, Colonel Crawshay had been wounded while out in No Man's Land inspecting the battalion wire: shot in the thigh by one of the 'rotten crowd' of his letter, who mistook him for a German and fired without challenging. He has been in and out of nursing homes ever since.

Doctor Dunn asked me with kindly disapproval what I meant by returning so soon. I said: 'I couldn't stand England any longer.' He told the acting CO that I was, in his opinion, unfit for trench service, so I took command of the headquarter company and went to live with transport, back at Frises, where the Somme made a bend. My company consisted of regimental clerks, cooks, tailors, shoemakers, pioneers, transport men, and so on, who in a break-through could turn riflemen and be used as a combatant force, as at the First Battle of Ypres. We lived in dug-outs, close to the river, which was frozen over completely but for a narrow stretch of fast-running water in the middle. I have never been so cold in all my life. I used to go up to the trenches every night with the rations, Yates being sick; it was about a twelve-mile walk there and back.

General Pinney, now commanding the Thirty-third Division, felt teetotal convictions on behalf of his men and stopped their issue of rum, unless in emergencies; the immediate result being the heaviest sick-list that the battalion had ever known. Our men looked forward to their tot of rum at the dawn stand-to as the brightest moment of the twenty-four hours; when this was denied them, their resistance weakened. I took the rations up through Cléry, not long before a wattle-and-daub village with some hundreds of inhabitants. The highest part of it now standing was a short course of brick wall about three feet high; the remainder consisted of enormous overlapping shell-craters. A broken-down steamroller by the roadside had 'CLÉRY' chalked on it as a guide to travellers. We often lost a horse or two at Cléry, which the Germans went on shelling from habit.

Our reserve billets for these Bouchavesnes trenches were at Suzanne: not really billets, but dug-outs and shelters. Suzanne also lay in ruins. This winter was the hardest since 1894–5. The men played inter-company football matches on the river, now frozen two feet thick. I remember a meal here, in a shelter-billet: stew and tinned tomatoes on aluminium plates. Though the food arrived hot from the kitchen next-door, ice had formed on the edge of our plates before we finished eating. In all this area one saw no French civilians, no unshelled houses, no signs of cultivation. The only living creatures besides soldiers, horses, and mules, were a few moorhen and duck paddling in the unfrozen central stream of the river. The fodder ration for the horses, many of them sick, was down to three pounds a day, and they had open standings only. I have kept no records of this time, but the memory of its misery survives . . .

Brigade appointed me a member of a field general court-martial that was to sit on an Irish sergeant charged with 'shamefully casting away his arms in the presence of the enemy'. I had heard about the case unofficially; the man, maddened by an intense bombardment, had thrown away his rifle and run with the rest of his platoon. An army order, secret and confidential, addressed to officers of captain's rank and above, laid down that, in the case of men tried for their life on other charges, sentence might be mitigated if conduct in the field had been exemplary; but cowardice was punishable only with death, and no medical excuses could be accepted. Therefore I saw no choice between sentencing the man to death and refusing to take part in the proceedings. If I refused, I should be court-martialled myself, and a reconstituted court would sentence the sergeant to death anyhow. Yet I could not sign a death-verdict for an offence which I might have committed myself in similar circumstances. I evaded the dilemma. One other officer in the battalion, besides the acting CO, had the necessary year's service as a captain entitling him to sit on a field general court-martial. I found him willing enough to take my place. He was hard-boiled and glad of a trip to Amiens, and I took over his duties.

Executions were frequent in France. I had my first direct experience of official lying when I arrived at Le Havre in May 1915, and read the back-files of army orders at the rest camp. They contained something like twenty reports of men shot for cowardice or desertion; yet a few days later the responsible minister in the House of Commons, answering a question from a pacifist, denied that sentence of death for a military offence had been carried out in France on any member of His Majesty's Forces.

James Cuthbert, the acting CO, a Special Reserve major, felt the strain badly and took a lot of whisky. Dr Dunn pronounced him too sick to be in the trenches; so he came to Frises, where he shared a dug-out with Yates and myself. Sitting in my arm-chair, reading the Bible, I stumbled on the text: 'The bed is too narrow to lie therein and the coverlet too small to wrap myself therewith.' 'Listen, James,' I said, 'here's something pretty appropriate for this dug-out.' I read it out.

He raised himself on an elbow, genuinely furious. 'Look here, von Runicke,' he shouted, 'I am not a religious man. I've cracked a good many of the commandments since I've been in France; but while I'm in command here I refuse to hear you, or anyone bloody else blaspheme the Bible!'

I liked James, whom I had first met on the day I arrived at Wrexham to join the Regiment. He was then just back from Canada, and how hilariously he threw the chairs about in the junior anteroom of the mess! He had been driving a plough through virgin soil, he told us, and reciting Kipling to the prairie-dogs. His favourite piece was (I may be misquoting):

Are ye there, are ye there, are ye there?
Four points on a ninety-mile square –
With a helio winking like fun in the sun,
Are ye there, are ye there, are ye there?

James, who had served with the Special Reserve a year or two before he emigrated, cared for nobody, was most courageous, inclined to sentimentality, and probably saw longer service with the Second Battalion in the war than any officer except Yates.

A day or two later, because James was still sick, I found myself in temporary command of the battalion, and attended a commanding officers' conference at brigade headquarters – 'that it should ever have come to this!' I thought. Opposite our trenches a German salient protruded, and the brigadier wanted to 'bite it off' in proof of the division's offensive spirit. Trench soldiers could never understand the Staff's desire to bite off an enemy salient. It was hardly desirable to be fired at from both flanks; if the Germans had got caught in a salient, our obvious duty must be to keep them there as long as they could be persuaded to stay. We concluded that a passion for straight lines, for which headquarters were well known, had dictated this plan, which had no strategic or tactical excuse. The attack had been twice postponed, and twice cancelled. I still have a field-message referring to it, dated February 21st.

Please	cancel	Form 4	of	my
AA 202	units	will	draw	from
19th	brigade	B. Echelon	the	following
issue	of	rum	which	will
be	issued	to	troops	taking
part	in	the	forth	coming
operations	at	the	discretion	of
O.C.	units	*2nd R.W.F.*	7½	gallons.

Even this promise of special rum could not, however, hearten the battalion. Everyone agreed that the attack was unnecessary, foolish, and impossible. A thaw had now set in, and the four company commanders assured me that to cross three hundred yards of No Man's Land, which constant shelling and the thaw had turned into a morass of mud more than knee-deep, would take even lightly armed troops four or five minutes. Not a man would be able to reach the enemy lines so long as a single section of Germans with rifles remained to defend them.

The general, when I arrived, inquired in a fatherly way whether I were not proud to be attending a commanding officers' conference at the age of twenty-one. I answered irritably that I had not examined my feelings, but that I was an old enough soldier to realize the impossibility of the attack. The colonel of the Cameronians, who were also to be engaged, took the same line. So the brigadier finally called off the show. That night, I went up with rations as usual; the officers were much relieved to hear of my stand at the conference.

We had been heavily shelled on the way, and while I took a drink at battalion headquarters, someone sent me a message about a direct hit on 'D' Company limber. Going off to inspect the damage, I passed our chaplain, who had come up with me from Frises Bend, and a group of three or four men. The chaplain was gabbling the burial service over a corpse lying on the ground covered with a waterproof sheet – the miserable weather and fear of the impending attack were responsible for his death. This, as it turned out, was the last dead man I saw in France and, like the first, he had shot himself.

Court Martial

The Irish poet Francis Ledwidge, born in 1887, author of gentle lyrics inspired by love, mythology and the countryside, was nevertheless a fierce nationalist. But he enlisted in the Royal Inniskilling Fusiliers in October 1914. 'I joined the British Army because she stood between Ireland and an enemy common to our civilization and I would not have her say that she defended us while we did nothing at home but pass resolutions.' Before he was killed in Flanders in July 1917 he saw fighting at Gallipoli and in Serbia.

He was on home leave when the Volunteers who had been his comrades rose in Dublin against British rule at Easter 1916 (q.v. Yeats's 'Easter 1916'). Despite his painfully conflicting loyalties he did not desert, but he was court-martialled for making insulting remarks to a superior officer.

AFTER COURT MARTIAL

My mind is not my mind, therefore
I take no heed of what men say,
I lived ten thousand years before
God cursed the town of Nineveh.

The Present is a dream I see
Of horror and loud sufferings,
At dawn a bird will waken me
Unto my place among the kings.

And though men called me a vile name,
And all my dream companions gone,
'Tis I the soldier bears the shame,
Not I the king of Babylon.

Georg Trakl

Georg Trakl, one of the major German poets, died in November 1914, aged twenty-eight. His powerful Expressionist idiom had found an 'objective correlative' in poems reacting to the war. His translator notes that Grodek was a 'town in Galicia, Poland, where Trakl served as a chemist with the Austrian army. A battle was fought there, after which he was placed in charge of a large number of serious casualties, whose sufferings he could not relieve; he tried to shoot himself, but was prevented.' 'Grodek' was 'his last poem: soon after writing it, he was sent to Cracow to be placed under observation as a mental case. He died in a military hospital there, from an overdose of drugs.'

LAMENT (*KLAGE*)

Sleep and death, the dark eagles
Around this head swoop all night long:
Eternity's icy wave
Would swallow the golden image
Of man; against horrible reefs
His purple body is shattered.
And the dark voice laments
Over the sea.
Sister of stormy sadness,
Look, a timorous boat goes down
Under stars,
The silent face of the night.

GRODEK

At nightfall the autumn woods cry out
With deadly weapons and the golden plains,
The deep blue lakes, above which more darkly
Rolls the sun; the night embraces

Dying warriors, the wild lament
Of their broken mouths.
But quietly there in the pastureland
Red clouds in which an angry god resides,
The shed blood gathers, lunar coolness.
All the roads lead to blackest carrion.
Under golden twigs of the night and stars
The sister's shade now sways through the silent copse
To greet the ghosts of the heroes, the bleeding heads;
And softly the dark flutes of autumn sound in the reeds.
O prouder grief! You brazen altars,
Today a great pain feeds the hot flame of the spirit,
The grandsons yet unborn.

All Quiet on the Western Front

Erich Maria Remarque's book, filmed by Hollywood soon after its publication in 1929, probably had wider international influence than other accounts of the carnage on the Western Front which appeared around the same time in English. Essentially, the novel presents the experience of four teenagers from the same school in Germany who volunteer at the same time, and the four close comrades they acquire in their regiment – a locksmith, a peat-digger, a peasant and the resourceful, forty-year-old leader of the group, Katczinsky. All die, including the narrator Paul Baumer. The book is very seriously 'anti-war'.

But Remarque projects very strongly the 'bonding' which military historians have identified as a prime reason why men go on fighting – for mates, for buddies – when disaster is clearly before them and the political and ideological motives offered them by politicians have proved hollow.

Instead of going to Russia, we go up the line again. On the way we pass through a devastated wood with the tree trunks shattered and the ground ploughed up.

At several places there are tremendous craters. 'Great guns, something's hit that,' I say to Kat.

'Trench mortars,' he replies, and then points up at one of the trees.

In the branches dead men are hanging. A naked soldier is squatting in the fork of a tree, he still has his helmet on, otherwise he is entirely unclad. There is only half of him sitting up there, the top half; the legs are missing.

'What can that mean?' I ask.

'He's been blown out of his clothes,' mutters Tjaden. 'It's funny,' says Kat, 'we have seen that several times now. If a mortar get you it blows you clean out of your clothes. It's the concussion that does it.'

I search around. And so it is. Here hang bits of uniform, and somewhere else is plastered a bloody mess that was once a human limb. Over there lies a body with nothing but a piece of the underpants on one leg and the collar of the tunic around its neck. Otherwise it is naked and the clothes are hanging up in the tree. Both arms are missing as though they had been pulled out. I discover one of them twenty yards off in a shrub.

The dead man lies on his face. There, where the arm wounds are, the earth is black with blood. Underfoot the leaves are scratched up as though the man had been kicking.

'That's no joke, Kat,' say I.

'No more is a shell splinter in the belly,' he replies, shrugging his shoulders.

'But don't get tender-hearted,' says Tjaden.

All this can only have happened a little while ago, the blood is still fresh. As everybody we see there is dead we do not waste any more time, but report the affair at the next stretcher-bearers' post. After all, it is not our business to take these stretcher-bearers' jobs away from them . . .

. . .

We have dropped in for a good job. Eight of us have to guard a village that has been abandoned because it is being shelled too heavily.

In particular we have to watch the supply dump, as that is not empty yet. We are supposed to provision ourselves from the same store. We are just the right people for that; – Kat, Albert, Müller, Tjaden, Detering, our whole gang is there. Haie is dead, though. But we are mighty lucky all the same; all the other squads have had more casualties than we have.

We select, as a dug-out, a reinforced concrete cellar into which steps lead down from above. The entrance is protected by a separate concrete wall.

Now we develop an immense industry. This is an opportunity not only to stretch one's legs, but to stretch one's soul also. We make the best use of such opportunities. The war is too desperate to allow us to be sentimental for long. That is only possible so long as things are not going too badly. After all, we cannot afford to be anything but matter-of-fact. So matter-of-fact, indeed, that I often shudder when a thought from the days before the war comes momentarily into my head. But it does not stay long.

We have to take things as lightly as we can, so we make the most of every opportunity, and nonsense stands stark and immediate beside horror. It cannot be otherwise; that is how we hearten ourselves. So we zealously set to work to create an idyll – an idyll of eating and sleeping, of course.

The floor is first covered with mattresses which we haul in from the houses. Even a soldier's behind likes to sit soft. Only in the middle of the floor is there any clear space. Then we furnish ourselves with blankets, and eiderdowns, luxurious soft affairs. There is plenty of everything to be had in the village. Albert and I find a mahogany bed which can be taken to pieces with a sky of blue silk and a lace coverlet. We sweat like monkeys moving it in, but a man cannot let a thing like that slip, and it would certainly be shot to pieces in a day or two.

Kat and I do a little patrolling through the houses. In very short time we have collected a dozen eggs and two pounds of fairly fresh butter. Suddenly there is a crash in the drawing-room, and an iron stove hurtles through the wall past us and on, a yard from us out through the wall behind. Two holes. It comes from the house opposite where a shell has just landed. 'The swine,' grimaces Kat, and we continue our search. All at once we prick up our ears, hurry across, and suddenly stand petrified – there running up and down in a little sty are two live sucking pigs. We rub our eyes and look once again to make certain. Yes, they are still there. We seize hold of them – no doubt about it, two real young pigs.

This will make a grand feed. About twenty yards from our dug-out there is a small house that was used as an officers' billet. In the kitchen is an immense fireplace with two ranges, pots, pans, and kettles – everything, even to a stack of small chopped wood in an outhouse – a regular cook's paradise.

Two of our fellows have been out in the fields all the morning hunting for potatoes, carrots and green peas. We are quite uppish and sniff at the tinned stuff in the supply dump; we want fresh vegetables. In the dining-room there are already two heads of cauliflower.

The sucking pigs are slaughtered. Kat sees to them. We want to make potato-cakes to go with the roast. But we cannot find a grater for the potatoes. However, that difficulty is soon got over. With a nail we punch a lot of holes in a pot lid and there we have a grater. Three fellows put on thick gloves to protect their fingers against the grater, two others peel the potatoes, and the business gets going.

Kat takes charge of the sucking pigs, the carrots, the peas, and the cauliflower. He even mixes a white sauce for the cauliflower. I fry the pancakes, four at a time. After ten minutes I get the knack of tossing the pan so that the pancakes which are done on one side sail up, turn in the air and are caught as they come down. The sucking pigs are roasted whole. We all stand round them as before an altar.

In the meantime we receive visitors, a couple of wireless-men, who are generously invited to the feed. They sit in the living-room where there is a piano. One of them plays, the other sings 'An der Weser'. He sings feelingly, but with a rather Saxon accent. All the same it moves us as we stand at the fireplace preparing the good things.

Then we begin to realize we are in for trouble. The observation balloons have spotted the smoke from our chimney, and the shells start to drop on us. They are those damned spraying little daisy-cutters that make only a small hole and scatter widely close to the ground. They keep dropping closer and closer all round us; still we cannot leave the grub in the lurch. A couple of splinters whizz through the top of the kitchen window. The roast is ready. But frying the pancakes is getting difficult. The explosions come so fast that the splinters strike again and again against the wall of the house and sweep in through the window. Whenever I hear a shell coming I drop down on one knee with the pan and the pancakes, and duck behind the wall of the window. Immediately afterwards I am up again and going on with the frying.

The Saxon stops singing – a fragment has smashed the piano. At last everything is ready and we organize the transport of it back to the dug-out. After the next explosion two men dash across the fifty yards to the dug-out with the pots of vegetables. We see them disappear.

The next shot. Everyone ducks and then two more trot off, each with a big can of finest grade coffee, and reach the dug-out before the next explosion.

Then Kat and Kropp seize the masterpiece – the big dish with the brown, roasted sucking pigs. A screech, a knee bend, and away they race over the fifty yards of open country.

I stay to finish my last four pancakes; twice I have to drop on the floor; – after all, it means four pancakes more, and they are my favourite dish.

Then I grab the plate with the great pile of cakes and squeeze myself behind the house door. A hiss, a crash, and I gallop off with the plate clamped against my chest with both hands. I am almost in, there is a rising screech, I bound, I run like a deer, sweep round the wall, fragments clatter against the concrete, I tumble down the cellar steps, my elbows are skinned, but I have not lost a single pancake, nor even upset the plate.

At two o'clock we start the meal. It lasts till six. We drink coffee until half-past six – officers' coffee from the supply dump – and smoke officers' cigars and cigarettes – also from the supply dump. Punctually at half-past six we begin supper. At ten o'clock we throw the bones of the sucking pigs outside the door. Then there is cognac and rum – also from the blessed supply dump – and once again long, fat cigars with belly-bands. Tjaden says that it lacks only one thing: Girls from an officers' brothel.

Late in the evening we hear mewing. A little grey cat sits in the entrance. We entice it in and give it something to eat. And that wakes up our own appetites once more. Still chewing, we lie down to sleep.

But the night is bad. We have eaten too much fat. Fresh baby pig is very griping to the bowels. There is an everlasting coming and going in the dug-out. Two, three men with their pants down are always sitting about outside and cursing. I have been out nine times myself. About four o'clock in the morning we reach a record: all eleven men, guards and visitors, are squatting outside.

Burning houses stand out like torches against the night. Shells lumber across and crash down. Munition columns tear along the street. On one side the supply dump has been ripped open. In spite of all the flying fragments the drivers of the munition columns pour in like a swarm of bees and pounce on the bread. We let them have their own way. If we said anything it would only mean a good hiding for us. So we go differently about it. We explain that we are the guard and so know our way about, we get hold of the tinned stuff and exchange it for things we are short of. What does it matter anyhow – in a while it will all be blown to pieces. For ourselves we take some chocolate from the depot and eat it in slabs. Kat says it is good for loose bowels.

Almost a fortnight passes thus in eating, drinking and roaming about. No one disturbs us. The village gradually vanishes under the shells and we lead a charmed life. So long as any part of the supply dump still stands we don't worry; we desire nothing better than to stay here till the end of the war.

Tjaden has become so fastidious that he only half smokes his cigars. With his nose in the air he explains to us that he was brought up that way. And Kat is most cheerful. In the morning his first call is: 'Emil, bring in the caviare and coffee.' We put on extraordinary airs, every man treats the other as his valet, bounces him and gives him orders.

'There is something itching under my foot; Kropp my man, catch that louse at once,' says Leer, poking out his leg at him like a ballet girl, and Albert drags him up the stairs by the foot. 'Tjaden!' – 'What?' – 'Stand at ease, Tjaden; and what's more, don't say "What," say "Yes, Sir," – now: Tjaden!' Tjaden retorts in the well-known phrase from Goethe's 'Gotz von Berlichingen', with which he is always free.

After eight more days we receive orders to go back. The palmy days are over. Two big motor lorries take us away. They are stacked high with planks. Nevertheless, Albert and I erect on top our four-poster bed complete with blue silk canopy, mattress, and two lace coverlets. And behind it at the head is stowed a bag full of choicest edibles. We often dip into it, and the tough ham sausages, the tins of liver sausages, the conserves, the boxes of cigarettes rejoice our hearts. Each man has a bag to himself.

Kropp and I have rescued two big red armchairs as well. They stand inside the bed, and we sprawl back in them as in a theatre box. Above us swells the silken cover like a baldaquin. Each man has a long cigar in his mouth. And thus from aloft we survey the scene.

Between us stands a parrot cage that we found for the cat. She is coming with us, and lies in the cage before her saucer of meat, and purrs.

Slowly the lorries roll down the road. We sing. Behind us shells are sending up fountains from the now utterly abandoned village.

An Unknown US Aviator

The USA entered the Great War in April 1917. By the end of the year only 175,000 troops had reached France, but on Armistice Day there were nearly four million Americans in uniform, nearly half of them in France.

A total of 210 American university students trained and flew with the British Royal Flying Corps. One wrote a diary, first published in a limited edition of 210 copies for the survivors and the next of kin of the fifty-one who were killed. It reached general circulation later as The Diary of an Unknown Aviator. *'Archie' was the RFC slang for 'Anti-Aircraft fire'.*

August 17th [1918]

I'm not feeling very well today. I fought Huns all night in my sleep and after two hours of real fighting today, I feel all washed out. Yesterday produced the worst scrap that I have yet had the honour to indulge in. It lasted about twenty minutes and the participants were nine little Fokkers and myself. I say participants because each Hun fired at me at least once and I fired at each of them several times, collectively and individually. We went down on a two-seater and I stuck with him and fought him on down after the others pulled up. It was one of these new Hannoveranners and he licked me properly. They just haven't got any blind spot at all and the pilot was using his front gun on me most of the time.

On the way back I spotted a flock of Fokkers about three thousand feet above me. I didn't know what was going on, but it looked to me as if the thing to do was to suck those Fokkers down on me and then there would be plenty of our machines up above to come down on them and get some easy picking.

I knew I was a good way over but I thought sure there would be a squadron of Dolphins about in addition to the SEs, so I climbed for all I was worth and waited for the Huns to see me and come down. Archie put up a burst as a signal and I didn't have long to wait. I turned towards the lines and two of them came down. I put my nose down and waited for them to catch up. As soon as one of them opened fire I pulled up in a long zoom and turned. One Hun overshot and I found myself level with the other one. He half rolled and I did a skid turn and opened up on him. He wasn't much of a pilot because I got about a hundred and fifty rounds into him. He went into a dive. But that first lad was all that could be expected. He got a burst in my right wing on his first crack and now he was stalling up under me and the first thing I knew about it was when I saw his tracer going by. I half rolled and sprayed a few rounds at him and went on down out of it too.

I was getting worried about where the rest of the boys were and couldn't see any signs of an SE. Three Huns came down on me from above and played their new game. They try to fight in threes. They have some prearranged method of attack by which one sits on your tail while the other two take time about shooting from angles. They were all three firing and all I could do was to stay in a tight bank and pray. I thought I was gone. One of them pulled up and then came straight down to finish me off. I turned towards him and forced him to pull up to keep from overshooting.

As soon as I saw his nose go by, I put mine down for I saw it was time to think more about rescuing the decoy than holding any bag for the rest of them. One Hun was on my tail in a flash and we were both doing about two hundred and fifty. I turned around to see what he was doing and as soon as his tracer showed up close, I pulled straight up. He tried to pull up but overshot and went on by, about fifty feet from me. I was close enough to see his goggles and note all the details of his plane, which was black and white checked with a white nose. I waved to him and I think he waved back, tho' I'm not sure. I tried to turn my guns on him but he went up like an elevator and tried to turn back to get on my tail. I put my nose down again and we more or less repeated. The rest of his crew did not seem to be in a fighting mood and only picked at me from a distance so I got away. I had to come back on the carpet and I shot up some infantry on the ground but it was too hot for me and I zigzagged on home. I felt fine then but before I got back I was shivering so I could hardly land. And I haven't been feeling right since. My heart seems to be trying to stunt all the time.

. . .

No Date

. . . The devastation of the country is too horrible to describe. It looks from the air as if the gods had made a gigantic steam roller, forty miles wide and run it from the coast to Switzerland, leaving its spike holes behind as it went.

I'm sick. At night when the colonel calls up to give us our orders, my ears are afire until I hear what we are to do the next morning. Then I can't sleep for thinking about it all night. And while I'm waiting round all day for the afternoon patrol, I think I am going crazy. I keep watching the clock and figuring how long I have to live. Then I go out to test my engine and guns and walk around and have a drink and try to write a little and try not to think. And I move my arms and legs around and think perhaps tomorrow I won't be able to.

Sometimes I think I am getting the same disease that Springs has when I get sick at my stomach. He always flies with a bottle of milk of magnesia in one pocket and a flask of gin in the other. If one doesn't help him he tries the other. It gives me a dizzy feeling every time I hear of the men that are gone. And they have gone so fast I can't keep track of them; every time two pilots meet it is only to swap news of who's killed. When a person takes sick, lingers in bed a few days, dies and is buried on the third day, it all seems regular and they pass on into the great beyond in an orderly manner and you accept their departure as an accomplished fact. But when you lunch with a man, talk to him, see him go out and get in his plane in the prime of his youth and the next day someone tells you that he is dead – it just doesn't sink in and you can't believe it. And the oftener it happens the harder it is to believe.

I've lost over a hundred friends, so they tell me – I've seen only seven or eight killed – but to me they aren't dead yet. They are just around the corner, I think, and I am still expecting to run into them any time. I dream about them at night when I do sleep a little and sometimes I dream that someone is killed who really isn't. Then I don't know who is and who isn't. I saw a man in Boulogne the other day that I had dreamed I saw killed and I thought I was seeing a ghost. I can't realize that any of them are gone. Surely human life is not a candle to be snuffed out. The English have all turned spiritualistic since the war. I used to think that was sort of far-fetched but now it's hard for me to believe that a man ever becomes even a ghost. I have sort of a feeling that he stays just as he is and simply jumps behind a cloud or steps through a mirror. Springs keeps talking about Purgatory and Hades and the Elysian Fields. Well, we sure are close to something.

When I go out to get into my plane my feet are like lead – I am just barely able to drag them after me. But as soon as I take off I am all right again. That is, I feel all right, though I know I am too reckless. Last week I actually tried to ram a Hun. I was in a tight place and it was the only thing I could do. He didn't have the nerve to stand the gaff and turned and I got him. I poured both guns into him with fiendish glee and stuck to him though three of them were on my tail. I laughed at them. I ran into an old Harry Tate over the lines the other day where he had no business to be. He waved and I waved back to him and we went after a balloon. Imagine it! An RE Eight out balloon strafing! I was glad to find someone else as crazy as I was. And yet if I had received orders to do it the night before, I wouldn't have slept a wink and would have chewed up a good pair of boots or gotten drunk. We didn't get the balloon – they pulled it down before we got to it, but it was a lot of fun. That lad deserves the VC. And he got all the Archie in the world on the way back. So did I, for I stayed with him. He had a high speed of about eighty and was a sitting shot for a good gunner but I don't think he got hit. I didn't.

I only hope I can stick it out and not turn yellow. I've heard of men landing in Germany when they didn't have to. They'd be better off dead because they've got to live with themselves the rest of their lives. I wouldn't mind being shot down; I've got no taste for glory and I'm no more good, but I've got to keep on until I can quit honourably. All I'm fighting for now is my own self-respect.

17 and 148 seem to get a lot of Huns these days. That's one thing about a Camel; you've got to shoot down all the Huns to get home yourself. There's not a chance to run for it. Clay, Springs and Vaughan are all piling up big scores. But their scores won't be anything to those piled up on the American and French fronts. Down there if six of them jump on one Hun and get him, all six of them get credit for one Hun apiece. On the British front each one of them would get credit for one-sixth of a Hun. Of course what happens up here is that the man who was nearest him and did most of the shooting gets credit for one Hun and the others withdraw their claims. Either that or the CO decided who should get credit for it and tears up the other combat reports. Cal has five or six now and I've got four to my credit.

. . . I saw Springs the other day in Boulogne. He said his girl at home sent him a pair of these Ninette and Rintintin luck charms. Since then he's lost five men, been shot down twice himself, lost all his money at blackjack and only gotten one Hun. He says he judges from that that she is unfaithful to him. So he had discarded them and says he is looking for a new charm and that the best one is a garter taken from the left leg of a virgin in the dark of the moon. I know they are lucky but I'd be afraid to risk one. Something might happen to her and then you'd be killed sure. A stocking to tie over my nose and a Columbian half-dollar and that last sixpence and a piece of my first crash seem to take care of me all right, though I am not superstitious.

[*The death of the author in air combat twenty miles behind German lines ended the diary at this point.*]

4

Revolution and Civil War

The word 'revolution' has many overlapping usages, one extending no further than 'coup', others embracing decades or hundreds of years of change in some areas of human affairs. Twentieth-century Europe saw one 'classic' revolution in Russia, and attempts to imitate it elsewhere – in Germany and, up to a point, in Spain. It is perhaps odd that the process by which the South of Ireland won independence from 1916 to 1921 is not usually referred to as 'revolutionary'. Nor are the superficially legal processes by which Mussolini and Hitler came to power.

Revolutions, typically, are betrayed. Stalinism curbed by murder and coercion the anarchic energies, joyful for some, of the Russian and Spanish left – a matter reserved here for oblique mention in a later section on the Eastern Front.

'Civil war' is easily defined. It is the battling out of internal differences within one country, such as followed the Bolshevik seizure of power in 1917, the Treaty which created the Irish Free State in 1922, Franco's 'Falangist' revolt in Spain in 1936 and the liberation of Greece from German rule in 1944. The situation in the former Yugoslavia in the 1990s was complicated by the existence of religious and ethnic distinctions which might define it as a war of nationalities. But it represented one grievous aspect of civil war. People who have formerly lived side by side on more or less neighbourly terms sort themselves out into groups and kill each other. The murder of Lorca by the Falangists of his home town Granada is one very famous case emphasized here.

The Capture of the Winter Palace

The 'October Revolution' of 1917 in Russia happened in November according to Western usage, which is followed here. It resulted directly from the strains which the First World War imposed on the country: bloodshed on the front against Germany and Austria and worsening living conditions for workers at home. These strains provoked revolutionary violence which forced the abdication of Tsar Nicholas II in March 1917. The Provisional Government now in charge was an uneasy coalition including Socialists and Liberal 'Kadets'. The Bolshevik faction, headed by Lenin, called for an end to the war. Soviets – councils of workers and soldiers – had sprung up. In July a Russian offensive in Galicia was countered and routed. Soldiers flooded back in retreat thereafter. In November, under the immediate leadership of Leon Trotsky, Chairman of the Petrograd Soviet, with its Military Revolutionary Committee, the Bolsheviks mounted a successful coup. Two years after his successful rival Stalin had deported him from the Soviet Union, Trotsky first published his own brilliant History of the Russian Revolution *(in Berlin, 1931). Its final chapter describes the 'storming' of Petrograd's Winter Palace, where the Provisional Government held out defended by the officer cadets known as 'Junkers', by members of the Uralsky Regiment and by a thousand-strong Women's Death Battalion. On the night of November 7/8, supported by the cruiser* Aurora, *some 18,000 Bolshevik-inspired soldiers, sailors and civilians took control of the Palace.*

The Women's Battalion suddenly announce their intention to make a sortie. According to their information the clerks in General Headquarters have gone over to Lenin, and after disarming some of the officers have arrested General Alexeiev – the sole man who can save Russia. He must be rescued at any cost. The commandant is powerless to restrain them from this hysterical undertaking. At the moment of their sortie the lights again suddenly flare up in the high electric lanterns on each side of the gate. Seeking an electrician the officer jumps furiously upon the palace servants: in these former lackeys of the tsar he sees agents of revolution. He puts still less trust in the court electrician: 'I would have sent you to the next world long ago if I hadn't needed you.' In spite of revolver threats, the electrician is powerless to help. His switch-board is disconnected. Sailors have occupied the electric station and are controlling the light. The women soldiers do not stand up under fire and the greater part of them surrender. The commandant of the defence sends a corporal to report to the government that the sortie of the women's battalion has 'led to their destruction', and that the palace is swarming with agitators. The failure of the sortie causes a lull lasting approximately from ten to eleven. The besiegers are busied with the preparation of artillery fire.

The unexpected lull awakens some hopes in the besieged. The ministers again try to encourage their partisans in the city and throughout the country: 'The government in full attendance, with the exception of Prokopovich, is at its post. The situation is considered favourable . . . The Palace is under fire, but only rifle fire and without results. It is clear that the enemy is weak.' In reality the enemy is all-powerful but cannot make up his mind to use his power. The government sends out through the country communications about the ultimatum, about the *Aurora*, about how it, the government, can only transfer the power to the Constituent Assembly, and how the first assault on the Winter Palace has been repulsed. 'Let the army and the people answer!' But just how they are to answer the ministers do not suggest.

Lashevich meantime has sent two sailor gunners to the fortress. To be sure, they are none too experienced, but they are at least Bolsheviks, and quite ready to shoot from rusty guns without oil in the compressors. That is all that is demanded of them. A noise of artillery is more important at the moment than a well-aimed blow. Antonov gives the order to begin. The gradations indicated in advance are completely followed out. 'After a signal shot from the fortress,' relates Flerovsky, 'the *Aurora* thundered out. The boom and flash of blank fire are much bigger than from a loaded gun. The curious onlookers jumped back from the granite parapet of the quay, fell down and crawled away . . .' Chudnovsky promptly raises the question: How about proposing to the besieged to surrender. Antonov as promptly agrees with him. Again an interruption. Some groups of women and junkers are surrendering. Chudnovsky wants to leave them their arms, but Antonov revolts in time against this too beautiful magnanimity. Laying the rifles on the sidewalk the prisoners go out under convoy along Milliony Street.

The palace still holds out. It is time to have an end. The order is given. Firing begins – not frequent and still less effectual. Out of thirty-five shots fired in the course of an hour and a half or two hours, only two hit the mark, and they only injure the plaster. The other shells go high, fortunately not doing any damage in the city. Is lack of skill the real cause? They were shooting across the Neva with a direct aim at a target as impressive as the Winter Palace: that does not demand a great deal of artistry. Would it not be truer to assume that even Lashevich's artillerymen intentionally aimed high in the hope that things would be settled without destruction and death? It is very difficult now to hunt out any trace of the motive which guided the two nameless sailors. They themselves have spoken no word. Have they dissolved in the immeasurable Russian land, or, like so many of the October fighters, did they lay down their heads in the civil wars of the coming months and years?

Shortly after the first shots, Palchinsky brought the ministers a fragment of shell. Admiral Verderevsky recognized the shell as his own – from a naval gun, from the *Aurora*. But they were shooting blank from the cruiser. It had been thus agreed, was thus testified by Flerovsky, and thus reported to the Congress of Soviets later by a sailor. Was the admiral mistaken? Was the sailor mistaken? Who can ascertain the truth about a cannon shot fired in the thick of night from a mutinous ship at a tsar's palace where the last government of the possessing classes is going out like an oilless lamp?

The garrison of the palace was greatly reduced in number. If at the moment of the arrival of the Uraltsi, the cripples and the women's battalion, it rose to a thousand and a half, or perhaps even two thousand, it was now reduced to a thousand, and perhaps considerably less. Nothing can save the day now but a miracle. And suddenly into the despairing atmosphere of the Winter Palace there bursts – not, to be sure, a miracle, but the news of its approach. Palchinsky announces: They have just telephoned from the City Duma that the citizens are getting ready to march from there for the rescue of the government. 'Tell everybody,' he gives orders to Sinegub, 'that the people are coming.' The officer runs up and down stairs and through the corridors with the joyful news. On the way he stumbles upon some drunken officers fighting each other with rapiers – shedding no blood, however. The junkers lift up their heads. Passing from mouth to mouth the news becomes more colourful and impressive. The public men, the merchantry, the people, with the clergy at their head, are marching, this way to free the beleaguered palace. The people with the clergy! 'That will be strikingly beautiful!' A last remnant of energy flares up: 'Hurrah! Long live Russia!' The Oranienbaum junkers, who by that time had quite decided to leave, changed their minds and stayed.

But the people with the clergy come very slowly. The number of agitators in the palace is growing. In a minute the Aurora will open fire. There is a whispering in the corridors. And this whisper passes from lip to lip. Suddenly two explosions. Sailors have got into the palace and either thrown or dropped from the gallery two hand grenades, lightly wounding two junkers. The sailors are arrested and the wounded bound up by Kishkin, a physician by profession.

The inner resolution of the workers and sailors is great, but it has not yet become bitter. Lest they call it down on their heads, the besieged, being the incomparably weaker side, dare not deal severely with these agents of the enemy who have penetrated the palace. There are no executions. Uninvited guests now begin to appear no longer one by one, but in groups. The palace is getting more and more like a sieve. When the junkers fall upon these intruders, the latter permit themselves to be disarmed. 'What cowardly scoundrels!' says Palchinsky scornfully. No, these men were not cowardly. It required a high courage to make one's way into that palace crowded with officers and junkers. In the labyrinth of an unknown building, in dark corridors, among innumerable doors leading nobody knew where, and threatening nobody knew what, the daredevils had nothing to do but surrender. The number of captives grows. New groups break in. It is no longer quite clear who is surrendering to whom, who is disarming whom. The artillery continues to boom.

With the exception of the district immediately adjoining the Winter Palace, the life of the streets did not cease until late at night. The theatres and moving-picture houses were open. To the respectable and educated strata of the capital it was of no consequence apparently that their government was under fire. Redemeister on the Troitsky Bridge saw quietly approaching pedestrians whom the sailors stopped. 'There was nothing unusual to be seen.' From acquaintances coming from the direction of the People's House Redemeister learned, to the tune of a cannonade, that Chaliapin had been incomparable in *Don Carlos*. The ministers continued to tramp the floors of their mousetrap.

'It is clear that the attackers are weak'; maybe if we hold out an extra hour reinforcements will still arrive. Late at night Kishkin summoned Assistant-Minister of Finance Khrushchev, also a Kadet, to the telephone, and asked him to tell the leaders of the party that the government needed at least a little bit of help in order to hold out until the morning hours, when Kerensky ought finally to arrive with the troops. 'What kind of a party is this,' shouts Kishkin indignantly, 'that can't send us three hundred armed men!' And he is right. What kind of a party is it? These Kadets who had assembled tens of thousands of votes at the elections in Petrograd, could not put out three hundred fighters at the moment of mortal danger to the bourgeois regime. If the ministers had only thought to hunt up in the palace library the books of the materialist Hobbes, they could have read in his dialogues about civil war that there is no use expecting or demanding courage from store-keepers who have gotten rich, 'since, they see nothing but their own momentary advantage . . . and completely lose their heads at the mere thought of the possibility of being robbed.' But after all Hobbes was hardly to be found in the tsar's library. The ministers, too, were hardly up to the philosophy of history. Kishkin's telephone call was the last ring from the Winter Palace.

Smolny was categorically demanding an end. We must not drag out the siege till morning, keep the city in a tension, rasp the nerves of the Congress, put a question-mark against the whole victory. Lenin sends angry notes. Call follows call from the Military Revolutionary Committee. Podvoisky talks back. It is possible to throw the masses against the palace. Plenty are eager to go. But how many victims will there be, and what will be left of the ministers and the junkers? However, the necessity of carrying the thing through is too imperious. Nothing remains but to make the naval artillery speak. A sailor from Peter and Paul takes a slip of paper to the *Aurora*. Open fire on the palace immediately. Now, it seems, all will be clear. The gunners on the *Aurora* are ready for business, but the leaders still lack resolution. There is a new attempt at evasion. 'We decided to wait just another quarter of an hour,' writes Flerovsky, 'sensing by instinct the possibility of a change of circumstances.' By 'instinct' here it is necessary to understand a stubborn hope that the thing would be settled by mere demonstrative methods. And this time 'instinct' did not deceive. Towards the end of that quarter of an hour a new courier arrived straight from the Winter Palace. The palace is taken!

The palace did not surrender but was taken by storm – this, however, at a moment when the power of resistance of the besieged had already completely evaporated. Hundreds of enemies broke into the corridor – not by the secret entrance this time but through the defended door – and they were taken by the demoralized defenders for the Duma deputation. Even so they were successfully disarmed. A considerable group of junkers got away in the confusion. The rest – at least a number of them – still continued to stand guard. But the barrier of bayonets and rifle-fire between the attackers and defenders is finally broken down.

That part of the palace adjoining the Hermitage is already filled with the enemy. The junkers make an attempt to come at them from the rear. In the corridors phantasmagoric meetings and clashes take place. All are armed to the teeth. Lifted hands hold revolvers. Hand-grenades hang from belts. But nobody shoots and nobody throws a grenade. For they and their enemy are so mixed together that they cannot drag themselves apart. Never mind the fate of the palace is already decided.

Workers, sailors, soldiers are pushing up from outside in chains and groups, flinging the junkers from the barricades, bursting through the court, stumbling into the junkers on the staircase, crowding them back, toppling them over, driving them upstairs. Another wave comes on behind. The square pours into the court. The court pours into the palace, and floods up and down stairways and through corridors. On the befouled parquets, among mattresses and chunks of bread, people, rifles, hand-grenades are wallowing. The conquerors find out that Kerensky is not there, and a momentary pang of disappointment interrupts their furious joy. Antonov and Chudnovsky are now in the palace. Where is the government? That is the door – there where the junkers stand frozen in the last pose of resistance. The head sentry rushes to the ministers with a question: Are we commanded to resist to the end? No, no, the ministers do not command that. After all, the palace is taken. There is no need of bloodshed. We must yield to force. The ministers desire to surrender with dignity, and sit at the table in imitation of a session of the government. The commandant has already surrendered the palace, negotiating for the lives of the junkers, against which in any case nobody had made the slightest attempt. As to the fate of the government, Antonov refuses to enter into any negotiations whatever.

The junkers at the last guarded doors were disarmed. The victors burst into the room of the ministers. 'In front of the crowd and trying to hold back the onpressing ranks strode a rather small, unimpressive man. His clothes were in disorder, a wide-brimmed hat askew on his head, eyeglasses balanced uncertainly on his nose, but his little eyes gleamed with the joy of victory and spite against the conquered.' In these annihilating strokes the conquered have described Antonov. It is not hard to believe that his clothes and his hat were in disorder: It is sufficient to remember the nocturnal journey through the puddles of the Peter and Paul fortress. The joy of victory might also doubtless have been read in his eyes; but hardly any spite against the conquered in those eyes – I announce to you, members of the Provisional Government, that you are under arrest – exclaimed Antonov in the name of the Military Revolutionary Committee. The clock then pointed to 2.10 in the morning of October 26. – The members of the Provisional Government submit to force and surrender in order to avoid bloodshed – answered Konovaby. The most important part of the ritual was thus observed.

Blok's Twelve

Aleksandr Blok was the major Russian lyric poet of his generation. His response to the Revolution implied that it was a necessary Apocalypse, and he became the first chairman of the Petrograd branch of the All-Russian Union of Poets. But he died in despair of what had happened to his beloved country – 'The poet dies because he cannot breathe.'

THE TWELVE

I

Darkness – and white
snow hurled
by the wind. The wind!
You cannot stand upright
for the wind: the wind
scouring God's world.

The wind ruffles
the white snow, pulls
that treacherous
wool over the wicked ice.
Everyone out walking
slips. Look – poor thing!

From building to building over
the street a rope skips nimbly,
a banner on the rope – ALL POWER
TO THE CONSTITUENT ASSEMBLY.
This old weeping woman is worried to death,
she doesn't know what it's all about:
that banner – for God's sake –
so many yards of cloth!
How many children's leggings it would make –
and they without shirts – without boots – without . . .

The old girl like a puffed hen picks
her way between drifts of snow.
'Mother of God, these Bolsheviks
will be the death of us, I know!'

Will the frost never lose its grip
or the wind lay its whips aside?
The bourgeois where the roads divide
stands chin on chest, his collar up.

But who's this with the mane
of hair, saying in a
whisper: 'They've sold us down
the river. Russia's down and out.'?
A pen-pusher, no doubt,
a word-spinner . . .

There's someone in a long coat, sidling
over there where the snow's less thick.
'What's happened to your joyful tidings,
comrade cleric?'

Do you remember the old days:
waddling belly-first to prayer,
when the cross on your belly would blaze
on the faithful there?

A lady in a fur
is turning to a friend:
'We cried our eyes out, dear . . .'
She slips up –
smack! – on her beam end.

Heave ho
and up she rises – so!

The wind rejoices,
mischievous and spry,
ballooning dresses
and skittling passers-by.
It buffets with a shower
of snow the banner-cloth: ALL POWER
TO THE CONSTITUENT ASSEMBLY,
and carries voices.

. . . Us girls had a session . . .
. . . in there on the right . . .
. . . had a discussion . . .
. . . carried a motion:
ten for a time, twenty-five for the night . . .
and not a rouble less
for anybody . . . coming up . . . ?

Evening ebbs out.
The crowds decamp.
Only a tramp
potters about.
And the wind screams . . .

Hey you! Hey
chum,
going my way . . . ?

A crust!
What will become
of us? Get lost!

Black sky grows blacker.

Anger, sorrowful anger
seethes in the breast . . .
Black anger, holy anger . . .

Friend!
Keep your eyes skinned!

II

The wind plays up: snow flutters down.
Twelve men are marching through the town.

Their rifle-butts on black slings sway.
Lights left, right, left, wink all the way . . .

Cap tilted, fag drooping, every one
looks like a jailbird on the run.

Freedom, freedom,
down with the cross!

Rat-a-tat-tat!

It's cold, boys, and I'm numb!

Johnny and Kate are living it up . . .
She's banknotes in her stocking-top.

John's in the money, too, and how!
He *was* one of us; he's gone over now!

Well, mister John, you son of a whore,
just you kiss my girl once more!

Freedom, freedom,
down with the cross!
Johnny right now is busy with Kate.
What do you think they're busy at?

Rat-a-tat-tat!

Lights left, right, left, lights all the way . . .
Rifles on their shoulders sway . . .

Keep A Revolutionary Step!
The Relentless Enemy Will Not Stop!

Grip your gun like a man, brother!
Let's have a crack at Holy Russia,
Mother
Russia
with her big, fat arse!
Freedom, freedom! Down with the cross!

III

The lads have all gone to the wars
to serve in the Red Guard –
to serve in the Red Guard –
and risk their hot heads for the cause.

Hell and damnation,
life is such fun
with a ragged greatcoat
and a Jerry gun!

To smoke the nobs out of their holes
we'll light a fire through all the world,
a bloody fire through all the world –
Lord, bless our souls!

IV

The blizzard whirls; a cabby shouts;
away fly Johnny and Kate
with a 'lectric lamp
between the shafts . . .
Hey there, look out!

He's in an Army overcoat,
a silly grin upon his snout.

He's twirling a moustachio,
twirling it about,
joking as they go . . .

Young Johnny's a mighty lover
with a gift of the gab that charms!
He takes her in his arms,
he's talking her over . . .

She throws her head back as they hug
and her teeth are white as pearl . . .
Ah, Kate, my Katey girl,
with your little round mug!

V

Across your collar-bone, my Kate,
a knife has scarred the flesh;
and there below your bosom, Kate,
that little scratch is fresh!

Hey there, honey, honey, what
a lovely pair of legs you've got!

You carried on in lace and furs –
carry on, dear, while you can!
You frisked about with officers –
frisk about, dear, while you can!

Honey, honey, swing your skirt!
My heart is knocking at my shirt!

Do you remember that officer –
the knife put an end to him . . .
do you remember that, you whore,
or does your memory dim?

Honey, honey, let him be!
You've got room in bed for me!

Once upon a time you wore grey spats,
scoffed chocolates in gold foil,
went out with officer-cadets –
now it's the rank and file!

Honey, honey, don't be cruel!
Roll with me to ease your soul!

VI

Carriage again and cabby's shout
came storming past: 'Look out! Look out!'

Stop, you, stop! Help, Andy – here!
Cut them off, Peter, from the rear!

Crack – crack – reload – crack – crack – reload!
The snow whirls skyward off the road.

Young Johnny and the cabman run
like the wind. Take aim. Give them one

for the road. Crack – crack! Now learn
. . . .
to leave another man's girl alone!

Running away, you bastard? Do.
Tomorrow I'll settle accounts with you!

But where is Kate? She's dead! She's dead!
A bullet hole clean through her head!

Kate, are you satisfied? Lost your tongue?
Lie in the snow-drift then, like dung!

Keep a Revolutionary Step!
The Relentless Enemy Will Not Stop!

VII

Onward the twelve advance,
their butts swinging together,
but the poor killer looks
at the end of his tether . . .

Fast, faster, he steps out.
Knotting a handkerchief
clumsily round his throat
his hand shakes like a leaf . . .

What's eating you, my friend?
Why so downhearted, mate?
Come, Peter, what's on your mind?
Still sorry for Kate?

Oh, brother, brother, brother,
I loved that girl . . .
such nights we had together,
me and that girl . . .
For the wicked come-hither
her eyes would shoot at me,
and for the crimson mole
in the crook of her arm,
I shot her in my fury –
like the fool I am . . .

Hey, Peter, shut your trap!
Are you a woman or
are you a man, to pour
your heart out like a tap?
Hold your head up
and take a grip!

This isn't the time now
for me to be your nurse!
Brother, tomorrow
will be ten times worse!

And shortening his stride,
slowing his step,
Peter lifts his head
and brightens up . . .

What the hell!
It's not a sin to have some fun!

Put your shutters up, I say –
There'll be broken locks today!

Open your cellars: quick, run down . . . !
The scum of the earth are hitting the town!

VIII

My God, what a life!
I've had enough!
I'm bored!

I'll scratch my head
and dream a dream . . .

I'll chew my quid
to pass the time . . .

I'll swig enough
to kill my drought . . .

I'll get my knife
and slit your throat!

Fly away, mister, like a starling,
before I drink your blue veins dry
for the sake of my poor darling
with her dark and roving eye . . .

Blessed are the dead which die in the Lord . . .

I'm bored!

IX

Out of the city spills no noise,
the prison tower reigns in peace.
'We've got no booze but cheer up, boys,
we've seen the last of the police!'

The bourgeois where the roads divide,
stands chin on chest, his collar up:
mangy and flea-bitten at his side
shivers a coarse-haired mongrel pup.

The bourgeois with a hangdog air
stands speechless, like a question mark,
and the old world behind him there
stands with its tail down in the dark.

X

Still the storm rages gust upon gust.
What weather! What a storm!
At arm's length you can only just
make out your neighbour's form.

Snow twists into a funnel,
a towering tunnel . . .

'Oh, what a blizzard! . . . Jesus Christ!'
Watch it, Pete, cut out that rot!
What did Christ and his bloody cross
ever do for the likes of us?
Look at your hands. Aren't they hot
with the blood of the girl you shot?

Keep A Revolutionary Step!
The Enemy Is Near And Won't Let Up!

Forward, and forward again
the working men!

XI

Abusing God's name as they go,
all twelve march onward into snow . . .
prepared for anything,
regretting nothing . . .

Their rifles at the ready
for the unseen enemy
in back streets, side roads
where only snow explodes
its shrapnel, and through quag-
mire drifts where the boots drag . . .

before their eyes
throbs a red flag.

Left, right,
the echo replies.

Keep your eyes skinned
lest the enemy strike!

Into their faces day and night
bellows the wind
without a break . . .

Forward, and forward again
the working men!

XII

. . . On they march with sovereign tread . . .
Who else goes there? Come out! I said
come out! It is the wind and the red
flag plunging gaily at their head.

The frozen snow-drift looms in front.
Who's in the drift? Come out! Come here!
There's only the homeless mongrel runt
limping wretchedly in the rear . . .

You mangy beast, out of the way
before you taste my bayonet.
Old mongrel world, clear off I say!
I'll have your hide to sole my boot!

The shivering cur, the mongrel cur
bares his teeth like a hungry wolf,
droops his tail, but does not stir . . .
Hey, answer, you there, show yourself.

Who's that waving the red flag?
Try and see! It's as dark as the tomb!
Who's that moving at a jog
trot, keeping to the back-street gloom?

Don't you worry – I'll catch you yet;
better surrender to me alive!
Come out, comrade, or you'll regret
it – we'll fire when I've counted five!

Crack – crack – crack! But only the echo
answers from among the eaves . . .
The blizzard splits his seams, the snow
laughs wildly up the whirlwind's sleeve . . .

Crack – crack – crack!
Crack – crack – crack!

. . . So they march with sovereign tread . . .
Behind them limps the hungry dog,
and wrapped in wild snow at their head
carrying a blood-red flag –
soft-footed where the blizzard swirls,
invulnerable where bullets crossed –
crowned with a crown of snowflake pearls,
a flowery diadem of frost,
ahead of them goes Jesus Christ.

January 1918

Red Cavalry

A sequel to the Bolshevik Revolution was civil war in Russia between 'Reds' and various 'White' opponents. The Western allies at first gave strong assistance, even troops, to the Whites, who appeared likely to succeed, but in October 1919 the Reds counter-attacked with success. With the West withdrawing support from the collapsing Whites, the Poles, newly independent from the Treaty of Versailles, were left to sustain their own drive for land and security, pushing deep into the Ukraine. Led by General Budenny, a former Tsarist officer, the Reds counter-attacked in the summer of 1920. Isaac Babel, a Jewish intellectual from Odessa, rode into Poland as a political commissar with Budenny's cavalry. His collection of stories Konarmiya *(1926) derives from his Polish experience. The Cossacks he served with were hereditary Jew-haters, but he writes of them with a combination of fastidious objectivity and relish. The commander, Maslak, soon betrayed the Reds.*

AFONKA BIDA

We were fighting at Leszniow. Wherever we turned we faced a wall of enemy cavalry. The compressed spring of the Polish defensive strategy was now being released with an ominous whistle. We were hard pressed. For the first time in the whole campaign, we felt stabbing pains on all sides: they were breaking through in the rear and pressing on our flanks – the merciless effects of the very strategy that had served us so long and so well.

The front at Leszniow was held by infantry. Along the unevenly dug trenches, the greyish, barefoot, Volhynian peasants came and went. These men had been taken from the plough only yesterday to form an infantry auxiliary for the Red Cavalry. The peasants had come eagerly, and they fought hard. Their snorting, peasant ferocity amazed even Budenny's men. Their hatred for the Polish landowners had built up only very gradually, but it was made of good, solid stuff.

In the second phase of the war, when our whooping had ceased to affect the enemy's imagination and cavalry attacks on our entrenched opponents became impossible, this homemade infantry might have been a great help to the Red Cavalry. But our poverty defeated us. The peasants were given one rifle for three men and cartridges that didn't fit. The idea had to be given up and this genuine people's militia was disbanded.

But to return to the fighting at Leszniow. The foot soldiers had dug in three miles from the little town. In front of their trenches, a round-shouldered youth in glasses paced up and down, his sabre trailing at his side. He hopped along, looking unhappy, as though his boots pinched. This was the peasants' leader, chosen and beloved by them. He was a Jew, a weak-eyed Jewish youth with the seedy, rapt face of a Talmudist. In battle he displayed a cautious courage and coolness that resembled the absent-mindedness of a dreamer.

It was going on three on a spacious July day. An iridescent web of heat shone in the air. Beyond the hills flashed a gay streak of uniforms and horses' manes braided with ribbons. The young man gave the signal to prepare. The peasants, stumping along in their bast shoes, ran to their places and raised their rifles. But it was a false alarm. It was Maslak's flamboyant cavalry troops which came riding out onto the Leszniow road. Their underfed but still spirited horses cantered along at a good pace; their ornate standards on gilded poles, loaded with velvet tassels, fluttered in fiery pillars of dust. The horsemen rode with cold, majestic arrogance. The unkempt foot soldiers crawled out of their ditches and, their mouths gaping, stared at the prancing elegance of this unhurried stream.

At the head of the regiment, on a jaded, bandy-legged steppe pony, rode Brigade Commander Maslak. He was full of drunken blood and the putrescence of his own fatty juices. His belly, like a large tomcat, rested on the silver-ornamented saddlebow. Catching sight of the infantry, he flushed purple with amusement and beckoned to Platoon Leader Afonka Bida. We had given this platoon leader the nickname 'Makhno' because of his resemblance to the guerrilla chief. The brigade commander and Afonka whispered together for a minute. Then the platoon leader turned to the first troop, leaned forward, and commanded in a low voice: 'Forward!' The Cossacks, one platoon after the other, increased their pace to a trot. Then, spurring on their horses, they charged at the trenches from which the infantry, delighted by the spectacle, were goggling at them.

'Prepare for action!' Afonka ordered in a monotonous, somehow distant-sounding voice.

Maslak, shouting hoarsely, coughing and having great fun, rode out of the way and the Cossacks threw themselves into the attack. The wretched infantry fled. But it was too late. The Cossack lashes were already working over their tattered coats. The horsemen circled around the field, their whips whirling in their hands with marvellous skill.

'What are you fooling around for?' I shouted to Afonka.

'For fun,' he answered, bouncing around in his saddle and seizing a fellow who had hidden himself in the bushes.

'Just for fun!' he yelled, jabbing at the lad, who was frightened out of his wits.

The fun ended when Maslak, softened and magnanimous, waved a plump hand.

'Keep a lookout, foot soldiers!' Afonka cried, haughtily straightening up his puny body. 'Go and catch your fleas . . .'

The laughing Cossacks re-formed ranks. The infantry had vanished; the trenches were empty. Only the round-shouldered Jew stood where he had stood before, gazing intently and scornfully at the Cossacks through his glasses.

The firing from the direction of Leszniow didn't abate; the Poles were hemming us in. Through our binoculars, we could see the isolated figures of mounted scouts. They kept popping up from the small town, then vanishing, like so many jack-in-the-boxes. Maslak deployed a troop along both sides of the road. The shining sky stood over Leszniow and it looked strikingly empty, as it always does in an hour of danger. The young Jew threw back his head and blew bitterly and mournfully on his metal whistle. The foot soldiers who had just taken a whipping returned to their posts.

Bullets were flying toward us in dense streams. The brigade staff found itself in the line of enemy machine-gun fire. We bolted into the forest and began making our way through a thicket on the right-hand side of the road. Branches broken by bullets creaked over our heads. When we came out of the thicket, the Cossacks were no longer there: on the orders of the division commander, they were withdrawing toward Brody. Only the peasants snapped back at the enemy, firing occasional shots from their trenches. Afonka, who had stayed behind, was now riding to catch up with his platoon.

He rode along the very edge of the road, looking around intently and sniffing the air. For a moment the firing abated a little and Afonka, deciding to take advantage of the lull, set off at a gallop. At that very instant a bullet hit his horse in the neck. It went on running for another hundred yards or so, then its front legs bent jerkily and it collapsed on the ground.

Unhurriedly Afonka freed his foot, which was caught in the stirrup, squatted down by the animal, and poked at its wound with his copper-coloured finger. Then he got up, straightened himself, and mournfully scanned the horizon.

'Good-bye, Stepan,' Afonka said woodenly. He took a step back from the dying animal and bowed to it from the waist. 'How will I get back to our village without you? What will I do with your embossed saddle? Good-bye, Stepan!' he repeated louder than before. He choked, squeaked like a trapped mouse, and broke into a wail. His spasmodic howls reached our ears and we saw him bowing and swaying like a praying dervish. 'No, I won't take it from that bitch Fate!' he screamed, removing his hands from his deadened face. 'I'll make those damn Polish landowners pay for this! I'll go and chop them up without pity! I'll tear their hearts out and listen to them sigh. I'll go on till they give their last gasp and swear by the blood of their Virgin – I promise you that, Stepan, in the name of our dear brother villagers . . .'

Afonka lay down, put his face against the wound, and grew quiet. With its deep, shining, violet eye fixed on its master, the horse listened to the man's rasping breath. In a gentle torpor, the animal moved its slack mouth against the ground as two ruby streamlets trickled down its white, muscle-inlaid chest.

Afonka lay without stirring. Then Maslak, sprightly on his fat legs, walked up to them, put his gun into the horse's ear, and fired. Afonka jumped up and turned his pockmarked face to Maslak.

'Take the harness, Afanasy,' Maslak said gently, 'and then go and join your men.'

From our hillock we saw Afonka bent in two under the weight of the saddle, his face raw and red as freshly cut meat, trudging toward his troop. He looked infinitely lonely in the dusty, sweltering emptiness of the fields.

Late that evening, I came across him in the wagon train. He was sleeping in a wagon among his possessions: swords, tunics, and pierced gold coins. His head was covered with clotted blood and his stiff, twisted mouth lay on the bend of the saddle; it looked like the head of one crucified. Next to him he had placed the harness of his dead horse, the complicated and indicative trappings of a Cossack mount – the black tasselled breastpieces, the soft leather crupper straps, studded with multicoloured stones, and the silver-plated snaffle.

The darkness was growing thicker about us. The supply column stretched along the Brody road in an endless file. Small, pale stars rolled down the Milky Way and, deep in the cool night, distant villages were burning. Orlov, the troop leader's assistant, and the mustachioed Bitsenko sat in Afonka's wagon and discussed Afonka's bereavement. 'He brought his horse all the way from home,' Bitsenko said. 'Where do you expect him to get a horse like that here?'

'A horse – he's your friend,' Orlov said.

'A horse – he's like a father to you,' Bitsenko sighed. 'The number of times a horse saves your life! I think Bida is lost without his horse.'

Next morning, Afonka had vanished. The battle for Brody began and ended. The defeat had turned into a temporary victory. We had a new division commander. But Afonka still didn't reappear. And only hushed murmurs in the villages about Afonka's looting and his vicious savagery indicated his arduous trail.

'He's getting himself a horse,' they said of their leader in the platoon, and during the endless evenings of our peregrinations, I heard many stories about Afonka's silent and vicious hunt.

Men from other units reported seeing Afonka Bida tens of miles away from our position. He would sit in ambush for straggling Polish cavalrymen or roam through the forests trying to find herds of horses hidden by the peasants. He set fire to Polish villages and shot their elders for concealing the smallest possessions. Rumours about his fierce one-man war, echoes of the lone wolf's attacks on the population, reached us all the time.

Another week went by. The hardships of the fighting we were exposed to burned out of our conversation the grim exploits of Afonka Bida and we began to forget him. Then it was rumoured that he had been killed somewhere in the forest by Galician peasants. And so, the day we entered Beresteczko, Emelyan Budyak of the First Troop asked the division commander whether he could have Afonka's saddle with its yellow cloth. Emelyan wanted to ride in the victory parade with a new saddle. But he didn't get his wish.

We took Beresteczko on August 6. At the head of our division rode our new commander, wearing a long red Caucasian coat and a red shirt. Behind him rode Lyovka, his mad-dog flunky, leading a breeding mare.

The warlike march music, full of drawn-out threats, floated along the miserable but pretentious streets. Old alleys that went nowhere, a paint-covered forest of ramshackle, shaky board fences led into the town whose core, eaten away by time, breathed on us its sad decay. Smugglers and hypocrites hid in the large, dark houses. Only Pan Ludomirski, the bellringer, came out to meet us near his church. He wore a green coat.

We crossed the river and entered the village. We were approaching the priest's house when, from around a corner, riding a big grey stallion, appeared Afonka.

'Hello, hello!' he barked and pushing riders out of his way, took up his place in the formation.

Maslak fixed his eyes on the colourless horizon and without turning his head asked in a hoarse voice:

'Where did you get the horse?'

'It's my personal horse,' Afonka said, rolling a cigarette, wetting it with a flick of his tongue, and sticking it down.

The Cossacks, one after the other, rode up to him and shook him by the hand. Instead of his left eye, a revolting pink swelling stood out on his charred face.

The next morning, Bida had himself a good time. He smashed the St Valentine shrine in the Catholic church and tried his hand at playing the organ. He wore an azure jacket cut out of a rug with an embroidered lily on the back, and his long Cossack forelock was plastered down over the gouged-out eye.

After dinner, he saddled his horse and went to fire some rounds from his rifle into the broken windows of Count Raciborski's castle. The Cossacks formed a half circle around him, lifting his stallion's tail, feeling his legs, inspecting his teeth.

'Great horse,' Orlov, the troop leader's assistant, declared.

'He's all right, that's for sure,' the mustachioed Bitsenko confirmed.

A Terrible Beauty is Born

Irish nationalists hoped, with German support, to seize power while Britain was preoccupied with the Western Front, and planned a rising for Easter Sunday, 23 April 1916. The aim was to take over Dublin's chief buildings and defy the British Government, with popular support. In fact, the theatricality of this hopeless lunge was, for leading participants, virtually its point. The event took place a two day late, on April 24, and the Provisional Government of the Irish Republic was proclaimed, but, after a thousand rebels had held out for nearly a week, the rising was crushed and its leaders were executed. The sympathy which these deaths aroused was to prove important to the wider movement for independence which now gathered decisive momentum. W. B. Yeats heard the news in Oxford where he was dining with English notabilities. His response, as Ireland's leading nationalist poet, was both bardic and personal. In his youth he had known the aristocratic Constance Markiewicz, née Gore-Booth, 'that woman', who was spared execution on account of her sex. He disapproved of her socialism and that of the trade-unionist James Connolly. MacDonagh was a scholar and a poet whom Yeats respected; Pearse, a headmaster, wrote verse in Gaelic. The 'lout' John MacBride had married Yeats's great love Maude Gonne. He saw that their joint tragic gesture made them 'immortal', irrespective of their personal strengths and weaknesses.

EASTER 1916

I have met them at close of day
Coming with vivid faces
From counter or desk among grey
Eighteenth-century houses.
I have passed with a nod of the head
Or polite meaningless words,
Or have lingered awhile and said
Polite meaningless words,
And thought before I had done
Of a mocking tale or a gibe

To please a companion
Around the fire at the club,
Being certain that they and I
But lived where motley is worn:
All changed, changed utterly:
A terrible beauty is born.

That woman's days were spent
In ignorant good-will,
Her nights in argument
Until her voice grew shrill.
What voice more sweet than hers
When, young and beautiful,
She rode to harriers?
This man had kept a school
And rode our wingèd horse;
This other his helper and friend
Was coming into his force;
He might have won fame in the end,
So sensitive his nature seemed,
So daring and sweet his thought.
This other man I had dreamed
A drunken, vainglorious lout.
He had done most bitter wrong
To some who are near my heart,
Yet I number him in the song;
He, too, has resigned his part
In the casual comedy;
He, too, has been changed in his turn,
Transformed utterly:
A terrible beauty is born.

Hearts with one purpose alone
Through summer and winter seem
Enchanted to a stone
To trouble the living stream.
The horse that comes from the road,
The rider, the birds that range
From cloud to tumbling cloud,

Minute by minute they change;
A shadow of cloud on the stream
Changes minute by minute;
A horse-hoof slides on the brim,
And a horse plashes within it;
The long-legged moor-hens dive,
And hens to moor-cocks call;
Minute by minute they live:
The stone's in the midst of all.

Too long a sacrifice
Can make a stone of the heart.
O when may it suffice?
That is Heaven's part, our part
To murmur name upon name,
As a mother names her child
When sleep at last has come
On limbs that had run wild.
What is it but nightfall?
No, no, not night but death;
Was it needless death after all?
For England may keep faith
For all that is done and said.
We know their dream; enough
To know they dreamed and are dead;
And what if excess of love
Bewildered them till they died?
I write it out in a verse –
MacDonagh and MacBride
And Connolly and Pearse
Now and in time to be,
Wherever green is worn,
Are changed, changed utterly:
a terrible beauty is born.

THE ROSE TREE

'O words are lightly spoken,'
Said Pearse to Connolly,
'Maybe a breath of politic words
Has withered our Rose Tree;
Or maybe but a wind that blows
Across the bitter sea.'

'It needs to be but watered,'
James Connolly replied,
'To make the green come out again
And spread on every side,
And shake the blossom from the bud
To be the garden's pride.'

'But where can we draw water,'
Said Pearse to Connolly,
'When all the wells are parched away?
O plain as plain can be
There's nothing but our own red blood
Can make a right Rose Tree.'

25 September 1916

Juno and the Paycock

Sean O'Casey grew up in a Protestant family in the desperately poor slums of Dublin, where eviction for debt was normal experience. He served as James Connolly's assistant in the Irish Citizen Army, but sickened of the idea of armed struggle. Juno and the Paycock (1924) *was one of three plays by him performed at the Abbey Theatre, Dublin, which infuriated some by their negative images of the recent violence that had brought, but then followed, independence. When Michael Collins on behalf of the Sinn Fein leadership accepted in December 1921 the partition of the island and Dominion status for most of it under the British Crown, producing the Irish Free State, intransigent Republicans assassinated him and waged civil war against the new Government. 'Juno' is Mrs Boyle, 'the Paycock' is her braggart husband, Jack, whose toadying false friend is Joxer Daly. Their son Johnny has been crippled in the cause of independence, their daughter Mary is engaged to an ambitious and insincere middle-class man, Bentham, who has made her pregnant and deserts her.*

(ACT II)

[MARY *opens the door, and* MRS TANCRED *– a very old woman, obviously shaken by the death of her son – appears, accompanied by several* NEIGHBOURS. *The first few phrases are spoken before they appear.*]

FIRST NEIGHBOUR: It's a sad journey we're goin' on, but God's good, an' the Republicans won't be always down.

MRS TANCRED: Ah, what good is that to me now? Whether they're up or down – it won't bring me darlin' boy from the grave.

MRS BOYLE: Come in an' have a hot cup o' tay, Mrs Tancred, before you go.

MRS TANCRED: Ah, I can take nothin' now, Mrs Boyle – I won't be long afther him.

FIRST NEIGHBOUR: Still an all, he died a noble death, an' we'll bury him like a king.

MRS TANCRED: An' I'll go on livin' like a pauper. Ah, what's the pains I suffered bringin' him into the world to carry him to his cradle, to the pains I'm sufferin' now, carryin' him out o' the world to bring him to his grave!

MARY: It would be better for you not to go at all, Mrs Tancred, but to stay at home beside the fire with some o' the neighbours.

MRS TANCRED: I seen the first of him, an' I'll see the last of him.

MRS BOYLE: You'd want a shawl, Mrs Tancred; it's a cowld night, an' the win's blowin' sharp.

MRS MADIGAN [*rushing out*]: I've a shawl above.

MRS TANCRED: Me home is gone now; he was me only child, an' to think that he was lyin' for a whole night stretched out on the side of a lonely counthry lane, with his head, his darlin' head, that I ofen kissed an' fondled, half hidden in the wather of a runnin' brook. An' I'm told he was the leadher of the ambush where me nex' door neighbour, Mrs Mannin', lost her Free State soldier son. An' now here's the two of us oul' women, standin' one on each side of a scales o' sorra, balanced be the bodies of our two dead darlin' sons. [MRS MADIGAN *returns, and wraps a shawl around her.*] God bless you, Mrs Madigan . . . [*She moves slowly towards the door.*] Mother o' God, Mother o' God, have pity on the pair of us! . . . O Blessed Virgin, where were you when me darlin' son was riddled with bullets, when me darlin' son was riddled with bullets! . . . Sacred Heart of the Crucified Jesus, take away our hearts o' stone . . . an' give us hearts o' flesh! . . . Take away this murdherin' hate . . . an' give us Thine own eternal love! [*They pass out of the room.*]

MRS BOYLE [*explanatorily to* BENTHAM]: That was Mrs Tancred of the two-pair back; her son was found, e'er yesterday, lyin' out beyant Finglas riddled with bullets. A Diehard he was, be all accounts. He was a nice quiet boy, but lattherly he went to hell, with his Republic first, an' Republic last an' Republic over all. He often took tea with us here, in the oul' days, an' Johnny, there, an' him used to be always together.

JOHNNY: Am I always to be havin' to tell you that he was no friend o' mine? I never cared for him, an' he could never stick me. It's not because he was Commandant of the Battalion that I was Quarther-Masther of, that we were friends.

MRS BOYLE: He's gone now – the Lord be good to him! God help his pour oul' creature of a mother, for no matther whose friend or enemy he was, he was her poor son.

BENTHAM: The whole thing is terrible, Mrs Boyle; but the only way to deal with a mad dog is to destroy him.

MRS BOYLE: An' to think of me forgettin' about him bein' brought to the church tonight, an' we singin' an' all, but it was well we hadn't the gramophone goin', anyhow.

BOYLE: Even if we had aself. We've nothin' to do with these things, one way or t'other. That's the Government's business, an' let them do what we're payin' them for doin'.

MRS BOYLE: I'd like to know how a body's not to mind these things; look at the way they're afther leavin' the people in this very house. Hasn't the whole house, nearly, been massacreed? There's young Dougherty's husband with his leg off; Mrs Travers that had her son blew up be a mine in Inchegeela, in County Cork; Mrs Mannin' that lost wan of her sons in an ambush a few weeks ago, an' now, poor Mrs Tancred's only child gone west with his body made a collandher of. Sure, if it's not our business, I don't know whose business it is.

BOYLE: Here, there, that's enough about them things; they don't affect us, an' we needn't give a damn. If they want a wake, well, let them have a wake. When I was a sailor, I was always resigned to meet with a wathery grave; an' if they want to be soldiers, well, there's no use o' them squealin' when they meet a soldier's fate.

JOXER: Let me like a soldier fall – me breast expandin' to th' ball!

MRS BOYLE: In wan way, she deserves all she got; for lately, she let th' Diehards make an open house of th' place; an' for th' last couple of months, either when th' sun was risin' or when th' sun was settin', you had CID men burstin' into your room, assin' you where were you born, where were you christened, where were you married, an' where would you be buried!

JOHNNY: For God's sake, let us have no more o' this talk.

MRS MADIGAN: What about Mrs Boyle's song before we start th' gramophone?

MARY [*getting her hat, and putting it on*]: Mother, Charlie and I are goin' out for a little sthroll.

MRS BOYLE: All right, darlin'.

BENTHAM [*going out with* MARY]: We won't be long away. Mrs Boyle.

MRS MADIGAN: Gwan, Captain, gwan.

BOYLE: E-e-e-e-eh, I'd want to have a few more jars in me, before I'd be in fettle for singin'.

JOXER: Give us that poem you writ t'other day. [*To the rest:*] Aw, it's a darlin' poem, a daarlin' poem.

MRS BOYLE: God bless us, is he startin' to write poetry!

BOYLE [*rising to his feet*]: E-e-e-eh. [*He recites in an emotional, consequential manner the following verses:*]

Shawn an' I were friends, sir, to me he was all in all.
His work was very heavy and his wages were very small.
None betther on th' beach as Docker, I'll go bail,
'Tis now I'm feelin' lonely, for today he lies in jail.
He was not what some call pious – seldom at church or prayer;
For the greatest scoundrels I know, sir, goes every Sunday there.
Fond of his pint – well, rather, but hated the Boss by creed
But never refused a copper to comfort a pal in need.

E-e-e-e-eh. [*He sits down.*]

MRS MADIGAN: Grand, grand; you should folly that up, you should folly that up.

JOXER: It's a daarlin' poem!

BOYLE [*delightedly*]: E-e-e-e-eh.

JOHNNY: Are yous goin' to put on th' gramophone tonight, or are yous not?

MRS BOYLE: Gwan, Jack, put on a record.

MRS MADIGAN: Gwan, Captain, gwan.

BOYE: Well, yous'll want to keep a dead silence.

[*He sets a record, starts the machine, and it begins to play 'If You're Irish Come into the Parlour'. As the tune is in full blare, the door is suddenly opened by a brisk, little bald-headed man, dressed circumspectly in a black suit; he glares fiercely at all in the room; he is* 'NEEDLE' NUGENT, *a tailor. He carries his hat in his hand.*]

NUGENT [*loudly, above the noise of the gramophone*]: Are yous goin' to have that thing bawlin' an' the funeral of Mrs Tancred's son passin' the house? Have none of yous any respect for the Irish people's National regard for the dead? [BOYLE *stops the gramophone.*]

MRS BOYLE: Maybe, Needle Nugent, it's nearly time we had a little less respect for the dead, an' a little more regard for the livin'.

MRS MADIGAN: We don't want you, Mr Nugent, to teach us what we learned at our mother's knee. You don't look yourself as if you were dyin' of grief; if y'ass Maisie Madigan anything, I'd call you a real thrue Diehard an' live-soft Republican, attendin' Republican funerals in the day, an' stoppin' up half the night makin' suits for the Civic Guards!

[*Persons are heard running down the street, some saying 'Here it is, here it is.'* NUGENT *withdraws, and the rest, except* JOHNNY, *go to the widow looking into the street, and look out. Sounds of a crowd coming nearer are heard; portions are singing:*]

To Jesus' Heart all burning
With fervent love for men,
My heart with fondest yearning
Shall raise its joyful strain.
While ages course along,
Blest be with loudest song
The Sacred Heart of Jesus
By every heart and tongue.

MRS BOYLE: Here's the hearse, here's the hearse!
BOYLE: There's t'oul' mother walkin' behin' the coffin.
MRS MADIGAN: You can hardly see the coffin with the wreaths.
JOXER: Oh, it's a darlin' funeral, a daarlin' funeral!
MRS MADIGAN: We'd have a betther view from the street.
BOYLE: Yes – this place ud give you a crick in your neck.

[*They leave the room, and go down.* JOHNNY *sits moodily by the fire. A* YOUNG MAN *enters; he looks at* JOHNNY *for a moment.*]

YOUNG MAN: Quarther-Masther Boyle.
JOHNNY [*with a start*]: The Mobilizer!
YOUNG MAN: You're not at the funeral?
JOHNNY: I'm not well.
YOUNG MAN: I'm glad I've found you; you were stoppin' at your aunt's; I called there but you'd gone. I've to give you an ordher to attend a Battalion Staff meetin' the night afther tomorrow.
JOHNNY: Where?
YOUNG MAN: I don't know; you're to meet me at the Pillar at eight o'clock; then we're to go to a place I'll be told of tonight; there we'll

meet a mothor that'll bring us to the meeting. They think you might be able to know somethin' about them that gave the bend where Commandant Tancred was shelterin'.

JOHNNY: I'm not goin', then. I know nothing about Tancred.

YOUNG MAN [*at the door*]: You'd better come for your own sake – remember your oath.

JOHNNY [*passionately*]: I won't go! Haven't I done enough for Ireland? I've lost me arm, an' me hip's desthroyed so that I'll never be able to walk right agen! Good God, haven't I done enough for Ireland?

YOUNG MAN: Boyle, no man can do enough for Ireland! [*He goes.*]

[*Faintly in the distance the crowd is heard saying:*]

Hail, Mary, full of grace, the Lord is with Thee;
Blessed art Thou amongst women, and blessed [*etc.*].

(ACT III)

[*In debt, the Boyles are losing their possessions.*]

FIRST MAN: We can't wait any longer for t'oul' fella – sorry, Miss, but we have to live as well as th' nex' man. [*They carry out some things.*]

JOHNNY: Oh, isn't this terrible! . . . I suppose you told him everything . . . couldn't you have waited for a few days? . . . he'd have stopped th' takin' of the things, if you'd kep' your mouth shut. Are you burnin' to tell every one of the shame you've brought on us?

MARY [*snatching up her hat and coat*]: Oh, this is unbearable! [*She rushes out.*]

FIRST MAN [*re-entering*]: We'll take the chest o' drawers next – it's the heaviest.

[*The votive light flickers for a moment, and goes out.*]

JOHNNY [*in a cry of fear*]: Mother o' God, the light's afther goin' out!

FIRST MAN: You put the win' up me the way you bawled that time. The oil's all gone, that's all.

JOHNNY [*with an agonizing cry*]: Mother o' God, there's a shot I'm afther gettin'!

FIRST MAN: What's wrong with you, man? Is it a fit you're takin'?

JOHNNY: I'm afther feelin' a pain in me breast, like the tearin' by of a bullet!

FIRST MAN: He's goin' mad – it's a wondher they'd leave a chap like that here by myself.

[*Two* IRREGULARS *enter swiftly; they carry revolvers; one goes over to* JOHNNY*; the other covers the two furniture men.*]

FIRST IRREGULAR [*to the men, quietly and incisively*]: Who are you? – what are yous doin' here? – quick!

FIRST MAN: Removin' furniture that's not paid for.

IRREGULAR: Get over to the other end of the room an' turn your faces to the wall – quick! [*The two men turn their faces to the wall, with their hands up.*]

SECOND IRREGULAR [*to* JOHNNY]: Come on, Sean Boyle, you're wanted; some of us have a word to say to you.

JOHNNY: I'm sick, I can't – what do you want with me?

SECOND IRREGULAR: Come on, come on; we've a distance to go an' haven't much time – come on.

JOHNNY: I'm an oul' comrade – yous wouldn't shoot an oul' comrade.

SECOND IRREGULAR: Poor Tancred was an oul' comrade o' yours, but you didn't think o' that when you gave him away to the gang that sent him to his grave. But we've no time to waste; come on – here, Dermot, ketch his arm. [*To* JOHNNY:] Have you your beads?

JOHNNY: Me beads! Why do you ass me that, why do you ass me that?

SECOND IRREGULAR: Go on, go on, march!

JOHNNY: Are yous goin' to do in a comrade? – look at me arm, I lost it for Ireland.

SECOND IRREGULAR: Commandant Tancred lost his life for Ireland.

JOHNNY: Sacred Heart of Jesus, have mercy on me! Mother o' God, pray for me – be with me now in the agonies o' death! . . . Hail, Mary, full o' grace . . . the Lord is . . . with Thee.

[*They drag out* JOHNNY BOYLE, *and the curtain falls. When it rises again the most of the furniture is gone.* MARY *and* MRS BOYLE, *one on each side, are sitting in a darkened room, by the fire; it is an hour later.*]

MRS BOYLE: I'll not wait much longer ... what did they bring him away in the mothor for? Nugent says he thinks they had guns ... is me throubles never goin' to be over? ... If anything ud happen to poor Johnny, I think I'd lose me mind ... I'll go to the Police Station, surely they ought to be able to do somethin'.

[*Below is heard the sound of voices.*] Whisht, is that something? Maybe, it's your father, though when I left him in Foley's he was hardly able to lift his head. Whisht!

[*A knock at the door, and the voice of* MRS MADIGAN, *speaking very softly:*] Mrs Boyle, Mrs Boyle. [MRS BOYLE *opens the door.*] Oh, Mrs Boyle, God an' His Blessed Mother be with you this night!

MRS BOYLE [*calmly*]: What is it, Mrs Madigan? It's Johnny – something about Johnny.

MRS MADIGAN: God send it's not, God send it's not Johnny!

MRS BOYLE: Don't keep me waitin', Mrs Madigan; I've gone through so much lately that I feel able for anything.

MRS MADIGAN: Two polismen below wantin' you.

MRS BOYLE: Wantin' me; an' why do they want me?

MRS MADIGAN: Some poor fella's been found, an' they think it's, it's ...

MRS BOYLE: Johnny, Johnny!

MARY [*with her arms round her mother*]: Oh, mother, mother, me poor, darlin' mother.

MRS BOYLE: Hush, hush, darlin'; you'll shortly have your own throuble to bear. [*To* MRS MADIGAN*:*] An' why do the polis think it's Johnny, Mrs Madigan?

MRS MADIGAN: Because one o' the doctors knew him when he was attendin' with his poor arm.

MRS BOYLE: Oh, it's thrue, then; it's Johnny, it's me son, me own son!

MARY: Oh, it's thrue, it's thrue what Jerry Devine says – there isn't a God, there isn't a God; if there was He wouldn't let these things happen!

MRS BOYLE: Mary, Mary, you mustn't say them things. We'll want all the help we can get from God an' His Blessed Mother now! These things have nothin' to do with the Will o' God. Ah, what can God do agen the stupidity o' men!

MRS MADIGAN: The polis want you to go with them to the hospital to see the poor body – they're waitin' below.

MRS BOYLE: We'll go. Come, Mary, an' we'll never come back here agen. Let your father furrage for himself now; I've done all I could an' it was all no use – he'll be hopeless till the end of his days. I've got a little room in me sisther's where we'll stop till your throuble is over an' then we'll work together for the sake of the baby.

MARY: My poor little child that'll have no father!

MRS BOYLE: It'll have what's far betther – it'll have two mothers.

A ROUGH VOICE SHOUTING FROM BELOW: Are yous goin' to keep us waitin' for yous all night?

MRS MADIGAN [*going to the door, and shouting down*]: Take your hour, there, take your hour! If yous are in such a hurry, skip off, then, for nobody wants you here – if they did yous wouldn't be found. For you're the same as yous were undher the British Government – never where yous are wanted! As far as I can see, the Polis as Polis, in this city, is Null an' Void!

MRS BOYLE: We'll go, Mary, we'll go; you to see your poor dead brother, an' me to see me poor dead son!

MARY: I dhread it, mother, I dhread it!

MRS BOYLE: I forgot, Mary, I forgot; your poor oul' selfish mother was only thinkin' of herself. No, no, you mustn't come – it wouldn't be good for you. You go on to me sisther's an' I'll face th' ordeal meself. Maybe I didn't feel sorry enough for Mrs Tancred when her poor son was found as Johnny's been found now – because he was a Diehard! Ah, why didn't I remember that then he wasn't a Diehard or a Stater, but only a poor dead son! It's well I remember all that she said – an' it's my turn to say it now. What was the pain I suffered, Johnny, bringin' you into the world to carry you to your cradle, to the pains I'll suffer carryin' you out o' the world to bring you to your grave! Mother o' God, Mother o' God, have pity on us all! Blessed Virgin, where were you when me darlin' son was riddled with bullets, when me darlin' son was riddled with bullets? Sacred Heart o' Jesus, take away our hearts o' stone, and give us hearts o' flesh! Take away this murdherin' hate, an' give us Thine own eternal love! [*They all go slowly out.*]

[*There is a pause; then a sound of shuffling steps on the stairs outside. The door opens and* BOYLE *and* JOXER, *both of them very drunk, enter.*]

BOYLE: I'm able to go no farther . . . Two polis, ey . . . what were they doin' here, I wondher? . . . Up to no good, anyhow . . . an' Juno an' that lovely daughter o' mine with them. [*Taking a sixpence from his pocket and looking at it:*] Wan single, solitary tanner left out of all I borreyed . . . [*He lets it fall.*] The last o' the Mohecans . . . The blinds is down, Joxer, the blinds is down!

JOXER [*walking unsteadily across the room, and anchoring at the bed*]: Put all . . . your throubles . . . in your oul' kit-bag . . . an' smile . . . smile . . . smile!

BOYLE: The counthry'll have to steady itself . . . it's goin' . . . to hell. Where'r all . . . the chairs . . . gone to . . . steady itself, Joxer . . . Chairs'll . . . have to . . . steady themselves . . . No matther . . . what any one may . . . say . . . Irelan' sober . . . is Irelan' . . . free.

JOXER [*stretching himself on the bed*]: Chains . . . an' . . . slaveree . . . that's a darlin' motto . . . a daaarlin' . . . motto!

BOYLE: If th' worse comes . . . to th' worse . . . I can join a flyin' . . . column . . . I done . . . me bit . . . in Easther Week . . . had no business . . . to . . . be . . . there . . . but Captain Boyle's Captain Boyle!

JOXER: Breathes there a man with soul . . . so . . . de . . . ad . . . this . . . me . . . o . . . wn, me nat . . . ive I . . . an'!

BOYLE [*subsiding into a sitting posture on the floor*]: Commandant Kelly died . . . in them . . . arms . . . Joxer . . . Tell me Volunteer butties . . . says he . . . that . . . I died for . . . Irelan'!

JOXER: D'jever rade 'Willie . . . Reilly . . . an' His Own . . . Colleen . . . Bawn?' It's a darlin' story, a daarlin' story!

BOYLE: I'm telling you . . . Joxer . . . th' whole worl's . . . in a terr . . . ible state o' . . . chassis!

Holmgang and Bullfight

In 1969 'the Troubles' of Ireland erupted again when claims for full equality by Catholics in the Protestant-dominated North triggered sectarian violence and a revival of armed Republicanism. Seamus Heaney, himself a Northern Catholic, wrote his book North *(1975) in response to the crisis in his homeland, linking it here to another civil war and the emblematic violent death of the poet and playwright Federico García Lorca.*

SUMMER 1969

While the Constabulary covered the mob
Firing into the Falls, I was suffering
Only the bullying sun of Madrid.
Each afternoon, in the casserole heat
Of the flat, as I sweated my way through
The life of Joyce, stinks from the fishmarket
Rose like the reek off a flax-dam.
At night on the balcony, gules of wine,
A sense of children in their dark corners,
Old women in black shawls near open windows,
The air a canyon rivering in Spanish.
We talked our way home over starlit plains
Where patent leather of the Guardia Civil
Gleamed like fish-bellies, in flax-poisoned waters.

'Go back,' one said, 'try to touch the people.'
Another conjured Lorca from his hill.
We sat through death counts and bullfight reports
On the television, celebrities
Arrived from where the real thing still happened.

I retreated to the cool of the Prado.
Goya's 'Shootings of the Third of May'
Covered a wall – the thrown-up arms

And spasm of the rebel, the helmeted
And knapsacked military, the efficient
Rake of the fusillade. In the next room
His nightmares, grafted to the palace wall –
Dark cyclones, hosting, breaking; Saturn
Jewelled in the blood of his own children,
Gigantic Chaos turning his brute hips
Over the world. Also, that holmgang
Where two berserks club each other to death
For honour's sake, greaved in a bog, and sinking.

He painted with his fists and elbows, flourished
The stained cape of his heart as history charged.

A Surrealist at War With Himself

Lorca was arrested and executed by Franco's Falangist rebels as they took over Granada in August 1936.

Spain had been a constitutional monarchy until 1923 when Primo de Rivera had overthrown the politicians and established a dictatorship. In 1931 he in turn was overthrown, and with him the monarch. Elections in 1933 replaced the first, left-wing, republican government with one of the centre-right which provoked attempted revolutions in Asturias and Catalonia. It was defeated in elections of February 1936 by a 'Popular Front' of centrist Republicans, Socialists, Communists, Trotskyists, Syndicalists and Anarchists. The new Government had a substantial majority, but could not control a wave of strikes and unrest in which peasants seized land and churches were burnt. In July General Francisco Franco led an army mutiny in Spanish Morocco which spread at once to the mainland.

Luis Buñuel (1900–1983) is undoubtedly one of the major figures of twentieth-century cinema, associated in the 1930s with the international Surrealist movement in the arts which claimed a left-wing direction. The Residencia, where Buñnel had met Lorca, was a college in Madrid on the Oxford model. Buñnel's memoir My Last Sigh *was published in 1983.*

In July 1936, Franco arrived in Spain with his Moroccan troops and the firm intention of demolishing the Republic and re-establishing 'order'. My wife and son had gone back to Paris the month before, and I was alone in Madrid. Early one morning, I was jolted awake by a series of explosions and cannon fire; a Republican plane was bombing the Montaña army barracks.

At this time, all the barracks in Spain were filled with soldiers. A group of Falangists had ensconced themselves in the Montaña and had been firing from its windows for several days, wounding many civilians. On the morning of July 18, groups of workers, armed and supported by Azaña's Republican assault troops, attacked the barracks. It was all over by ten o'clock, the rebel officers and Falangists executed. The war had begun.

It was hard to believe. Listening to the distant machine-gun fire from my balcony, I watched a Schneider cannon roll by in the street below, pulled by a couple of workers and some gypsies. The revolution we'd felt gathering force for so many years, and which I personally had so ardently desired, was now going on before my eyes. All I felt was shock.

Two weeks later, Elie Faure, the famous art historian and an ardent supporter of the Republican cause, came to Madrid for a few days. I went to visit him one morning at his hotel and can still see him standing at his window in his long underwear, watching the demonstrations in the street below and weeping at the sight of the people in arms. One day, we watched a hundred peasants marching by, four abreast, some armed with hunting rifles and revolvers, some with sickles and pitchforks. In an obvious effort at discipline, they were trying very hard to march in step. Faure and I both wept.

It seemed as if nothing could defeat such a deep-seated popular force, but the joy and enthusiasm that coloured those early days soon gave way to arguments, disorganization, and uncertainty – all of which lasted until November 1936, when an efficient and disciplined Republican organization began to emerge. I make no claims to writing a serious account of the deep gash that ripped through my country in 1936. I'm not a historian, and I'm certainly not impartial. I can only try to describe what I saw and what I remember. At the same time, I do see those first months in Madrid very clearly. Theoretically, the city was still in the hands of the Republicans, but Franco had already reached Toledo, after occupying other cities like Salamanca and Burgos. Inside Madrid, there was constant sniping by Fascist sympathizers. The priests and the rich land-owners – in other words, those with conservative leanings, whom we assumed would support the Falange – were in constant danger of being executed by the Republicans. The moment the fighting began, the anarchists liberated all political prisoners and immediately incorporated them into the ranks of the Confederación Nacional de Trabajo, which was under the direct control of the anarchist federation. Certain members of this federation were such extremists that the mere presence of a religious icon in someone's room led automatically to Casa Campo, the public park on the outskirts of the city where the executions took place. People arrested at night were always told that they were going to 'take a little walk'.

It was advisable to use the intimate '*tu*' form of address for everyone, and to add an energetic *compañero* whenever you spoke to an anarchist, or a *camarada* to a Communist. Most cars carried a couple of mattresses tied to the roof as protection against snipers. It was dangerous even to hold out your hand to signal a turn, as the gesture might be interpreted as a Fascist salute and get you a fast round of gunfire. The *señoritos*, the sons of 'good' families, wore old caps and dirty clothes in order to look as much like workers as they could, while on the other side the Communist party recommended that the workers wear white shirts and ties.

. . .

The first three months were the worst, mostly because of the total absence of control. I, who had been such an ardent subversive, who had so desired the overthrow of the established order, now found myself in the middle of a volcano, and I was afraid. If certain exploits seemed to me both absurd and glorious – like the workers who climbed into a truck one day and drove out to the monument to the Sacred Heart of Jesus about twenty kilometres south of the city, forming a firing squad, and executed the statue of Christ – I none the less couldn't stomach the summary executions, the looting, the criminal acts. No sooner had the people risen and seized power than they split into factions and began tearing one another to pieces. This insane and indiscriminate settling of accounts made everyone forget the essential reasons for the war.

I went to nightly meetings of the Association of Writers and Artists for the Revolution, where I saw most of my friends – Alberti, Bergamín, the journalist Corpus Varga, and the poet Altolaguirre, who believed in God and who later produced my *Mexican Bus Ride*. The group was constantly erupting in passionate and interminable arguments, many of which concerned whether we should just act spontaneously or try to organize ourselves. As usual, I was torn between my intellectual (and emotional) attraction to anarchy and my fundamental need for order and peace. And there we sat, in a life-and-death situation, but spending all our time constructing theories.

Franco continued to advance. Certain towns and cities remained loyal to the Republic, but others surrendered to him without a struggle. Fascist repression was pitiless; anyone suspected of liberal tendencies was summarily executed. But instead of trying to form an organization, we debated – while the anarchists persecuted priests. I can still hear the old cry: 'Come down and see. There's a dead priest in the street.' As anti-clerical as I was, I couldn't condone this kind of massacre, even though the priests were not exactly innocent bystanders. They took up arms like everybody else, and did a fair bit of sniping from their bell towers. We even saw Dominicans with machine-guns. A few of the clergy joined the Republican side, but most went over to the Fascists. The war spared no one, and it was impossible to remain neutral, to declare allegiance to the utopian illusion of a *tercera España*.

Some days, I was very frightened. I lived in an extremely bourgeois apartment house and often wondered what would happen if a wild bunch of anarchists suddenly broke into my place in the middle of the night to 'take me for a walk'. Would I resist? How could I? What could I say to them? . . .

The Republican camp was riddled with dissension. The main goal of both Communists and Socialists was to win the war, while the anarchists, on the other hand, considered the war already won and had begun to organize their ideal society.

'We've started a commune at Torrelodones,' Gil Bel, the editor of the labour journal *El Sindicalista*, told me one day at the Café Castilla. 'We already have twenty houses, all occupied. You ought to take one.'

I was beside myself with rage and surprise. Those houses belonged to people who'd fled or been executed. And as if that weren't enough, Torrelodones stood at the foot of the Sierra de Guadarrama, only a few kilometres from the Fascist front lines. Within shooting distance of Franco's army, the anarchists were calmly laying out their utopia.

On another occasion, I was having lunch in a restaurant with the musician Remacha, one of the directors of the Filmofono Studios where I'd once worked. The son of the restaurant owner had been seriously wounded fighting the Falangists in the Sierra de Guadarrama. Suddenly, several armed anarchists burst into the restaurant yelling, '*Salud compañeros!*' and shouting for wine. Furious, I told them they should be in the mountains fighting instead of emptying the wine cellar of a good man whose son was fighting for his life in a hospital. They sobered up quickly and left, taking the bottles with them, of course.

Every evening, whole brigades of anarchists came down out of the hills to loot the hotel wine cellars. Their behaviour pushed many of us into the arms of the Communists. Few in number at the beginning of the war, they were none the less growing stronger with each passing day. Organized and disciplined, focused on the war itself, they seemed to me then, as they do now, irreproachable. It was sad but true that the anarchists hated them more than they hated the Fascists. This animosity had begun several years before the war when, in 1935, the Federación Anarquista Ibérica (FAI) announced a general strike among construction workers. The anarchist Ramón Acin, who financed *Las Hurdes*, told me about the time a Communist delegation went to see the head of the strike committee.

'There are three police stoolies in your ranks,' they told him, naming names.

'So what?' the anarchist retorted. 'We know all about it, but we like stoolies better than Communists.'

Despite my ideological sympathies with the anarchists, I couldn't stand their unpredictable and fanatical behaviour. Sometimes, it was sufficient merely to be an engineer or to have a university degree to be taken away to Casa Campo. When the Republican government moved its headquarters from Madrid to Barcelona because of the Fascist advance, the anarchists threw up a barricade near Cuenca on the only road that hadn't been cut. In Barcelona itself, they liquidated the director and the engineers in a metallurgy factory in order to prove that the factory could function perfectly well when run by the workers. Then they built a tank and proudly showed it to a Soviet delegate. (When he asked for a parabellum and fired at it, it fell apart.) . . .

All in all, the dominant feeling was one of insecurity and confusion, aggravated, despite the threat of Fascism on our very doorstep, by endless internal conflicts and diverging tendencies. As I watched the realization of an old dream, all I felt was sadness.

And then one day I learned of Lorca's death, from a Republican who'd somehow managed to slip through the lines . . .

It was difficult, of course, to have serious discussions about painting and poetry while the war raged around us. Four days before Franco's arrival, Lorca, who never got excited about politics, suddenly decided to leave for Granada, his native city.

'Federico,' I pleaded, trying to talk him out of it. 'Horrendous things are happening. You can't go down there now; it's safer to stay right here.'

He paid no attention to any of us, and left, tense and frightened, the following day. The news of his death was a terrific shock. Of all the human beings I've ever known, Federico was the finest. I don't mean his plays or his poetry; I mean him personally. He was his own masterpiece.

Whether sitting at the piano imitating Chopin, improvising a pantomime, or acting out a scene from a play, he was irresistible. He read beautifully, and he had passion, youth, and joy. When I first met him, at the Residencia, I was an unpolished rustic, interested primarily in sports. He transformed me, introduced me to a wholly different world. He was like a flame.

Homage to Catalonia

The Soviet Union quickly began to assist the Spanish Republic. Fascist Italy and Nazi Germany gave decisive material help, and scores of thousands of regular personnel, to Franco's forces. Britain and France decided on 'non-intervention'. But about 45,000 volunteers from many countries flocked to the Republic's side. An International Brigade was formed. One volunteer who did not join this was George Orwell, who went from Britain to Barcelona in December 1936 under the auspices of the small Independent Labour Party. His controversial account of his service in Spain, Homage to Catalonia, *was published in 1938.*

Republican militias were organized on political lines. The Communists, with Soviet aid, were best equipped. The largest were run by the anarcho-syndicalist and socialist trade unions. Orwell joined that of the United Marxist Workers' Party (POUM), which was smeared as 'Trotskyite' by the Communists, but actually represented a range of independent Marxist elements. Orwell's one-time service in the Burma Police of the British Empire had given him quasi-military experience, so he was soon put to work drilling men. Then he went to the Aragon front, between Saragossa and Huesca.

I had been made a corporal, or *cabo*, as it was called, as soon as we reached the front, and was in command of a guard of twelve men. It was no sinecure, especially at first. The *centuria* was an untrained mob composed mostly of boys in their teens. Here and there in the militia you came across children as young as eleven or twelve, usually refugees from Fascist territory who had been enlisted as militiamen as the easiest way of providing for them. As a rule they were employed on light work in the rear, but sometimes they managed to worm their way to the front line, where they were a public menace. I remember one little brute throwing a hand-grenade into the dug-out fire 'for a joke'. At Monte Pocero I do not think there was anyone younger than fifteen, but the average age must have been well under twenty. Boys of this age ought never to be used in the front line, because they cannot stand the lack of sleep which is inseparable from trench warfare. At the beginning it was almost impossible to keep our position properly guarded at night. The wretched children of my section could only be roused by dragging them out of their dug-outs feet foremost, and as soon as your back was turned they left their posts and slipped into shelter; or they would even, in spite of the frightful cold, lean up against the wall of the trench and fall fast asleep. Luckily the enemy were very unenterprising. There were nights when it seemed to me that our position could be stormed by twenty Boy Scouts armed with airguns, or twenty Girl Guides armed with battledores, for that matter.

At this time and until much later the Catalan militias were still on the same basis as they had been at the beginning of the war. In the early days of Franco's revolt the militias had been hurriedly raised by the various trade unions and political parties; each was essentially a political organization, owing allegiance to its party as much as to the central Government. When the Popular Army, which was a 'non-political' army organized on more or less ordinary lines, was raised at the beginning of 1937, the party militias were theoretically incorporated in it. But for a long time the only changes that occurred were on paper; the new Popular Army troops did not reach the Aragon front in any numbers till June, and until that time the militia-system remained unchanged. The essential point of the system was social equality between officers and men. Everyone from general to private drew the same pay, ate the same food, wore the same clothes, and mingled on terms of complete equality. If you wanted to slap the general commanding the division on the back and ask him for a cigarette, you could do so, and no one thought it curious. In theory at any rate each militia was a democracy and not a hierarchy. It was understood that orders had to be obeyed, but it was also understood that when you gave an order you gave it as comrade to comrade and not as superior to inferior. There were officers and NCOs, but there was no military rank in the ordinary sense; no titles, no badges, no heel-clicking and saluting. They had attempted to produce within the militias a sort of temporary working model of the classless society. Of course there was no perfect equality, but there was a nearer approach to it than I had ever seen or than I would have thought conceivable in time of war.

But I admit that at first sight the state of affairs at the front horrified me. How on earth could the war be won by an army of this type? It was what everyone was saying at the time, and though it was true it was also unreasonable. For in the circumstances the militias could not have been much better than they were. A modern mechanized army does not spring up out of the ground, and if the Government had waited until it had trained troops at its disposal, Franco would never have been resisted. Later it became the fashion to decry the militias, and therefore to pretend that the faults which were due to lack of training and weapons were the result of the equalitarian system. Actually, a newly raised draft of militia was an undisciplined mob not because the officers called the private 'Comrade' but because raw troops are *always* an undisciplined mob. In practice the democratic 'revolutionary' type of discipline is more reliable than might be expected. In a workers' army discipline is theoretically voluntary. It is based on class loyalty, whereas the discipline of a bourgeois conscript army is based ultimately on fear. (The Popular Army that replaced the militias was midway between the two types.) In the militias the bullying and abuse that go on in an ordinary army would never have been tolerated for a moment. The normal military punishments existed, but they were only invoked for very serious offences. When a man refused to obey an order you did not immediately get him punished; you first appealed to him in the name of comradeship. Cynical people with no experience of handling men will say instantly that this would never 'work', but as a matter of fact it does 'work' in the long run. The discipline of even the worst drafts of militia visibly improved as time went on. In January the job of keeping a dozen raw recruits up to the mark almost turned my hair grey. In May for a short while I was acting-lieutenant in command of about thirty men, English and Spanish. We had all been under fire for months, and I never had the slightest difficulty in getting an order obeyed or in getting men to volunteer for a dangerous job. 'Revolutionary' discipline depends on political consciousness – on an understanding of *why* orders must be obeyed; it takes time to diffuse this, but it also takes time to drill a man into an automaton on the barrack-square. The journalists who sneered at the militia-system seldom remembered that the militias had to hold the line while the Popular Army was training in the rear. And it is a tribute to the strength of 'revolutionary' discipline that the militias stayed in the field at all. For until about June 1937 there was nothing to keep them there, except class loyalty. Individual deserters could be shot – were shot, occasionally – but if a thousand men had decided to walk out of the line together there was no force to stop them. A conscript army in the same circumstances – with its battle-police removed – would have melted away. Yet the militias held the line, though God knows they won very few victories, and even individual desertions were not common. In four or five months in the POUM militia I only heard of four men deserting, and two of those were fairly certainly spies who had enlisted to obtain information. At the beginning the apparent chaos, the general lack of training, the fact that you often had to argue for five minutes before you could get an order obeyed, appalled and infuriated me. I had British Army ideas, and certainly the Spanish militias were very unlike the British Army. But considering the circumstances they were better troops than one had any right to expect.

Meanwhile, firewood – always firewood. Throughout that period there is probably no entry in my diary that does not mention firewood, or rather the lack of it. We were between two and three thousand feet above sea-level, it was mid winter and the cold was unspeakable. The temperature was not exceptionally low, on many nights it did not even freeze, and the wintry sun often shone for an hour in the middle of the day; but even if it was not really cold, I assure you that it seemed so. Sometimes there were shrieking winds that tore your cap off and twisted your hair in all directions, sometimes there were mists that poured into the trench like a liquid and seemed to penetrate your bones; frequently it rained, and even a quarter of an hour's rain was enough to make conditions intolerable. The thin skin of earth over the limestone turned promptly into a slippery grease, and as you were always walking on a slope it was impossible to keep your footing. On dark nights I have often fallen half a dozen times in twenty yards; and this was dangerous, because it meant that the lock of one's rifle became jammed with mud. For days together clothes, boots, blankets, and rifles were more or less coated with mud. I had brought as many thick clothes as I could carry, but many of the men were terribly underclad. For the whole garrison, about a hundred men, there were only twelve great-coats, which had to be handed from sentry to sentry, and most of the men had only one blanket. One icy night I made a list in my diary of the clothes I was wearing. It is of some interest as showing the amount of clothes the human body can carry. I was wearing a thick vest and pants, a flannel shirt, two pull-overs, a woollen jacket, a pigskin jacket, corduroy breeches, puttees, thick socks, boots, a stout trench-coat, a muffler, lined leather gloves and a woollen cap. Nevertheless I was shivering like a jelly. But I admit I am unusually sensitive to cold.

Firewood was the one thing that really mattered. The point about the firewood was that there was practically no firewood to be had. Our miserable mountain had not even at its best much vegetation, and for months it had been ranged over by freezing militiamen, with the result that everything thicker than one's finger had long since been burnt. When we were not eating, sleeping, on guard, or on fatigue-duty we were in the valley behind the position, scrounging for fuel. All my memories of that time are memories of scrambling up and down the almost perpendicular slopes, over the jagged limestone that knocked one's boots to pieces, pouncing eagerly on tiny twigs of wood. Three people searching for a couple of hours could collect enough fuel to keep the dug-out fire alight for about an hour. The eagerness of our search for firewood turned us all into botanists. We classified according to their burning qualities every plant that grew on the mountain-side; the various heaths and grasses that were good to start a fire with but burnt out in a few minutes, the wild rosemary and the tiny whin bushes that would burn when the fire was well alight, the stunted oak tree, smaller than a gooseberry bush, that was practically unburnable. There was a kind of dried-up reed that was very good for starting fires with, but these grew only on the hill-top to the left of the position, and you had to go under fire to get them. If the Fascist machine-gunners saw you they gave you a drum of ammunition all to yourself. Generally their aim was high and the bullets sang overhead like birds, but sometimes they crackled and chipped the limestone uncomfortably close, whereupon you flung yourself on your face. You went on gathering reeds, however; nothing mattered in comparison with firewood.

Beside the cold the other discomforts seemed petty. Of course all of us were permanently dirty. Our water, like our food, came on mule-back from Alcubierre, and each man's share worked out at about a quart a day. It was beastly water, hardly more transparent than milk. Theoretically it was for drinking only, but I always stole a pannikinful for washing in the mornings. I used to wash one day and shave the next; there was never enough water for both. The position stank abominably, and outside the little enclosure of the barricade there was excrement everywhere. Some of the militiamen habitually defecated in the trench, a disgusting thing when one had to walk round it in the darkness. But the dirt never worried me. Dirt is a thing people make too much fuss about. It is astonishing how quickly you get used to doing without a handkerchief and to eating out of the tin pannikin in which you also wash. Nor was sleeping in one's clothes any hardship after a day or two. It was of course impossible to take one's clothes and especially one's boots off at night;

one had to be ready to turn out instantly in case of an attack. In eighty nights I only took my clothes off three times, though I did occasionally manage to get them off in the daytime. It was too cold for lice as yet, but rats and mice abounded. It is often said that you don't find rats and mice in the same place, but you do when there is enough food for them.

In other ways we were not badly off. The food was good enough and there was plenty of wine. Cigarettes were still being issued at the rate of a packet a day, matches were issued every other day, and there was even an issue of candles. They were very thin candles, like those on a Christmas cake, and were popularly supposed to have been looted from churches. Every dug-out was issued daily with three inches of candle, which would burn for about twenty minutes. At that time it was still possible to buy candles, and I had brought several pounds of them with me. Later on the famine of matches and candles made life a misery. You do not realize the importance of these things until you lack them. In a night-alarm, for instance, when everyone in the dug-out is scrambling for his rifle and treading on everybody else's face, being able to strike a light may make the difference between life and death. Every militiaman possessed a tinder-lighter and several yards of yellow wick. Next to his rifle it was his most important possession. The tinder-lighters had the great advantage that they could be struck in a wind, but they would only smoulder, so that they were no use for lighting a fire. When the match famine was at its worst our only way of producing a flame was to pull the bullet out of a cartridge and touch the cordite off with a tinder-lighter.

It was an extraordinary life that we were living – an extraordinary way to be at war, if you could call it war. The whole militia chafed against the inaction and clamoured constantly to know why we were not allowed to attack. But it was perfectly obvious that there would be no battle for a long while yet, unless the enemy started it. Georges Kopp, on his periodical tours of inspection, was quite frank with us. 'This is not a war,' he used to say, 'it is a comic opera with an occasional death.' As a matter of fact the stagnation on the Aragon front had political causes of which I knew nothing at that time; but the purely military difficulties – quite apart from the lack of reserves of men – were obvious to anybody.

To begin with, there was the nature of the country. The front line, ours and the Fascists', lay in positions of immense natural strength, which as a rule could only be approached from one side. Provided a few trenches have been dug, such places cannot be taken by infantry, except in overwhelming numbers. In our own position or most of those round us a dozen men with two machine-guns could have held off a battalion. Perched on the hill-tops as we were, we should have made lovely marks for artillery; but there was no artillery. Sometimes I used to gaze round the landscape and long – oh, how passionately! – for a couple of batteries of guns. One could have destroyed the enemy positions one after another as easily as smashing nuts with a hammer. But on our side the guns simply did not exist. The Fascists did occasionally manage to bring a gun or two from Zaragoza and fire a very few shells, so few that they never even found the range and the shells plunged harmlessly into the empty ravines. Against machine-guns and without artillery there are only three things you can do: dig yourself in at a safe distance – four hundred yards, say – advance across the open and be massacred, or make small-scale night-attacks that will not alter the general situation. Practically the alternatives are stagnation or suicide.

And beyond this there was the complete lack of war materials of every description. It needs an effort to realize how badly the militias were armed at this time. Any public school OTC in England is far more like a modern army than we were. The badness of our weapons was so astonishing that it is worth recording in detail.

For this sector of the front the entire artillery consisted of four trench-mortars with *fifteen rounds* for each gun. Of course they were far too precious to be fired and the mortars were kept in Alcubierre. There were machine-guns at the rate of approximately one to fifty men; they were oldish guns, but fairly accurate up to three or four hundred yards. Beyond this we had only rifles, and the majority of the rifles were scrap-iron. There were three types of rifle in use. The first was the long Mauser. These were seldom less than twenty years old, their sights were about as much use as a broken speedometer, and in most of them the rifling was hopelessly corroded; about one rifle in ten was not bad, however. Then there was the short Mauser, or *mousqueton*, really a cavalry weapon. These were more popular than the others because they were lighter to carry and less nuisance in a trench, also because they were comparatively new and looked efficient. Actually they were almost useless. They were made out of reassembled parts, no bolt belonged to its rifle, and three-quarters of them could be counted on to jam after five shots. There were also a few Winchester rifles. These were nice to shoot with, but they were wildly inaccurate, and as their cartridges had no clips they could only be fired one shot at a time. Ammunition was so scarce that each man entering the line was only issued with fifty rounds, and most of it was exceedingly bad. The Spanish-made cartridges were all refills and would jam even the best rifles. The Mexican cartridges were better and were therefore reserved for the machine-guns. Best of all was the German-made ammunition, but as this came only from prisoners and deserters there was not much of it. I always kept a clip of German or Mexican ammunition in my pocket for use in an emergency. But in practice when the emergency came I seldom fired my rifle; I was too frightened of the beastly thing jamming and too anxious to reserve at any rate one round that would go off.

We had no tin hats, no bayonets, hardly any revolvers or pistols, and not more than one bomb between five or ten men. The bomb in use at this time was a frightful object known as the 'FAI bomb', it having been produced by the Anarchists in the early days of the war. It was on the principle of a Mills bomb, but the lever was held down not by a pin but a piece of tape. You broke the tape and then got rid of the bomb with the utmost possible speed. It was said of these bombs that they were 'impartial'; they killed the man they were thrown at and the man who threw them. There were several other types, even more primitive but probably a little less dangerous – to the thrower, I mean. It was not till late March that I saw a bomb worth throwing.

And apart from weapons there was a shortage of all the minor necessities of war. We had no maps or charts, for instance. Spain has never been fully surveyed, and the only detailed maps of this area were the old military ones, which were almost all in the possession of the Fascists. We had no range-finders, no telescopes, no periscopes, no field-glasses except for a few privately-owned pairs, no flares or Very lights, no wire-cutters, no armourers' tools, hardly even any cleaning materials. The Spaniards seemed never to have heard of a pull-through and looked on in surprise when I constructed one. When you wanted your rifle cleaned you took it to the sergeant, who possessed a long brass ramrod which was invariably bent and therefore scratched the rifling. There was not even any gun oil. You greased your rifle with olive oil, when you could get hold of it; at different times I have greased mine with vaseline, with cold cream, and even with bacon-fat. Moreover, there were no lanterns or electric torches – at this time there was not, I believe, such a thing as an electric torch throughout the whole of our sector of the front, and you could not buy one nearer than Barcelona, and only with difficulty even there.

As time went on, and the desultory rifle-fire rattled among the hills, I began to wonder with increasing scepticism whether anything would ever happen to bring a bit of life, or rather a bit of death, into this cock-eyed war. It was pneumonia that we were fighting against, not against men. When the trenches are more than five hundred yards apart no one gets hit except by accident. Of course there were casualties, but the majority of them were self-inflicted. If I remember rightly, the first five men I saw wounded in Spain were all wounded by our own weapons – I don't mean intentionally, but owing to accident or carelessness. Our worn-out rifles were a danger in themselves. Some of them had a nasty trick of going off if the butt was tapped on the ground; I saw a man shoot himself through the hand owing to this. And in the darkness the raw recruits were always firing at one another. One evening when it was barely even dusk a sentry let fly at me from a distance of twenty yards; but he missed me by a yard – goodness knows how many times the Spanish standard of marksmanship has saved my life.

Days of Hope

André Malraux had perhaps the most extraordinary career of any twentieth-century writer. Eventually Gaullist politician and Minister of Culture in the sixties, in the mid-twenties (which were also his own mid-twenties) he was a revolutionary activist in China before translating this experience into fiction. A dedicated anti-Fascist, he organized a volunteer air squadron to fight for the Spanish Republic, then, before that civil war was decided, published a very large novel, Days of Hope *(1938), surveying the early phases of the struggle from the Republican viewpoint – or, better say, various viewpoints. So close to the conflict, Malraux can yet write with objectivity about Republican shortcomings and engage sympathetically with the ideas and personalities of Communists, anarchists and Christian Republicans alike. He writes with vivid and convincing detail about the war in the air, in the provinces and in Madrid. The capital was bombed severely, and its suburbs were penetrated by Falangist troops.*

Madrid, 2nd December [1936]

Two corpses were lying in front of the window. A wounded man had been dragged back to cover, by the feet. Five of the Internationals were holding the staircase, with their dumps of hand-grenades beside them. There were some thirty members of the International Brigade occupying the fourth floor of the house painted pink.

An enormous loud-speaker, one of those which the Republicans drove round in propaganda lorries more than half-filled by the huge funnels, was bellowing through the failing light of the winter afternoon:

Comrades! Comrades! Hold on to your positions. The fascists will be out of munitions by this evening. The Uribarri column blew up thirty-two of their lorries this morning. Comrades! Comrades! Hold on!

The loud-speaker, knowing there was no answering it, reiterated . . .

The fascists would be out of munitions by the evening, but for the time being they had plenty; they had counter-attacked, and were holding the first two storeys of the building. The third floor was a no-man's-land. The Internationals occupied the fourth.

'Dirty swine!' a voice yelled up the chimney, in French. 'You'll soon see whether or not we have enough munitions to lay you out!'

That was one of the Tercios, down below. Chimneys make good speaking-tubes.

'Dirty ten-francs-a-day hirelings!' Maringaud yelled back, getting down on all fours. Heads were in the line of fire, even at the back of the room. Formerly Maringaud had believed all the usual romantic stuff about the Foreign Legion. Rebels, tough fellows, those boys! Well, there they were, just below, the Spanish foreign legionnaires, come here to defend they knew not what, full of vanity, and crazy to fight. Maringaud had been in a bayonet charge against them a month before, in the Western Park. What price the Tercios then? That pack of trained bloodhounds, servile to their unknown masters, now utterly disgusted him. The International Brigade, likewise a foreign legion, hates above all that other Foreign Legion.

The Republican six-inch guns continued to fire on the hospital at regular intervals.

The flat in which Maringaud and his mates were looking for good sniping posts had formerly been a dentist's. One of the rooms was locked. He decided to break open the door. Squat to the point of tubbiness, Maringaud had black eyebrows and a short nose set in a round, genial face, bringing to mind the 'bonny baby' of advertisement. Under his weight the door burst open, and the dentist's operating-room appeared. There, sprawling in the dentist's chair, was a dead Moor. The Republicans had been occupying the two lower floors of the building only the day before. The window in this room was wider and lower than the others. The enemy's bullets had broken the dentist's glassware only above a height of three yards from the floor. It would be possible to look out of the window and shoot from there.

Maringaud was not a commissioned officer as yet – he had not done his military service – but he was not without authority in his company. Everyone knew that he had been secretary of the Workers' Union in one of the largest munitions factories, and what he had done there. The Italians had given the firm an order for 2,000 machine-guns to be delivered for Franco. The factory manager was a fire-arms enthusiast, and would not let the packers box the arms for shipping until they were 'up to the dot'. So each night, when the day's work was over, lights burned until late in a portion of the factory where the old boss was working by himself indefatigably in a brightly lit work-room, tinkering with a bolt on a minute piece of mechanism, putting the last touch to an all-important gadget which would make those machine-guns 'top-notch, I'm telling you!' And at four in the morning, the militant workers, following Maringaud's instructions, would come, one after another, to the factory and, with a few strokes of a file, put out of gear the piece to which such patient industry had gone. So it went on for six weeks. For almost forty nights the dogged struggle persisted in the munitions factory between the workers' solidarity and the technical zeal of Maringaud's employer. (He was not a fascist, but his sons were.)

All the men knew – they now had reason to know! – that this work had not been in vain.

In the pink house, Maringaud's mates had at last installed themselves below the line of fire.

That house, in which fighting had been going on now for six days, with attacks and counter-attacks, was impregnable, except by the staircase, where five Internationals with hand-grenades kept constant guard. The space round the house would not permit of training a gun. Rifle-bullets took no effect on it. There remained the possibility of the place being mined. But so long as the Tercio held the lower floors, it was certain that the mine would not be set off.

The six-inch guns of the Republicans went on firing.

The street was empty. In a dozen houses insults were being bandied up and down the chimneys.

Now and then an attacking party from one side or the other made an effort to rush the street, failed, and fell back. Behind the windows the look-out men, bored even by death, waited idly. Had a misguided journalist come along to survey the situation, he would at once have had a load of lead in his body.

There was a machine-gun or a rifle behind every window. The loud-speaker drowned with its hoarse blare the insults bawled up the chimneys, and the street was empty, seemingly for ever.

But to the right stood the Hospital, the best fascist position on the Madrid front. A thick-set skyscraper, standing apart in wooded ground, it overlooked the whole suburban quarter. From their fourth floor, Maringaud's mates could see the Republicans in every street near by, crouching in the mud; had the Hospital not been visible, its proximity might have been inferred from the way the men kept below the line of fire from its windows.

The Hospital looked deserted, as did the neighbouring houses. But from all its windows machine-guns spat unceasingly. There it stood, stolid and ox-like, a gloomy, murderous skyscraper, a ruined Babylonian tower, amid the bursting shells that scoured it with flying debris.

One of the Internationals, after searching all the cupboards, had found a pair of opera-glasses.

Some grenades exploded suddenly in the stairs. Maringaud went out on the landing.

'It's nothing,' one of the International guards informed him, above the roar of bursting shells.

Nothing, only the Tercios trying again to come up the stairs.

Maringaud took the opera-glasses. In nearness, the Hospital changed colour, grew red. Its clean-cut outline was seen to be due merely to its bulk. That it was undamaged was an illusion. The glasses showed that under the pounding of the six-inch guns it was being hollowed out, dented, flattened, like red-hot iron under hammer-blows. A close-up view of the windows gave it the look of an abandoned beehive. Yet even at a considerable distance from that ruined fortress, men crept warily along the rain-drenched pavements and rusting tram-lines.

Suddenly Maringaud began waving frantically his fat arms. 'Oh boys, look! Look! It's begun! Our fellows are attacking!'

The men crowded up between the window and the dead Moor on the dentist's chair. Dynamiters and bombers could be seen, dark specks rising from the ground round the Hospital. They raised their arms, sank into the mud again, then re-appeared where, five minutes before, their dynamite cartridges and hand-grenades had made a ring of red beads.

Maringaud rushed to the chimney, and bellowed to the Tercios:

'Just have a look what's happening to your hospital, you bloody fools!'

Then he ran back to his place at the window. The dynamiters were closing in. From the smashed beehive a swarm of insects was pouring out towards the fascist lines, swept by their own machine-guns.

No reply had come from the chimney. One of the fellows, a Czech, suddenly crouched lower than his comrades and, bringing up his rifle, started banging away. From the houses on the opposite side of the street, some other besieged Internationals were also firing. Hugging the wall, the Tercios were filing out of the pink house. It was mined, and now that the Tercios had left, the mine would be set off.

Cautiously the Negus crept along the counter-mine. For a whole month he had ceased believing in the revolution. The Apocalypse was over.

There remained the struggle against fascism; and the Negus's respect for the defenders of Madrid. There were anarchist members of the Government; other anarchists, in Barcelona, were fiercely defending their doctrine and their status. Durruti was dead. But the fight against the bourgeoisie had been, for such a long time, the breath of life to the Negus that he found it easy to go on living for the fight against fascism. He had always fought for negative emotions. Yet things were not going well with him. He listened to the men of his clan making their radio appeals for 'discipline', and he envied the young communists who spoke after them. Their lives had not gone topsy-turvy in the last six months! With the Negus now was Gonzalez, the fat man with whom Pepe had attacked the Italian tanks advancing on Toledo. Gonzalez belonged to the CNT. But that made no difference to the Negus. The fascists must be mopped up first, he guessed; plenty of time to argue afterwards. 'You know,' the Negus once remarked, 'the communists are good workers. I can work with them. But as to liking – no! I done my bloody best, but I can't get to like 'em!' Gonzalez had been an Asturian miner; the Negus had been a dockhand in Barcelona.

Since his exploit with the flame-thrower at the Alcazar, the Negus had taken to mine-laying. He liked that underground warfare in which nearly all the fighters are foredoomed and know it; in which, for the most part, each plays a lone hand. When up against insoluble problems, the Negus always fell back on violence or self-sacrifice; best of all, on both together.

Now he was creeping forward, a thin figure, followed by fat Gonzalez, along the gallery which was believed to extend a little beyond the pink house. The ground sounded more and more hollow. That meant either that the enemy sap was very near (but he could hear no thud of spades), or –?

He set the detonator of a hand-grenade.

The last blow of the pick landed on emptiness, and his momentum carried the miner through the hole into a sort of chasm in front.

Groping round with his electric torch like a blind man with his hands, the Negus took stock of the cavern below. Earthenware jars were everywhere, jars the height of a man. Obviously, a cellar. The Negus switched off his light and jumped. In front of him shone another electric torch, groping about. The man who held it could not have seen the Negus's lamp, put out a moment before. A fascist. The Negus hesitated. Should he fire? No, he could not see the man. The pink house must be almost directly above them. Gonzalez was still in the sap. The Negus threw his grenade.

When the smoke-clouds, swirling across the ray of Gonzalez' torch, had lifted, two fascists came into view sprawling in a slimy pool of oil or wine, from which their heads emerged. Fragments of the enormous jars stood up like cliffs from the pool which, slowly deepening, rose to the dead men's shoulders, then to their mouths, then above their eyes.

The Republican counter-attack was over. Maringaud and his mates were rescued, Gonzalez and his men returned to brigade headquarters. They had to cross a district of Madrid to get there.

The city had acquired the routine of bombardment. As soon as pedestrians heard an explosion, they ran for shelter to the nearest doorway; then, when the danger was past, they went on their way. Here and there, smoke-streamers trailed in a languid breeze, recalling in the midst of tragedy the peaceful smoke of cottage chimneys when supper-time approaches. A dead man had fallen in the street. He was still holding a lawyer's briefcase, which no one had dared to touch. The cafés were open. A draggled crowd, like the denizens of some ill-famed doss-house, was streaming from each metro exit. Others were swarming down the entrances, with mattresses, towels, baby-carriages, hand-carts heaped with kitchen pots and pans, tables, family portraits, and children clasping cardboard bulls. A peasant was trying to push a stubborn donkey into one of the entrances. Since the twenty-first, the fascists had been shelling the city every day. Round the Salamanca quarter, queer negotiations were in progress to bespeak the tenancy of 'cushy' doorways. Sometimes a mass of wreckage in the street would begin moving, and a hand, with its fingers fantastically splayed, emerge. But in the bombarded areas, amongst the horror-stricken faces of the fugitives, children could be seen playing at 'pursuit planes'. Stories, worthy of the *Arabian Nights*, were going round of women who had come back to their homes in Madrid packed up in baskets or tucked inside mattresses . . . A tram-driver joined the soldiers who were returning to headquarters, and began talking to Gonzalez.

'I ain't grumbling at the life, nohow, but it's a rum go nowadays, this job of mine. I start off, I do my run, I reach the terminus – with half my fares alive! The others have been knocked out on the way. No. What I say is, I don't cotton to the job, not like it is now!'

Suddenly the tram-driver stopped. Gonzalez and Maringaud stopped.

All the people in the street stopped, or ran for doorways. Five Junkers, escorted by fourteen Heinkels, were approaching overhead.

'Keep your pecker up!' a voice said. 'You'll get used to it!'

And then, before Gonzalez or Maringaud had noticed anything in the grey evening sky, a huge crowd of people came pouring out of shelters, cellars, doorways, houses, underground railway-stations – with cigarettes in their mouths, kitchen-ware or newspapers in their hands – variously clad in overalls, jackets, blankets and pyjamas.

'Them's our planes!' someone, a civilian, was shouting.

'How the hell do *you* know?' Gonzalez asked.

'Can't you hear? The sound of the motors. It's louder, clearer.'

From the other side of Madrid, for the first time, thirty-six Republican pursuit planes were approaching; the planes sold by the USSR after the Soviet Union's denouncement of non-intervention, had at last been assembled. Some had already fought over Getafe, and the patched-up machines of the International Flight had flown over Madrid, dropping pamphlets announcing the reorganization of the Republican air force. But these four squadrons of nine planes each, in V formation, with Sembrano in command, were being used that day for the first time for the protection of Madrid.

The leading Junkers swerved to the right, swerved to the left, hesitated. The Republican squadron swooped all out upon the bombing planes. Men's hands gripped excitedly the shoulders of their women. In every street, on all the house-tops, at each cellar opening, at all the underground entrances, the people who for eighteen days had gone their ways in terror of the bombs raised their eyes, looked up in wonder and delight.

And then – they saw the enemy squadron turn tail towards Getafe; the roar of half a million voices, a wild, inhuman, exultant paean, rose to the dim sky, loud with the thunder of the people's planes.

5
Death Camps

'Concentration Camp' implies merely the aggregation of large numbers of prisoners in a given confined space. During the Boer War of 1899–1902 Kitchener, the British Commander-in-Chief, decided to follow a scorched earth policy, destroying farms and gathering the homeless families together in camps already established for refugees. Epidemics swept these overcrowded camps and 26,000 women and children died. So did thousands of British soldiers, doctors and camp staff. The 'barbarism' of the camps was denounced in Britain and abroad. The Nazis would later use this for propaganda purposes – the British had massacred virtuous Aryans.

More recently, appalling atrocities have been reported from concentration camps in the former Yugoslavia. There is a tendency to assimilate such horrors with those of the German death camps and apply the word 'genocide'. It should be resisted. The word 'genocide' is not synonymous with 'ethnic cleansing'.

Nowhere other than under the Nazis has the aim consciously been to destroy an ethnic group in its entirety – which is what genocide strictly means – and to introduce into this process of systematic killing experiments in medical science, minutely comprehensive pillaging and industrial by-production. The Nazi gas-chambers were major works of engineering, coldly planned and cleverly executed. If the dream of H. G. Wells had been a World State applying advanced science and technology for the good of all peoples, the Nazis devoted state-of-the-art techniques to the extermination of their enemies and, in particular, of one people, while reducing those not destroyed at once to the degradation of slave labour. In the Soviet Union under Stalin many innocent people were executed and myriad others suffered in the Gulag. But the Soviet labour camps were not dedicated to systematic murder.

The Nazis had defined 'Jewishness' in the Nuremberg Laws of 1935 as implicating any person with one Jewish grandparent. Being Christian did not mitigate Jewishness. Nor did service in the German army in 1914–18. Persecution of Germany's half million Jews had begun with the Nazis' arrival in power in 1933. Emigration was officially encouraged, and more than half Germany's Jews had gone by 1938. Meanwhile, between 1933 and 1938, fewer than a hundred Jews were among those enemies of Nazism murdered in concentration camps. When Austria was incorporated into the Reich in 1938, five out of eight Jews emigrated, still with official encouragement. German conquest of Poland brought another million and a half Jews under Nazi control. In the initial massacre of civilians many Jews died along with many Poles. A new 'solution' to 'the Jewish problem' was found. Jews were driven from the countryside where they had lived for generations into urban ghettoes, where many starved and survivors were used as forced labour. There were hundreds of thousands of Jews in western and south-eastern European countries occupied by German troops in 1940–41. They were persecuted but not slaughtered. A qualitative and quantitative change in Nazi policy began with invasion of the Soviet Union in June 1941. Here, death squads – Einsatzgruppen – were ordered to kill all Jews in occupied areas. Perhaps a million died in six months. Lithuanians, Ukrainians and Romanians participated with zeal in the slaughter.

The 'Final Solution' emerged in the latter part of 1941. Essentially, all Jews in Nazi-held areas were to be rounded up and transported to camps where they would be gassed. The nature of these camps was to be kept secret even from local inhabitants, if possible. From Norway and the Channel Islands to the Greek islands, Jews were ferreted out and sent to the camps. Four of these were in German-occupied Poland, one in the German-occupied USSR. In March 1942 a further death-installation was established at the village of Birkenau, close to Auschwitz in Silesia, formerly Polish. In this region rich in coal, where several hundred German factories had been relocated, only children, old people and the sick were gassed on arrival. The able-bodied were put to work as slaves, but three quarters of these died – worked to exhaustion, prey for sadistic guards or sent to be gassed when they fell sick. Altogether at least two and a quarter million Jews died in Auschwitz alone, and the name of this murder-factory became a metonym for the Final Solution.

The Final Solution was not efficient. Only 83,000 French Jews were deported – 200,000 escaped the hunters, as did 35,000 out of Italy's

43,000 Jews. Of Hungarian Jews 400,000 went to Auschwitz, but 300,000 were saved, at least temporarily, by pressure on the Fascist Horthy regime from the Pope and the King of Sweden. But from Holland, Yugoslavia and Greece the vast majority of Jews were taken. As the Soviet Army approached the death camps, slave labourers were evacuated in forced marches to work in central Germany. Many of these died en route or from evil conditions on arrival.

Altogether some six million people – one third of the world's Jewish population – were murdered in what Jews call in Hebrew Shoah, *'The Catastrophe'. That six and a half million Germans were also killed in the war is important information, but irrelevant to consideration of 'the Holocaust'. No one, not even 'Bomber Harris' of the RAF, deliberately set out to kill all Germans.*

Industrialized Killing

The Holocaust has often been referred to as if it was an atavistic aberration, a barbaric application of science and technology out of harmony with their peaceful, fertile and spectacular development elsewhere at other times in the twentieth century. The Israeli historian Omer Bartov argues in Murder in Our Midst *(1996) that, on the contrary, 'industrialized killing' is centrally part of our modernity, with the Holocaust following logically from the First World War.*

MURDER IN OUR MIDST

War, slaughter and genocide, are of course as old as human civilization itself. Industrial killing, however, is a much newer phenomenon, not only in that its main precondition was the industrialization of human society, but also in the sense that this process of industrialization came to be associated with progress and improvement, hope and optimism, liberty and democracy, science and the rule of law. Industrial killing was not the dark side of modernity, some aberration of a generally salutary process; rather, it was and is inherent to it, a perpetual potential of precisely the same energies and ideas, technologies and ideologies, that have brought about the 'great transformation' of humanity. But precisely because modernity means to many of us progress and improvement, we cannot easily come to terms with the idea that it also means mass annihilation. We see genocide as a throwback to another, pre-modern, barbarous past, a perversion, an error, an accident. All evidence to the contrary, we repeatedly believe that *this* time, in *this* war, it will finally be stamped out and eradicated, never to reappear again. Yet even this well-meant urge reveals our complicity in modernity's destructive, unrelenting, intolerant nature. We wish to annihilate destruction, to kill war, to eradicate genocide, by the most effective and deadly means at our disposal. And we want to marginalize the evil, repress it, push it out of our own time and context, attribute it to everything that we are not, to anything that is foreign to our civilization. We thus elect to exist in an illusory reality, occasionally jarred by disturbing incidents of déjà vu, which in turn unleash in us precisely that sense of fear and confusion, that desire for drastic solutions, that anger at a world that refuses to conform to our expectations, that is at the root of modern society's destructive impulse.

The most spectacular and terrifying instance of industrial killing in this century was the Nazi attempted genocide of the Jews. Neither the idea, nor its implementation, however, can be understood without reference to the Great War, the first truly industrial military confrontation in history. This war differed from its predecessors by the magnitude, intensity and mechanized nature of the killing. To be sure, there were precedents, such as the Russo-Japanese War and the American Civil War; but not only was the Great War a much improved version of those earlier attempts at industrial military confrontations, it was also distinguished by its direct and profound impact on a whole generation of Europeans, both combatants and civilians, as well as their offspring. And it was these European men and women who became the immediate perpetrators, victims, and bystanders of the Holocaust, acting out one of modernity's extreme, yet inherent potentials, whose traumatic effect on subsequent generations is only matched by their desperate attempts to deny its relevance to their post-Auschwitz realities.

It has rightly been pointed out that the Holocaust was not only directly related to the Nazi euthanasia program of killing the mentally handicapped, both conceptually and administratively, but also to a whole complex of scientific thinking on the need and legitimacy of treating human society as an organism to be manipulated by means of a vast surgical operation. Yet it must be stressed that in another respect the genocide of the Jews both differed from the T-4 campaign and was directly related to the Great War, since the very concept of mass killing of human beings by states, as well as the technological and administrative means for actually organizing such vast operations, were lifted directly from the realities of 1914–18. Unlike the killing facilities of the euthanasia campaign, the death camps did not resemble medical installations, but were architecturally and organizationally modelled on the experience of the Great War, incorporating all the attributes of a military environment, such as uniforms and barbed wire, watch towers and roll calls, hierarchy and order, drill and commands. The Holocaust was therefore a militarized genocide, made all the more effective both by killing *all* those targeted for murder and in being safe for *all* those who carried it out. In another sense, however, the experience of the Great War was also linked to the concept of racial hygiene. Prewar fears of the degeneration of humanity were greatly enhanced by the carnage in the trenches, which threatened to bring about the total extinction of the combatants' 'healthy' genes and the consequent predominance of the 'unhealthy' genes of the shirkers and handicapped. Hence the post-1918 conceptualization of industrial extermination was also meant to redress the balance upset by that first major bout of mechanical killing by means of a massive cleansing operation that would eliminate the threat of genetic degeneration. It is this that we must bear in mind today when we read new/old theories about the potential pollution of the genetic pool in the United States by a genetically (and therefore both socially and intellectually) inferior, but numerically ever-expanding underclass.

. . .

With the outbreak of the Second World War, escape from industrial killing by evasion became increasingly difficult; only a few people in Europe could safely remain pacifist, at least as long as they did not join the fascists. Nazi Germany had chosen the other path, escape by perpetration. This did not save Germany from being ultimately devastated, although not before it had destroyed large parts of Europe and brought about the death of even greater numbers of people than in 1914–18. But it did make for the creation in the most concrete form possible of the nightmare of industrial killing that had haunted the European imagination since the Great War. The killing was more efficient, the victims more varied in age and gender, and the cost for the killers minuscule in comparison. Had it not been for the war raging around this 'concentrationary universe', it would have indeed been the ideal answer to the Western Front of 1914–18. It even resembled images of Hell more closely. George Steiner has suggested that 'The camp embodies . . . the images and chronicles of Hell in European art and thought from the twelfth to the eighteenth centuries', and that 'these representations . . . gave the deranged horrors of Belsen a kind of "expected logic"'. Indeed, to his mind the death camps 'are *Hell made immanent*. They are the transference of Hell from below the earth to its surface. They are the deliberate enactment of a long, precise imagining'. To be sure, images of Hell force themselves on us whenever we read descriptions of the Holocaust, and such images often also haunted the inmates and cheered the perpetrators. But this was a hell whose immediate origins were geographically and chronologically much closer, one which had already been seen on earth. For the Holocaust was far more directly the almost perfect re-enactment of the Great War (and its own imagery of hell), with the important correction that all the perpetrators were on one side and all the victims on the other. Everything else was there: the barbed wire, the machine-guns, the charred bodies, the gas, the uniforms, the military discipline, the barracks. But this re-enactment had the great advantage that it was *totally* lethal for the inmates and *totally* safe for the guards. And the killing too, needless to say, was *total*.

. . .

While there is clearly a distinction to be made between the mutual killing of soldiers and the wholesale massacre of defenceless populations, it is crucial to realize that total war and genocide are closely related. For modern war provides the occasion and the tools, the manpower and the organization, the mentality and the imagery necessary for the perpetration of genocide. With the introduction of industrial killing to the battlefield, the systematic murder of whole peoples became both practical and thinkable: those who had experienced the former could imagine and plan, organize, and perpetrate the latter. All that was needed was the will to act, and by the end of the Great War there were not a few men who believed that their only escape from the hell of modern war was to subject others to the industrial killing they had barely survived.

Commandant of Auschwitz

Rudolf Höss, born in 1900, became a Nazi as early as 1922 and joined the SS in 1933. As Commandant at Auschwitz he oversaw the execution of Poles, Russians and Gypsies, as well as Jews. He was condemned after the war by a Polish court and hanged. His own account of his experiences was posthumously published in 1951.

By the will of the Reichsführer SS, Auschwitz became the greatest human extermination centre of all time.

When in the summer of 1941 he himself gave me the order to prepare installations at Auschwitz where mass exterminations could take place, and personally to carry out these exterminations, I did not have the slightest idea of their scale or consequences. It was certainly an extraordinary and monstrous order. Nevertheless the reasons behind the extermination programme seemed to me right. I did not reflect on it at the time: I had been given an order, and I had to carry it out. Whether this mass extermination of the Jews was necessary or not was something on which I could not allow myself to form an opinion, for I lacked the necessary breadth of view.

If the Führer had himself given the order for the 'Final solution of the Jewish question', then, for a veteran National-Socialist and even more so for an SS officer, there could be no question of considering its merits. 'The Führer commands, we follow' was never a mere phrase or slogan. It was meant in bitter earnest.

Since my arrest it has been said to me repeatedly that I could have disobeyed this order, and that I might even have assassinated Himmler. I do not believe that of all the thousands of SS officers there could have been found a single one capable of such a thought. It was completely impossible. Certainly many SS officers grumbled and complained about some of the harsh orders that came from the Reichsführer SS, but they nevertheless always carried them out.

Many orders of the Reichsführer SS deeply offended a great number of his SS officers, but I am perfectly certain that not a single one of them would have dared to raise a hand against him, or would have even contemplated doing so in his most secret thoughts. As Reichsführer SS, his person was inviolable. His basic orders, issued in the name of the Führer, were sacred. They brooked no consideration, no argument, no interpretation. They were carried out ruthlessly and regardless of consequences, even though these might well mean the death of the officer concerned, as happened to not a few SS officers during the war.

It was not for nothing that during training the self-sacrifice of the Japanese for their country and their emperor, who was also their god, was held up as a shining example to the SS.

SS training was not comparable to a university course which can have as little lasting effect on the students as water on a duck's back. It was on the contrary something that was deeply engrained, and the Reichsführer SS knew very well what he could demand of his men . . .

Before the mass extermination of the Jews began, the Russian *politruks* and political commissars were liquidated in almost all the concentration camps during 1941 and 1942.

In accordance with a secret order issued by Hitler, these Russian *politruks* and political commissars were combed out of all the prisoner-of-war camps by special detachments from the Gestapo. When identified, they were transferred to the nearest concentration camp for liquidation. It was made known that these measures were taken because the Russians had been killing all German soldiers who were party members or belonged to special sections of the NSDAP, especially members of the SS, and also because the political officials of the Red Army had been ordered, if taken prisoner, to create every kind of disturbance in the prisoner-of-war camps and their places of employment and to carry out sabotage wherever possible.

The political officials of the Red Army thus identified were brought to Auschwitz for liquidation. The first, smaller transports of them were executed by firing squads.

When I was away on duty, my deputy, Fritzsch, the commander of the protective custody camp, first tried gas for these killings. It was a preparation of prussic acid, called Cyclon B, which was used in the camp as an insecticide and of which there was always a stock on hand. On my return, Fritzsch reported this to me, and the gas was used again for the next transport.

The gassing was carried out in the detention cells of Block II. Protected by a gas-mask, I watched the killing myself. In the crowded cells death came instantaneously the moment the Cyclon B was thrown in. A short, almost smothered cry, and it was all over. During this first experience of gassing people, I did not fully realize what was happening, perhaps because I was too impressed by the whole procedure. I have a clearer recollection of the gassing of nine hundred Russians which took place shortly afterwards in the old crematorium, since the use of Block II for this purpose caused too much trouble. While the transport was detraining, holes were pierced in the earth and concrete ceiling of the mortuary. The Russians were ordered to undress in an anteroom; they then quietly entered the mortuary, for they had been told they were to be deloused. The whole transport exactly filled the mortuary to capacity. The doors were then sealed and the gas shaken down through the holes in the roof. I do not know how long this killing took. For a little while a humming sound could be heard. When the powder was thrown in, there were cries of 'Gas!', then a great bellowing, and the trapped prisoners hurled themselves against both the doors. But the doors held. They were opened several hours later, so that the place might be aired. It was then that I saw, for the first time, gassed bodies in the mass.

It made me feel uncomfortable and I shuddered, although I had imagined that death by gassing would be worse than it was. I had always thought that the victims would experience a terrible choking sensation. But the bodies, without exception, showed no signs of convulsion. The doctors explained to me that the prussic acid had a paralysing effect on the lungs, but its action was so quick and strong that death came before the convulsions could set in, and in this its effects differed from those produced by carbon monoxide or by a general oxygen deficiency.

The killing of these Russian prisoners-of-war did not cause me much concern at the time. The order had been given, and I had to carry it out. I must even admit that this gassing set my mind at rest, for the mass extermination of the Jews was to start soon and at that time neither Eichmann nor I was certain how these mass killings were to be carried out. It would be by gas, but we did not know which gas or how it was to be used. Now we had the gas, and we had established a procedure. I always shuddered at the prospect of carrying out exterminations by shooting, when I thought of the vast numbers concerned, and of the women and children. The shooting of hostages, and the group executions ordered by the Reichsführer SS or by the Reich Security Head Office had been enough for me. I was therefore relieved to think that we were to be spared all these blood-baths, and that the victims too would be spared suffering until their last moment came. It was precisely this which had caused me the greatest concern when I had heard Eichmann's description of Jews being mown down by the Special Squads armed with machine-guns and machine-pistols. Many gruesome scenes are said to have taken place, people running away after being shot, the finishing off of the wounded and particularly of the women and children. Many members of the *Einsatzkommandos*, unable to endure wading through blood any longer, had committed suicide. Some had even gone mad. Most of the members of these *Kommandos* had to rely on alcohol when carrying out their horrible work. According to Hofle's description, the men employed at Globocnik's extermination centres consumed amazing quantities of alcohol.

In the spring of 1942 the first transports of Jews, all earmarked for extermination, arrived from Upper Silesia.

They were taken from the detraining platform to the 'Cottage' – to Bunker I – across the meadows where later Building Site II was located. The transport was conducted by Aumeier and Palitzsch and some of the block leaders. They talked with the Jews about general topics, inquiring concerning their qualifications and trades, with a view to misleading them. On arrival at the 'Cottage', they were told to undress. At first they went calmly into the rooms where they were supposed to be disinfected. But some of them showed signs of alarm, and spoke of death by suffocation and of annihilation. A sort of panic set in at once. Immediately all the Jews still outside were pushed into the chambers, and the doors were screwed shut. With subsequent transports the difficult individuals were picked out early on and most carefully supervised. At the first signs of unrest, those responsible were unobtrusively led behind the building and killed with a small-calibre gun that was inaudible to the others. The presence and calm behaviour of the Special Detachment served to reassure those who were worried or who suspected what was about to happen. A further calming effect was obtained by members of the Special Detachment accompanying them into the rooms and remaining with them until the last moment, while an SS-man also stood in the doorway until the end.

It was most important that the whole business of arriving and undressing should take place in an atmosphere of the greatest possible calm. People reluctant to take off their clothes had to be helped by those of their companions who had already undressed, or by men of the Special Detachment.

The refractory ones were calmed down and encouraged to undress.

The prisoners of the Special Detachment also saw to it that the process of undressing was carried out quickly, so that the victims would have little time to wonder what was happening.

The eager help given by the Special Detachment in encouraging them to undress and in conducting them into the gas-chambers was most remarkable. I have never known, nor heard, of any of its members giving these people who were about to be gassed the slightest hint of what lay ahead of them. On the contrary, they did everything in their power to deceive them and particularly to pacify the suspicious ones. Though they might refuse to believe the SS-men, they had complete faith in these members of their own race, and to reassure them and keep them calm the Special Detachments therefore always consisted of Jews who themselves came from the same districts as did the people on whom a particular action was to be carried out.

They would talk about life in the camp, and most of them asked for news of friends or relations who had arrived in earlier transports. It was interesting to hear the lies that the Special Detachment told them with such conviction, and to see the emphatic gestures with which they underlined them.

Many of the women hid their babies among the piles of clothing. The men of the Special Detachment were particularly on the look-out for this, and would speak words of encouragement to the woman until they had persuaded her to take the child with her. The women believed that the disinfectant might be bad for their smaller children, hence their efforts to conceal them.

The smaller children usually cried because of the strangeness of being undressed in this fashion, but when their mothers or members of the Special Detachment comforted them, they became calm and entered the gas-chambers, playing or joking with one another and carrying their toys.

I noticed that women who either guessed or knew what awaited them nevertheless found the courage to joke with the children to encourage them, despite the mortal terror visible in their own eyes.

One woman approached me as she walked past and, pointing to her four children who were manfully helping the smallest ones over the rough ground, whispered:

'How can you bring yourself to kill such beautiful, darling children? Have you no heart at all?'

One old man, as he passed by me, hissed:

'Germany will pay a heavy penance for this mass murder of the Jews.'

His eyes glowed with hatred as he said this. Nevertheless he walked calmly into the gas-chamber, without worrying about the others.

One young woman caught my attention particularly as she ran busily hither and thither, helping the smallest children and the old women to undress. During the selection she had two small children with her, and her agitated behaviour and appearance had brought her to my notice at once. She did not look in the least like a Jewess. Now her children were no longer with her. She waited until the end, helping the women who were not undressed and who had several children with them, encouraging them and calming the children. She went with the very last ones into the gas-chamber. Standing in the doorway, she said:

'I knew all the time that we were being brought to Auschwitz to be gassed. When the selection took place I avoided being put with the able-bodied ones, as I wished to look after the children. I wanted to go through it all, fully conscious of what was happening. I hope that it will be quick. Goodbye!'

...

On one occasion two small children were so absorbed in some game that they quite refused to let their mother tear them away from it. Even the Jews of the Special Detachment were reluctant to pick the children up. The imploring look in the eyes of the mother, who certainly knew what was happening, is something I shall never forget. The people were already in the gas-chamber and becoming restive, and I had to act. Everyone was looking at me. I nodded to the junior non-commissioned officer on duty and he picked up the screaming, struggling children in his arms and carried them into the gas-chamber, accompanied by their mother who was weeping in the most heart-rending fashion. My pity was so great that I longed to vanish from the scene: yet I might not show the slightest trace of emotion.

I had to see everything. I had to watch hour after hour, by day and by night, the removal and burning of the bodies, the extraction of the teeth, the cutting of the hair, the whole grisly, interminable business. I had to stand for hours on end in the ghastly stench, while the mass graves were being opened and the bodies dragged out and burned.

I had to look through the peep-hole of the gas-chambers and watch the process of death itself, because the doctors wanted me to see it.

I had to do all this because I was the one to whom everyone looked, because I had to show them all that I did not merely issue the orders and make the regulations but was also prepared myself to be present at whatever task I had assigned to my subordinates.

The Reichsführer SS sent various high-ranking Party leaders and SS officers to Auschwitz so that they might see for themselves the process of extermination of the Jews. They were all deeply impressed by what they saw. Some who had previously spoken most loudly about the necessity for this extermination fell silent once they had actually seen the 'final solution of the Jewish problem'. I was repeatedly asked how I and my men could go on watching these operations, and how we were able to stand it.

My invariable answer was that the iron determination with which we must carry out Hitler's orders could only be obtained by a stifling of all human emotions. Each of these gentlemen declared that he was glad the job had not been given to him.

. . .

It would often happen, when at home, that my thoughts suddenly turned to incidents that had occurred during the extermination. I then had to go out. I could no longer bear to be in my homely family circle. When I saw my children happily playing, or observed my wife's delight over our youngest, the thought would often come to me: how long will our happiness last? My wife could never understand these gloomy moods of mine, and ascribed them to some annoyance connected with my work . . .

My family, to be sure, were well provided for in Auschwitz. Every wish that my wife or children expressed was granted them. The children could lead a free and untrammelled life. My wife's garden was a paradise of flowers. The prisoners never missed an opportunity for doing some little act of kindness to my wife or children, and thus attracting their attention.

No former prisoner can ever say that he was in any way or at any time badly treated in our house. My wife's greatest pleasure would have been to give a present to every prisoner who was in any way connected with our household.

The children were perpetually begging me for cigarettes for the prisoners. They were particularly fond of the ones who worked in the garden.

My whole family displayed an intense love of agriculture and particularly for animals of all sorts. Every Sunday I had to walk them all across the fields, and visit the stables, and we might never miss out the kennels where the dogs were kept. Our two horses and the foal were especially beloved.

The children always kept animals in the garden, creatures the prisoners were forever bringing them. Tortoises, martens, cats, lizards: there was always something new and interesting to be seen there. In summer they splashed in the paddling pool in the garden, or in the Sola. But their greatest joy was when Daddy bathed with them. He had, however, so little time for all these childish pleasures. Today I deeply regret that I did not devote more time to my family. I always felt that I had to be on duty the whole time. This exaggerated sense of duty has always made life more difficult for me than it actually need have been. Again and again my wife reproached me and said: 'You must think not only of the service always, but of your family too.'

Yet what did my wife know about all that lay so heavily on my mind? She has never been told.

Science of Death

William Shirer bore witness against Nazism as an American journalist in Berlin under the Reich. After the war he immersed himself in the Nazi archives. His history of The Rise and Fall of the Third Reich *(1960) became a major bestseller, and remains a monument to his perseverance and his humanity.*

THE MEDICAL EXPERIMENTS

There were some practices of the Germans during the short-lived New Order that resulted from sheer sadism rather than a lust for mass murder. Perhaps to a psychiatrist there is a difference between the two lusts though the end result of the first differed from the second only in the scale of deaths.

The Nazi medical experiments are an example of this sadism, for in the use of concentration camp inmates and prisoners of war as human guinea pigs very little, if any, benefit to science was achieved. It is a tale of horror of which the German medical profession cannot be proud. Although the 'experiments' were conducted by fewer than two hundred murderous quacks – albeit some of them held eminent posts in the medical world – their criminal work was known to thousands of leading physicians of the Reich, not a single one of whom, so far as the record shows, ever uttered the slightest public protest.

In the murders in this field the Jews were not the only victims. The Nazi doctors also used Russian prisoners of war, Polish concentration camp inmates, women as well as men, and even Germans. The 'experiments' were quite varied. Prisoners were placed in pressure chambers and subjected to high-altitude tests until they ceased breathing. They were injected with lethal doses of typhus and jaundice. They were subjected to 'freezing' experiments in icy water or exposed naked in the snow outdoors until they froze to death. Poison bullets were tried out on them as was mustard gas. At the Ravensbrueck concentration camp for women hundreds of Polish inmates – the 'rabbit girls' they were called – were given gas gangrene wounds while others were subjected to 'experiments' in bone grafting. At Dachau and Buchenwald gypsies were selected to see how long, and in what manner, they could live on salt water. Sterilization experiments were carried out on a large scale at several camps by a variety of means on both men and women; for, as an SS physician, Dr Adolf Pokorny, wrote Himmler on one occasion, 'the enemy must be not only conquered but exterminated'. If he could not be slaughtered – and the need for slave labour toward the end of the war made that practice questionable, as we have seen – then he could be prevented from propagating. In fact Dr Pokorny told Himmler he thought he had found just the right means, the plant *Caladium seguinum*, which, he said, induced lasting sterility.

> The thought alone [the good doctor wrote the SS Fuehrer] that the three million Bolsheviks now in German captivity could be sterilized, so that they would be available for work but precluded from propagation, opens up the most far-reaching perspectives.

Another German doctor who had 'far-reaching perspectives' was Professor August Hirt, head of the Anatomical Institute of the University of Strasbourg. His special field was somewhat different from those of the others and he explained it in a letter at Christmas time of 1941 to SS Lieutenant General Rudolf Brandt, Himmler's adjutant.

> We have large collections of skulls of almost all races and peoples at our disposal. Of the Jewish race, however, only very few specimens of skulls are available . . . The war in the East now presents us with the opportunity to overcome this deficiency. By procuring the skulls of the Jewish-Bolshevik commissars, who represent the prototype of the repulsive, but characteristic, subhuman, we have the chance now to obtain scientific material.

Professor Hirt did not want the skulls of 'Jewish-Bolshevik commissars' already dead. He proposed that the heads of these persons first be measured while they were alive. Then –

> Following the subsequently induced death of the Jew, whose head should not be damaged, the physician will sever the head from the body and will forward it . . . in a hermetically sealed tin can.

Whereupon Dr Hirt would go to work, he promised, on further scientific measurements. Himmler was delighted. He directed that Professor Hirt 'be supplied with everything needed for his research work'.

He was well supplied. The actual supplier was an interesting Nazi individual by the name of Wolfram Sievers, who spent considerable time on the witness stand at the main Nuremberg trial and at the subsequent 'Doctors' Trial', in the latter of which he was a defendant. Sievers, a former bookseller, had risen to be a colonel of the SS and executive secretary of the Ahnenerbe, the Institute for Research into Heredity, one of the ridiculous 'cultural' organizations established by Himmler to pursue one of his many lunacies. It had, according to Sievers, fifty 'research branches', of which one was called the 'Institute for Military Scientific Research', which Sievers also headed. He was a shifty-eyed, Mephistophelean-looking fellow with a thick, ink-black beard, and at Nuremberg he was dubbed the 'Nazi Bluebeard', after the famous French killer. Like so many other characters in this history, he kept a meticulous diary, and this and his correspondence, both of which survived, contributed to his gallows end.

By June 1943 Sievers had collected at Auschwitz the men and women who were to furnish the skeletons for the 'scientific measurements' of Professor Dr Hirt at the University of Strasbourg. 'A total of 115 persons, including 79 Jews, 30 Jewesses, 4 "Asiatics" and 2 Poles were processed,' Sievers reported, requesting the SS main office in Berlin for transportation for them from Auschwitz to the Natzweiler concentration camp near Strasbourg. The British cross-examiner at Nuremberg inquired as to the meaning of 'processing'.

'Anthropological measurements,' Sievers replied.

'Before they were murdered they were anthropologically measured? That was all there was to it, was it?'

'And casts were taken,' Sievers added.

What followed was narrated by SS Captain Josef Kramer, himself a veteran exterminator from Auschwitz, Mauthausen, Dachau and other camps and who achieved fleeting fame as the 'Beast of Belsen' and was condemned to death by a British court at Lueneburg.

> Professor Hirt of the Strasbourg Anatomical Institute told me of the prisoner convoy en route from Auschwitz. He said these persons were to be killed by poison gas in the gas-chamber of the Natzweiler camp, their bodies then to be taken to the Anatomical Institute for his disposal. He gave me a bottle containing about half a pint of salts – I think they were cyanide salts – and told me the approximate dosage I would have to use to poison the arriving inmates from Auschwitz . . .

Captain Kramer testified that he repeated the performance until all eighty inmates had been killed and turned the bodies over to Professor Hirt, 'as requested'. He was asked by his interrogator what his feelings were at the time, and he gave a memorable answer that gives insight into a phenomenon in the Third Reich that has seemed so elusive of human understanding.

> I had no feelings in carrying out these things because I had received an order to kill the eighty inmates in the way I already told you.
>
> *That, by the way, was the way I was trained.*

Another witness testified as to what happened next. He was Henry Herypierre, a Frenchman who worked in the Anatomical Institute at Strasbourg as Professor Hirt's laboratory assistant until the Allies arrived.

> The first shipment we received was of the bodies of thirty women. These thirty female bodies arrived still warm. The eyes were wide open and shining. They were red and bloodshot and were popping from their sockets. There were also traces of blood about the nose and mouth. No *rigor mortis* was evident.

Herypierre suspected that they had been done to death and secretly copied down their prison numbers which were tattooed on their left arms. Two more shipments of fifty-six men arrived, he said, in exactly the same condition. They were pickled in alcohol under the expert direction of Dr Hirt. But the professor was a little nervous about the whole thing. 'Peter,' he said to Herypierre, 'if you can't keep your trap shut, you'll be one of them.'

. . .

Not only skeletons but human skins were collected by the masters of the New Order though in the latter case the pretence could not be made that the cause of scientific research was being served. The skins of concentration camp prisoners, especially executed for this ghoulish purpose, had merely decorative value. They made, it was found, excellent lamp shades, several of which were expressly fitted up for Frau Ilse Koch, the wife of the commandant of Buchenwald and nicknamed by the inmates the 'Bitch of Buchenwald'. Tattooed skins appear to have been the most sought after. A German inmate, Andreas Pfaffenberger, deposed at Nuremberg on this.

> All prisoners with tattooing on them were ordered to report to the dispensary . . . After the prisoners had been examined the ones with the best and most artistic specimens were killed by injections. The corpses were then turned over to the pathological department where the desired pieces of tattooed skin were detached from the bodies and treated further. The finished products were turned over to Koch's wife, who had them fashioned into lamp shades, and other ornamental household articles.

One piece of skin which apparently struck Frau Koch's fancy had the words 'Haensel and Gretel' tattooed on it.

The Museum, Auschwitz

The poet Tadeusz Różewicz, born in 1921, fought in the Polish Resistance during the war.

PIGTAIL

When all the women in the transport
had their heads shaved
four workmen with brooms made of birch twigs
swept up
and gathered up the hair

Behind clean glass
the stiff hair lies
of those suffocated in gas chambers
there are pins and side combs
in this hair

The hair is not shot through with light
is not parted by the breeze
is not touched by any hand
or rain or lips

In huge chests
clouds of dry hair
of those suffocated
and a faded plait
a pigtail with a ribbon
pulled at school
by naughty boys.

1948
The Museum, Auschwitz

MASSACRE OF THE BOYS

The children cried 'Mummy!
But I have been good!
It's dark in here! Dark!'

See them They are going to the bottom
See the small feet
they went to the bottom Do you see
that print
of a small foot here and there

pockets bulging
with string and stones
and little horses made of wire

A great closed plain
like a figure of geometry
and a tree of black smoke
a vertical
dead tree
with no star in its crown.

1948
The Museum, Auschwitz

If This Is A Man

Primo Levi was an Italian Jew, a young chemist, active in the Resistance, who was captured by Fascist militia late in 1943 and detained in a camp at Fossoli. On 22 February 1944 all the Jews in the camp were deported to Auschwitz. Of 125 people sent to Auschwitz in that consignment from Italy, only three returned to their homeland after the war. Levi was saved from a 'death march' when the SS evacuated 20,000 prisoners as the Soviet army approached in January 1945 because he was ill in the camp hospital. The Russians arrived on January 27. Levi eventually regained Italy after an extraordinary journey through the Ukraine, Belorus, Romania, Hungary and Austria, detailed in his book The Truce *(1963).*

On his return Levi immediately wrote If This Is A Man, *an account of his months in Auschwitz. Important publishers turned it down. A small publisher brought it out in 1947, printed 2500 copies, and promptly folded. 'So this first book of mine fell into oblivion for many years; perhaps also because in all of Europe those were difficult times of mourning and reconstruction and the public did not want to return in memory to the painful years of the war that had just ended.' Republished by Einaudi in 1958, it sold hundreds of thousands of copies in Italy and was translated into eight languages.*

It is difficult to praise this book in terms that do not trivialize its achievement. Levi recognizes – as his title suggests – that Jewish and other prisoners might be dehumanized by their systematically brutal treatment in Auschwitz. His project, it might be said, is to salvage what still testifies to the true human spirit from his memories of degradation. Short extracts cannot do justice to the book's range – its modest and controlled presentation of suffering, its vivid characterization of so many men condemned to facelessness.

ON THE BOTTOM

The journey did not last more than twenty minutes. Then the lorry stopped, and we saw a large door, and above it a sign, brightly illuminated (its memory still strikes me in my dreams): *Arbeit Macht Frei*, work gives freedom.

We climb down, they make us enter an enormous empty room that is poorly heated. We have a terrible thirst. The weak gurgle of the water in the radiators makes us ferocious; we have had nothing to drink for four days. But there is also a tap – and above it a card which says that it is forbidden to drink as the water is dirty. Nonsense. It seems obvious that the card is a joke, 'they' know that we are dying of thirst and they put us in a room, and there is a tap, and *Wassertrinken Verboten*. I drink and I incite my companions to do likewise, but I have to spit it out, the water is tepid and sweetish, with the smell of a swamp.

This is hell. Today, in our times, hell must be like this. A huge, empty room: we are tired, standing on our feet, with a tap which drips while we cannot drink the water, and we wait for something which will certainly be terrible, and nothing happens and nothing continues to happen. What can one think about? One cannot think any more, it is like being already dead. Someone sits down on the ground. The time passes drop by drop.

We are not dead. The door is opened and an SS man enters, smoking. He looks at us slowly and asks, '*Wer kann Deutsch?*' One of us whom I have never seen, named Flesch, moves forward; he will be our interpreter. The SS man makes a long calm speech; the interpreter translates. We have to form rows of five, with intervals of two yards between man and man; then we have to undress and make a bundle of the clothes in a special manner, the woollen garments on one side, all the rest on the other, we must take off our shoes but pay great attention that they are not stolen.

Stolen by whom? Why should our shoes be stolen? And what about our documents, the few things we have in our pockets, our watches? We all look at the interpreter, and the interpreter asks the German, and the German smokes and looks him through and through as if he were transparent, as if no one had spoken.

I had never seen old men naked. Mr Bergmann wore a truss and asked the interpreter if he should take it off, and the interpreter hesitated. But the German understood and spoke seriously to the interpreter pointing to someone. We saw the interpreter swallow and then he said: 'The officer says, take off the truss, and you will be given that of Mr Coen.' One could see the words coming bitterly out of Flesch's mouth; this was the German manner of laughing.

Now another German comes and tells us to put the shoes in a certain corner, and we put them there, because now it is all over and we feel outside this world and the only thing is to obey. Someone comes with a broom and sweeps away all the shoes, outside the door in a heap. He is crazy, he is mixing them all together, ninety-six pairs, they will be all unmatched. The outside door opens, a freezing wind enters and we are naked and cover ourselves up with our arms. The wind blows and slams the door; the German reopens it and stands watching with interest how we writhe to hide from the wind, one behind the other. Then he leaves and closes it.

Now the second act begins. Four men with razors, soapbrushes and clippers burst in; they have trousers and jackets with stripes, with a number sewn on the front; perhaps they are the same sort as those others of this evening (this evening or yesterday evening?); but these are robust and flourishing. We ask many questions but they catch hold of us and in a moment we find ourselves shaved and sheared. What comic faces we have without hair! The four speak a language which does not seem of this world. It is certainly not German, for I understand a little German.

Finally another door is opened: here we are, locked in, naked, sheared and standing, with our feet in water – it is a shower-room. We are alone. Slowly the astonishment dissolves, and we speak, and everyone asks questions and no one answers. If we are naked in a shower-room, it means that we will have a shower. If we have a shower it is because they are not going to kill us yet. But why then do they keep us standing, and give us nothing to drink, while nobody explains anything, and we have no shoes or clothes, but we are all naked with our feet in the water, and we have been travelling five days and cannot even sit down.

And our women?

Mr Levi asks me if I think that our women are like us at this moment, and where they are, and if we will be able to see them again. I say yes, because he is married and has a daughter; certainly we will see them again. But by now my belief is that all this is a game to mock and sneer at us. Clearly they will kill us, whoever thinks he is going to live is mad, it means that he has swallowed the bait, but I have not; I have understood that it will soon all be over, perhaps in this same room, when they get bored of seeing us naked, dancing from foot to foot and trying every now and again to sit down on the floor. But there are two inches of cold water and we cannot sit down.

We walk up and down without sense, and we talk, everybody talks to everybody else, we make a great noise. The door opens, and a German enters; it is the officer of before. He speaks briefly, the interpreter translates. 'The officer says you must be quiet, because this is not a rabbinical school.' One sees the words which are not his, the bad words, twist his mouth as they come out, as if he was spitting out a foul taste. We beg him to ask what we are waiting for, how long we will stay here, about our women, everything; but he says no, that he does not want to ask. This Flesch, who is most unwilling to translate into Italian the hard cold German phrases and refuses to turn into German our questions because he knows that it is useless, is a German Jew of about fifty, who has a large scar on his face from a wound received fighting the Italians on the Piave. He is a closed, taciturn man, for whom I feel an instinctive respect as I feel that he has begun to suffer before us.

The German goes and we remain silent, although we are a little ashamed of our silence. It is still night and we wonder if the day will ever come. The door opens again, and someone else dressed in stripes comes in. He is different from the others, older, with glasses, a more civilized face, and much less robust. He speaks to us in Italian.

By now we are tired of being amazed. We seem to be watching some mad play, one of those plays in which the witches, the Holy Spirit and the devil appear. He speaks Italian badly, with a strong foreign accent. He makes a long speech, is very polite, and tries to reply to all our questions.

We are at Monowitz, near Auschwitz, in Upper Silesia, a region inhabited by both Poles and Germans. This camp is a work-camp, in German one says *Arbeitslager*; all the prisoners (there are about ten thousand) work in a factory which produces a type of rubber called Buna, so that the camp itself is called Buna.

We will be given shoes and clothes – no, not our own – other shoes, other clothes, like his. We are naked now because we are waiting for the shower and the disinfection, which will take place immediately after the reveille, because one cannot enter the camp without being disinfected.

Certainly there will be work to do, everyone must work here. But there is work and work: he, for example, acts as doctor. He is a Hungarian doctor who studied in Italy and he is the dentist of the Lager. He has been in the Lager for four and a half years (not in this one: Buna has only been open for a year and a half), but we can see that he is still quite well, not very thin. Why is he in the Lager? Is he Jewish like us? 'No,' he says simply, 'I am a criminal.'

We ask him many questions. He laughs, replies to some and not to others, and it is clear that he avoids certain subjects. He does not speak of the women: he says they are well, that we will see them again soon, but he does not say how or where. Instead he tells us other things, strange and crazy things, perhaps he too is playing with us. Perhaps he is mad – one goes mad in the Lager. He says that every Sunday there are concerts and football matches. He says that whoever boxes well can become cook. He says that whoever works well receives prize-coupons with which to buy tobacco and soap. He says that the water is really not drinkable, and that instead a coffee substitute is distributed every day, but generally nobody drinks it as the soup itself is sufficiently watery to quench thirst. We beg him to find us something to drink, but he says he cannot, that he has come to see us secretly, against SS orders, as we still have to be disinfected, and that he must leave at once; he has come because he has a liking for Italians, and because, he says, he 'has a little heart'. We ask him if there are other Italians in the camp and he says there are some, a few, he does not know how many; and he at once changes the subject. Meanwhile a bell rang and he immediately hurried off and left us stunned and disconcerted. Some feel refreshed but I do not. I still think that even this dentist, this incomprehensible person, wanted to amuse himself at our expense, and I do not want to believe a word of what he said.

At the sound of the bell, we can hear the still dark camp waking up. Unexpectedly the water gushes out boiling from the showers – five minutes of bliss; but immediately after, four men (perhaps they are the barbers) burst in yelling and shoving and drive us out, wet and steaming, into the adjoining room which is freezing; here other shouting people throw at us unrecognizable rags and thrust into our hands a pair of broken-down boots with wooden soles; we have no time to understand and we already find ourselves in the open, in the blue and icy snow of dawn, barefoot and naked, with all our clothing in our hands, with a hundred yards to run to the next hut. There we are finally allowed to get dressed.

When we finish, everyone remains in his own corner and we do not dare lift our eyes to look at one another. There is nowhere to look in a mirror, but our appearance stands in front of us, reflected in a hundred livid faces, in a hundred miserable and sordid puppets. We are transformed into the phantoms glimpsed yesterday evening.

Then for the first time we became aware that our language lacks words to express this offence, the demolition of a man. In a moment, with almost prophetic intuition, the reality was revealed to us: we had reached the bottom. It is not possible to sink lower than this; no human condition is more miserable than this, nor could it conceivably be so. Nothing belongs to us any more; they have taken away our clothes, our shoes, even our hair; if we speak, they will not listen to us, and if they listen, they will not understand. They will even take away our name and if we want to keep it, we will have to find ourselves the strength to do so, to manage somehow so that behind the name something of us, of us as we were, still remains.

We know that we will have difficulty in being understood, and this is as it should be. But consider what value, what meaning is enclosed even in the smallest of our daily habits, in the hundred possessions which even the poorest beggar owns: a handkerchief, an old letter, the photo of a cherished person. These things are part of us, almost like limbs of our body; nor is it conceivable that we can be deprived of them in our world, for we immediately find others to substitute the old ones, other objects which are ours in their personification and evocation of our memories.

Imagine now a man who is deprived of everyone he loves, and at the same time of his house, his habits, his clothes, in short, of everything he possesses: he will be a hollow man, reduced to suffering and needs, forgetful of dignity and restraint, for he who loses all often easily loses himself. He will be a man whose life or death can be lightly decided with no sense of human affinity, in the most fortunate of cases, on the basis of a pure judgement of utility. It is in this way that one can understand the double sense of the term 'extermination camp', and it is now clear what we seek to express with the phrase: 'to lie on the bottom'.

Häftling [prisoner]: I have learnt that I am Häftling. My number is 174517; we have been baptized, we will carry the tattoo on our left arm until we die.

The operation was slightly painful and extraordinarily rapid: they placed us all in a row, and one by one, according to the alphabetical order of our names, we filed past a skilful official, armed with a sort of pointed tool with a very short needle. It seems that this is the real, true initiation: only by 'showing one's number' can one get bread and soup. Several days passed, and not a few cuffs and punches, before we became used to showing our number promptly enough not to disorder the daily operation of food-distribution: weeks and months were needed to learn its sound in the German language. And for many days, while the habits of freedom still led me to look for the time on my wristwatch, my new name ironically appeared instead, a number tattooed in bluish characters under the skin.

Only much later, and slowly, a few of us learnt something of the funereal science of the numbers of Auschwitz, which epitomize the stages of destruction of European Judaism. To the old hands of the camp, the numbers told everything: the period of entry into the camp, the convoy of which one formed a part, and consequently the nationality. Everyone will treat with respect the numbers from 30,000 to 80,000: there are only a few hundred left and they represented the few survivals from the Polish ghettos. It is as well to watch out in commercial dealings with a 116,000 or a 117,000: they now number only about forty, but they represent the Greeks of Salonica, so take care they do not pull the wool over your eyes. As for the high numbers, they carry an essentially comic air about them, like the words 'freshman' or 'conscript' in ordinary life. The typical high number is a corpulent, docile and stupid fellow: he can be convinced that leather shoes are distributed at the infirmary to all those with delicate feet, and can be persuaded to run there and leave his bowl of soup 'in your custody'; you can sell him a spoon for three rations of bread; you can send him to the most ferocious of the Kapos to ask him (as happened to me!) if it is true that his is the *Kartoffelschalenkommando*, the 'Potato Peeling Command', and if one can be enrolled in it.

In fact, the whole process of introduction to what was for us a new order took place in a grotesque and sarcastic manner. When the tattooing operation was finished, they shut us in a vacant hut. The bunks are made, but we are severely forbidden to touch or sit on them: so we wander around aimlessly for half the day in the limited space available, still tormented by the parching thirst of the journey. Then the door opens and a boy in a striped suit comes in, with a fairly civilized air, small, thin and blond. He speaks French and we throng around him with a flood of questions which till now we had asked each other in vain.

But he does not speak willingly; no one here speaks willingly. We are new, we have nothing and we know nothing; why waste time on us? He reluctantly explains to us that all the others are out at work and will come back in the evening. He has come out of the infirmary this morning and is exempt from work for today. I asked him (with an ingenuousness that only a few days later already seemed incredible to me) if at least they would give us back our toothbrushes. He did not laugh, but with his face animated by fierce contempt, he threw at me '*Vous n'êtes pas à la maison*.' And it is this refrain that we hear repeated by everyone. You are not at home, this is not a sanatorium, the only exit is by way of the Chimney. (What did it mean? Soon we were all to learn what it meant.)

And it was in fact so. Driven by thirst, I eyed a fine icicle outside the window, within hand's reach. I opened the window and broke off the icicle but at once a large, heavy guard prowling outside brutally snatched it away from me. '*Warum?*' I asked him in my poor German. '*Hier ist kein warum*' (there is no why here), he replied, pushing me inside with a shove.

The explanation is repugnant but simple: in this place everything is forbidden, not for hidden reasons, but because the camp has been created for that purpose. If one wants to live one must learn this quickly and well:

> 'No Sacred Face will help thee here! it's not
> A Serchio bathing-party . . .'

Hour after hour, this first long day of limbo draws to its end. While the sun sets in a tumult of fierce, blood-red clouds, they finally make us come out of the hut. Will they give us something to drink? No, they place us in line again, they lead us to a huge square which takes up the centre of the camp and they arrange us meticulously in squads. Then nothing happens for another hour: it seems that we are waiting for someone.

A band begins to play, next to the entrance of the camp: it plays *Rosamunda*, the well-known sentimental song, and this seems so strange to us that we look sniggering at each other; we feel a shadow of relief, perhaps all these ceremonies are nothing but a colossal farce in Teutonic taste. But the band, on finishing *Rosamunda*, continues to play other marches, one after the other, and suddenly the squads of our comrades appear, returning from work. They walk in columns of five with a strange, unnatural hard gait, like stiff puppets made of jointless bones; but they walk scrupulously in time to the band.

They also arrange themselves like us in the huge square, according to a precise order; when the last squad has returned, they count and recount us for over an hour. Long checks are made which all seem to go to a man dressed in stripes, who accounts for them to a group of SS men in full battledress.

Finally (it is dark by now, but the camp is brightly lit by headlamps and reflectors) one hears the shout '*Absperre!*' at which all the squads break up in a confused and turbulent movement. They no longer walk stiffly and erectly as before: each one drags himself along with obvious effort. I see that all of them carry in their hand or attached to their belt a steel bowl as large as a basin.

We new arrivals also wander among the crowd, searching for a voice, a friendly face or a guide. Against the wooden wall of a hut two boys are seated on the ground: they seem very young, sixteen years old at the outside, both with their face and hands dirty with soot. One of the two, as we are passing by, calls me and asks me in German some questions which I do not understand; then he asks where we come from. '*Italien*,' I reply: I want to ask him many things, but my German vocabulary is very limited.

'Are you a Jew?' I asked him.

'Yes, a Polish Jew.'

'How long have you been in the Lager?'

'Three years,' and he lifts up three fingers. He must have been a child when he entered, I think with horror; on the other hand this means that at least some manage to live here.

'What is your work?'

'*Schlosser*,' he replies. I do not understand. '*Eisen, Feuer*' (iron, fire), he insists, and makes a play with his hands of someone beating with a hammer on an anvil. So he is an ironsmith.

'*Ich Chemiker*,' I state; and he nods earnestly with his head, '*Chemiker gut*.' But this all has to do with the distant future: what torments me at the moment is my thirst.

'Drink, water. We no water,' I tell him.

He looks at me with a serious face, almost severe, and states clearly: 'Do not drink water, comrade,' and then other words that I do not understand.

'*Warum?*'

'*Geschwollen*,' he replies cryptically. I shake my head. I have not understood. '*Swollen*,' he makes me understand, blowing out his cheeks and sketching with his hands a monstrous tumefaction of the face and belly. '*Warten bis heute Abend.*' 'Wait until this evening,' I translate word by word.

Then he says: '*Ich Schlome. Du?*' I tell him my name and he asks me: 'Where your mother?'

'In Italy.' Schlome is amazed: a Jew in Italy? 'Yes,' I explain as best I can, 'hidden, no one knows, run away, does not speak, no one sees her.' He has understood; he now gets up, approaches me and timidly embraces me. The adventure is over, and I now feel filled with a serene sadness that is almost joy. I have never seen Schlome since, but I have not forgotten his serious and gentle face of a child, which welcomed me on the threshold of the house of the dead . . .

. . .

The hours of work vary with the season. All hours of light are working hours: so that from a minimum winter working day (8–12 a.m. and 12.30–4 p.m.) one rises to a maximum summer one (6.20–12 a.m. and 1–6 p.m.). Under no excuse are the *Häftlinge* allowed to be at work during the hours of darkness or when there is a thick fog, but they work regularly even if it rains or snows or (as occurs quite frequently) if the fierce wind of the Carpathians blows; the reason being that the darkness or fog might provide opportunities to escape.

One Sunday in every two is a regular working day; on the so-called holiday Sundays, instead of working at Buna, one works normally on the upkeep of the Lager, so that days of real rest are extremely rare.

Such will be our life. Every day, according to the established rhythm, *Ausrücken* and *Einrücken*, go out and come in; work, sleep and eat; fall ill, get better or die.

And for how long? But the old ones laugh at this question: they recognize the new arrivals by this question. They laugh and they do not reply. For months and years, the problem of the remote future has grown pale to them and has lost all intensity in face of the far more urgent and concrete problems of the near future: how much one will eat today, if it will snow, if there will be coal to unload.

If we were logical, we would resign ourselves to the evidence that our fate is beyond knowledge, that every conjecture is arbitrary and demonstrably devoid of foundation. But men are rarely logical when their own fate is at stake; on every occasion, they prefer the extreme positions. According to our character, some of us are immediately convinced that all is lost, that one cannot live here, that the end is near and sure; others are convinced that however hard the present life may be, salvation is probable and not far off, and if we have faith and strength, we will see our houses and our dear ones again. The two classes of pessimists and optimists are not so clearly defined, however, not because there are many agnostics, but because the majority, without memory or coherence, drift between the two extremes, according to the moment and the mood of the person they happen to meet.

Here I am, then, on the bottom. One learns quickly enough to wipe out the past and the future when one is forced to. A fortnight after my arrival I already had the prescribed hunger, that chronic hunger unknown to free men, which makes one dream at night, and settles in all the limbs of one's body. I have already learnt not to let myself be robbed, and in fact if I find a spoon lying around, a piece of string, a button which I can acquire without danger of punishment, I pocket them and consider them mine by full right. On the back of my feet I already have those numb sores that will not heal. I push wagons, I work with a shovel, I turn rotten in the rain, I shiver in the wind; already my own body is no longer mine: my belly is swollen, my limbs emaciated, my face is thick in the morning, hollow in the evening; some of us have yellow skin, others grey. When we do not meet for a few days we hardly recognize each other.

We Italians had decided to meet every Sunday evening in a corner of the Lager, but we stopped it at once, because it was too sad to count our numbers and find fewer each time, and to see each other ever more deformed and more squalid. And it was so tiring to walk those few steps and then, meeting each other, to remember and to think. It was better not to think.

. . .

October 1944

We fought with all our strength to prevent the arrival of winter. We clung to all the warm hours, at every dusk we tried to keep the sun in the sky for a little longer, but it was all in vain. Yesterday evening the sun went down irrevocably behind a confusion of dirty clouds, chimney stacks and wires, and today it is winter.

We know what it means because we were here last winter; and the others will soon learn. It means that in the course of these months, from October till April, seven out of ten of us will die. Whoever does not die will suffer minute by minute, all day, every day: from the morning before dawn until the distribution of the evening soup we will have to keep our muscles continually tensed, dance from foot to foot, beat our arms under our shoulders against the cold. We will have to spend bread to acquire gloves, and lose hours of sleep to repair them when they become unstitched. As it will no longer be possible to eat in the open, we will have to eat our meals in the hut, on our feet, everyone will be assigned an area of floor as large as a hand, as it is forbidden to rest against the bunks. Wounds will open on everyone's hands, and to be given a bandage will mean waiting every evening for hours on one's feet in the snow and wind.

Just as our hunger is not that feeling of missing a meal, so our way of being cold has need of a new word. We say 'hunger', we say 'tiredness', 'fear', 'pain', we say 'winter' and they are different things. They are free words, created and used by free men who lived in comfort and suffering in their homes. If the Lagers had lasted longer a new, harsh language would have been born; and only this language could express what it means to toil the whole day in the wind, with the temperature below freezing, wearing only a shirt, underpants, cloth jacket and trousers, and in one's body nothing but weakness, hunger and knowledge of the end drawing nearer.

In the same way in which one sees a hope end, winter arrived this morning. We realized it when we left the hut to go and wash: there were no stars, the dark cold air had the smell of snow. In roll-call square, in the grey of dawn, when we assembled for work, no one spoke. When we saw the first flakes of snow, we thought that if at the same time last year they had told us that we would have seen another winter in Lager, we would have gone and touched the electric wire-fence; and that even now we would go if we were logical, were it not for this last senseless crazy residue of unavoidable hope.

Because 'winter' means yet another thing.

Last spring the Germans had constructed huge tents in an open space in the Lager. For the whole of the good season each of them had catered for over a thousand men: now the tents had been taken down, and an excess two thousand guests crowded our huts. We old prisoners knew that the Germans did not like these irregularities and that something would soon happen to reduce our number.

One feels the selections arriving. '*Selekcja*': the hybrid Latin and Polish word is heard once, twice, many times, interpolated in foreign conversations; at first we cannot distinguish it, then it forces itself on our attention, and in the end it persecutes us.

This morning the Poles had said '*Selekcja*'. The Poles are the first to find out the news, and they generally try not to let it spread around, because to know something which the others still do not know can always be useful. By the time that everyone realizes that a selection is imminent, the few possibilities of evading it (corrupting some doctor or some prominent with bread or tobacco; leaving the hut for Ka-Be [the infirmary] or vice-versa at the right moment so as to cross with the commission) are already their monopoly.

In the days which follow, the atmosphere of the Lager and the yard is filled with '*Selekcja*': nobody knows anything definite, but all speak about it, even the Polish, Italian, French civilian workers whom we secretly see in the yard. Yet the result is hardly a wave of despondency: our collective morale is too inarticulate and flat to be unstable. The fight against hunger, cold and work leaves little margin for thought, even for this thought. Everybody reacts in his own way, but hardly anyone with those attitudes which would seem the most plausible as the most realistic, that is with resignation or despair.

All those able to find a way out, try to take it; but they are the minority because it is very difficult to escape from a selection. The Germans apply themselves to these things with great skill and diligence.

Whoever is unable to prepare for it materially, seeks defence elsewhere. In the latrines, in the washroom, we show each other our chests, our buttocks, our thighs, and our comrades reassure us. 'You are all right, it will certainly not be your turn this time, . . . *du bist kein Muselmann* . . . more probably mine . . .' and they undo their braces in turn and pull up their shirts.

Nobody refuses this charity to another: nobody is so sure of his own lot to be able to condemn others. I brazenly lied to old Wertheimer; I told him that if they questioned him, he should reply that he was forty-five, and he should not forget to have a shave the evening before, even if it cost him a quarter-ration of bread; apart from that he need have no fears, and in any case it was by no means certain that it was a selection for the gas-chamber; had he not heard the *Blockältester* say that those chosen would go to Jaworszno to a convalescent camp?

It is absurd of Wertheimer to hope: he looks sixty, he has enormous varicose veins, he hardly even notices the hunger any more. But he lies down on his bed, serene and quiet, and replies to someone who asks him with my own words; they are the command-words in the camp these days: I myself repeated them just as – apart from details – Chajim told them to me, Chajim, who has been in Lager for three years, and being strong and robust is wonderfully sure of himself; and I believed them.

On this slender basis I also lived through the great selection of October 1944 with inconceivable tranquillity. I was tranquil because I managed to lie to myself sufficiently. The fact that I was not selected depended above all on chance and does not prove that my faith was well-founded.

Monsieur Pinkert is also, a priori, condemned: it is enough to look at his eyes. He calls me over with a sign, and with a confidential air tells me that he has been informed – he cannot tell me the source of information – that this time there is really something new: the Holy See, by means of the International Red Cross . . . in short, he personally guarantees both for himself and for me, in the most absolute manner, that every danger is ruled out; as a civilian he was, as is well known, attached to the Belgian embassy at Warsaw.

Thus in various ways, even those days of vigil, which in the telling seem as if they ought to have passed every limit of human torment, went by not very differently from other days.

The discipline in both the Lager and Buna is in no way relaxed: the work, cold and hunger are sufficient to fill up every thinking moment.

Today is working Sunday, *Arbeitssonntag*: we work until 1 p.m., then we return to camp for the shower, shave and general control for skin diseases and lice. And in the yards, everyone knew mysteriously that the selection would be today.

The news arrived, as always, surrounded by a halo of contradictory or suspect details: the selection in the infirmary took place this morning; the percentage was seven per cent of the whole camp, thirty, fifty per cent of the patients. At Birkenau, the crematorium chimney has been smoking for ten days. Room has to be made for an enormous convoy arriving from the Poznan ghetto. The young tell the young that all the old ones will be chosen. The healthy tell the healthy that only the ill will be chosen. Specialists will be excluded. German Jews will be excluded. Low Numbers will be excluded. You will be chosen. I will be excluded.

At 1 p.m. exactly the yard empties in orderly fashion, and for two hours the grey unending army files past the two control stations where, as on every day, we are counted and recounted, and past the military band which for two hours without interruption plays, as on every day, those marches to which we must synchronize our steps at our entrance and our exit.

It seems like every day, the kitchen chimney smokes as usual, the distribution of the soup is already beginning. But then the bell is heard, and at that moment we realize that we have arrived.

Because this bell always sounds at dawn, when it means the reveille; but if it sounds during the day, it means '*Blocksperre*', enclosure in huts, and this happens when there is a selection to prevent anyone avoiding it, or when those selected leave for the gas, to prevent anyone seeing them leave.

Our *Blockältester* knows his business. He has made sure that we have all entered, he has the door locked, he has given everyone his card with his number, name, profession, age and nationality and he has ordered everyone to undress completely, except for shoes. We wait like this, naked, with the card in our hands, for the commission to reach our hut. We are hut 48, but one can never tell if they are going to begin at hut 1 or hut 60. At any rate, we can rest quietly at least for an hour, and there is no reason why we should not get under the blankets on the bunk and keep warm.

Many are already drowsing when a barrage of orders, oaths and blows proclaims the imminent arrival of the commission. The *Blockältester* and his helpers, starting at the end of the dormitory, drive the crowd of frightened, naked people in front of them and cram them in the *Tagesraum* which is the Quartermaster's office. The *Tagesraum* is a room seven yards by four: when the drive is over, a warm and compact human mass is jammed into the *Tagesraum*, perfectly filling all the corners, exercising such a pressure on the wooden walls as to make them creak.

Now we are all in the *Tagesraum*, and besides there being no time, there is not even any room in which to be afraid. The feeling of the warm flesh pressing all around is unusual and not unpleasant. One has to take care to hold up one's nose so as to breathe, and not to crumple or lose the card in one's hand.

The *Blockältester* has closed the connecting-door and has opened the other two which lead from the dormitory and the *Tagesraum* outside. Here, in front of the two doors, stands the arbiter of our fate, an SS subaltern. On his right is the *Blockältester*, on his left, the quartermaster of the hut. Each one of us as he comes naked out of the *Tagesraum* into the cold October air, has to run the few steps between the two doors, give the card to the SS man and enter the dormitory door. The SS man, in the fraction of a second between two successive crossings, with a glance at one's back and front, judges everyone's fate, and in turn gives the card to the man on his right or his left, and this is the life or death of each of us. In three or four minutes a hut of two hundred men is 'done', as is the whole camp of twelve thousand men in the course of the afternoon.

Jammed in the charnel-house of the *Tagesraum*, I gradually felt the human pressure around me slacken, and in a short time it was my turn. Like everyone, I passed by with a brisk and elastic step, trying to hold my head high, my chest forward and my muscles contracted and conspicuous. With the corner of my eye I tried to look behind my shoulders, and my card seemed to end on the right.

As we gradually come back into the dormitory we are allowed to dress ourselves. Nobody yet knows with certainty his own fate, it has first of all to be established whether the condemned cards were those on the right or the left. By now there is no longer any point in sparing each other's feelings with superstitious scruples. Everybody crowds around the oldest, the most wasted-away, and most 'muselmann'; if their cards went to the left, the left is certainly the side of the condemned.

Even before the selection is over, everybody knows that the left was effectively the '*schlechte Seite*', the bad side. There have naturally been some irregularities: René, for example, so young and robust, ended on the left; perhaps it was because he has glasses, perhaps because he walks a little stooped like a myope, but more probably because of a simple mistake: René passed the commission immediately in front of me and there could have been a mistake with our cards. I think about it, discuss it with Alberto, and we agree that the hypothesis is probable;

I do not know what I will think tomorrow and later; today I feel no distinct emotion.

It must equally have been a mistake about Sattler, a huge Transylvanian peasant who was still at home only twenty days ago; Sattler does not understand German, he has understood nothing of what has taken place, and stands in a corner mending his shirt. Must I go and tell him that his shirt will be of no more use?

There is nothing surprising about these mistakes: the examination is too quick and summary, and in any case, the important thing for the Lager is not that the most useless prisoners be eliminated, but that free posts be quickly created, according to a certain percentage previously fixed.

The selection is now over in our hut, but it continues in the others, so that we are still locked in. But as the soup-pots have arrived in the meantime, the *Blockältester* decides to proceed with the distribution at once. A double ration will be given to those selected. I have never discovered if this was a ridiculously charitable initiative of the *Blockältester*, or an explicit disposition of the SS, but in fact, in the interval of two or three days (sometimes even much longer) between the selection and the departure, the victims at Monowitz-Auschwitz enjoyed this privilege.

Ziegler holds out his bowl, collects his normal ration and then waits there expectantly. 'What do you want?' asks the *Blockältester*: according to him, Ziegler is entitled to no supplement, and he drives him away, but Ziegler returns and humbly persists. He was on the left, everybody saw it, let the *Blockältester* check the cards; he has the right to a double ration. When he is given it, he goes quietly to his bunk to eat.

Now everyone is busy scraping the bottom of his bowl with his spoon so as not to waste the last drops of the soup; a confused, metallic clatter, signifying the end of the day. Silence slowly prevails and then, from my bunk on the top row, I see and hear old Kuhn praying aloud, with his beret on his head, swaying backwards and forwards violently. Kuhn is thanking God because he has not been chosen.

Kuhn is out of his senses. Does he not see Beppo the Greek in the bunk next to him, Beppo who is twenty years old and is going to the gas-chamber the day after tomorrow and knows it and lies there looking fixedly at the light without saying anything and without even thinking any more? Can Kuhn fail to realize that next time it will be his turn? Does

Kuhn not understand that what has happened today is an abomination, which no propitiatory prayer, no pardon, no expiation by the guilty, which nothing at all in the power of man can ever clean again? If I was God, I would spit at Kuhn's prayer.

Kaddish in Buchenwald

Jorge Semprun, son of a diplomat for the Spanish Republic, emigrated to France after Franco's victory. He joined the Resistance and was arrested and sent to Buchenwald in 1943. He survived, became a published writer of distinction, and was Spain's Minister of Culture from 1988 to 1991.

Buchenwald had not been opened in 1937 to kill Jews. Communists, other political enemies of Nazism and common criminals were its constituency. However, out of 238,980 prisoners held there over eight years, 56,545 died. Towards the end of the war, Jews were decanted there from the death camps. On 11 April 1945 the camp's inmates revolted and liberated themselves before the US Army arrived.

Semprun's Literature or Life *(1994) is a meditation moving between past and present, the art of writing and reality.*

THE GAZE

They stand amazed before me, and suddenly, in that terror-stricken gaze, I see myself – in their horror.

For two years, I had lived without a face. No mirrors, in Buchenwald. I saw my body, its increasing emaciation, once a week, in the shower. Faceless, that absurd body. Sometimes I gently touched the jutting bones of the eye sockets, the hollow of a cheek. I could have got myself a mirror, I suppose. You could find anything on the camp's black market in exchange for bread, tobacco, margarine. Even tenderness, on occasion.

But I wasn't interested in such niceties.

I watched my body grow more and more vague beneath the weekly shower. Wasted but alive: the blood still circulated, nothing to fear. It would be enough, that thinned down but available body, fit for a much dreamed of – although most unlikely – survival.

The proof, moreover: here I am.

They stare at me, wild-eyed with panic.

It can't be because of my close-cropped hair. Young recruits and country boys, among others, innocently wear short hair. It's no big deal.

A louse cut never bothered anyone. Nothing frightening about it. My outfit, then? A curious one, I admit: mismatched cast-offs. But my boots are Russian, of soft leather. Across my chest hangs a German submachine gun, an obvious sign of authority these days. Authority isn't alarming; on the whole, it's even reassuring. My thinness? They must have seen worse by now. If they're following the Allied armies' drive into Germany this spring, they've already seen worse. Other camps, living corpses . . .

The stubble on my head, my worn and ill-assorted clothing – such particulars can be startling, intriguing. But these men aren't startled or intrigued. What I read in their eyes is fear.

It must be my gaze, I conclude, that they find so riveting. It's the horror of my gaze that I see reflected in their own. And if their eyes are a mirror, then mine must look like those of a madman.

They got out of the car just now, only a moment ago. Took a few steps in the sunshine, stretching their legs. Then saw me, and moved forward.

Three officers, in British uniforms.

A fourth soldier, the driver, stayed near the automobile, a large grey Mercedes still bearing its German licence plates.

The men came toward me.

Two of them are about thirty, blond, rather pink-complexioned. The third one is younger, darker, wearing a badge with a cross of Lorraine on which is written the word 'France'.

I remember the last French soldiers I saw, in June 1940. From the regular army, of course. Because after that I'd seen irregulars, guerrillas – plenty of them. Enough for me to have remembered them, in any case.

In the Tabou, for example, a Burgundian *maquis* between Laignes and Larrey.

But the last regular soldiers of the French Army – that was in June 1940, in the streets of Redon: wretched men falling back in disorder, in shame and misfortune, grey with dust and defeat. Five years later, in the April sunlight, the man in front of me doesn't look defeated. He wears a badge of France over his heart, over the left pocket of his uniform jacket.

Triumphantly, or at least joyfully.

He must be my age, a few years older. I could try being friendly.

He stares at me, bewildered by fright.

'What's the matter?' I ask irritably, and doubtless harshly. 'You're surprised to find the woods so quiet?'

He looks around at the trees encircling us. The other men do the same. Listening. No, it's not the silence. They hadn't noticed, hadn't heard the silence. I'm what's scaring them, obviously, and nothing else.

'No birds left,' I continue, pursuing my idea. 'They say the smoke from the crematory drove them away. Never any birds in this forest . . .'

They listen closely, straining to understand.

'The smell of burned flesh, that's what did it!'

They wince, glance at one another. In almost palpable distress. A sort of gasp, a heave of revulsion.

. . .

I'm laughing, laughing to find myself alive.

The springtime, the sun, my companions, the pack of Camels given to me that night by a young American soldier from New Mexico who spoke a lilting Castilian Spanish – it's all rather amusing to me.

Perhaps I shouldn't have laughed. Perhaps laughter is indecent, given what I must look like. Judging from the expressions of the British officers, laughter doesn't much suit me at the moment.

And it seems my face is no laughing matter, either.

They're standing silently a few steps away. They avoid looking at me. One officer's mouth has gone dry, I can tell. The other Britisher has a twitching eyelid. Nerves. As for the Frenchman, he's looking for something in a pocket of his military jacket, which allows him to avert his gaze.

I laugh again – too bad if it's out of place.

'The crematory shut down yesterday,' I tell them. 'No more smoke over the countryside, ever again. Maybe the birds will come back.'

They wince, vaguely nauseated.

But they can't really understand. They probably know what the words mean. Smoke: you know what that is, you think you know. Throughout historic memory, there have been smoking chimneys. Sometimes country hearths, domestic firesides: the smoke of household gods.

This smoke, however, is beyond them. And they will never really understand it. Not these people, that day. Nor all the others, afterward. They will never know – they cannot imagine, whatever their good intentions may be.

Ever-present, billowing or spiralling over the squat smoke-stack of the crematory of Buchenwald, not far from the administrative offices of the Labour Service, the *Arbeitsstatistik*, where I was assigned during that last year.

I had only to bend a little, without leaving my duties at the central card index, and look out one of the windows facing the forest. There was the crematory, massive, surrounded by a high palisade, crowned with smoke.

Or flames, at night.

When the Allied aircraft flew deep into the heart of Germany on night bombing runs, the SS ordered that the fire in the crematory ovens be extinguished. The flames, which actually shot out of the chimney, were an ideal landmark for the English and American pilots.

'*Krematorium, ausmachen!*' A curt, impatient shout would crackle over the camp loudspeakers.

'Crematory, shut down!'

Sleeping, we would awaken to the hollow voice of the SS officer on duty in the control tower. Or rather: the voice would first become a part of our slumber, reverberating through our dreams, before waking us. In Buchenwald, while our bodies and our souls struggled blindly, during the brief nights, to return to life with a tenacious and carnal yearning belied by reason in the returning light of day, these two words – *Krematorium, ausmachen!* – exploded over and over in our dreams, filling them with echoes, bringing us back to the reality of death. Tearing us away from the dream of life.

Later, after we had returned from that absence, whenever we heard them (not necessarily during a nightmare: in a daydream or an idle moment, even in the midst of a friendly conversation, it makes no difference), these two German words – and it is always these two words, only these, that ring out: *Krematorium, ausmachen!* – would still bring us back to reality.

And so, in the jolt of awakening, or of returning self-awareness, we sometimes suspected that life had been only a dream, albeit occasionally a pleasant one, since our release from Buchenwald. A dream from which these two words would jar us awake, plunging us into a strangely serene despair. For it wasn't the reality of death, suddenly recalled, that was anguishing. It was the dream of life, even a peaceful one, even one filled with little joys. It was the fact of being alive, even in a dream, that was alarming.

'To leave by the chimney', 'to go up in smoke': common expressions in Buchenwald slang, in the slang spoken in all the camps – there's ample evidence. These expressions were used at every turn and in every tone, including the rasp of sarcasm. The sarcastic edge even predominated, among ourselves, at least. The SS and the civilian foremen, the *Meisters*, always adopted a threatening manner or a tone of dire prediction.

They cannot understand, not really, these three officers. They'd have to be told the story of the smoke: sometimes dense, a sooty black against the variable sky. Or light and grey, almost vaporous, drifting with the winds over the assembled living like a portent, a farewell.

Smoke for a shroud as vast as the heavens, the last trace of the passing, body and soul, of our companions.

It would take hours, entire seasons, an eternity of telling to come close to accounting for them all.

There will be survivors, of course. Me, for example. Here I am, the survivor on duty, appearing opportunely before these three Allied officers to tell them of the crematory smoke, the smell of burned flesh hanging over the Ettersberg, the roll calls out in the falling snow, the murderous work details, the exhaustion of life, the inexhaustibility of hope, the savagery of the human animal, the nobility of man, the fraternity and devastation in the naked gaze of our comrades . . .

KADDISH

All of a sudden, a voice, behind us.

A voice? More like a bestial moan. The inarticulate groaning of a wounded animal. A blood-curdling wail of lamentation.

We froze on the threshold of the hut, just as we were stepping back out into the fresh air, Albert and I. Standing stock-still at the boundary between the stinking murkiness inside and the April sunlight outdoors. In front of us, blue sky faintly streaked with fleecy clouds. Around us, the mostly green mass of the forest, beyond the huts and tents of the Little Camp. Off in the distance, the mountains of Thuringia. In short, the timeless landscape Goethe and Eckermann must have contemplated during their walks on the Ettersberg.

It really was a human voice, though: an eerie, guttural humming.

Albert and I were still standing there, petrified.

Albert was a Hungarian Jew, stocky, indefatigable, always cheerful. Or at least optimistic. I was accompanying him, that day, on a last tour of inspection. For the past two days we had been regrouping the Jewish survivors of Auschwitz and the other camps in Poland. Children and adolescents, in particular, had been gathered together in a building in the SS section.

Albert was in charge of this rescue operation.

We went back into the unspeakable gloom, in icy apprehension. Where was the inhuman voice coming from? Because we had just determined that no one in there was still alive. We had just walked the entire length of the central aisle in that hut. Faces were turned toward us, as we passed by. The wasted bodies, covered in rags, lay on three tiers of bunks aligned in rows. The corpses were all mixed up with one another, and sometimes stiffened into a ghastly immobility. They stared out at us, into the centre aisle; often they'd had to twist their necks violently around. Dozens of protruding eyes had watched us pass.

Watched without seeing us.

There had been no more survivors in that hut in the Little Camp. The wide-open eyes, their dilated pupils glaring inscrutably at the abomination of the world, were lifeless, their light snuffed out.

We had passed by, Albert and I, choked with emotion, walking as lightly as possible in the viscous silence where death was in its element, setting off the stone-cold fireworks of all those eyes gazing at the hellish scene, the underside of the world.

From time to time, Albert – I myself hadn't had the courage – had drawn closer to the jumbled bodies piled on the bare planks of the bunks. The corpses would move all of a piece, like tangled roots on a tree stump. Albert shoved this deadwood aside with a firm hand. He peered into the hollows, the interstices between the bodies, still hoping to find life.

But there hadn't seemed to be any survivors there that day on April 14, 1945. All who could must have fled the hut upon hearing that the camp had been liberated.

I can be certain of that date, April 14, and speak of it with confidence, yet the period of my life between the liberation of Buchenwald and my return to Paris is confused, my memory clouded by forgetfulness. By vagueness, in any case.

I've often tallied up the days and nights. I always obtain a disconcerting result. Between the liberation of Buchenwald and my return to Paris, eighteen days passed: that much is certain. I have very few memories of this time, however. The rare images are startlingly clear, it's true, and bathed in a bleak radiance, but they're surrounded by a thick halo of shadowy mist. I remember enough to fill a few short hours in a life, no more.

It's easy to establish the date at the beginning of this period. It's in the history books: April 11, 1945, the day Buchenwald was liberated. It's possible to figure out when I arrived in Paris, but I'll spare you the data behind my calculations. It was two days before May Day, which makes it April 29. In the afternoon, to be absolutely precise. It was on the afternoon of April 29 that I arrived in Paris, on the rue de Vaugirard, with a convoy of the repatriation mission carried out by the Abbé Rodhain.

I provide all these facts, which are probably superfluous and even silly, to show that my memory is fine, that it's not because of failing powers of remembrance that I have more or less forgotten those two long weeks of existence before my return to life, to what is called life.

Nevertheless, there it is: I have only a few scattered recollections of this period, barely enough to fill several hours out of those two long weeks. Memories that shine with a garish light, to be sure, but which are enveloped in the greyish haze of nonbeing. Of something almost impossible to pin down, at any rate.

So the day in question was April 14, 1945.

That morning I'd reflected that the date was an important one in my childhood: Spain was declared a republic on that same day in 1931. Crowds poured in from the outlying neighbourhoods, heading for the centre of Madrid beneath a rippling forest of flags. 'We've changed regimes without breaking a single window!' announced the leaders of the republican parties triumphantly – and in some amazement. History caught up with itself five years later in a long and bloody civil war.

But on April 14, 1945, there hadn't been any survivors in that hut in the Little Camp at Buchenwald.

There had been only dead eyes, wide open on the horror of the world. The corpses, which were as contorted as the figures of El Greco, seemed to have used their last reserves of strength to crawl across the planks to the edge of the bunks nearest to the centre aisle, where their last hope of rescue might finally have appeared. Their glazed eyes, dulled by the agony of waiting, had no doubt watched until the end for some sudden salvation. The despair visible in those eyes bespoke the torment of that vigil, of the violence of their last hope.

I abruptly understood the mistrustful, fearful astonishment of the three Allied officers of the previous day. If my gaze reflected, in fact, even a mere hundredth part of the terror discernible in the dead eyes we had contemplated, Albert and I, then it was no wonder the three officers in British uniform had been appalled.

'You hear that?' murmured Albert.

It wasn't really a question. How could I not hear it? I listened to that inhuman voice, that crooned sobbing, that strangely rhythmic death-rattle, that rhapsody from the great beyond.

I turned back towards the outdoors: the balmy April breeze, the blue sky. I took a deep draught of spring.

'What is it?' asked Albert in a low, toneless voice.

'Death,' I told him. 'Who else?'

Albert made a gesture of irritation.

It was death that was humming, no doubt, somewhere amid the heaps of corpses. The life of death, in other words, making itself heard. The agony of death, its shining and mournfully loquacious presence. But why point out the obvious? That's what Albert's gesture seemed to say. Why bother, indeed?

I kept quiet.

The crematory furnace had been shut down three days earlier. When the camp's International Committee and the American military authorities had restored the essential services of Buchenwald in order to feed, clothe, care for, and reorganize the several tens of thousands of survivors, no one had considered restarting the crematory. It was truly unthinkable. The smoke from the crematory had to disappear forever: there was no question of seeing it drift across the landscape ever again. Even though we no longer went up in smoke, however, that didn't mean that death had taken a holiday. The end of the crematory wasn't the end of death, which had merely ceased hovering overhead, in dense clouds or ragged wisps, depending on the circumstances. Death was no longer smoke that was sometimes almost immaterial, a practically impalpable fall of grey ash upon the countryside. Death had become carnal again, incarnate once more in the dozens of tortured, emaciated bodies that still constituted its daily harvest.

To avoid risking an epidemic, the American military authorities had decided to collect and identify the corpses and then bury them in common graves. Which was why Albert and I were making one final sweep through the Little Camp that day hoping to find some last survivors too enfeebled to have rejoined, on their own, the communal life of Buchenwald since its liberation.

Albert's face went livid. He strained to hear, and suddenly became frantic, squeezing my arm painfully.

'Yiddish!' he shouted. 'It's speaking Yiddish!'

So, death spoke Yiddish.

Albert was more able than I was to glean this information from the guttural (and to me, meaningless) sounds of that ghostly singsong.

After all, it was hardly surprising that death spoke Yiddish. Now, there was a language it had certainly been forced to learn over the last few years. If indeed it hadn't already known it from the very beginning.

But Albert has grabbed my arm and is clutching it tightly. He drags me back into the hut.

We take a few steps down the centre aisle, and stop. We listen hard, trying to determine where the voice is coming from.

Albert is panting.

'It's the prayer for the dead,' he whispers.

I shrug. Of course it's a funeral chant. No one expects death to serenade us with funny songs. Or words of love, either.

We let ourselves be guided by that prayer for the dead. Sometimes we have to wait, motionless, holding our breath. Death has fallen silent, leaving us no way to locate the source of that monotonous threnody. But it always starts up again: inexhaustible, the voice of death. Immortal.

Suddenly as we grope around in a short lateral aisle, I feel we're almost there: now the voice – hoarse, mumbling – is quite near.

Albert rushes over to the bunk where the voice is rattling faintly.

Two minutes later, we have extracted from a heap of corpses the dying man through whose mouth death is singing to us. Reciting its prayer to us, actually. We carry the man out in front of the hut, into the April sunshine. We lay him down on a pile of rags that Albert has collected. The man doesn't open his eyes, but he hasn't stopped singing, in a rough, barely audible voice.

I have never seen a human face that more closely resembled that of the crucified Christ. Not the stern but serene countenance of a Roman Jesus, but the tormented face of a Spanish Gothic Jesus. Of course, Christ on the Cross does not usually intone the Jewish prayer for the dead, but this is a minor detail. There is nothing from a theological point of view, I presume, to prevent Christ from chanting the Kaddish.

'Wait for me here,' says Albert firmly. 'I'll dash over to the *Revier* for a stretcher!'

He takes a few steps, then comes back to me.

'You'll take care of him, right?'

That strikes me as so stupid, so outrageous, even, that I blow up.

'What is it you think I should do for him? We could have a little chat? How about if I sing him a song? "La Paloma", maybe?'

But Albert doesn't lose control.

'Just stay with him, that's all!'

And he runs off to the camp infirmary.

I turned back toward the man. Eyes closed, he lies there, still singing faintly. More and more faintly, it seems to me.

I had mentioned 'La Paloma' just like that, out of nowhere. But it reminds me of something I can't remember. Reminds me that I ought to remember something, anyway. Something I could remember, if I tried. 'La Paloma'? The beginning of the song pops into my mind . . . and strange as it may seem, the words are in German.

Kommt eine weisse Taube zur Dir geflogen . . .

I mutter the beginning of 'La Paloma', in German. Now I know what story I could remember.

I really think back, deliberately, since I'm going to have to remember it anyway.

The German was young, he was tall, and he was blond. He was the absolute embodiment of the German ideal: all in all, a perfect German. This was a year and a half earlier, in 1943. It was autumn, in the area of Semur-en-Auxois. At a bend in the river, there was a kind of natural dam, and there the surface of the water was almost completely still: a liquid looking-glass beneath the autumn sun. Shadows of trees moved upon this translucent, silvery mirror.

The German had appeared on the crest of the riverbank. His motor cycle rumbled softly as he guided it along the path leading down to the water's edge.

We were waiting for him, Julien and I.

That is to say, we weren't waiting for that particular German. That blond, blue-eyed youth. (Watch out – I'm fabricating: I wasn't able to see the colour of his eyes at that point. Not until later, when he was dead. But he certainly looked like the blue-eyed type to me.) We were waiting for a German, for some Germans. No matter which ones. We knew that the soldiers of the Wehrmacht had taken to coming in groups, toward the end of the afternoon, to refresh themselves at that spot. Julien and I had come to study the terrain, to see if it would be possible to stage an ambush with the help of the local Resistance fighters.

This German appeared to be alone, however. No other motor cycle, no other vehicle had appeared behind him on the road at the top of the riverbank. Admittedly, it wasn't the soldiers' usual visiting time, either. It was around midmorning.

He went down to the water, got off his bike, and parked it on its kickstand. There he stood, breathing the mild air of the French countryside. He unfastened the collar of his jacket. He was relaxed, obviously. He hadn't let down his guard, though: he had a machine-gun slung across his chest, hanging from a strap around his neck.

Julien and I looked at each other. The same idea occurred to us. We had our Smith and Wessons, and the German was alone, within easy range. There was a motor cycle for the taking, and a machine-gun.

We were on the lookout, under cover. We had a perfect target. So the same thought came into our minds.

But the young German soldier suddenly looked up at the sky and began to sing.

Kommt eine weisse Taube zu Dir geflogen . . .

Startled, I almost gave us away by knocking the barrel of my Smith and Wesson against the rock that concealed us. Julien gave me a furious look.

Perhaps that song meant nothing to him. Perhaps he didn't even know that it was 'La Paloma'. Even if he'd known that, perhaps the song wouldn't have brought back any memories for him. Childhood, the maids singing in the pantry, music from the bandstands in shady village squares . . . 'La Paloma'! How could I not have started when I heard that song?

The German went on singing, in a lovely blond voice. My hand began to shake. It had become impossible for me to shoot at that young soldier singing 'La Paloma'. As though singing that melody from my childhood, that refrain so full of nostalgia, had suddenly made him innocent. Not personally innocent, which perhaps he was, in any case, whether he'd ever sung 'La Paloma' or not. Maybe he had nothing to reproach himself for, this young soldier, nothing besides having been born a German in the time of Adolf Hitler. No – it was as though he'd just become innocent in a completely different way. Innocent not only of being born a German under Hitler, of belonging to an army of occupation, of involuntarily embodying the brute force of Fascism. But fundamentally innocent, in the fullness of his existence, because he was singing 'La Paloma'. It was absurd, and I knew it. Still, I was incapable of shooting at this young German singing 'La Paloma', with his face turned to the sky in the candid enjoyment of an autumn morning, utterly immersed in the mellow beauty of a French countryside.

I lowered the long barrel of my Smith and Wesson, brightly painted with red lead to keep it from rusting.

Julien had seen me hesitate, and he lowered his arm as well.

Now he looks at me anxiously, doubtless wondering what's happening to me.

'La Paloma' is happening to me, that's all: my Spanish childhood, right in the face.

But the young soldier has turned around and is walking slowly back to where his bike waits motionless on its kickstand.

Then I grab my weapon with both hands. Aiming at the German's back, I squeeze the trigger of the Smith and Wesson. I hear the reports of Julien's revolver beside me: he, too, has fired several times.

The German soldier leaps forward, as though pushed violently from the back. Because he actually has been pushed from the back, by the brutal impact of the bullets.

He falls full length.

I collapse, with my face in the cool grass, and pound my fist furiously on the flat rock that had concealed us.

'Shit, shit, shit!'

I shout louder and louder, frightening Julien.

He shakes me, screaming that now is not the moment to go into hysterics – we have to get out of there. Take the motor cycle, and the German's machine-gun, and beat it.

He's right. There's nothing else to do.

We get up and cross the river, scrambling over the rocks that block the watercourse. Julien takes the dead man's gun, after turning over his body. And it's true: the German does have blue eyes, wide open with surprise.

We flee on the motor cycle, which starts up on the first kick.

. . .

I can't hear the Kaddish anymore. I no longer hear death singing in Yiddish. I've been lost among my memories, not paying any attention. How long ago did he stop his chanting? Did he really die, just now, sneaking off while my thoughts were elsewhere for a moment?

I lean over him, listening to his heart. I think I hear something, still beating inside his sunken chest. Something quite muffled, and very far off: a sigh that's fading away, running out of breath. A heart that's stopping, that's what it sounds like to me.

It's pretty pathetic.

I look around for help. There is none. There's no one. The Little Camp was cleared the day after the liberation of Buchenwald. The survivors were installed in the most comfortable building of the main camp, or else in the barracks formerly used by the SS *Totenkopf* Division.

I look around: no one. There is only the sound of the wind blowing, as always, on this slope of the Ettersberg. In spring or winter, mild breeze or icy blast, there is always the wind on the Ettersberg. A wind for all seasons on Goethe's hillside, stirring the smoke from the crematory.

In the Habitations of Death

Nellie Sachs, born in Berlin in 1891 and a published poet in the 1920s, emigrated to Sweden in 1940. Her first book after the war, In the Habitations of Death, *commemorates its Jewish victims.*

O THE CHIMNEYS

And though after my skin worms destroy this
body, yet in my flesh shall I see God – Job, 19:26

O the chimneys
On the ingeniously devised habitations of death
When Israel's body drifted as smoke
Through the air –
Was welcomed by a star, a chimney sweep,
A star that turned black
Or was it a ray of sun?

O the chimneys!
Freedomway for Jeremiah and Job's dust –
Who devised you and laid stone upon stone
The road for refugees of smoke?

O the habitations of death,
Invitingly appointed
For the host who used to be a guest –
O you fingers
Laying the threshold
Like a knife between life and death –

O you chimneys,
O you fingers
And Israel's body as smoke through the air!

YOU ONLOOKERS

Whose eyes watched the killing.
As one feels a stare at one's back
You feel on your bodies
The glances of the dead.

How many dying eyes will look at you
When you pluck a violet from its hiding place?
How many hands be raised in supplication
In the twisted martyr-like branches
Of old oaks?
How much memory grows in the blood
Of the evening sun?

O the unsung cradlesongs
In the night cry of the turtledove –
Many a one might have plucked stars from the sky,
Now the old well must do it for them!

You onlookers,
You who raised no hand in murder,
But who did not shake the dust
From your longing,
You who halted there, where dust is changed
To light.

6
World War II

Blitzkrieg

The term 'Blitzkrieg' *(lightning war) was invented by the Nazis during the German campaign against Poland which precipitated the British and French declarations of war in September 1939. It then denoted the use of tanks, air power, subversion, and later paratroops, swiftly to undermine a target country. Opposing forces were outpaced and enveloped. In May 1940 the Nazi invasion of the Low Countries and France exemplified* Blitzkrieg *at its most terrifying, when a major power was brought to surrender in barely six weeks. Troops in retreat were impeded by panicking civilian refugees as the Stuka dive-bombers screamed overhead.*

That momentum of Blitzkrieg *stalled when the Nazis found it was impossible to proceed to invade Britain. But the term was soon appropriated and familiarized by the British to refer to the nightly Luftwaffe raids over their own country. London's blitz was followed by blitzes – air attacks in force – on other British cities. As time went on, it would not seem odd to talk about Germany itself being blitzed by Allied bombers.*

It has been easy to forget that service in bombing planes was as risky as any undertaken in war. Yet whereas fighter pilots were seen, in Britain, as sacrificial heroes, the men of Bomber Command attracted little sympathy after the war ended, and their commander, Harris, was the only British military man of such rank not to be awarded a peerage. The traumas of active service in the USAAF are represented in this anthology by two of Randall Jarrell's poems and extracts from Joseph Heller's Catch-22.

Poland 1939

The poet Czesław Miłosz was in his late twenties when the Nazi army invaded Poland. He remembered his emotions in his memoirs Native Realm *(1968).*

When the blitzkrieg began I felt a need to carry out orders of some sort, and thus to relieve myself of responsibility. Unfortunately, it was not easy to find someone to give orders. But very soon I was wearing something like a uniform made up of ill-matching pieces, unable, however, to revel in any more glorious deeds than taking part in the retreat. The shock of disaster followed immediately. Yet for me that September of 1939 was a breakthrough, which must be hard to imagine for anyone who has never lived through a sudden collapse of the whole structure of collective life. In France, the blitzkrieg did not have the same effect.

I could reduce all that happened to me then to a few things. Lying in the field near a highway bombarded by airplanes, I riveted my eyes on a stone and two blades of grass in front of me. Listening to the whistle of a bomb, I suddenly understood the value of matter: that stone and those two blades of grass formed a whole kingdom, an infinity of forms, shades, textures, lights. They were the universe. I had always refused to accept the division into macro- and micro-cosmos; I preferred to contemplate a piece of bark or a bird's wing rather than sunsets or sunrises. But now I saw into the depths of matter with exceptional intensity.

Something else was the mixture of fury and relief I felt when I realized that nothing was left of the ministries, offices and Army. I slept a deep sleep in the hay barns along the way. The nonsense was over at last. That long-dreaded fulfilment had freed us from the self-reassuring lies, illusions, subterfuges; the opaque had become transparent; only a village well, the roof of a hut, or a plough were real, not the speeches of statesmen recalled now with ferocious irony. The land was singularly naked, as it can only be for people without a state, torn from the safety of their habits.

The Fall of France, 1940

In May 1940, when the German army suddenly burst through Belgium into France, Claude Simon was a twenty-six-year-old cavalryman. His novel The Flanders Road, *published in 1960, centres on the critical moment when the captain commanding him was shot dead by a sniper and the unit disintegrated. (Simon himself was rounded up and sent as a POW to Saxony.) But 'Georges' whose consciousness is central to the novel is not Simon. The actual Captain Rey becomes 'de Reixach', a distant relative of Georges, and also in the unit there is Iglésia, who has been de Reixach's jockey and was the lover of de Reixach's wife Corinne. The central symbol of the novel, a dead horse rotting in the roadway, helps to hold together a complex of considerations of history, sexuality and mortality. Simon's method is that of the French* nouveau roman, *in which minute perceptions of things seen are accorded great importance, but his techniques also recall the 'modernist' stream-of-consciousness novels of Joyce and Woolf. We begin here with Georges reminiscing with Blum, a colleague in the cavalry and now a fellow-prisoner in Germany. Georges assumes that de Reixach, disillusioned by his wife's adultery, deliberately exposed himself to death. He and Iglésia, in flight, found temporary refuge in a café where they got very drunk.*

. . . Saying aloud (Georges): 'But the General killed himself too: not only the one seeking and finding on that road a decent and disguised suicide, but the other one too in his villa, his garden with the raked gravel paths . . . You remember that military review, that ceremony, the soaking field that winter morning in the Ardennes, and he – it's the only time we saw him – with his little jockey's head, that kind of tiny, wrinkled, wizened and parboiled apple, his little jockey's legs in the tiny shiny boots that splattered indifferently through the mud while he passed in front of us without looking at us: a little old man or rather a little old foetus that had just been taken out of its jar of formaldehyde, marvellously well preserved, unchangeable, alert, expeditious and dry, quickly walking along the serried squadrons trailing behind him that group of beribboned, gloved officers, the hilts of their sabres at the hollow of their elbows, and panting as they followed him over the spongy field while he walked on without turning back, probably talking to the veterinary officer – the only one he would have spoken to – of the state of the horses and the bad case of thrush the ground gave them – or the climate – in this part of the country; and then when he learned, that is when he realized, finally understood that his brigade no longer existed, had been not annihilated, destroyed according to the rules – or at least what he thought were the rules – of war: normally, correctly, as for instance, by attacking an impregnable position or even by an artillery pounding, or even – he might have accepted this as a last resort – submerged by an enemy attack: but so to speak absorbed, diluted, dissolved, erased from the general-staff charts without his knowing where nor how nor when: only the couriers returning one after the other without having seen a thing at the place – the village, the woods, the hill, the bridge – where a squadron or a combat group was supposed to be, and even that resulting, according to all appearances, not from a panic, a flight, a rout – a mishap that he could also have acknowledged perhaps, at least have recognized as being in the realm of disastrous but, all in all, normal possibilities, comprising part of the anticipated, the inevitable risks of any battle and which could be remedied by means equally anticipated, as for instance a police barrier at the crossroads and a few summary executions – not a rout, then, since the order the courier was carrying, was supposed to transmit, was invariably an order to fall back and since the position the unit was supposed to be holding and towards which it was headed was itself a retreat position but which, apparently, no one had ever reached, the couriers then continuing farther, in other words towards the preceding retreat position, without ever seeing, on either side of the road, anything but that inextricable, monotonous and enigmatic wake of disasters, in other words not even trucks or burned wagons, or men, or children, or soldiers, or women, or dead horses, but simply detritus, something like a vast public discharge spread over kilometres and kilometres and exuding not the traditional and heroic odour of carrion, of corpses in a state of decomposition, but only of ordure, simply stinking, the way a pile of old tin cans, potato peels and burnt rags can stink, and no more affecting or tragic than a pile of ordure, and just barely usable for scrap-metal collectors or ragpickers, and nothing more until, still advancing, they (the couriers) took – at a turn of the road – another burst of gunfire, which made one more corpse at the bottom of the ditch, the overturned motorcycle still sputtering or catching fire, which made one more of those black cadavers still sitting on one of those twisted and rusty iron carcasses (have you noticed how fast it goes, that acceleration of time, the extraordinary speed with which the war produces phenomena – rust, stains, putrefaction, corruption of bodies – which in ordinary times usually take months or years to happen?) like some macabre caricatures of motor-cyclists still leaning over their handle-bars, riding at a terrible speed, decomposing that way (spreading beneath them in the green grass the bituminous and excremental brownish blob – oil, grease, burnt flesh – consisting of a dark sticky liquid) at a terrible speed –, the couriers, then, returning one after the other without having found anything, or not coming back at all, his brigade somehow evaporated, conjured away, erased, sponged out without leaving a trace save a few dazed, wandering men hidden in the woods or drunk and finally I had a minimum of consciousness left, sitting in front of that tiny cone of gin that now I no longer even had the strength to empty while slumped down on the bench overpowered by my own weight I was trying with that obstinate consciousness of drunkards to get up and go away, realizing that they (Iglésia and that old man whom we had first robbed then almost killed and who had then offered to take us through the lines after dark) were just as drunk as I was, starting again without being discouraged to lean my body forward so that its own weight helped me get up from that bench to which I seemed to be nailed at the same time that my hands attempted to push back the table, realizing at the same moment that these various movements remained at the stage of impulses and that I was still absolutely motionless, a kind of ghostly and transparent double of myself – and without the slightest effect – repeating over and over the same gestures leaning my body forward the simultaneous effort of the thighs the arms pushing until it realized that nothing had happened coming back then melting back into my own body that was still sitting there which it tried to encourage once again but without any more success that was why I was trying to get my head clear thinking that if I could manage to settle clarify my perceptions I would also manage to order and direct my movements and then in succession:

first that door which I had first to reach and then walk through, seeing it reflected in the mirror over the bar one of those rectangular mirrors like the ones you can see or rather in which you can see yourself at the barber's the upper corners rounded the frame not enamelled white like in barber-shops but covered with a coat of brown paint, threadlike reliefs like noodles decorating the moulding like astragals asterisks starting with a central honeysuckle motif in the middle of each side, and since the mirror was tilted the verticals reflected in it were also tilted, starting at the bottom with the row of necks and spigots of bottles lined up on the shelf immediately underneath then the raw wood floor that seemed to tilt upwards at an angle of about twenty degrees, grey in the shadow, yellow in the rectangle of sunshine extending obliquely from the door open on to the street, the two jambs tilted too as if the wall were falling in, the doorstep a stone block then the pavement then the long rectangular stones forming the kerb then the first rows of cobbles in the street to which I had my back turned

and probably because of the drunkenness, impossible to be visually aware of anything but that that mirror and what was reflected in it my eyes clinging to it so to speak the way a drunkard clings to a lamppost as to the only fixed point in a vague invisible and colourless universe from which only voices reached me probably that of the woman (the proprietress) and of the two or three men who were there, and then one of them saying The front has collapsed but sounding to me like The runt has collapsed, able to see the little dead dog floating downstream with the current its pink and white belly swollen the hair stiff already stinking

then the rectangle of sunlight on the floor disappearing then reappearing then disappearing again but not entirely: this time I could see thanks to the mirror the bottom of the woman's skirt her two calves and her two feet in slippers all tilted as if she were falling over backward

then her voice coming from outside coming into the café over her shoulder probably talking with her head half turned in other words if the mirror had been high enough I would have seen her in profile; that way she could go on watching what she had just seen and still be heard from inside the café saying Here come some soldiers

and this time I found myself managing to get up clinging to the table hearing one of the conical glasses overturn roll across the table describing what was probably a circle round its base until it reached the edge of the table and fell hearing it break just as I reached the woman and looked over her shoulder seeing the grey car with the strange top like a kind of coffin with square-cut sides and four backs and four round helmets and Good God those are . . . Good God you

and she Oh you know I never pay any attention to uniforms

and I Good God

and she I've already met one this morning on my way to get the milk, he spoke French it must have been an officer because he was looking at a map sitting in a side-car, he asked me if this was the road I told him Yes It was only afterwards that I thought he looked funny

then crossing the café again shaking Iglésia who was asleep his elbows spread out on the table his cheek on his arm saying Wake up Good God wake up we have got to get out of here Good God let's get going

the woman still on the doorstep saying a moment later Here come some more

this time I was right behind her looking in the same direction in other words the direction opposite where the car had vanished so that the two cyclists looked as though they were chasing the car but they were wearing khaki

for a second I saw the soldiers of the two armies chasing each other round and round the block of houses like in the Opera or those comic films people dashing in those parodic and burlesque chases the lover the husband brandishing a revolver the hotel chambermaid the adulterous wife the bellboy the little pastrycook the police then again the lover in pants and garters running his body straight up and down his elbows pressed to his sides raising his knees high the husband with the revolver the woman in panties black stockings and camisole and so on everything went round in the sunlight I didn't see the step down to the pavement and almost landed head first I took a few strides my body almost horizontal at the limit of disequilibrium then I grabbed hold of his handle-bars

the face of the man under the helmet fat red unshaven and streaming with sweat furious his eyes furious and wild his mouth furious shouting What is it what Get out of here let go, then I saw the truck a dispatch car vaguely camouflaged hastily daubed with yellow brown and green paint off balance leaning on one side as it took the turn then straightening I waved my arms standing in the middle of the road

I saw from his insignia he was an engineer he must have been from the reserve staff he looked like an official with his steel-rimmed glasses, walking towards me as soon as he had stepped out of the cab furious feverish already shouting not listening to me and he repeating too What do you want what is it you want I tried to explain but he was still furious feverish constantly glancing over his shoulder in the direction they had come from holding his revolver first turning towards me then he forgot it waving it gesticulating holding me by a button of my jacket the work clothes the man had given me, shouting What are those clothes, again I tried to explain to him but he wasn't listening constantly turning round to look at the turn in the road, nervous, I took out my *livret* my identity disc that I had kept but he kept looking over his shoulder then I said That way, pointing to the place where the little grey car had disappeared and he What? and I They just went by five minutes ago four of them in a little car, and he shouting What if I had you shot? I tried to begin explaining again but he let go of me heading for the truck again still glancing in the direction they had come from (I looked too almost expecting to see the little coffin-shaped car appear that meanwhile must have had time to get round the block of houses) then he went back inside sat down closed the door from the window frame the window was rolled down he was holding the revolver now the barrel aimed at me his thin greyish sweating face leaning forward still looking behind him his myopic eyes behind the glasses the truck started up

running behind: there were about ten of them under the canvas sitting on the two benches on each side, I hung on to the back flap running trying to get in but they pushed me back they looked drunk too I managed to get one leg in one of them tried to hit me with his gun butt he was probably too drunk the butt coming down next to my hand then I let go still having time to see one of them head thrown back drinking greedily out of a bottle then he aimed at me one eye closed and threw it but they were already too far away and it fell at least a yard in front of my feet broke there was still some wine in it that made a dark spot on the cobbles with tentacles splinters of greenish black glass scattered around then I heard a shot but not even the bullet passing, drunk as they were and shaken up jolted in that truck it wasn't surprising then it disappeared

he had managed to wake up and was standing in front of the door in front of the woman his big bulging eyes looking at me with an offended expression, I screamed We've got to get out of here We've got to get our clothes back on He wanted to have me shot one of those boys took a shot at me

but he didn't move went on looking at me with that same expression of outrage reproving sullen then he raised his arm towards the café behind him, saying He said he'd cook us a duck tonight

and I A duck?

and he He's going to give us something to eat He said he

then I stopped listening, I headed overland climbing back up the hill the sun had that insistent obsessive presence of long afternoons in spring when it lingers endlessly lingering still high in the sky days that never end as if it were immobilized on the verge of setting but not able to move held motionless by some Joshua there must have been at least two or three days that it had forgotten to set since it had risen reddening at first softly tinting the sky purple the rosy-fingered dawn but I hadn't seen the moment when it had appeared only my shadow elongated and diaphanous, a quadruped's shadow on the road where there was nothing but those motionless heaps like rags and the idiot face of Wack lying back staring at me I had it right in my eyes back now motionless in the white sky

turning round I saw he was following me; so he had finally made up his mind, he was still at the foot of the hill had just passed the last houses walking up the meadow staggering a little once he stumbled fell but got up again then I stopped and waited for him when he caught up with me he stumbled again and fell on all fours for a moment vomiting then he stood up again wiping his mouth on his sleeves and started walking.

Perhaps it was at this same moment that the General had killed himself? He had nevertheless a car, a driver, petrol. All he had to do was put on his helmet, pull on his gloves and leave, walking down the front steps of that villa (I suppose it must have been a villa: that's the usual place where a brigadier general's command post is installed, the chateaux being traditionally reserved to the division generals and the farms to mere colonels): a villa then, with probably a plum tree in bloom on the lawn, a gateway painted white, a gravel driveway turning between the aucuba hedges with their mottled leaves, and a middle-class salon decorated with the inevitable bouquet of holly branches or dyed feathers – silver or autumnal red – on the corner of the mantelpiece or the grand piano, the vase pushed back to make room for the sprawled-out maps, and from which (the villa) had issued for the last eight days, orders and directives almost all as useful as those given during the same period by the strategist of a provincial café commenting on the daily communiqué he had, then, only to walk down those steps, climb calmly into his car with its flag, and drive straight ahead without stopping to the division headquarters or to his army corps headquarters, and to wait around there long enough for someone to give him a new command, as they did to the others. And instead of that, when his officers were installed in the second car, the motors already running, the motorcycles of the three or four couriers still sputtering, the car with its flags waiting with the door open, he blew his brains out. And in the racket of the motors and the cars no one even heard it. And perhaps it wasn't even the dishonour, the sudden revelation of his incapacity (after all perhaps he wasn't absolutely a fool – how could anyone tell? – perhaps it wasn't impossible to imagine that his orders weren't stupid but the best, the most pertinent, even inspired – but again how could anyone tell since none of them ever reached its destination?): probably something else: a kind of void a hole. Bottomless. Absolute.'

. . .

. . . standing there (Georges) without making a move, without daring to move, trying to hold his breath, to calm the deafening murmur of his blood, the green and transparent May twilight like glass too, and in his throat that kind of nausea he tried to choke down, swallowing, thinking between two deafening rushes of air: It's from running too much, thinking: But maybe it's all that alcohol? thinking that he should have tried to vomit the way Iglésia did a little while ago in the field, thinking: But vomit what? trying to remember the last time he had eaten oh yes that piece of sausage this morning in the forest (but was it in the morning or when?), his stomach full of the gin he seemed to feel inside him like an alien body, unassimilable, a solidified ball or rather half-solidified and heavy, something like a mercury, so a little while ago he should have put a finger down his throat and vomited, at least he would have been relieved, when they were in the house putting on their uniforms again, and then standing (again stiff, heavy, exhausted, in his stiff, heavy cocoon of cloth and leather) alone in the room, still wondering if he was going to vomit or not and where could Iglésia have gone, while out of the window he watched the engineers' trucks retreating down the road, no bigger than toys, following each other in a regular, hurried flight, then Iglésia there again without his being able to say when and how he had returned (any more than when he had vanished), Georges starting, turning round, looking at him with that same exhausted, incredulous look, and Iglésia: 'Those poor nags, after all they have to eat too,' and he thinking: 'Good God, he's even managed to think of that. Almost dead drunk. Like the other one this morning to let them drink. As if . . .', then no longer thinking, not finishing his train of thought, no longer interested in it turning and looking at what Iglésia's bulging, yellowish, astonished and incredulous eyes were looking at now, both of them standing there motionless for a minute while in the distance beyond the sloping fields the little toy cars went on following each other: then jogging down the staircase, running across the farm's deserted courtyard and taking the lane they had followed that morning – but in the opposite direction and all he could see now (lying flat on his belly in the grass of the ditch, panting, still trying to choke down the terrible wheezing sound in his chest) with the narrow horizontal strip to which the world now reduced itself limited above by the visor of his helmet, below by the crisscrossing of the blades of grass in the ditch just in front of his eyes, vague, then more distinct, then no longer blades of grass: a green blur in the green twilight, thinning out then stopping at the place where the lane joined the road, then the stones of the road and the sentry's two black boots, carefully polished, with their shiny accordion pleats at the ankle, the axis of the boots forming the base of an inverted V in the opening of which, on the other side of the road, the dead horse appeared and disappeared between the wheels of the trucks jolting across the cobbles, still in the same place as that morning but apparently flattened out, as though it had gradually melted during the day like those snowmen who seem to sink imperceptibly into the earth, as though attacked at their base, gradually shrinking with the thaw until finally only the largest masses and the struts are left – broomsticks, laths – that have served as an armature: here the belly, enormous now, swollen, distended, and the bones, as if the middle of the body had absorbed the whole substance of the endless carcass, the bones with their round heads holding up as well they could the crust of peeling mud that served as an envelope: but no more flies now, as if they had abandoned it, as if there were nothing left to take from it, as if there were already – but that wasn't possible, Georges thought, not in one day –, no longer rotten and stinking meat, but transmuted, assimilated by the deep earth that hides beneath its hair of grass and leaves the bones of every defunct Rosinante and every defunct Bucephalus (and the defunct riders, the defunct coachmen and the defunct Alexanders) reverted to crumbling lime or . . . (but he was wrong: suddenly one flew out – this time from inside the nostrils – and although he was more than fifteen yards away he saw it (probably thanks to that nauseating and minute visual acuity drunkenness affords) as distinctly (hairy, blue-black, shiny, and though his ears were splintered by the incessant racket of the trucks moving at high speed, hearing it too: its impetuous, voracious, furious buzzing) as the nailheads in the four horse-shoes lying on the edge beside the road and now, in relation to Georges, in the foreground) . . . reverted, then, to the state of crumbling lime, of fossils, which he himself was probably becoming out of immobility, watching, impotent, the slow transmutation of his own substance starting with his arm that he could feel dying gradually, growing numb, devoured not by worms but by a slowly mounting tingle that was perhaps the secret stirring of atoms in the process of permutating in order to organize themselves according to a different structure, mineral or crystalline, in the crystalline twilight from which he was still separated by the thickness of a leaf of cigarette paper, unless it wasn't a leaf of cigarette paper at all but the contact of the twilight itself on his skin for such, he thought, is the exquisite delicacy of women's flesh that you hesitate to believe you're really touching them, the skin like feathers, grass leaves, transparent air, fragile as crystal, so that he could still hear her panting faintly, unless it was his own breathing, unless he was now as dead as the horse and already half swallowed up, taken back by the earth his flesh mingling with the moist clay, his bones mingling with the stones, for perhaps it was a simple matter of immobility and then you simply became a little chalk, sand and mud again . . .

Fighter

After Marshal Pétain sued for peace on 17 June 1940, the next target for German invasion became Britain. The embittered British troops evacuated through Dunkirk around the beginning of the month were short of arms. So was the civilian 'Home Guard', raised from May onwards, which numbered one and a half million men by September. But the Royal Navy retained command of the seas. And RAF Fighter Command had planes of high quality. From July through to September Fighter Command, though desperately hard pressed, denied the Luftwaffe that mastery of the air which was essential if the invasion force now massed across the Channel was to succeed. In the south-east of England civilians were enthralled by 'dog-fights' in the sky between British and German planes. Exaggerated accounts of German losses greatly boosted morale. Spitfire and Hurricane pilots were acclaimed as the 'knights of the air'.

Len Deighton's study Fighter *(1977) looks coolly, in impressive detail, at the personnel, tactics, strategies and machines of the 'Battle of Britain'.*

[German aircraft destroyed]

	RAF claim 1940	*RAF claim post-war*	*German High Command diary*
15 August	185	76	55
18 August	155	71	49
15 September	185	56	50
27 September	153	55	42
Totals	678	258	196

Wild claims for each day's total victories had to be supported, so the RAF accepted the exaggerated reports of the individual pilots. For instance, the victory claims for Bader's wing alone, on 15 September, were greater than the German figures for the entire day's extensive air fighting. To avoid the consequences of their policy, the Air Ministry refused to investigate their pilots' claims, and simply said that individual scores were not recognized by the RAF.

The RAF's evasive attitude is revealed in the secret letters and instructions on the subject. A secret letter from Fighter Command HQ on 23 September describes the inflated RAF claims as disquieting. An accompanying analysis of the five weeks from 8 August to 11 September showed that the RAF announced that 1,631 enemy aircraft were destroyed and 584 aircraft were 'probably destroyed'. If one assumes that half of the probables were downed, this makes a claim of well over 1,900 aircraft for the five weeks under review. Yet during this period a mere 316 enemy aircraft wrecks were counted. Even allowing for the fact that the pilot of a crippled German plane will head for home (and so possibly fall into the sea), this is obviously highly inaccurate.

The Luftwaffe formed an *Abschusskommission* to investigate the individual claims of its pilots. Sometimes it took a year to reach a decision, and there was a firm rule that *without a witness no claim would be even considered*. Its regulations were stringent and its results conservative. Although the RAF usually awarded a half-share to all the pilots who contributed to the destruction of a downed enemy aircraft, the Germans simply credited the unit with one victory but did not allow any individuals to share it. For this reason, German unit scores do not tally with the sum of their individual pilots' victories. But German unit scores for this period come remarkably close to known RAF losses. (The average *Jagdgruppe* shot down fifty-five aircraft.)

Anyone reading about 'official RAF scores' should remember that there are no such things. But in the light of recent research, the scores generally accepted as the largest are seventeen aircraft shot down by Sergeant Frantisek, a Czech flying with 303 (Polish) Squadron, and sixteen destroyed by Flight Lieutenant McKellar of 605 (County of Warwick) Squadron.

The tactics of the air war – as they emerged – were not very much different from the lessons that had been learned from 1914 to 1918. Height was still the trump card, with attacks out of the sun the most reliable tactic. Heavier fighters, that accelerated more quickly into the dive, were often forgiven other faults. Acceleration in level flight is a quality not listed in any aircraft specification, but for a pilot coming under fire, it often meant the difference between life and death. The twin-engined [Messerschmitt] Bf 110 and the Hurricane were sluggish in this respect.

The most common type of attack was a dive out of the sun, pulling out behind, and under the tail of, the enemy, and firing while in this blind spot. A cliché of the fiction inspired by the First World War, this tactic continued in use right until the end of the war in 1945.

The head-on formation attacks that were invented by the pilots of 111 Squadron were abandoned during the Battle, because of the number of collisions suffered. However, this tactic was reintroduced by German fighter pilots and used against the big USAAF daylight formations later in the war. It became a standard tactic because it minimized the ability of the bombers to return fire during the head-on approach, while the heavy cannon of the fighters gave them a good chance of inflicting fatal damage.

The fighter pilots themselves had the same physical advantages that marked the First World War's aces: above average eyesight and the ability to see distant aircraft (not quite the same thing), coupled with very quick reactions. For this reason, many of the younger pilots were more successful than their more experienced elders, although experience improved a pilot's chance to survive.

No less vital than eyesight was the ability – and the willingness – to fly very close to the enemy. The aces would not open fire until they were 100 yards away, while the average pilot was breaking off attacks at that distance. The design of the reflector gun-sights – used by both sides – did nothing to help. When the German gun-sight ring was completely filled by the wings of a Spitfire, the two aircraft were still 335 yards apart, too far away for effective shooting.

Scrutiny of Air Ministry secret records (only now released) shows the cloud-cuckoo-land that the RAF High Command enjoyed at this time. Fictitious German fighter aircraft are reported in great detail, and the writers of Intelligence Summaries are obsessed with highly unlikely secret devices, such as tin boxes thrown by bomber crews at RAF fighters, and repeatedly report that the Germans are using captured RAF aircraft in all kinds of bizarre colour schemes.

About 3,000 RAF men flew in the Battle of Britain, although this number is marginally reduced if only single-seat fighters are included. Over 80 per cent of these flyers were from the United Kingdom; the remainder included 147 Poles, eighty-seven Czechs, twenty-nine Belgians, fourteen Frenchmen, seven Americans, ten Irishmen, a Palestinian, and many men from the Commonwealth nations, including ninety-four Canadians and 101 New Zealanders.

But these figures do not reflect the skill, daring, and determination of this 'remainder'. Poles and Czechs were not permitted to participate in the air fighting until they had mastered the rudiments of the English language and flying procedures. When they did start operations these homeless men, motivated often by a hatred bordering upon despair, fought with a terrible and merciless dedication.

The Australians, New Zealanders, Rhodesians, and Canadians were often men who had paid their own fare to England in order to join the peacetime RAF. Perhaps this sort of determination explains why their contribution was of an exceptional kind. The Commonwealth provided some of the best and bravest flyers and suffered disproportionate casualties. For instance, of twenty-two Australians, fourteen were killed. South Africa also contributed twenty-two flyers, and of these nine were killed during a period in which the average air-crew fatalities in Fighter Command were 17 per cent.

And the skills of this 'remainder' can be recognized among the aces of the Battle. Of the top ten fighter pilots (scoring fourteen or more victories), one was Czech, one was Polish, two were New Zealanders, and one Australian. Only five were from the UK. From such tiny samplings it would be reckless to draw any conclusions, but it is interesting to note that in this list of aces the Hurricane and Spitfire are distributed evenly down the list from top to bottom, with one pilot flying both types of aircraft.

German fighter pilots came to the end of 1940 with considerable reservations about the Bf 109E. When the new Bf 109F arrived, some liked it even less. The difficulties with the Messerschmitt wings had now persuaded the design team to omit any kind of wing guns. A vastly improved cannon, firing through the airscrew boss, had been made to function, but this was now the sole armament, apart from two machine-guns mounted on the cowling. Galland, who thought machine-guns ineffective for air fighting, said that such armament was quite inadequate for the average fighter pilot. *Major* Walter Oesau, a Battle of Britain ace, preferred his old E model and kept it going until lack of replacement parts forced him to fly the Bf 109F. Mölders, on the other hand, thought one centrally mounted cannon was worth two in the wings. Armament experts pointed out that any kind of wing gun suffered a high rate of jamming. A compromise was reached by sending a kit of parts to the front-line units, so that an extra cannon (20-mm MG 151) could be bolted under each wing. It up-gunned the Messerschmitt but it impoverished its performance and made it unwieldy in combat.

Men who had been watching the intense rivalry between Galland and Mölders throughout that summer were perhaps amused to see both of these legendary air fighters' totals (fifty-two and fifty-four respectively) passed by *Major* Helmut Wick, whose string of fifty-six successes had made him *Kommodore* of JG 2 (*Richthofen*), which he took over from Harry von Bülow-Bothkamp, the First World War ace. At forty victories Wick was, like his rivals, awarded the oak leaves to the Knight's Cross.

The twenty-five-year-old Wick was highly regarded by the lower ranks in the fighter force for his readiness to answer back to the top brass. When Wick's unit was paraded for a visit by *Feldmarschall* Sperrle, Wick was gently told that his ground crews were unmilitary in appearance. Wick asked his Air Fleet commander innocently if he didn't think that refuelling, rearming, and servicing the fighters, to maximize the operational status, wasn't more important than getting a haircut.

As the Battle came to an end, the most successful fighter pilot the RAF had put into the air – Sergeant pilot Josef Frantisek – died. The Czech, who declined to fly with the Czech Squadron, preferring to remain 'a guest' of the Poles with whom he got on so well, failed to get home. Soon after this, Wick also was killed in action. He parachuted down into the wintry waters of the Channel while his men circled, unable to save him. 'It was as if a curtain went down, and the play ended,' remembered one of Wick's flyers.

As already described, the importance of the German fighter squadrons became more and more evident as the Battle progressed. In the later stages, the bomber fleets were greatly outnumbered by the necessary fighter escort, and the bombers' use was limited by the availability of fighters. And so it seems incomprehensible that the Luftwaffe did not provide their single-seat fighters with an external fuel tank, until the E-7 version came along too late for the battle.

The first thing that must be said is that the range and endurance of the Spitfire and Hurricane were no better than those of the Bf 109E that fought in the Battle. And certainly the Spitfire and Hurricane had no long-range tanks at this time. But this comparison does not take into account the role of the Luftwaffe as an offence arm, used with the army, to penetrate enemy air space. The RAF Fighter Command was designed entirely to defend Britain from foreign attackers.

Luftwaffe planners saw no need for long-range fighters because of the extraordinary fleet of Junkers Ju 52/3m, three-engined transport aircraft available to them to move their support units forward to captured airfields. By this means German squadrons could leap-frog ahead, always operating from fields near to the front line . . .

In 1940 the Bf 109 averaged about ninety minutes' flying time. But climbing and getting into formation, as well as finding airfields on the return, meant that the German fighters never had more than about thirty minutes over English soil.

External fuel tanks would have eliminated the relay escorts that forced fighter pilots to fly four or five sorties a day, and consequently would have changed the tactical map. Luftwaffe fighter units could have been situated in Holland, beyond British radar coverage, and raids could have been flown by indirect routes over the water. Many pilots lost at sea in 1940 would have had enough fuel to get home safely and have flown again.

But instead of extra fuel, the rack under the new Bf 109E-7 usually held a bomb. This made these aircraft suitable only as nuisance raiders. Most pilots were anxious to release their bomb as soon as possible rather than risk combat while carrying it. Relegating the Bf 109E-7 to such a role demonstrated a profound misunderstanding of the importance of the single-seat fighter . . .

The Battle of Britain saw the end of the Luftwaffe's reputation as an invincible force. The 'yellow-nosed Abbeville boys', a unit of Bf 109 fighters with yellow-painted cowlings that had achieved an awesome reputation during the summer of 1940, proved no more than a reflection of Fighter Command's state of mind. There were no 'Abbeville boys': many Bf 109 units had painted their cowling with a yellow patch so that friend and foe could be easily distinguished in battle.

For the RAF, the quantity and quality of pilots had come nearest to bringing disaster. Bravery was no substitute for training, skill, and experience, and as the Battle progressed, Fighter Command put into combat squadrons of men who should not have been asked to meet the Germans on equal terms. There were fifty-eight naval pilots, an American parachutist with virtually no experience of military flying, and Polish pilots who had had only a brief experience of the British high-speed monoplanes and even less of the English language. As the fighting progressed, and the men leading the formations suffered unduly heavy casualties, too many of them were replaced by outside officers without combat experience. This extraordinary procedure had a doubly bad effect upon the other pilots, for it deprived them of promotion and sent them into battle with inadequate leaders. Worst of all was the way in which pilots 'went operational' before they had properly mastered their machines – ten hours on fighters was not unusual – and without any realistic operational training.

The American Newsmen See the London Blitz Begin

On 7 September 1940 the Luftwaffe, which had almost extinguished Fighter Command by accurate bombing of airfields, was foolishly switched to attack civilian London, which was bombarded nightly for more than two months, then frequently until mid-May the following year. As this development occurred, the most important allies that beleaguered Britain had were the US journalists in London, most of them strongly anti-Nazi, and using all the influence they possessed to draw their own nation into the war against Hitler.

Among these often hard-edged people Vincent Sheean might have stood seigneurially apart. Cosmopolitan, at home with the 'high arts', he had dined pre-war with Europe's great men, as his memoir Between the Thunder and the Sun *(1943) was at pains to demonstrate. But it also pays tribute to American colleagues.*

On Saturday, September 7, 1940, Ed Murrow, Ben Robertson and I drove down the Thames to Tilbury and crossed to Gravesend. There had been considerable bombing in the Thames estuary for some weeks. Tilbury in particular had been repeatedly hit, and we wanted to get some idea of the extent of the damage and how it was being repaired.

Edward Murrow, dark and taciturn and often beset by gloom, was at the same time capable of sustained hilarity and high spirits; the range of his moral orchestra was great. He was the European director for the Columbia Broadcasting System, and even before the war I had sometimes spoken to America over his air. He was now using that air himself to such purpose that he became – particularly in 1940 and 1941 – one of the familiar voices of the nation; I discovered afterward that he was as well known to families throughout the country as their own members. The men and women who speak from that inexplicable instrument in the American living-room have a place in the national mind unlike that of politicians, journalists or writers; they live in the house, so to speak. Ed was talking to millions of Americans at certain stated hours every day, and for many of them he was like part of the evening meal, as indispensable as a knife and fork. He used this new, strange potency with caution, as did most of his colleagues, restricting himself to an account of the latest news with little or no comment upon it, and yet (like Bill Shirer, who did the same thing from Berlin) there was sometimes a world of significance in the turn of a phrase, the accent of the voice. He was fiercely in earnest about the war, fiercely impatient with sham, incompetence and muddle; he liked the English people well enough to be savagely critical of their government; and yet he was capable of putting forward a calm, uncoloured version of all the vast drama of the day so that it passed both the British censors and the radio regulations at home. For a sustained effort, his daily broadcasts to America during 1940 and 1941 seem to me the finest thing the new instrument of communication has given us. The instrument is a thing of the moment, like the air over which it breathes; these broadcasts are not the same thing in print. They depend upon the events of a single day, the quality of a voice which has been tempered by fury, fatigue or sorrow, the particular phrasing of an hour. I used to hear Ed, seated in a stuffy little room in the bowels of the earth underneath the BBC building, and imagine the thousands upon thousands of American living-rooms and dining-rooms in which these words were being heard with all the possible combinations and gradations of attention or inattention . . .

As a correspondent – that is, going about the ways of the world, seeing things and talking to people – Ed Murrow seemed to me as remarkable as he was at his own microphone. His courage, endurance and obliviousness to fatigue made it possible for him to survive many months of a cruel schedule. He could go without sleep as long as might be necessary, broadcasting at all sorts of hours and working like a slave between times. His courage was of the kind I most respect: that is, it did not consist in lack of sensitivity to danger, but in a professional determination to ignore it in the interests of his job. I have been whirled around London in his open car while the bombs were thundering down and the searchlights made fantastic patterns in the sky; I am always prompt to proclaim my fear on such occasions. Ed would get a little grimmer, a little wrier and drier, and say little or nothing. In the first air raid over London (August 24, 1940), when areas far to the east were bombed and great fires started in the night sky, Ed and I were broadcasting in a sort of round-up with several other speakers stationed throughout London. Ed himself was on the steps of St Martin-in-the-Fields, in Trafalgar Square; I was on a balcony of the Piccadilly Hotel, overlooking Piccadilly; Eric Sevareid was at the Palais de Danse in Hammersmith; Mr J. B. Priestley was, I think, at the Cenotaph. The sirens sounded just as Ed was beginning to speak. We did not hear each other broadcast; we began and ended on a light signal without having any idea of what the others had said; it was all improvised, and must have sounded extraordinarily unreal to the listeners across the sea. Your truly realistic air-raid broadcast could only be made, I should imagine, in a magnificent New York studio with an infinity of gadgets for sound effects and ample time for rehearsal. Our air-raid broadcast involved nothing more than the connivance of time and space (an intersection of time-space lines), so that as we described the behaviour of the people in our line of vision, and spoke of the glow in the sky, we were all aware that it very probably would convince the listener less than any well-drilled studio performance.

Yet it was real, and none of us is likely to forget it. The bombs did not come near us – none fell in the centre of London – and the guns, too, were mostly down the river; but it was the first raid. The Germans used screaming bombs that night (I heard two of them) and the long wail was indeed a dreadful sound. The fire down the river glowed all night.

. . .

We drove through ruined areas in Tilbury's mean streets and saw how the people would creep back to the very edge of the ruins, into houses which had been condemned as unsafe. An old man in his shirt-sleeves, smoking a pipe on the doorstep of a more or less intact house on the brink of a crater, was watching his granddaughter play in the gutter. A woman hung out clothes on the line; the dust had hardly settled properly from the last night's bombing. The children, like children of other races all over the earth, found toys in the wreckage and treasured bits of shrapnel. (Down at Dover a Messerschmitt cannon shell was worth three big chunks of shrapnel, in the barter of their kind.) The barrage balloons, which had become far more numerous of late, swung lazily in the clouded sunlight. We lunched at the riverside inn and crossed in the automobile ferry to Gravesend. The vast river, which used to be crowded with every kind of shipping at this point, was almost deserted. Launches and small craft belonging to the patrols were to be seen making their rounds; the ferry still ran; we saw one freighter making its way up to the docks. At Gravesend the inn beside the river was open and seemed to be doing good business; we had difficulty getting rooms for the night.

From Gravesend, busy with Saturday afternoon shoppers, we drove up the hill and off in the direction of Chatham. The road over the hill was dotted with signs of the air war. At one crossroads a crew stood guard over an air-raid siren installation. Ben told us about the siren near the Bank of England, which neither Ed nor I had noticed: it flowered in a big horn from the feet of the Duke of Wellington's statue. At one wayside inn the mistress of the house was cheerful. 'We always go upstairs when the sirens sound,' she said. 'We get worried downstairs; we think it's safer up there.' A week or so later this inn – which was a landmark for us after this day – had ceased to exist. There had been scattered bombs all over this area, and we saw a good many craters which represented little or no real damage. We spent some hours vainly chasing the ghost of a Dornier plane which was said to have crashed the day before somewhere in the neighbourhood. Ed's car nosed its way through shaded lanes into forgotten villages where it was difficult to imagine that such an invention as the airplane was even known. The Dornier was elusive: everybody had heard of it, nobody had seen it, and, of course, we had new directions in each village. After some hours of this we turned back toward the Thames and were driving through flat fields when we noticed some aircraftmen working on a wrecked plane. We got out to investigate and found a Hurricane which had crashed some days before. It was being stripped for everything of value or use that was left intact on it. We had bought some apples at a farmhouse where we stopped during the afternoon; now, on a sloping bank beside the road, we stretched out to eat apples and feel the warmth of the late afternoon sun.

At this point it began – the great air attack which was to last for weeks and end in a confession of failure (one of the very few) by the Germans.

The first thing we heard was a far-off hum of many motors. The familiar sound brought us to our feet at once, and before we had had time to get our bearings the first formation was directly over us. The roar of anti-aircraft and bombs had come swiftly nearer until it now seemed very close. The first formation was of thirty or more planes at a considerable altitude, fifteen thousand feet (perhaps) or above. Each plane was distinct and black in the clear afternoon sky, and they took their orderly, undisturbed course straight up the river. The thunder of the bombs grew heavier as we stood there in the road, peering up under our tin hats. To the left of us a flight of Hurricanes rushed into the sky like larks and pursued the black visitors further up the river. The rat-tat-tat of the machine-guns died away.

'This is a bad place to be,' said I, ever mindful of security, 'in case there are more of them. Let's get farther up from the river, where we can see without catching bombs.'

We got into the car and drove toward the hill-top, where the main road ran from Chatham to Gravesend. Whilst we were driving another formation went over and the bombs thundered again. Without attempting to go farther we left the car at the side of the main road and took refuge in a sunken road – a small old road that had seen many wars – cutting into it at right angles. Interception from the airdromes down-river was going on meanwhile, and the machine-gun chatter could be heard in intervals of bombing and cannonade.

Our sunken road had all the properties of a good ditch. I have ever been a partisan of the good ditch, and think every modern road should be built with one alongside. Here we could flatten ourselves against the tufted side bank when the planes were directly overhead, and when they had passed beyond us we could crawl up and look over the edge. Before we had been here long, a bus on the Chatham–Gravesend line stopped at our refuge and disgorged its few passengers, a conductor and a guard. During the next half-hour, when all hell seemed to have broken loose in the air above and all around us, the conductor sat beside the sunken road and totted up his totals of passengers, fares and journeys. The guard was a little more communicative. He told us a story.

'There was a bloody monkey hanging by his bloody tail in the jungle,' he narrated, 'and along came a bloody air-raid warden. One monkey says to the other monkey, "Look out, Jock, here's this bloody bastard comin' along to civilize us." '

From time to time we crawled to the edge of our ditch – an ancient and honourable road, but a ditch to me – and looked over it. Dense clouds of smoke were rising along the banks of the river. Flames had broken out here and there, particularly in the part of the river opposite us. The roar of anti-aircraft was the principal and most persistent noise, but it was punctuated by the deep, reverberant thunder of the bombs, heard more penetratingly here because we were beneath and against the earth. During the battle, Hurricanes returned to their roost to refuel and rearm; we saw two or three such returns; we saw them, or others like them, take off soon thereafter. The sun was setting when it was all over.

At last there was silence in our area, although an occasional far-off boom reminded us that the Germans were making their way home to France by another route. We got up from our refuge and shook off the dust. After a brief consultation we decided to return to Gravesend to see what had been hit in our part of the river.

As we drove along the highway we had many clear views of the Thames bank on the other side and a little lower down. Great blobs of flame, identifiable as the flame from oil fires, rose in the air, were swallowed by black smoke and rose again, monstrous signals of destruction over a wide area. This was Thameshaven, where there had been vast petroleum tanks. Farther up the river, where the docks were, dense black clouds had formed but no flame was yet to be seen from this point. All the way up the river these clouds were in process of formation. A crazy rhyme from childhood ran in my head then and all through the night: London's burning, London's burning. It was hard to realize that this thing, so long expected, so certain of advent, had come to pass. The three of us looked, estimated, calculated. It seemed (and, as it turned out afterward, was) the most destructive foray the enemy had yet made upon us.

We went down to the inn by the waterside and had dinner. There was a crowd of navy and river patrol people there, discussing the raid. Nothing had been seriously damaged in Gravesend – although when we went to the police station to report our presence before dinner we found it propped up as the result of a previous raid – and all the speculation was upon places opposite, on the other side of the river. Tilbury had, as they said, taken 'another packet'. The docks were in flames further up. Thameshaven was gone.

Ed and Ben and I were – for no clear reason – quite certain that the Germans would return that night. My feeling was that they would not have made such a tremendous attack in daylight, when it was bound to be costly, if they did not intend a continuation in the inexpensive hours of darkness. We voted to get through our dinner and return to our ditch, which had suited our purposes well, as soon as it got quite dark.

By the time we had done so we could already hear gunfire afar off on the coast beyond the estuary. We explored the field near our ditch and discovered a convenient haystack. 'This will come in handy,' Ed said, 'if we get cold later on.' We knew that there was at least one fighter station near us – more probably two – and an anti-aircraft battery somewhere in the neighbourhood, since the shrapnel had fallen here in the afternoon. For purposes of observation we decided to divide our time between the haystack and the ditch, depending upon the amount of stuff that might be falling in the neighbourhood.

We had been there no time at all – scarcely ten minutes – when the first German planes came over, heralded by very heavy anti-aircraft fire from the coast. We heard the anti-aircraft before we heard the German motors, and then, steady and relentless, the throb of the desynchronized engines. We had all grown so familiar with this intermittent purr – the tiger's purr – that we could distinguish it quite easily from any other, and no expert testimony to the contrary could make us think otherwise. The intermittent throb came closer, stronger, and, as we cowered beside the haystack, passed directly over our heads. By the sound we judged it to be two or at most three airplanes. There was a flash in the moonlight; we thought this might be wings; it was impossible to be sure. About three minutes later the same thing happened again: the roar of anti-aircraft on the coast heralded the approach of another pair or trio of German planes which throbbed over our heads and were gone up the river. This happened a third, fourth, fifth time: by now it seemed that all the anti-aircraft in England were active, filling all the air with sound. The bombs were falling now, too – falling on London, far up the Thames, far beyond the area reached by this afternoon's raids. The fires that had been started in the afternoon now lined the river with flame. Great solid blobs of flame rose from high up the river, were obliterated and rose again, like those at Thameshaven opposite us: more petroleum was afire. 'They're following the line of the river,' Ed said, 'as easily as if it were a main street. They come in at Margate and curve round the water line and all the way up. Are you glad you're not in London tonight?' We wondered what was happening in London, what would be left, whether our own houses had been hit, what was to become of the homeless, whether there would be many casualties and whether the surface shelters – so trumpery-looking in the middle of the street – would survive the shock.

So far as we could estimate there seemed to be about two German bombers at a time coming over at three-minute intervals. As we were afterward informed by those who should know, this observation was correct. Except for a very occasional flash of metal high up in the sky, caught by the beam of a searchlight, we saw none of these machines, but we could hear them most distinctly, singly and in pairs, as they made their way up the firelit river. Hour after hour they came on, cruelly disturbed, or so it seemed to us, by the efforts of anti-aircraft gunnery. Chatham was now letting loose a terrific fire, probably, as we thought (and were again proved right by subsequent information), from naval guns. The flames seemed to spread far beyond the unseen horizon, into the farthest reaches of the dark. The monstrous inferno before us was like nothing I or anybody else in this century had ever seen. The burning of Smyrna by the Turks in 1922 (I had often heard of it) could only have been insignificant in comparison. It was like a vision of the end of the world.

It grew cold; we crawled under the haystack and lit our cigarettes with great care, lest a small fire be added to the immensity of London burning. We were subdued, horror-struck at the possibilities. No city could endure much of this punishment and survive. There seemed no end to it; hour upon hour passed and the bombers were still coming on, two at a time at three-minute intervals, directly over our heads.

Belfast Takes It

From November 1940 the Luftwaffe often switched its main nightly attention from London to provincial British cities – seaports and centres of industrial production. Belfast's turn came late, in April 1941. Though fatalities were numbered in hundreds, rather than the thousands later killed by Allied raids on Germany, the effect was especially traumatic. Ireland had seemed a long way from the war.

Moira Hedges, a social worker in the city, kept a diary for the London-based social-survey organization, Mass Observation. It should be noted that the phenomenon of 'trekking' from bombed towns had become commonplace in British cities much better-prepared psychologically than Belfast had been.

16th [April 1941]

Where to begin? Dazed and mentally battered after 5½ hours of Blitz last night, one does not feel at one's most coherent. Perhaps put personal reactions first. Sirens went about 10.30 pm as I was in the bath and the bombs started falling at 10.45. I went to bed and tried to sleep, but this proved impossible. After an hour or so one started listening and waiting for the bomb, wondering why the barrage wasn't louder and trying to analyse peculiar sounds. Nazi planes kept coming back, for all the world like some giant swarm of insects, whose drone was only ineffectually interrupted by bangs and crashes. For lengthy periods no noise could be heard but the planes kept flying about. One fretted 'why don't they fire at them' and 'where are our fighters'? At 3 am I could stand it no longer and feeling desperately frightened and somewhat hysterical, put on a dressing-gown and went down to join my husband in his vigil below the stairs. I grabbed the whiskey decanter, and with shaking hands drank off about a quarter tumbler neat to try and pull myself together, (usually I dislike whiskey and I never touch it). We then sat down in the pantry under the stairs, and just waited. After a while I recovered my self-control and began to reflect mournfully that this was civilization in 1941! – Sitting shivering bored and frightened in a cubby hole at 3.30 am. I thought too of Madrid and how the Spanish people had neither defences, nor the sympathy of the outside world. Well, now it's our turn, and one derives a sort of bitter consolation from feeling 'we told you so'.

Things eased off a bit around 4.30 am, and I went back to bed with a splitting headache and dozed till morning. My maid returned at 10.00 am, having had to walk several miles from her own house in another part of the city. She told a hair-raising story of time-bombs, craters, direct hits on shelters and houses, etc., and said that she and her family had left their house in the middle of it all, and walked out to the end of the bus lines, where they spent the rest of the night sitting in an immobilized trolley bus.

Went downtown on my bike shopping. Atmosphere completely different from the morning after our previous 'sample' raid last week. People are quiet and looked harassed and weary. 'Isn't it awful!' is the most frequent comment. There seems less tendency to dilate personal experiences. Everyone is asking: 'Why don't we have a proper barrage?' 'They did just as they liked' is being said on all sides.

Centre of town comparatively undamaged, numbers of plate-glass windows gone, several areas roped off for time-bombs. People are shopping with anxious faces, but there is little to buy, for as well as Blitz dislocation it's the day after the holiday. Blackened faces, bandaged heads, parties of mothers and children with bundles are to be seen. Old lady of 70, owner of my fruit shop, describes how her house was hit, how she escaped under the kitchen table. Assistant in grocers tells me his house is in ruins, yet they were both on the job. I think these people are wonderful.

Passed railway station after lunch on my way to refugee committee, I have never seen anything like it. Thousands of people crowding in, cars, buses, carts and lorries, bathchairs, women pushing prams and go-karts with anything up to 6 or 8 children trailing along, belongings in blankets, pillowcases, baskets and boxes.

Coming back from the committee at 4.00 pm, found that the station doors had been shut. Crowds were waiting outside, mothers and children sitting on the pavement all round, constant stream of people arriving on foot and on buses, many looking exhausted. It was a heartbreaking sight.

Went up to see some friends, living on road which leads out of town. Such an exodus, on foot, in trains, lorries, trailers, cattle floats, bicycles, delivery vans, anything that would move would be utilized. Private cars streamed past laden with women and children, with mattresses tied on top and all sorts of paraphernalia roped on behind. Hundreds were waiting at the main bus-stops. Anxiety on every face.

Came home to find a message awaiting me from one of our refugees asking could I help to find somebody in the country for his wife and child. As he lived in a reported Blitz area, it sounded urgent, so after supper I got on my bike again and resolved to try and get through to them. (They live across town about 4 miles away.) Found that the road had only just been opened and was being policed by military. What awful scenes met me as I proceeded. It looked like photographs of Spain or China or some town in the last war. Houses roofless, windowless, burnt out or burning; familiar landmarks gone and in their place vast craters and mounds of rubble. The desolation is indescribable. Thousands and thousands must be homeless, and as for the death toll, I shuddered to think of the horrors and ghastly injuries and death which have occurred. Reached my refugees eventually to find them unharmed but terribly nervous and exhausted. Dr F— said he had been through the last war on several fronts but never known such a hell as last night. Made some plans for them and tried to cheer them up.

Coming home through the gathering darkness was a horrible experience, and I admit to being rather frightened. Small parties of people were still trailing on feet towards the country, (trains of course could not run on account of craters and broken wires), but no one seemed to be returning to the city but me. Road most of the way was inches deep in subsoil mud thrown up from the craters, and at one point I skidded and fell flat on my face with the bike on top. A kindly policeman picked me up, and led me into a bombed house where he found some water and wiped the mud off with his handkerchief. It was a peculiar experience to stand in someone else's scullery in the gathering darkness surrounded by debris and have a policeman direct the removal of mud from one's face. Mirrors, of course, were all shattered.

Continued my ride somewhat shaken, through more mud and passed fresh fires and crashing slates. Found 2 weary-eyed friends at home. We opened some wine rather than let Hitler have it and drank a bottle before collapsing into bed.

17th April

It has now been discovered that what we had was as severe as Coventry or Glasgow. Hundreds of planes were used. Everyone I meet has some terrible story of death and damage and disorganization. Electricity and water still okay but gas off. I spent half the morning running around trying to boil water on picnic outfits, and ancient spirit burners resuscitated from the attic; called in a plumber to see if the oven on our ancient (coal) range could be made workable. Rang up gas works to order some coke, and the clerk started telling about his experiences as a warden and about dead bodies. He said among other things that the many soldiers about were swearing in their impotence . . . 'if we could only get at them' was being heard on all sides. This raiding only seems to make people more bitter and determined than ever. I myself begin to feel that I should have tried to add some WVS work to my already overcrowded life.

My mother telephones to say that she took 8 evacuees last night, 2 mothers and 6 children. Says one mother is about to have another baby any minute, but they are all filthy, the smell in the room is terrible, they refuse all food except bread and tea, the children have made puddles all over the floor etc. She is terribly sorry for them and kindliness itself but finds this revelation of how the other half live rather overpowering . . .

Evacuation is taking on panic proportions. Roads out of town are still one stream of cars with mattresses and bedding tied on top. Everything on wheels is being pressed into service. People are leaving from all parts of town and not only from the bombed areas. Where they are going, or what they will find even when they get there, nobody knows . . . Belfast is the only large town in Ulster, most of the country towns have also been bombed, and there is absolutely no provision for the reception of and feeding of those vast numbers.

18th

Only now 3 days afterwards are people beginning to realize the results of the raid. Paper is full of cancellations, notices of changes of addresses, lists of names under 'by enemy action' in obituary column, instructions to homeless, etc. Unidentified bodies have been collected at the market and there is talk of a mass funeral.

One encouraging piece of news is that in spite of enmity between North and South and the almost total lack of petrol in Eire, fire brigades came up from Drogheda, Dundalk and even from Cork to help in putting out the blaze. An action like this does more for Irish Unity than any words of politicians. I hear that the brigades were wildly cheered in towns and villages in Ulster as they passed through and going back. The arrival too, of a large detachment of AFS from Glasgow complete with equipment makes us conscious of a comforting solidarity with Britain.

. . .

30th

Out on Welfare case work in the blitzed area. Bitterly cold, and a wind which swirled dust, plaster and ashes about the ruins so that one could scarcely see. I had 5 families to visit, and found one burnt out and departed, whereabouts unknown; 3 others also gone from houses uninhabitable though still standing; and the 5th evacuated from an undamaged house. It was a scene of desolation: whole streets of roofless and windowless houses, with an occasional notice chalked on the door: 'Gone to Ballymena', or some other country address. Nor a soul about, except demolition workers. Enormous gaps, or mounds of bricks, where formerly some familiar building had stood. More than a fortnight now since the raid, yet it still looks raw and obscene. People who survived that night of horror there will surely never be the same again. Easy to understand why even still habitable houses are deserted.

The Battle of Hamburg, 1943

Martin Middlebrook, an assiduous collector of facts and figures about Britain's involvement in the two world wars, edited the Bomber Command War Diaries *(1985). Chris Everitt, who did all the British research for the book, had joined the RAF as a Regular in 1939, and served as groundstaff in North Africa throughout the war. They provide details of the 'Battle of Hamburg'. Since February 1942 Air Chief Marshal Harris, at the head of Bomber Command, had been committed to the strategic policy of 'area bombing'. Though it was not of his devising, it was to his liking. The idea was to knock out Germany by destroying not only industrial installations but the homes and lives of the workers employed by them. In spite of huge raids, German production of war materials tripled between 1942 and 1944.*

H2S *was a 'forerunner of the simple airborne ground-scanning radar set which most aircraft now have . . .' It was a useful navigation aid and could be used as a rough-and-ready aiming device beyond the range of the sophisticated* Oboe *system of radio-directed 'blind bombing'.*

The scale of civilian deaths from bombing in this brief battle can be set against the total of 60,595 civilians killed by bombs, flying bombs and V2 rockets in Britain during the whole course of the war.

24/25 July to 3 August 1943

Sir Arthur Harris had decided upon his next step well before the Battle of the Ruhr was over. As early as 27 May, he had circulated an order to his group commanders to start preparing for a series of heavy raids on Hamburg – Europe's largest port and the second largest city in Germany, with one and three-quarter million people. Bomber Command had attacked this target ninety-eight times so far in the war. But Hamburg had twice missed being the target for 1,000-bomber raids in 1942 and it had never been seriously hit as had Cologne and many of the Ruhr communities. Harris felt that the time was now ripe for this target to receive the full attentions of Bomber Command.

. . . The aiming points and approach routes for the coming raids would all be chosen so that the now familiar creepback would fall across various sections of the main residential areas of this huge city which were on the north bank of the Elbe. Hamburg was a famous shipyard city; the battleship *Bismarck* – now at the bottom of the Atlantic – and at least 200 U-boats had already been built there. But the port and shipbuilding areas, which were on the south bank of the Elbe, were not to be targets in the coming raids. It was hoped to slow down production by the indirect means of crippling the general life of the city.

For the first time, the heavy daylight bombers of the American Eighth Air Force were invited to join directly in with a Bomber Command 'battle'. B-17 Fortresses would fly 252 sorties in the two days immediately following the first RAF night raid. The American targets were all industrial and included the U-boat yards. But the American effort would run into difficulties, mainly caused by the dense smoke from the fires started by the RAF bombing still obscuring their targets. The Americans quickly withdrew from the Battle of Hamburg and were not keen to follow immediately on the heels of RAF raids, in future, because of the smoke problem.

This diary shows that Sir Arthur Harris directed four major raids on Hamburg in the space of ten nights. A total of 3,091 sorties were flown and nearly 10,000 tons of bombs dropped, though not all of these would hit Hamburg. Because of the firestorm which developed in the city on the second RAF raid, it is often suggested that Bomber Command carried an unusually high proportion of incendiary bombs in these attacks and was launching 'firestorm raids'. This was not true. Just under half the total tonnage dropped on Hamburg was incendiary, a proportion which was actually lower than on many of the recent Ruhr raids. It cannot be stressed too strongly that the raids to be carried out against Hamburg at this time were no more than Bomber Command's normal area attacks for this period of the bombing war. The Hamburg firestorm was caused by other, unexpected, factors which will be described later.

There was, however, one major tactical innovation in the Battle of Hamburg – a device which enabled the bombers to pass through the German defences and to reach Hamburg in greater safety and numbers. This was *Window*, strips of coarse black paper exactly 27 centimetres long and 2 centimetres wide with thin aluminium foil stuck to one side of the strips. It had been proved in trials that, if sufficient of these were released by a force of bombers, the German *Würzburg* radar sets on the ground which controlled both the night-fighter interceptions and the radar-laid Flak guns, as well as the smaller airborne *Lichtenstein* radar sets which the night-fighter crews used for their final part of the bomber interception process, would be swamped by false echoes and rendered virtually useless. *Window* had been ready since April 1942 but Bomber Command had not been allowed to use it for fear that the Luftwaffe would copy it and use it in raids against England. It was a bad decision. The Luftwaffe was mainly in Russia at this time and the weak German raids on England had been of only the most minor nature compared with the Bomber Command night offensive against Germany. Bomber Command lost 2,200 aircraft during the *Window* embargo period, a large proportion of them to German radar-assisted defences. *Window* was released in time for Bomber Command to use it for the Battle of Hamburg and would be carried by RAF bombers for the remainder of the war. It can be estimated that, in the six major raids carried out in the ten nights of operations which comprised the Battle of Hamburg, *Window* saved 100–130 Bomber Command aircraft which would otherwise have been lost. The German defensive system was rendered obsolete at a stroke, although they started to recover and reorganize remarkably quickly . . .

24/25 July 1943
Hamburg

791 aircraft – 347 Lancasters, 246 Halifaxes, 125 Stirlings, 73 Wellingtons. 12 aircraft – 4 Halifaxes, 4 Lancasters, 3 Stirlings, 1 Wellington – lost, 1.5 per cent of the force.

Window was used for the first time on this night. Conditions over Hamburg were clear with only a gentle wind. The marking – a mixture of *H2S* and visual – was a little scattered but most of the target indicators fell near enough to the centre of Hamburg for a concentrated raid to develop quickly. 728 aircraft dropped 2,284 tons of bombs in 50 minutes. Bombing photographs showed that less than half of the force bombed within 3 miles of the centre of Hamburg and a creepback 6 miles long E developed. But, because Hamburg was such a large city, severe damage was caused in the central and north-western districts, particularly in Altona, Eimsbüttel and Hoheluft. The Rathaus, the Nikolaikirche, the main police station, the main telephone exchange and the Hagenbeck Zoo (where 140 animals died) were among the well-known Hamburg landmarks to be hit. Approximately 1,500 people were killed.

. . .

27/28 July 1943
Hamburg

787 aircraft – 353 Lancasters, 244 Halifaxes, 116 Stirlings, 74 Wellingtons. 17 aircraft – 11 Lancasters, 4 Halifaxes, 1 Stirling, 1 Wellington – lost, 2.2 per cent of the force. The American commander, Brigadier-General Anderson, again flew in a Lancaster and watched this raid.

The centre of the Pathfinder marking – all carried out by *H2S* on this night – was about 2 miles east of the planned aiming point in the centre of the city, but the marking was particularly well concentrated and the Main Force bombing 'crept back' only slightly. 729 aircraft dropped 2,326 tons of bombs.

This was the night of the firestorm, which started through an unusual and unexpected chain of events. The temperature was particularly high (30° centigrade at 6 o'clock in the evening) and the humidity was only 30 per cent, compared with an average of 40–50 per cent for this time of the year. There had been no rain for some time and everything was very dry. The concentrated bombing caused a large number of fires in the densely built-up working-class districts of Hammerbrook, Hamm and Borgfeld. Most of Hamburg's fire vehicles had been in the western parts of the city, damping down the fires still smouldering there from the raid of three nights earlier, and only a few units were able to pass through roads which were blocked by the rubble of buildings destroyed by high-explosive bombs early in this raid. About half-way through the raid, the fires in Hammerbrook started joining together and competing with each other for the oxygen in the surrounding air. Suddenly, the whole area became one big fire with air being drawn into it with the force of a storm. The bombing continued for another half hour, spreading the firestorm area gradually eastwards. It is estimated that 550–600 bomb loads fell into an area measuring only 2 miles by 1 mile. The firestorm raged for about three hours and only subsided when all burnable material was consumed.

The burnt-out area was almost entirely residential. Approximately 16,000 multi-storeyed apartment buildings were destroyed. There were few survivors from the firestorm area and approximately 40,000 people died, most of them by carbon monoxide poisoning when all the air was drawn out of their basement shelters. In the period immediately following this raid, approximately 1,200,000 people – two thirds of Hamburg's population – fled the city in fear of further raids.

. . .

29/30 July 1943
Hamburg

777 aircraft – 340 Lancasters, 244 Halifaxes, 119 Stirlings, 70 Wellingtons, 4 Mosquitoes. 28 aircraft – 11 Halifaxes, 11 Lancasters, 4 Stirlings, 2 Wellingtons – lost, 3.6 per cent of the force.

The marking for this raid was again all by *H2S*. The intention was to approach Hamburg from almost due north and bomb those northern and north-eastern districts which had so far not been bombed. The Pathfinders actually came in more than 2 miles too far to the east and marked an area just south of the devastated firestorm area. The Main Force bombing crept back about 4 miles, through the devastated area, but then produced very heavy bombing in the Wandsbek and Barmbek districts and parts of the Uhlenhorst and Winterhude districts. These were all residential areas. 707 aircraft dropped 2,318 tons of bombs. There was a widespread fire area – though no firestorm – which the exhausted Hamburg fire units could do little to check. The worst incident was in the shelter of a large department store in Wandsbek. The building collapsed and blocked the exits from the shelter which was in the basement of the store. 370 people died, poisoned by carbon monoxide fumes from a burning coke store near by.

. . .

1/2 August 1943
Hamburg

740 aircraft – 329 Lancasters, 235 Halifaxes, 105 Stirlings, 66 Wellingtons, 5 Mosquitoes. 30 aircraft – 13 Lancasters, 10 Halifaxes, 4 Wellingtons, 3 Stirlings – lost, 4.1 per cent of the force.

The bombing force encountered a large thunderstorm area over Germany and the raid was a failure. Many crews turned back early or bombed alternative targets. At least 4 aircraft, probably more, were lost because of icing, turbulence or were struck by lightning. No Pathfinder marking was possible at Hamburg and only scattered bombing took place there. Many other towns in a 100-mile area of Northern Germany received a few bombs. A sizeable raid developed on the small town of Elmshorn, 2 miles from Hamburg. It is believed that a flash of lightning set a house on fire here and bomber crews saw this through a gap in the storm clouds and started to bomb the fire. 254 houses were destroyed in Elmshorn and 57 people were killed, some of them refugees from recent raids on Hamburg.

[*The percentages of British Aircraft lost may seem quite slight. But, cumulatively, Bomber Command suffered enormous losses.*]

Aircrew Casualties

Approximately 125,000 aircrew served in the squadrons and the operational training and conversion units of Bomber Command during the war. Nearly 60 per cent of Bomber Command aircrew became casualties. Approximately 85 per cent of these casualties were suffered on operations and 15 per cent in training and other accidents. The Air Ministry was able to compile the following figures up to 31 May 1947:

Killed in action or died while prisoners of war	47,268	
Killed in flying or ground accidents	8,195	
Killed in ground-battle action	37	
Total fatal casualties to aircrew		55,500
Prisoners of war, including many wounded		9,838
Wounded in aircraft which returned from operations	4,200	
Wounded in flying or ground accidents in UK	4,203	
Total wounded, other than prisoners of war		8,403
Total aircrew casualties		73,741

USAAF Losses

Randall Jarrell, a notable literary critic as well as a major poet, entered the US Army Air Force in 1942, failed to qualify as a flier and became a training navigator.

THE DEATH OF THE BALL TURRET GUNNER

From my mother's sleep I fell into the State,
And I hunched in its belly till my wet fur froze.
Six miles from earth, loosed from its dream of life,
I woke to black flak and the nightmare fighters.
When I died they washed me out of the turret with a hose.

LOSSES

It was not dying: everybody died.
It was not dying: we had died before
In the routine crashes – and our fields
Called up the papers, wrote home to our folks,
And the rates rose, all because of us.
We died on the wrong page of the almanac,
Scattered on mountains fifty miles away;
Diving on haystacks, fighting with a friend,
We blazed up on the lines we never saw.
We died like aunts or pets or foreigners.
(When we left high school nothing else had died
For us to figure we had died like.)

In our new planes, with our new crews, we bombed
The ranges by the desert or the shore,
Fired at towed targets, waited for our scores –
And turned into replacements and woke up
One morning, over England, operational.

It wasn't different: but if we died
It was not an accident but a mistake
(But an easy one for anyone to make).
We read our mail and counted up our missions –
In bombers named for girls, we burned
The cities we had learned about in school –
Till our lives wore out; our bodies lay among
The people we had killed and never seen.
When we lasted long enough they gave us medals;
When we died they said, 'Our casualties were low.'
They said, 'Here are the maps'; we burned the cities.

It was not dying – no, not ever dying;
But the night I died I dreamed that I was dead,
And the cities said to me: 'Why are you dying?
We are satisfied, if you are; but why did I die?'

In Pilsen

Like other patriotic Czechs, Miroslav Holub welcomed the Allied air raids on his country which might bring nearer the end of Nazi occupation. But the consequences of bombs for individual Czechs were the same as those for civilians everywhere.

FIVE MINUTES AFTER THE AIR RAID

In Pilsen,
twenty-six Station Road,
she climbed to the third floor
up stairs which were all that was left
of the whole house,
she opened her door
full on to the sky,
stood gaping over the edge.

For this was the place
the world ended.

Then
she locked up carefully
lest someone steal
Sirius
or Aldebaran
from her kitchen,
went back downstairs
and settled herself
to wait
for the house to rise again
and for her husband to rise from the ashes
and for her children's hands and feet to be stuck back in place.

In the morning they found her
still as stone,
sparrows pecking her hands.

South and West

Having failed to put Britain out of the war quickly, Hitler concentrated German efforts on 'Barbarossa', his plan for the conquest of the Soviet Union. The Germans' southern flank was a problem. Rommel was sent to stiffen Italian resistance to the British in North Africa (q.v. above). Italy had occupied Albania in 1939. In October 1940 Mussolini had launched an invasion from there of Greece. British, Australian and New Zealand troops were sent to fight on the Greek side. In April 1941 the Germans invaded Yugoslavia, and by the end of that month whatever Greek and Imperial troops were still combatant had been evacuated to Crete. They held the island with scant reinforcements and air cover which dwindled to nil. A German paratroop attack on May 20 suffered heavy losses, but, with total command of the air, could not long be resisted.

Late in 1942 the British assembled a force able to confront and beat Rommel at El Alamein (23 October–4 November). As the Germans retreated American troops were landed in French Morocco and Algeria. This US First Army converged on Tunisia with Montgomery's Eighth Army, and in May 1943 the Germans and Italians there capitulated. Invasion of Italy through Sicily followed. In September Italy surrendered, but Germans fought on fiercely in the peninsula down to the very end in 1945, despite the valour of a very significant Resistance movement.

Meanwhile, the Western Allies (USA, British Empire, Free French, Free Poles, etc.) prepared the decisive 'Second Front' which the Soviet Union had been clamouring for. The D-Day landings of June 1944 preluded the liberation of Paris in August, but also nearly a year of bitter German resistance, particularly frustrating for the inhabitants of Holland, which was by-passed by Montgomery's force as it headed east. General von Runstedt's counter-attack in the Ardennes in December 1944 briefly rocked Allied confidence, while the Germans launched V2 rockets against Britain. But Allied bombers continued to batter the German cities and, more pertinently, oil installations. With Soviet troops in Berlin and Hitler dead by suicide in his bunker, the German army surrendered in May 1945.

Waugh's War

The English novelist Evelyn Waugh volunteered for the army in 1939 at the advanced age of thirty-five, and served with acute frustration till near the end. He saw significant action only when he went to Crete as liaison officer for Colonel Robert Laycock, leader of a specially created 'Commando', LAYFORCE. When they arrived the battle against air-borne German soldiers was already lost, and General Freyberg, the New Zealander in command, knew it. Eighteen thousand British and Commonwealth troops were taken off the island by the Royal Navy; twelve thousand left behind became prisoners of war. A suicidally brave man himself, Waugh, in a 'Memorandum' written soon after he got back to Egypt, did not allow for the effect of several days' uncontested pounding by the Luftwaffe, coupled with a severe shortage of transport and food, on the morale of British troops whom he despised as cowards. 'Hound' is not the real name of the senior officer who collapsed with shell-shock, but that given to a partly equivalent figure in Waugh's novel Sword of Honour *(final version, 1965), which reproduces in fictional mode several episodes described here.*

FROM 'MEMORANDUM ON LAYFORCE'

At about 11 o'clock that night we sailed into Suda Bay. We had three hours to land ourselves and stores. Lighters should have come alongside immediately but did not do so for three-quarters of an hour. When they did, they were full of wounded. The first indication which we received of conditions in Crete was the arrival in the captain's cabin, where HQ were waiting, of a stocky, bald, terrified naval commander named Roberts or Robertson. He was wearing shorts and a greatcoat and could not speak intelligibly on account of weariness and panic. 'My God, it's hell,' he said. 'We're pulling out. Look at me, no gear. O my God, it's hell. Bombs all the time. Left all my gear behind, etc., etc.' We took this to be an exceptionally cowardly fellow, but in a few hours realized that he was typical of British forces in the island.

No light could be shown on deck and there was confusion between the wounded and runaways and our troops waiting in the dusk to disembark. The ships could not prolong their stay because they had to get as far clear as they could before light. It was soon plain that we had barely time to get the men ashore and would have to leave most of our stores. A large quantity of valuable signalling stores – 9 and 18 wireless transmitting sets – was wantonly thrown overboard. We landed in tank landing craft which we heard were to be scuttled behind us. The quay on which we landed seemed to have been badly bombarded; it was full of craters and littered with loose stones, burned-out vehicles, abandoned stores, etc. There were groups of wounded sitting about and swearing moodily.

Liaison officers met us from General Weston and Lt.-Col. Hound. They said the Germans were in Canea. Weston had sent a truck so Bob and I set off to find him, leaving Freddy Graham to look after the troops and get them to the defensive positions Bob chose off the map in a shed with a torch. In the dark Suda seemed to be burned out but this was, I think, a trick of the starlight. We drove forward into the country somewhere between Suda and Canea to a farm which was Weston's HQ. He was asleep on the floor. A Marine told us that the New Zealand Brigade had packed up at Maleme and were in retreat. There was also an Australian Brigade in retreat, also various British and Greek units. The Marines and ourselves were to form a rearguard covering their withdrawal to Sphakia on the south coast. This was barely thirty miles but the road led through the mountains and was longer than it looked on the map. We then went to Hound's headquarters, gave him his orders for the line he was to hold next day; his liaison officer spoke in a quavering undertone which I learned to recognize as the voice of the force. Hound himself did not seem particularly nervous that night; I think he was encouraged by our coming and thought he would now be able to leave things to Bob. He spoke of bombing but had suffered no serious casualties.

We next went to Freyberg's headquarters; he was in a camouflaged tent off the Suda–Heraklion road, east of the junction with the Sphakia road. He was composed but obtuse.

Bob said he was worried about his left flank which was in the air.

'My dear boy, don't worry about that. The Boche never work off the roads.'

Bob asked if it was a defence to be held to the last man and last round.

'No, a rearguard. Withdraw when you are hard pressed.'

It was now light. We kept our truck and drove to the further side of the first rise of the south road where we found Graham and brigade HQ and D Battalion. All the road which we travelled was densely packed with motor transport and marching men. When we were going forward we had to plough slowly through them; coming back they climbed onto the truck presuming we were heading for Sphakia.

We picked up one man in colonel's uniform who spoke in the most affected voice I ever heard, saying, 'By Jove don't cher know old man.' He said he had been in charge of a transit camp at Canea. It was too dark to see his face but he seemed quite young. I wondered at the time and have continued to wonder since if he were a German. I had decided to make investigations when the truck got stuck temporarily and he disappeared into the dark and the mob saying, 'Thanks no end.' It occurs to me now he may have been a private soldier masquerading as an officer to get transport.

Our headquarters were off the road on the side of a hill, facing south, covered in rock and gorse. Freddy made an attempt to arrange tactical groups of the sort he had heard about at the Staff College. The signallers were useless since their apparatus was all sunk in Suda Bay. Sergeant Lane had shown intelligence in getting hold of a few tinned stores. We each got a packet of biscuits and some bully beef. Most of us were already tired and thirsty but not hungry. Besides our usual headquarters we had attached a Presbyterian minister and a caddish fellow, sacked by Pedder, called Murdoch.

At 8 o'clock the German aeroplanes appeared and remained in the sky more or less continually all day. There were seldom less than half a dozen or more than a dozen overhead at a time. They were bombing the country to the west of us and in Suda Bay, but did not trouble us that morning. As soon as they appeared the rabble on the roads went to ground. When there was half an hour's pause they resumed their retreat.

Bob produced some written orders for a timed rearguard action lasting two days. A Battalion was to fall back through D and take up an intermediate position, etc. Bob sent me forward in the truck to give Hound his orders. I had rather vague memories of his position from the night before and drove about for some time in no-man's-land. There were plenty of aeroplanes about. When they came directly overhead we pulled into the shade and sheltered in the ditch.

At one point in our journey General Weston popped out of the hedge; he seemed to have lost his staff and his head.

'Who the hell are you and where are you going?'

I told him.

'Where's Laycock?'

I showed him on my map.

'Don't you know better than to show a map? It's the best way of telling the enemy where headquarters are.'

It did not seem worth pointing out that we were not headquarters, just two lost officers meeting at the side of the road. He said he wanted a lift back to Laycock. I said I was going forward to find Hound. 'I used to command here once,' he said wistfully.

At length I came across a Layforce anti-tank rifleman concealed in the hedge about a mile east of Suda on the coast road. He said that headquarters were vaguely on his left. I put the truck under the best cover available, left my servant and the driver, and went forward on foot. There were vineyards and olive groves south of the road running up to the edge of the hills where the country became scrub and rock.

Quarter of a mile off the road was a domed church and some scattered farm buildings. The olive groves were full of trenches and weapon pits. I walked about for half an hour trying to find Hound. Some of the trenches had stray colonials or Royal Army Medical Corps details in them; some had Layforce. A Battalion kept no lookouts although they were not being directly bombed. They just crouched as low as possible and hid their heads. The bombing was all going on in the hills, three-quarters of a mile or more to the south; here the enemy were systematically working over the scrub with dive-bombing and machine-gunning. I knew there were no British there, except a few stragglers taking a short cut for home, and thought that a way was being cleared for an infantry advance. I reported this later but we had no troops to spare and nothing could be done. Late that evening the Germans worked through and cut off a company of D Battalion holding the road between Suda and the junction. I do not know if this company surrendered or fought it out.

After asking two officers who made excuses for not leaving their holes I found one who cheerfully consented to take me to Hound. He took me to the furthest of the farm buildings and went back to his company. I went into a tin-roofed shed and found two NCOs sitting at a table.

I said, 'I was told Colonel Hound was here.'

'He is,' they said.

I looked round, saw no one. Then they pointed under the table where

I saw their commanding officer sitting hunched up like a disconsolate ape. I saluted and gave him his orders. He did not seem able to take them in at all.

He said, 'Where's Colonel Bob? I must see him.'

I said I was on my way back there now.

'Wait till the blitz is over. I'll come too.'

After a time the aeroplanes went home for refreshment and Hound emerged He still looked a soldierly figure when he was on his feet. 'We had a burst of machine-gun right through the roof,' he said half apologetically. I think this was a lie as the aeroplanes were concentrated on the hillside all that forenoon.

I took him to Bob. He showed no inclination to go back to his battalion but could still talk quite reasonably when there was no aeroplane overhead. Soon they came back and he lay rigid with his face in the gorse for about four hours. If anyone stretched a leg, he groaned as though he had broken all his limbs and was being jolted. 'For Christ's sake keep still.'

A squadron of dive-bombers now started work to the east of us; they came round and round regularly and monotonously like the horses at Captain Hance's [riding school]. Just below us there was a very prominent circular cornfield in a hollow and they used this as their pivot so that they were always directly overhead flying quite low, then they climbed as they swung right, dived and let go their bombs about a mile away. I do not know what their target was; Freyberg's headquarters had been somewhere in that area. At first it was impressive, but after half an hour deadly monotonous. It was like everything German – overdone.

It was intolerably hot on the hillside; blankets served the double purpose of camouflage and protection from the sun. It was then I learned that the most valuable piece of equipment one can have in action is a pillow. From then on I always carried mine under my arm and did not relinquish it until it went into the captain's wastepaper basket in Alexandria harbour; it was then threadbare and soaked in oil.

At sunset Hound went back towards his battalion who were to withdraw that night to a position about seven miles inland. D Battalion moved out to a position in their rear. Hound's second-in-command, with the newly arrived A Battalion detachment, were to hold the most forward position. There was also the company which got cut off, of D Battalion, which should have fallen back through A Battalion's forward position. I think that was the plan but I have no copy of the orders and, anyway, it did not work out that way the next day. Bob and Freddy went out in the truck to look for Weston. We did not once, in the five days' action, receive an order from any higher formation without going to ask for it. The rest of HQ settled down to sleep. An hour or two later – I think about 9 o'clock – Bob moved HQ to the road. The Germans had worked along the hills to our flank and were very close, he said. We took up firing positions along the road facing east, posted sentries and went to sleep.

Within an hour, Bob having gone off again in the truck, we were woken up. Hound had arrived with a confused account of having been ambushed on a motor cycle. His battalion was fiercely engaged he said (this was balls), and without explaining why he was not with them he gave us the order to withdraw. It all seemed fishy but Murdoch was in command of brigade HQ troops so off we set, I presumed to fall back about a mile.

We marched on and on all through the night, through two villages. I protested but Hound kept saying, 'We must get as far as we can before light.' The roads were full of troops retreating without any discipline. All the officers seemed to have made off in the motor transport. After the second village the road ran along the side of a valley with steep bare slopes on either side. When I suggested a halt Hound said, 'We must find cover.' Nothing but daylight would stop him. The moment that came he popped into a drain under the road and sat there.

I got an hour's sleep. When I woke up the road was full of a strange procession carrying white sheets as banners; they were a ragged, bearded troop of about 2,000. I thought at first it was some demonstration by the local inhabitants. Then I realized that they were Italians, taken prisoner in Greece, and now liberated. They advanced towards freedom with the least possible enthusiasm.

Some troops of A Battalion now arrived with a few wounded. One man had marched all the way with a bullet through his guts. When he lay down he stayed down and the doctor finished him with morphia. I asked Captain Mackintosh-Flood what the situation was. He said, 'I don't know and I don't care.' So I went off to look for myself, leaving my servant and the intelligence section behind.

It was always exhilarating as soon as one was alone; despondent troops were a dead weight on one's spirits and usefulness. I set off along the road we had come. Presently I met a subaltern (not one of ours but, I think, English) accompanied by, one could not say in command of, half a platoon. He was in a great hurry.

He said, 'You can't go any further on this road. The enemy landed parachutists in the night. They're firing on it with machine-guns.'

I asked where they were firing from.

'I don't know.'

'Were any of your men hit?'

'I didn't stop to look,' he said, laughing at me for asking so silly a question.

So I left the road and cut across the hills to the village we had passed in the night. It was a pretty, simple place with a well in the square. I wanted to fill my bottle but the rope had been cut and the bucket stolen. I asked a peasant, in gesture, for water; he went away grumbling a refusal but I followed him into his cottage and after a bit he gave me a cupful from a stone jar.

In the square a peasant girl came and pulled at my sleeve; she was in tears. I followed her to the church, where in the yard was a British soldier on a stretcher. Flies were all over his mouth and he was dead. There was another girl by him also in tears. I think they had been looking after him. There was also a bearded peasant who shrugged and made signs that might have been meant to describe the ascent of a balloon, but which told me what I could already see. Again with signs, I told them to bury him.

Then I went on through the next village at the furthest house of which a motor cyclist had told me I should find some sort of headquarters. The enemy were being held about half a mile up the road from there. In an arbour of sweet jasmine I found Bob and Freddy and two brigadiers; they had had an adventure, being attacked at close quarters by tommy-gunners. Bob had jumped into a tank and Ken Wiley, second-in-command of A Battalion, redeemed the Commandos' honour by leading a vigorous and successful counter-attack. A few New Zealanders, mostly Maoris, had rallied and were joining us in the rearguard. A plan was decided on which I cannot now remember and, anyway, was never put into effect.

Presently Bob, Freddy and I got into the truck and drove back to where I had left Hound. A number of his battalion had got together there but he was still in his drain. Bob as politely as possible relieved him of command saying, 'You're done up. Ken will take over from you.' Then we went to set up brigade headquarters in the next village back.

This was called, I think, Babali Inn. There was certainly an inn there with some tipsy stragglers and pools of wine spilled about but some jars still full. We had had no food that day, and two mugs of the wine, brown and sweet, made us all more cheerful. We broke into a house and called it brigade HQ after Bob had rejected a very nice barn I found him. D Battalion took up a line on the edge of the village in a deep ditch near a well. Presently A Battalion appeared at a good pace. They should have been covering D while they took up position but Hound had gone forward and told them to withdraw. Bob now relieved him of command in terms which could not be misunderstood. (The Presbyterian minister had also taken his part, telling Christie Laurence, 'It's *sauve qui peut*, now.') If the enemy had cared to push on they could have caught D Battalion before they were in position, but they were tired by now and, anyway, seldom advanced far without air preparation. From now on the air support slackened a great deal. There were frequent reconnaissance planes and some desultory attacks but no longer the skyful of the preceding week.

After Hound's unexpected retreat Babali Inn became the front line so brigade HQ withdrew a mile or so to a place of great beauty. It was a little roadside shrine with a spring running down to a brook. There had been a kind of terrace there once and the spring was built round with stone, and fell into stone basins. Presumably the place had some medical properties once. There was a grove of five trees round the spring and although there were gross evidences of previous occupation it was still an enchanting spot. Sergeant Lane had prudently filled a large bottle with wine. We kept it cool in the spring. Bob had a box of cigars and a book of crossword puzzles. We had a few hours' rest here. Fatigue and hunger were beginning to affect us.

At about 5 in the afternoon Bob and I went up to visit George Young. He was still in his ditch at Babali Inn in uncomfortable circumstances, being shot at from three sides by sub-machine-gunners in the trees. The enemy also had a four-inch mortar ranged on him and on the road which was accurate and damaging. Bob and I had some bullets near us in getting to the trench and bombs very close on the return journey. We found Young's headquarters, and all his battalion whom we saw, in the steadiest condition. He was now commanding what was left of A Battalion. He held his position until told to withdraw when it became dark.

As night fell stragglers emerged from the ditches, like ghosts from their graves, and began silently crawling along towards the coast. None that I saw in this area were under any kind of control, but the majority still had their rifles. They had all thrown away their packs, had beards and the lassitude of hunger and extreme exhaustion; a pitiful spectacle.

The 51st Highland Division's Farewell to Sicily, 1943

Hamish Henderson, Information Officer with the 51st Highland Division, already harboured the passion for traditional music which would make him in the decades after the war Scotland's most distinguished folklorist. He was with the Division when, having fought all the way from El Alamein, it moved out of Sicily. He later promoted the 'D-Day Dodgers' ditty quoted by John Ellis above.

Getting my driver to park the jeep, and asking him to stay with it, I moved forward with some difficulty through a dense crowd of enthusiastic Sicilians, shouting things like, 'Viva la Scozia!' and 'Viva i Scozzesi', till I got to the top of the approach road leading to the piazza, and saw there a heart-warming sight. It was the massed pipe band of 153 Brigade – two Gordons battalions, and one Black Watch battalion – and they were playing the beautiful retreat air 'Magersfontein'. Presiding over the occasion was the immense bulk of Etna, with a plume of smoke drifting lazily from its crater.

In the silence after the retreat air finished I stood wondering what the Pipe Major was going to get his boys to play for a March, Strathspey and Reel. When they struck up again, the March turned out to be one of my favourite pipe tunes – 'Farewell to the Creeks', a tune composed during the First World War by Pipe Major James Robertson of Banff. And while I listened to it, words began to form in my head, particularly one recurrent line 'Puir bluidy swaddies are weary'.

And they were too! Since Alamein some of the companies of that splendid division had been more or less totally 'made up' due to heavy losses – and I knew that shortly they were going home, presumably to take part in yet another D-Day in north-west Europe. By the time I had elbowed my way through the crowd back to the jeep, I had the beginnings of a song half completed; that night it had its first airing in a Gordons Officers' Mess, and I was soon scribbling the words out in pencil for all ranks. It took off with amazing speed and, in the event, preceded me back to Scotland. When I was collecting songs with Alan Lomax in the north-east in 1951, we were occasionally offered it – sandwiched between classic ballads, lyric love songs and comic ditties by ex-soldiers who had been in Sicily!

. . .

THE HIGHLAND DIVISION'S FAREWELL TO SICILY

The pipe is dozie, the pipie is fey,
He winna come roon for his vino the day:
The sky ow'r Messina is unco an' grey,
And a' the bricht chaulmers are eerie.

Then fareweel ye banks o' Sicily,
Fare ye weel, ye valley an' shaw.
There's nae Jock will mourn the kyles o' ye.
Puir bluidy swaddies are weary.

Then fareweel ye banks o' Sicily,
Fare ye weel, ye valley an' shaw.
There's nae hame can smoor the wiles o' ye.
Puir bluidy swaddies are weary.

Then doon the stair an' line the waterside,
Wait your turn, the ferry's awa'.
Then doon the stair an' line the waterside.
A' the bricht chaulmers are eerie.

The drummie is polisht, the drummie is braw,
He cannae be seen for his webbin' ava.
He's beezed himsel' up for a photy an' a'
Tae leave wi' his Lola, his dearie.

Sae fare weel, ye dives o' Sicily,
(Fare ye weel, ye shieling an' ha')
We'll a' mind shebeens and bothies
Whaur Jock made a date wi' his dearie.

Then fareweel, ye dives o' Sicily
(Fare ye weel, ye shieling an' ha').
We'll a' mind shebeens and bothies
Whaur kind signorine were cheerie.

Then tune the pipes an' drub the tenor drum,
(Leave your kit this side o' the wa'),
Then tune the pipes an' drub the tenor drum,
A' the bricht chaulmers are eerie.

Lilli Marlene

In 1917 a German infantryman, Hans Leip (1894–1983), wrote verses expressing nostalgia for two girls (he said much later) called Lili and Marleen (sic) *whom he had met on leave in Berlin. In 1938 Norbert Schultz set them to music. The first recording in Germany, by Lale Andersen, and issued in 1939, sold only 700 copies. When the Germans occupied Belgrade in the spring of 1941 they set up a radio station with a signal which could reach their comrades in North Africa. Serbo-Croat ditties were not quite the thing, so they played 'Lili Marleen'.*

The Italians serving alongside Rommel heard it. So did Montgomery's Eighth Army. While the Italian music industry developed a version sung by operatic tenors, Tommie Connor constructed for Tin Pan Alley an English version designed to oust the bawdy parodies now heard in the desert. A very young, up-and-coming English singer, Ann Shelton, recorded 'Lilli Marlene' and sold more than a million copies. When she got her own regular radio show this was the signature tune.

LILLI MARLENE

Underneath the lantern by the barrack gate,
Darling, I remember how you used to wait;
'Twas there that you whispered tenderly,
That you lov'd me,
You'd always be
My Lilli of the lamp-light,
My own LILLI MARLENE.

Time would come for roll call, time for us to part,
Darling I'd caress you and press you to my heart;
And there 'neath that far off lantern light,
I'd hold you tight,
We'd kiss 'Good-night',
My Lilli of the lamp-light,
My own LILLI MARLENE.

Orders came for sailing somewhere over there,
All confined to barracks was more than I could bear;
I knew that you were waiting in the street,
I heard your feet,
But could not meet;
My Lilli of the lamp-light,
My own LILLI MARLENE.

Resting in a billet just behind the line,
Even tho' we're parted your lips are close to mine;
You wait where that lantern softly gleams,
Your sweet face seems,
To haunt my dreams,
My Lilli of the lamp-light,
My own LILLI MARLENE.

With Tito

After the German conquest of Yugoslavia in April 1941, King Peter made his way to London. Colonel Mihailović organized a Serbian Royalist resistance movement, the 'Chetniks'. In December 1943 Churchill decided to break with the inactive and compromised Mihailović and to commit Allied support to Josip Broz, war-name 'Tito', a Croat Communist who successfully persuaded members of all ethnic and religious groups to work together in his movement of Partisans. Fitzroy Maclean, a British officer who had formerly been a diplomat in the USSR and a founder member of the SAS, raiding behind Rommel's lines in North Africa, joined Tito in his Bosnian base as Churchill's personal representative and Commander of the British Military Mission to the Partisans. Tito's eventual success was the basis of a multicultural state in which the southern Slavs cohabited with each other for four decades.

By the time Maclean published his memoir Eastern Approaches *in 1949, Tito had broken with his erstwhile masters in Moscow, confirming Maclean's impression that he was first and foremost a southern Slav patriot.*

Sometimes at night, before going to sleep, we would turn on our receiving set and listen to Radio Belgrade. For months now, the flower of the Afrika Korps had been languishing behind the barbed wire of Allied prison camps. But still, punctually at ten o'clock, came Lili Marlene singing their special song, with the same unvarying, heart-rending sweetness that we knew so well from the desert.

> Unter der Laterne,
> Vor dem grössen Tor . . .

Belgrade was still remote. But, now that we ourselves were in Jugoslavia, it had acquired a new significance for us. It had become our ultimate goal, which Lili Marlene and her nostalgic little tune seemed somehow to symbolize. 'When we get to Belgrade . . .' we would say. And then we would switch off the wireless a little guiltily, for the

Partisans, we knew, were shocked at the strange pleasure we got from listening to the singing of the German woman who was queening it in their capital.

It grew colder: sharp, crackling autumn weather. The leaves and a bitter wind swept up the valley, ruffling the waters of the lake. Winter was not far off; a hard time for guerrillas. For the Partisans it would be the third spent in the woods, '*u šume*'. Already food was scarcer and the lack of proper boots and clothing was making itself felt.

Once again the Germans were attacking. Split had fallen, and, with the enemy in strength at Banjaluka and Travnik, just up the road, our position was none too secure. Daily their patrols pushed closer. Between us and the coast the Germans were forcing their way back into the areas which the Italians had evacuated.

War breaks down the barriers which divide us in peace time. Living as we did amongst the Partisans, we came to know them well, from Tito and the other leaders to the dozen or so rank and file who acted as our bodyguard and provided for our daily needs.

All had one thing in common: an intense pride in their Movement and in its achievements. For them the outside world did not seem of immediate interest or importance. What mattered was *their* War of National Liberation, *their* struggle against the invader, *their* victories, *their* sacrifices. Of this they were proudest of all, that they owed nothing to anyone; that they had got so far without outside help. In their eyes we acquired merit from the mere fact of our presence among them. We were living proof of the interest which the outside world was at last beginning to take in them. We were with them 'in the woods'. This, in itself, was a bond.

With this pride went a spirit of dedication, hard not to admire. The life of every one of them was ruled by rigid self-discipline, complete austerity; no drinking, no looting, no love-making. It was as though each one of them were bound by a vow, a vow part ideological and part military, for, in the conditions under which they were fighting, any relaxation of discipline would have been disastrous; nor could private desires and feelings be allowed to count for anything.

But, for all that, the Partisans were not dull people to live among. They would not have been Jugoslavs if they had been. Their innate turbulence, their natural independence, their deep-seated sense of the dramatic kept bubbling up in a number of unexpected ways.

Tito stood head and shoulders above the rest. When there were decisions to be taken, he took them; whether they were political or military, took them calmly and collectedly, after hearing the arguments on both sides. My own dealings were with him exclusively. From him I could be certain of getting a prompt and straightforward answer, one way or the other, on any subject, however important or however trivial it might be. Often enough we disagreed, but Tito was always ready to argue out any question on its merits, showing himself open to conviction, if a strong enough case could be made out. Often, where a deadlock had been reached owing to the stubbornness of his subordinates, he, on being approached, would intervene and reverse their decision.

One line of approach, I soon found, carried great weight with him: the suggestion, advanced at the psychological moment, that this or that line of conduct did or did not befit an honourable and civilized nation. By a discreet use of this argument I was able to dissuade him more than once from a course of action which would have had a calamitous effect on our relations. At the same time he reacted equally strongly to anything that, by the widest stretch of the imagination, might be regarded as a slight on the national dignity of Jugoslavia. This national pride, it struck me, was an unexpected characteristic in one whose first loyalty, as a Communist, must needs be to a foreign power, the Soviet Union.

There were many unexpected things about Tito: his surprisingly broad outlook; his never-failing sense of humour; his unashamed delight in the minor pleasures of life; a natural diffidence in human relationships, giving way to a natural friendliness; a violent temper, flaring up in sudden rages; a considerateness and a generosity constantly manifesting themselves in a dozen small ways; a surprising readiness to see two sides of a question. These were human qualities, hard to reconcile with the usual conception of a Communist puppet, and making possible better personal relations between us than I had dared hope for. And yet I did not for a moment forget that I was dealing with a man whose tenets would justify him in going to any lengths of deception or violence to attain his ends, and that these, outside our immediate military objectives, were in all probability, diametrically opposed to my own.

Of the men round Tito, we saw most during those early days of his gaunt Montenegrin Chief of Staff, Arso Jovanović, who as a regular officer of the old Jugoslav Army had studied at the Belgrade Staff College under General Mihajlović. A stiff, angular, unbending, unlovable man, he kept strictly to the business in hand, unimaginative, but coldly competent, supporting his arguments with facts and figures and frequent references to a captured German map. During Tito's outbursts of anger or merriment he would remain silent. Then, when he had finished, he would resume his accurate and conscientious appreciation of the situation.

But Arso was not one of Tito's real intimates. These, we soon found, were men with the same background as himself; professional revolutionaries, who had shared his exiles and imprisonments, helped him to organize workers' cells and promote strikes, run with him the gauntlet of police persecution. Gradually we got to know them.

Perhaps the most important of all was Edo Kardelj, a small, stocky, pale-skinned, black-haired Slovene in the early thirties, with steel-rimmed spectacles and a neat little dark moustache, looking like a provincial schoolmaster, which, as it happened, was what he was. He, I found, was the theoretician of the Party, the expert Marxist dialectician.

There were a lot of questions about the theory and practice of Communism that I had always wanted an answer to. Now was my opportunity. Kardelj knew all the answers. He was a fascinating man to talk to. You could never catch him out or make him angry. He was perfectly frank, perfectly logical, perfectly calm and unruffled. Muddle; murder; distortion; deception. It was quite true. Such things happened under Communism, might even be an intentional part of Communist policy. But it would be worth it in the long run. The end would justify the means. Some day they would get their way; some day their difficulties would disappear; their enemies would be eliminated; the people educated; and a Communist millennium make the world a happier and a better place. Then the need for strong measures would disappear. He might not live to see this happen. But he was quite ready, as they all were, not only to die himself, but to sacrifice everybody and everything that was near and dear to him to the cause which he had chosen, to liquidate anybody who stood in his way. Such sacrifices, such liquidations, would be for the greater good of humanity. What worthier cause could there be? And he looked at me steadily and amiably through his spectacles.

Then there was Marko, a Serb whose real name was Aleksander Ranković. 'Marko', it seemed, was his conspiratorial code-name. And indeed, everything about him was conspiratorial. He had a way of keeping in the background, and it was not for some time that I realized what an important part he played in the Movement. Chiefly as an organizer. He it was who, under Tito's supervision, operated the Party machine; got rid of unreliable characters, promoted good men in their place; planted underground workers in the big towns; penetrated the quisling forces; penetrated the Gestapo. Still, like Kardelj, in his early thirties, he had been in prison before the war; had been with Tito from the start, taking an active part in the first uprising in Serbia in the summer of 1941. The son of a peasant, he had the stubborn, rather sly look which peasants often have. Not, you felt, a man who would come off worst in a bargain. And yet, somehow, a rather engaging character. '*Konspiracia!*' he would say gleefully, winking and laying his finger at the side of his nose, '*Konspiracia!*'

There was Džilas, too, Montenegrin, young, intolerant and good-looking, with a shock of hair like a golliwog; and Moše Pijade, an elderly intellectual from Belgrade, who, as almost the only Jew amongst the Partisans, became a favourite target for Nazi propaganda; both high up in the Party hierarchy. And the girls, Zdenka and Olga, who took turns at working for Tito, keeping his maps and lists and bundles of signals. Zdenka, a strange, pale, fanatical little creature. Olga, tall and well-built, in her black breeches and boots, with a pistol hanging at her belt, speaking perfect English, for before the war she had been sent to a smart finishing school in London by her father, a Minister in the Royal Jugoslav Government, in the hope of keeping her out of trouble. A hope which was doomed to disappointment, for no sooner was she back in her own country than, despite her background and upbringing, she joined the Communist Party, pledged to overthrow the Government of which her father was a member, and for her part in Communist disturbances was promptly thrown into prison by that same Government's police. Now, for two years, she had hidden in the woods and tramped the hills, had been bombed and machine-gunned, an outlaw, a rebel, a revolutionary, a Partisan. But when she spoke English, it was like talking to a young girl at home before the war; the same words and expressions, the same way of talking, the same youthful tastes and enthusiasms – all pleasantly refreshing in these grim surroundings. Somehow one never thought of her as being married, but she had a husband who was a Bosnian Moslem and a baby that she had left behind when she joined the Partisans. Now the baby – a little girl – was in Mostar, a German garrison town down towards the coast, at the mercy of the Gestapo and of frequent RAF bombings. She wondered if she would ever see her again. Once a photograph was smuggled out by an agent who had been working underground in Mostar for the Partisans, a tiny, blurred snapshot, which, as Vlatko Velebit said, made the child look like a tadpole. But Olga was delighted. At least her baby had been alive a week ago.

Finally, to complete Tito's entourage, there were Boiko and Prija, his bodyguards, a formidable pair of toughs who never left his side, and his dog, Tigger, an enormous wolfhound, originally captured from the Germans and now his constant companion.

Two things struck me about this strange group over which Tito presided with a kind of amused benevolence; first their complete devotion to the Old Man, as they called him, and secondly the fact that all of them, young and old, men and women, intellectuals and artisans, Serbs and Croats, had been with him in the woods from the early days of the resistance, sharing with him hardships and dangers, setbacks and successes. This common experience had overcome all differences of class or race or temperament and forged between them lasting bonds of loyalty and affection.

Calvino's Fear on the Footpath

Italo Calvino fought with the Italian Resistance as a very young man. His first novel The Path to the Nest of Spiders *(1947) and his collection of short stories* The Crown Comes Last *(1949), published in English in* Adam One Afternoon, *draw directly on this experience. But at a time when Italian cinema was famous for 'realism' Calvino's interest in folklore and folktales prompted him to craft fables which transcend 'realism'.*

FEAR ON THE FOOTPATH

At a quarter past nine, just as the moon was getting up, he reached the Colla Bracca meadow; at ten he was already at the crossroads of the two trees; by half past twelve he'd be at the fountain; he might reach Vendetta's camp by one – ten hours of walking at a normal speed, but six hours at the most for Binda, the courier of the first battalion, the fastest courier in the partisan brigade.

He went hard at it, did Binda, flinging himself headlong down short cuts, never making a mistake at turnings which all looked alike, recognizing stones and bushes in the dark. His firm chest never changed the rhythm of his breathing, his legs went like pistons. 'Hurry up, Binda!' his comrades would say as they saw him from a distance climbing up towards their camp. They tried to read in his face if the news and orders he was bringing were good or bad; but Binda's face was shut like a fist, a narrow mountaineer's face with hairy lips on a short bony body more like a boy's than a youth's, with muscles like stones.

It was a tough and solitary job, his was, being woken at all hours, sent out even to Serpe's camp or Pelle's, having to march in the dark valleys at night, accompanied only by a French tommy-gun, light as a little wooden rifle, hanging on his shoulder; and when he reached a detachment he had to move on to another or return with the answer; he would wake up the cook and grope around in the cold pots, then leave again with a panful of chestnuts still sticking in his throat. But it was the natural job for him, as he never got lost in the woods and knew all the paths, from having led goats about them or gone there for wood or hay since he was a child; and he never went lame or rubbed the skin off his feet scrambling about the rocks as so many partisans did who'd come up from the towns or the navy.

Glimpses seen as he went along: a chestnut tree with a hollow trunk, blue lichen on a stone, the bare space round a charcoal pit, linked themselves in his mind to his remotest memories – an escaped goat, a pole-cat driven from its lair, the raised skirt of a girl. And now the war in these parts was like a continuation of his normal life; work, play, hunting, all turned into war; the smell of gunpowder at the Loreto bridge, escapes down the bushy slopes, minefields sewn with death.

The war twisted closely round and round in those valleys like a dog trying to bite its tail; partisans elbow to elbow with Bersaglieri and Fascist militia; each side alternating between mountain and valley, making wide turns round the crests so as not to run into each other and find themselves fired on; and always someone killed, either on hill or valley. Binda's village, San Faustino, was down among fields, three groups of houses on each side of the valley. His girl, Regina, hung out sheets from her window on days when there were round ups. Binda's village was a short halt on his way up and down; a sip of milk, a clean vest ready washed by his mother; then off he had to hurry, in case the Fascists suddenly arrived, for there hadn't been enough partisans killed at San Faustino.

All winter it was a game of hide and seek; the Bersaglieri at Baiardo, the Militia at Molini, the Germans at Briga, and in the middle of them the partisans squeezed into two corners of the valley, avoiding the round ups by moving from one to the other during the night. That very night a German column was marching on Briga, had perhaps already reached Carmo, and the Militia were getting ready to reinforce Molini. The partisan detachments were sleeping in stalls around half spent braziers; Binda marched along in the dark woods, with their salvation in his legs, for the order he carried was: 'Evacuate the valleys at once. Entire battalion and heavy machine-guns to be on Mount Pellegrino by dawn.'

Binda felt anxiety fluttering in his lungs like bats' wings; he longed to grasp the slope two miles away, pull himself up it, whisper the order like a breath of wind into the grass and hear it flowing off through his moustache and nostrils, till it reached Vendetta, Serpe, Gueriglia; then scoop himself out a hole in the chestnut leaves and bury himself in there, he and Regina, first taking out the cones that might prick Regina's legs; but the more leaves he scooped out the more cones he found – it was impossible to make a place for Regina's legs there, her big soft legs with their smooth thin skin.

The dry leaves and the chestnut cones rustled, almost gurgled, under Binda's feet; the squirrels with their round glittering eyes ran to hide at the tops of the trees. 'Be quick, Binda!' the commander, Fegato, had said to him when giving him the message. Sleep rose from the heart of the night, there was a velvety feel on the inside of his eyelids; Binda would have liked to lose the path, plunge into a sea of dry leaves and swim in them until they submerged him. 'Be quick, Binda!'

He was now walking on a narrow path along the upper slopes of the Tumena valley, which was still covered with ice. It was the widest valley in the area, and had high sides wide apart; the one opposite him was glimmering in the dark, the one on which he was walking had bare slopes scattered with an occasional bush from which, in daytime, rose fluttering groups of partridges. Binda felt he saw a distant light, down in lower Tumena, moving ahead of him. It zig-zagged every now and again as if going round a curve, vanished, and reappeared a little farther on in an unexpected part. Who on earth could it be at that hour? Sometimes it seemed to Binda that the light was much farther away, on the other side of the valley, sometimes that it had stopped, and sometimes that it was behind him. Who could be carrying so many different lights along all the paths of lower Tumena, perhaps in front of him too, in higher Tumena, winking on and off like that? The Germans!

Following on Binda's tracks was an animal roused from deep back in his childhood; it was coming after him, would soon catch him up; the animal of fear. Those lights were the Germans searching Tumena, bush by bush, in battalions. Impossible, Binda knew that, although it would be almost pleasant to believe it, to abandon himself to the blandishments of that animal from childhood which was following him so close. Time was drumming, gulping in Binda's throat. Perhaps it was too late now to arrive before the Germans and save his comrades. Already Binda could see Vendetta's hut at Gastagna burnt out, the bleeding bodies of his comrades, the heads of some of them hanging by their long hair on branches of larch trees. 'Be quick, Binda!'

He was amazed at where he was, he seemed to have gone such a little way in such a long time; perhaps he had slowed down or even stopped without realizing it. He did not change his pace, however; he knew well that it was always regular and sure, that he mustn't trust that animal which came to visit him on these night missions, wetting his temples with its invisible fingers slimy with saliva. He was a healthy lad,

Binda, with good nerves, cool in every eventuality; and he kept intact all his power to act even though he was carrying that animal around with him like a monkey tethered to his neck.

The surface of the Colla Bracca meadow looked soft in the moonlight. 'Mines!' thought Binda. There were no mines up there, Binda knew that; they were a long way off, on the other slope of the mountain. But Binda now began thinking that the mines might have moved underground from one part of the mountain to the other, following his steps like enormous underground spiders. The earth above mines produces strange funguses, disastrous to knock over; everything would go up in a second, but each second would become as long as a century and the world would have stopped as if by magic.

Now Binda was going down through the wood. Drowsiness and darkness drew gloomy masks on the tree trunks and bushes. There were Germans all round. They must have seen him pass the Colla Bracca meadow in the moonlight, they were following him, waiting for him at the entrance to the wood. An owl hooted nearby: it was a whistle, a signal for the Germans to close in round him. There, another whistle, he was surrounded! An animal moved at the back of a bush of heather; perhaps it was a hare, perhaps a fox, perhaps a German lying in the thickets keeping him covered. There was a German in every thicket, a German perched on the top of every tree, with the squirrels. The stones were pullulating with helmets, rifles were sprouting among the branches, the roots of the trees ended in human feet. Binda was walking between a double row of hidden Germans, who were looking at him with glistening eyes from between the leaves; the farther he walked the deeper he got in among them. At the third, the fourth, the sixth hoot of the owl all the Germans would jump to their feet round him, their guns pointed, their chests crossed by sten-gun straps.

One called Gund, in the middle of them, with a terrible white smile under his helmet, would stretch out huge hands to seize him. Binda was afraid to turn round in case he saw Gund looming above his shoulders, sten-gun at the ready, hands open in the air. Or perhaps Gund would appear on the path ahead, pointing a finger at him, or come up and begin walking silently along beside him.

Suddenly he thought he had missed the way; and yet he recognized the path, the stones, the trees, the smell of musk. But they were stones, trees, musk from another place far away, from a thousand different far away places. After these stone steps there should be a short drop, not a bramble bush. After that slope a bush of broom, not of holly; the side of the path should be dry, not full of water and frogs. The frogs were in another valley, they were near the Germans; at the turn of the path there was a German ambush waiting and he'd suddenly fall into their hands, find himself facing the big German called Gund who is deep down in all of us, and who opens his enormous hands above us all, yet never succeeds in catching us.

To drive away Gund he must think of Regina, scoop a niche for Regina in the snow; but the snow is hard and frozen – Regina can't sit on it in her thin dress; nor can she sit under the pines – there are endless layers of pine needles; the earth underneath is all ant heaps, and Gund is already above, lowering his hands on to their heads and throats, lowering still . . . he gave a shriek. No, he must think of Regina, the girl who is in all of us and for whom we all want to scoop a niche deep in the woods – the girl with big hips and dressed only in hair which falls down over her shoulders.

But the pursuit between Binda and Gund is nearing its end; Vendetta's camp is now only fifteen, twenty minutes away. Binda's thoughts run ahead; but his feet go on placing themselves regularly one in front of the other so as not to lose breath. When he reaches his comrades his fear will have vanished, cancelled even from the bottom of his memory as something impossible. He must think of waking up Vendetta and Sciabola, the commissar, to explain Fegato's order to them; then he'd set off again for Serpe's camp.

But would he ever reach the hut? Wasn't he tied by a wire which dragged him farther away the nearer he got? And as he arrived wouldn't he hear *ausch ausch* from Germans sitting round the fire eating up the remaining chestnuts? Binda imagined himself arriving at the hut to find it half burnt out and deserted. He went inside: empty. But in a corner, huge, sitting on his haunches, with his helmet touching the ceiling, was Gund, with his eyes round and glistening like the squirrels' and his white toothy smile between damp lips. Gund would make a sign to him: 'Sit down.' And Binda would sit down.

There, a hundred yards off, a light! It was them! Which of them? He longed to turn back, to flee, as if all the danger was up there in the hut. But he went on walking quickly along, his face hard and closed like a fist. Now the fire suddenly seemed to be getting too near; was it moving to meet him? Now to be getting farther off; was it running away? But it was motionless, a camp-fire which had not yet gone out, Binda knew that.

'Who goes there?' He did not quiver an eyelash. 'Binda,' he said.

Sentry: 'I'm Civetta. Any news, Binda?'

'Is Vendetta asleep?'

Now he was inside the hut, with sleeping comrades breathing all round him. Comrades, of course; who could ever have thought there'd be anything else?

'Germans down at Briga, Fascists up at Molni. Evacuate. By dawn you've all to be up on the crest of Mount Pellegrino with the heavies.'

Vendetta was scarcely awake and fluttering his eyelids. 'God,' he said. Then he got up, clapped his hands. 'Wake up, everyone, we've got to go out and fight.'

Binda was now sucking at a can of boiled chestnuts, spitting out the bits of skin sticking to them. The men divided up into shifts for carrying the ammunition and the tripod of the heavy. He set off. 'I'm going on to Serpe's,' he said. 'Be quick, Binda!' exclaimed his comrades.

Villers-Bocage

After the Allies' D-Day invasion of France in June 1944, Montgomery's British troops soon fell behind schedule. The bocage *country of Normandy, with its deep lanes and high hedges, steep valleys and wooded hills, was ideal defensive terrain for the Germans. Carlo D'Este, retired Lieutenant Colonel of the US Army, turned military historian, describes one embarrassing engagement in his book* Decision in Normandy.

The order for the 7th Armoured Division to disengage and initiate a right hook aimed at the crossroads town of Villers-Bocage came none too soon for General Erskine who, according to one of his former operations officers, 'thought that he should have been given the opportunity to go for Villers-Bocage twenty-four hours earlier' . . .

As the 7th Armoured implied by breaking contact with Panzer Lehr and beginning their drive in less than four hours, far too much time had been spent in making plans: Erskine was delighted by the order and, understanding at once the urgency conveyed by Dempsey, promptly ordered Brigadier Robert Hinde's 22nd Armoured Brigade to spearhead the drive. As far as Erskine was concerned the order was long overdue. Hinde's Brigade Major recently recalled that the pre-D-Day planning clearly specified that the 7th Armoured was to take Villers-Bocage almost immediately and then push quickly south to seize Mont Pinçon. During the afternoon the brigade successfully disengaged from Panzer Lehr and by 1600 hours was on the move towards Villers-Bocage. Hinde had acquired a reputation in North Africa as a fearless commander, so fearless in fact that he was known as 'Looney'. His former brigade major has described him as 'One of the most colourful personalities I came across in the Army. He believed in leading from the front but against that he had little regard for staff work and administration which he regarded as a responsibility of others.'

The predicted gap west of the Aure was indeed there in the disorganized German lines and by late evening of 12 June leading elements of the 22nd Armoured Brigade reached the Caumont–Villers-Bocage road five miles west of the town. After meeting light resistance, Hinde wisely decided not to continue further movement against Villers-Bocage that night, as it was not known what German opposition might be encountered there and a reconnaissance in force might prematurely disclose British intentions. In the early morning hours of 13 June the drive resumed and within a short time a tank-infantry force stormed virtually unopposed into Villers-Bocage at 0800 hours, led by the 4th County of London Yeomanry (Sharpshooters) and 'A' Company, 1st Battalion the Rifle Brigade.

After being so effectively contained by Panzer Lehr, the men of the London Yeomanry found the easy capture of the important crossroads town an exhilarating experience, perhaps too exhilarating in the light of what shortly transpired. In eighteen hours they had advanced to an objective which the day before had seemed unattainable . . .

A lieutenant of the Rifle Brigade later wrote of the astonishing welcome given the British by the townspeople. 'Once in the main street of Villers-Bocage we were amazed at the terrific reception which we received from the dense crowd of gaily dressed civilians who thronged the pavements. Everything seemed normal and even the gendarmes had turned out in their khaki and blue uniforms to guide us through the town.' This mutual joy was shortlived.

Villers-Bocage had strategic importance to both the British and the German armies. Situated at the head of the Seulles valley, the town was the gateway to Mont Pinçon ten miles to the south and to the Odon valley and Caen in the east. The road network for the entire area originated from Villers-Bocage and, as with another famous market town – Bastogne – the force controlling the town and its environs controlled this network.

Brigadier Hinde knew that Villers-Bocage could not remain effectively in British hands without control of the high ground north-east of it on the Caen–Villers-Bocage highway, known as Point 213, less than a mile from the edge of town. 'A' Squadron was ordered to continue north-east to seize Point 213, followed shortly thereafter by the motorized infantry of 'A' Company of the Rifle Brigade which parked along the highway nearby while two troops of 'A' Squadron deployed around the high ground. From the moment it was captured, the veteran regiment commander, Lieutenant Colonel (Viscount) Arthur Cranley, was apprehensive about advancing beyond Villers-Bocage until a reconnaissance could be made of the area to the east. Several German armoured cars were seen in the distance observing the Sharpshooters and Cranley knew this information would quickly be passed to all German units operating in the area. Hinde's brigade major, Major Lever, observed that Cranley 'was undoubtedly cautious in his progress. I seem to recall that my operations map had as many reports of German 88-mm guns than perhaps ever existed at the time ... Hinde was right up with Cranley urging him on as fast as possible.' Cranley made his misgivings known to Hinde but his requests for additional time to conduct a more thorough reconnaissance were, according to eyewitnesses, 'repeatedly refused and [he] was ordered to continue his advance to secure the high ground beyond Villers-Bocage ...' Obviously still troubled by the unknown situation around Point 213, Cranley left the four tanks of his Regimental HQ parked on the main street of Villers-Bocage while he went forward in his scout car to inspect the new 'A' Squadron positions.

In anticipation of a British flanking movement aimed at Villers-Bocage, the 2nd Panzer Division had been alerted to move from its position north of the Seine near Amiens to Normandy, to establish blocking positions in the Villers sector. Unknown to the British, two companies of the 1st SS Panzer Corps panzer reserve had already arrived and were in position outside Villers-Bocage the morning of 13 June. One of these units, No. 2 Company, 501st Heavy Tank Battalion, was commanded by a young SS Obersturmführer (captain) named Michael Wittmann, who had already achieved fame as a panzer ace and who, that day, would earn the plaudits of friend and foe as the most acclaimed tank commander in history. This Tiger force now lying in wait for the 7th Armoured was the first of the German reinforcements hastily ordered up to help plug the dangerous gap in the German defences on the left flank of 1 SS Panzer Corps. Not far behind advance elements of the 2nd Panzer Division would later reinforce Panzer Lehr in the Villers-Bocage area. Their hasty forced march across the Seine had been completely undetected by Allied intelligence, so that their presence, along with the Tigers, was a complete surprise to the British. Certainly, the 22nd Armoured Brigade had no inkling of what awaited the London Yeomanry. Major Lever recalls that 'Intelligence indicated enemy forces along the way including armour but with absolutely no suggestion that these included Tiger or Panther tanks.' As a post-war German account of 1 SS Panzer Corps' operations was to relate:

> Panzer Lehr Division was not able to establish a continuous front, and we had to consider the possibility of enemy tanks breaking through along

> the road Villers-Bocage–Caen. The weak reconnaissance elements of this division's reconnaissance battalion committed in this gap on the flank of adjacent LXXXIV Corps reported advancing United States forces, which as it seemed, intended to capture the mountainous terrain west of Tilly . . . By 10 June the appearance of British tanks on the left wing of Panzer Lehr Division and of United States forces within this gap made it appear probable that the enemy had discovered few German troops were in the area of Tilly – south of Bayeux-Balleroy. Early on the morning of 12 June [sic], the commander of the five tanks [Tiger], which had been placed in readiness north of Villers-Bocage sighted an enemy motorized column, including tanks, on the march from Tilly toward Villers-Bocage.

What is now known is that Wittmann and his company of four other Tigers and a Mark IV Special had a similar mission to the 4th CLY – that of occupying the commanding terrain around Point 213 – and of doing whatever possible to stem any British advance to the east into the Odon valley. 'From the evidence of his executive officer his objective was the same as the British – the road junction [north-east] of town. He must have been surprised to see a squadron of British armour leave Villers-Bocage and advance to occupy positions to its south. Wittmann's first thoughts are now known to be that he must endeavour to stop the British and protect the flanks of Panzer Lehr.'

One of the most amazing engagements in the history of armoured warfare was about to begin near Point 213. From various published and unpublished accounts, the encounter between Wittmann and the 22nd Armoured Brigade can be reconstructed.

At 0800 'A' Squadron, 4th CLY and 'A' Company, 1st Battalion the Rifle Brigade pass through Villers-Bocage. At 0905 lead elements of the Yeomanry reach Point 213 accompanied by an advance party of the infantry from 'A' Company. The main tank-infantry column consisting of some twenty-five half-tracks and tanks of both units halt several hundred yards behind on a hedge-lined section of the highway awaiting instructions before moving forward to deploy with 'A' Squadron around Point 213. The infantry is summoned forward at the same moment that two or three Tigers are spotted running parallel to the column, screened by a hedge. The Tigers swing around and face the column whose crews have just dismounted. Wittmann, who has observed the column halt from a position on the wooded high ground several hundred yards north of the highway, recognizes its extreme vulnerability and decides to attack at once on his own without waiting for the other Tigers to assist.

Wittmann was in the better tactical position. He paused only to explain his intention which was, without waiting for support, to attack the British column using

> speed and fire-power to block the road and thus prevent the British vehicles from being reinforced or from withdrawing. He knew that the high hedge banks were too thick to be pierced by the light-armoured vehicles and that there was too little room on the road to allow the enemy machines to turn round and escape. Running to the left of, and parallel to, the road on which the British column lay there was a narrow cart track. This led from the high ground to the road at a point almost at the crest of 213. Wittmann decided to approach the column via this track and to destroy, as his first victim, the personnel carrier near the road and track junction. The high velocity gun was laid, aimed and fired. The half-track, swung across the road by the force of the impact, caught fire and began to pour out dense clouds of black smoke . . . the heavy Tiger thundered towards the British, shuddering only slightly as the heavy gun fired shell after shell into the mass of machines. Half-tracks, carriers and tanks were smashed by 8.8cm shells, and then with a final burst of speed the 55-ton steel monster, destroying in its rush a British tank which it met on the narrow path, crashed through the junction, was swung in a tight arc onto the roadway and began its descent upon the vehicles lined up outside the village and along the narrow high street.

Wittmann's Tiger entered the main street where it immediately encountered the RHQ tanks whose crews were also caught dismounted and unable to react to the menacing sight of a lone Tiger roaring unexpectedly into view. What happened next is recounted by several of the participants:

> [The Tiger] immediately knocked out Colonel Arthur's tank, then that of the Regimental second in command, Major Carr, whom he seriously wounded, followed by the Regimental Sergeant-Major's tank. Captain [Pat] Dyas in the fourth tank, reversed and backed into the front garden of a nearby house. His own gunner was at that moment out of the tank, so he had to watch helplessly as the tank commander, with his head well out of his turret, presented the vulnerable side of his Tiger tank as he continued through the main street towards the road junction [on the western edge of Villers-Bocage].

The Tiger had so far been unmolested during its destructive sally through town but at the road junction it encountered the leading tanks of 'B' Squadron.

> He exchanged shots with Sergeant Lockwood in a Cromwell and was hit at least once which was possibly the cause of his missing the British tank. The road junction was effectively in British hands. The Tiger had seen enough and done enough to stop the British advance. The main danger to Panzer Lehr was still 'A' Squadron. He must have reversed away to disengage from Sergeant Lockwood, who was somewhat handicapped by the part of a house which he had demolished because it contained a German sniper. On his return through the main street [the Tiger] came face to face with Pat Dyas in his Cromwell, still bent on stalking him. He knocked out Dyas and killed two of his crew, one by machine-gun fire whilst escaping. Dyas, although wounded, succeeded in getting away, as did the other member of his crew.

After creating havoc within the town, Wittmann prudently withdrew into the woods south-east of Villers-Bocage. With the aid of a French girl, Captain Dyas managed to reach the commander of 'B' Squadron. 'From the latter's tank he spoke to Viscount Cranley still in his Scout car on the high ground and told him of the events within the town. In reply Colonel Arthur said he realized the situation was desperate and that 'A' Squadron was at that moment being heavily attacked by German Tiger tanks. No further messages were received from him.'

Within the space of some *five minutes* a single Tiger had devastated Cranley's force and left behind a trail of wrecked and burning vehicles, the shattered leading element of the 22nd Armoured Brigade. It was only the beginning. Wittmann now withdrew and returned to his unit to re-arm and re-fuel his Tiger. In the early afternoon, this time with four other Tigers and the Mark IV Special, and possibly three other tanks plus infantry in support, he returned to Point 213 to renew the attack against the remnants of Cranley's outgunned and outnumbered tank-infantry force. It was a total mismatch and what was left of 'A' Squadron was soon overwhelmed. Cranley, along with many others, was captured. From what is known, apparently only one survivor managed to escape the débâcle at Point 213. 'He, although wounded, got back to Villers-Bocage where a French butcher hid him until, three days later, after surviving the Allied bombing of the town, he escaped back to British lines.' This survivor told of the tank crews attempting to escape but being killed, wounded or captured by the German infantry supporting the Tigers. All attempts to reinforce the isolated squadron were rebuffed by other German elements which were now engaging the British in and around Villers-Bocage.

After dealing with Cranley at Point 213 the Germans returned to mop up the remaining infantrymen of the Rifle Brigade. Individual acts of heroism by the infantrymen were in vain. One corporal, for example, bravely charged the Tigers with only a Sten gun. British casualties were high. The 4th CLY lost 4 killed in action, 5 wounded and 76 men missing. Accounts vary as to the material losses but at least 20 Cromwell tanks, 4 Fireflys, 3 light tanks, 3 scout cars and a half-track were knocked out. 'A' Company lost some 80 infantrymen including 3 officers killed. By early afternoon both British units had virtually ceased to exist. Nearly 30 infantrymen managed to escape and the first safely to reach British lines on 14 June was Captain Christopher Milner, who had made a dramatic escape after being stalked along a hedge by a German officer who kept shouting at him: 'Englishman, surrender! Englishman, surrender!' The remainder of the 4th CLY now came under the command of 'B' Squadron, whose commander tightened his defences within the town and attempted – in vain – to learn the fate of his sister unit, 'A' Squadron.

Wittmann, however, had not yet finished performing his task of giant killer. With the same force he returned to Villers-Bocage later that day, along with fresh tank support from the first arriving units of the 2nd Panzer Division. This time he pushed his luck too far, for the Sharpshooters were prepared and had baited a trap. In the ensuing engagement the Mark IV Special and three Tigers were knocked out, including Wittmann's, which was hit by a six-pounder anti-tank gun situated on a side street. Wittmann, his crew and those of the other tanks got away on foot: most of the British supporting infantry had been lost at Point 213, so there was no way to prevent their escape. The four German tanks were set on fire to prevent their later recovery.

Almost single-handedly, this one audacious and brilliant German tank commander had crushed the British advance around Villers-Bocage and forced the 7th Armoured Division on to the defensive.

Louis Simpson's 'Carentan'

Louis Simpson, born in Jamaica, enlisted in the US Army in 1943 and served with the 101st Airborne Division in France, Holland, Belgium and Germany. Back in the USA he suffered a severe nervous breakdown, involving amnesia. The war was blacked out in his mind. When he left hospital, he began to write poetry. In 1948 he wrote out a dream he had had as 'Carentan O Carentan', then realized that it was in fact a memory – of his first time under fire.

CARENTAN O CARENTAN

Trees in the old days used to stand
And shape a shady lane
Where lovers wandered hand in hand
Who came from Carentan.

This was the shining green canal
Where we came two by two
Walking at combat-interval.
Such trees we never knew.

The day was early June, the ground
Was soft and bright with dew.
Far away the guns did sound,
But here the sky was blue.

The sky was blue, but there a smoke
Hung still above the sea
Where the ships together spoke
To towns we could not see.

Could you have seen us through a glass
You would have said a walk
Of farmers out to turn the grass,
Each with his own hay-fork.

The watchers in their leopard suits
Waited till it was time,
And aimed between the belt and boot
And let the barrel climb.

I must lie down at once, there is
A hammer at my knee.
And call it death or cowardice,
Don't count again on me.

Everything's all right, Mother,
Everyone gets the same
At one time or another.
It's all in the game.

I never strolled, nor ever shall,
Down such a leafy lane.
I never drank in a canal,
Nor ever shall again.

There is a whistling in the leaves
And it is not the wind,
The twigs are falling from the knives
That cut men to the ground.

Tell me, Master-Sergeant,
The way to turn and shoot.
But the Sergeant's silent
That taught me how to do it.

O Captain, show us quickly
Our place upon the map.
But the Captain's sickly
And taking a long nap.

Lieutenant, what's my duty,
My place in the platoon?
He too's a sleeping beauty,
Charmed by that strange tune.

Carentan O Carentan
Before we met with you
We never yet had lost a man
Or known what death could do.

The *Duce* Dies

Eventually Germans could protect Mussolini no longer. Partisans caught him on 29 April 1945, attempting to flee to Switzerland, and hanged his body, upside down, with that of his mistress, in the streets of Milan. The Sicilian poet Salvatore Quasimodo responded.

LAUDE, 29 APRIL 1945

SON:
Mother, why do you spit at a corpse
hanging tied by the feet from a beam, head down?
And the others dangling beside him, don't they
disgust you? Ah! that woman with the ghoulish can-can
stockings, and mouth and throat of trampled
flowers! No, mother, stop! Shout
to the crowd to go. This is not grief but leering
and joy. The horseflies are glued already
to the knots of veins. Now you have aimed at that face:
mother, mother, mother!

MOTHER:
We have always spat at corpses, son:
hanging from window-bars and masts of ships,
burnt at the stake, torn to pieces
by hounds on estate bounds for the sake of a little
grass. An eye for an eye, a tooth
for a tooth, turmoil or quiet no matter:
after two thousand years of eucharist
our heart wants open the heart that opened yours
my son. They have gouged your eyes, maimed
your hands, just for a name to be betrayed.
Show me your eyes, give me your hands:
you are dead, son, and because you are dead, my son,
you can pardon, my son, my son.

SON:

This sickening, sultry heat, this smoke
of ruins, the fat green flies bunched on the hooks:
justly the anger and blood are flowing.
Not for you, mother, and mother, not for me:
tomorrow they will pierce my eyes and hands
again. All down the ages pity
has been the howl of the murdered.

7

The Eastern Front

If it had not coincided with the horrors of the Sino-Japanese and Allied-Japanese war further East, and been followed by the USA's operations in Vietnam, one might say without hesitation that the German–Soviet war of 1941–45 was the most barbaric of the twentieth, or any other, century. Statistics numb the mind – four million men, for instance, 13,000 vehicles and 12,000 aircraft were involved in the decisive Battle of Kursk in July 1943. Richard Overy, in Russia's War *(Allen Lane, 1998), discusses the problems which we have in assessing new estimates from Russian researchers following the collapse of the Soviet Union. For instance, Soviet military 'losses' of 11,444,100 include over four and a half million people taken prisoner by the Germans (mortality among these was enormous), or listed as 'missing', beside 6,885,100 personnel killed in action, mortally wounded and so on. Richard Overy regards 8.6 million as the likeliest figure for Soviet military deaths that we can get. Quite apart from these, estimates of civilian deaths range from 16.9 million up to a stupefying 25 million. It seems most likely that, including military personnel, about 25 million Soviet citizens died prematurely because of the war. Adding three million German military and 2.5 million German civilians, the Eastern Front contributed about half the world's war-related mortality. The initial German onslaught from June 1941 eliminated 98 out of 170 Soviet divisions from the line of battle. But over the full forty-seven months of fighting, the huge Red Army inflicted 70 per cent of the total losses of men and weapons suffered by the Wehrmacht, knocking out 607 German divisions as compared to the Anglo-American tally of 176.*

The statistics would be shocking enough in themselves, but the character of this war between two ruthless totalitarian regimes was brutal beyond compare. Germans were instructed to kill all Jews under Soviet rule, and counselled to regard even Slavs as subhuman. Horrific German atrocities provoked ruthless behaviour in return. To compound this disaster for humanity, the German lands and Russia were perhaps the two countries above all others which had defined contemporary humanity through literature, music and thought. The compatriots of Mozart and Goethe practised genocide against the people of Heine and Mahler, and this scandal was sadly echoed as people brought up to adore Pushkin and Tolstoy and Chekhov behaved in ways that these men would have denounced.

British and US propaganda – often sincerely representing the thoughts and feelings of the propagandists – projected the Russians as valiant patriots whose efforts were saving the world from Fascism. But while the ideology of Nazism had been drilled into German soldiers, commissars on the Soviet side kept strict account of backslidings from 'Leninist' orthodoxy and inflamed by their reports the malignant paranoia of Stalin and his creatures. Granted that Stalinists and Nazis had in fact learnt a great deal from each other, it is still possible to discriminate between the German doctrine of absolute unquestioning loyalty to the Führer and his concept of an Aryan master race and Communist obeisance to the idea that the interests of workers of all races in all lands were the same. A sincere Communist might find the brutality displayed by his compatriots towards Germans especially painful.

Entering Kaunas, 1941

Joannes Bobrowski was born in East Prussia in 1917. A student of art history, he was conscripted at the outbreak of war and fought on the Eastern Front where he became a prisoner of war. His first poems appeared in a Nazi cultural periodical in 1943. He did not publish again until he was settled post-war in the Communist DDR. His verse evokes the territory which the Romans, who never conquered it, called 'Sarmatia' – those plains of Eastern Europe disputed between Poles and Germans, Ukrainians and Lithuanians, where millions of Jews had come to live in a terrain of impoverished cultivators and changeable boundaries. (Tilsit, Bobrowski's birthplace, became part of the USSR in 1945.) Under everything he heard the language of the Prussian Slavs overrun by the German Teutonic Knights in the Middle Ages – a language which became extinct in the eighteenth century. From a savagely contested land he asserted the common humanity of the contestants.

KAUNAS 1941

Town,
branches over the river,
copper-coloured, like branching candles.
The banks call from the deep.
Then the lame girl
walked before dusk,
her skirt of darkest red.

And I know the steps,
the slope, this house. There is no
fire. Under this roof
lives the Jewess, lives whispering
in the Jews' silence
– the faces of the daughters
a white water. Noisily
the murderers pass the gate. We walk
softly, in musty air, in the track of wolves.

At evening we looked out
over a stony valley. The hawk
swept round the broad dome.
We saw the old town, house after house
running down to the river.

Will you walk over
the hill? The grey processions
– old men and sometimes boys –
die there. They walk
up the slope ahead of the slavering wolves.

Did my eyes avoid yours
brother? Sleep struck us
at the bloody wall. So we went on
blind to everything. We looked
like gipsies at the villages
in the oakwood, the summer
snow on the roofs.

I shall walk on the stone banks
under the rainy bushes,
listen in the haze of the plains.
There were swallows upstream
and the woodpigeon called
in the green night:
My dark is already come.

Hitler's Army

Omer Bartov, an Israeli, made his international reputation with The Eastern Front, 1941–1945: German Troops and the Barbarisation of War *(1985). His view – that the German Army, as distinct from the wholly politicized SS, was not the ideologically neutral body of brave patriots which its admirers and defenders have proclaimed – has run into bitter opposition. But Bartov's case has great weight. The army mostly consisted of young men educated in schools where Nazi ideas were paramount from 1933, then, at the Front, subjected to Goebbels' propaganda about the subhuman 'Jewish Commissars' who were their prime adversaries, and confronted by him with a horrific vision of wives, sisters and mothers raped by oncoming Slav hordes if they did not fight to the death in Russia. As Bartov further demonstrates, the appalling conditions which they had to endure were likely to confirm them in paranoia and brutality.*

Why did Hitler's Army *(the title of Bartov's study published in 1991 and extracted below) fight so long against impossible odds? Because, Bartov suggests, it had been successfully Nazified.*

The risks of Blitzkrieg tactics and strategy, and the fundamental limitations of Germany's production capacity, became glaringly visible during the first six months of the Russian campaign. The Reich's war industries succeeded in raising tank production from 2,235 in 1940 to 5,290 in 1941; and the Wehrmacht doubled the number of its armoured divisions to twenty-one (though at the price of reducing the number of tanks per division by a third). Yet this expansion of the modern combat elements proved far from sufficient in view of the tremendous losses at the front, and the size of the enemy's own armoured forces. It is indeed quite revealing that judging by the ratio between manpower and fighting machines, the Soviet forces directly facing the *Ostheer* were more modern, even if just like the Western Allies, they too had not yet learned to make effective use of their material strength. In June 1941 the *Ostheer*'s 3,600,000 troops attacked with 3,648 tanks out of a total German stock of 5,694; once again, only 444 of these were of the relatively advanced Panzer IV model. Facing it in Western Russia were 2,900,000 Soviet soldiers supported by no less than 15,000 tanks out of a total armoured force of 24,000, more than all the tanks in the rest of the world put together. To be sure, the vast majority of Soviet machines were quite obsolete, but 1,861 were T-34 and heavy KV tanks, significantly superior to the best machines produced at the time in Germany. And, whereas in 1940 only 358 such tanks were built in the Soviet Union, in the first half of 1941 alone their number rose to 1,503, and even in the second half of that year, in spite of the occupation of Russia's primary industrial regions, a further 4,740 advanced models were turned out. Similarly, the *Ostheer* was supported by only 2,510 aircraft, considerably less than it had deployed in the West, whereas the Russians had up to 9,000, though in this case they were generally inferior to German planes. Worse still, once the Blitzkrieg faltered, the Soviet Union's greater manpower and industrial resources came into play and rapidly widened the technological margin between the Red Army and the *Ostheer*.

It should again be stressed that following the débâcle of winter 1941–42, the Third Reich both immensely expanded its overall war production and made considerable strides in the development of some highly sophisticated weapons and machines. Yet the experience of the average combat soldier at the front did not reflect Germany's switch to total war production. This was so both because proportionately the enemy became ever stronger and better equipped, and because due to the vast expanse of the territories occupied by the Wehrmacht, the Reich's rising production figures seemed far less impressive at the receiving end. In the relatively constricted spaces of the West, the Wehrmacht's policy of maintaining a few well-equipped divisions at the expense of the great bulk of infantry formations had proved effective. In the East, one of the keys to the failure of the Blitzkrieg was the infantry's inability to keep up with the armoured spearheads over a long distance. Consequently the nature of the war changed drastically as a more or less stable front emerged which could only be held by the Wehrmacht's ill-equipped infantry formations, along with a growing number of armoured divisions which had lost most of their tanks. Only a few élite units were kept well supplied with modern fighting machines, but they were no longer able fundamentally to change the overall situation. This was the reason that although as viewed in overall production figures the Wehrmacht seemed to be undergoing a process of modernization, the experience of most troops on the ground was of profound demodernization, of a return to the trench warfare of the Great War made worse by the enemy's growing technological capacity.

It is of some interest to examine these developments at greater detail. As far as war production was concerned, Germany managed to raise the annual turnout of light and medium tanks to as many as 22,110 by 1944, at which time it was also producing 5,235 super-heavy tanks. Yet the Soviet Union maintained an annual production rate of 30,000 tanks as of 1943; Britain produced 36,720 tanks between late 1941 and the end of 1943; and the United States turned out a total of 88,410 tanks. Similarly, the Third Reich raised aircraft production from 12,401 in 1941 to 40,593 in 1944. But the Soviet Union achieved a monthly production rate of between 2,000 and 3,000 aircraft in the last years of the war, and the United States produced just under 100,000 fighter planes and more than 90,000 bombers, of which more than a third were four-engined long-range machines. All this was apart from the tremendous output of the American motor industry, which turned out well over four million armoured, combat, and supply vehicles of all kinds, a large proportion of which were instrumental in the motorization of the Red Army.

From the perspective of the front, the length of the Soviet frontier meant that the *Ostheer* could repeat its Blitzkrieg tactics only by splitting its armour among three army groups, making each of its spearheads weaker than the single and decisive armoured concentration of the Western campaign. In the central sector of the front, where the most powerful grouping of German forces was to be found, it was necessary once more to split the armoured formations between two Panzer groups in order to encircle the large Soviet forces in Belorussia. As the Germans charged deeper into Russia, the length of the front almost doubled, from 800 to 1,500 miles, and lines of supply extended some 1,000 miles to the rear. This further increased the dispersal of tank units, and caused tremendous difficulties with maintaining their crucial logistical links to the depots. Matters were made worse due to the fact that while the *Ostheer*'s supply apparatus was inadequately motorized, unlike western Europe, in Russia roads were sparse and mostly unpaved, and the railroad used a different gauge. It is indicative of the partial modernization of the Wehrmacht that although the Panzer divisions were given their own motor supply columns, fully 77 infantry divisions, or about half of the entire invasion force, relied strictly on horse-drawn wagons for their provisions from the railheads. Moreover, lack of spare parts meant that damaged vehicles could not be repaired, while over-exertion and lack of food greatly diminished the number of horses. Because the northern and southern army groups failed to reach their operational goals with their own limited tank forces, armoured units in the centre had to come to their assistance, thereby greatly weakening the *Ostheer*'s thrust toward Moscow. By the time the Germans finally made up their minds to attack the Russian capital, their material strength had already significantly diminished, and their logistical system was in increasing disarray. In retrospect it can be said that the attempt to repeat the risky Blitzkrieg tactics employed in the West with an even less favourable ratio between space and machines was thus bound to fail.

Matériel and mentality were closely related matters in the *Ostheer*. As the number of tanks diminished, the troops had to dig in and revert to trench warfare; as the trucks broke down and the trains failed to arrive, provisions of ammunition, food, and clothes decreased. The demodernization of the front was thus a process whereby the disappearance of the machine forced the individual soldier into living conditions of the utmost primitiveness. The nature of this process can be seen from the following instances. Panzer Group 4, the armoured element of Army Group North, raced over 200 miles into Soviet territory in the first five days of the campaign, but then had to wait a whole week for its supply basis to be pushed forward before it could renew its advance. Even then, it was necessary to divert all army group provisions and transport resources to the tank units, with the result that the infantry was left far behind. Hence when the armoured divisions reached the gates of Leningrad, they had to wait so long for the infantry to catch up with them that in the meanwhile the city's defences were reinforced and it was no longer possible to capture it. From this point on the front solidified and the remaining tanks were diverted to the centre. Similarly, further south the infantry soldiers of 16 Army marched on foot over 600 miles during the first five weeks of the campaign, and then found themselves in an area of swamps east of the Lovat River where they were to remain for the next fourteen months in the most wretched conditions conceivable. The exertions of infantry troops in the initial stages of 'Barbarossa' were not unusual, albeit especially great, for an army which had conducted all its Blitzkrieg campaigns with a small motorized element supported by a vast mass of walking infantry. But when the tanks got bogged down, and the whole army became stranded deep inside the Soviet Union, the infantry became the backbone of the front, clinging to it with the same desperation as the men of 1914–18, and with just as little hope of ever being rescued from their predicament by this or that technological means. Throughout the front lack of fighting machines combined with the climatic and geographical peculiarities of Russia to deprive this former Blitzkrieg army of all semblance of modernity. The commander of 16 Army's II Corps reported as early as 28 October 1941 that

> The recent rainy weather has made the roads and terrain . . . so impassable, that only tractors, [Russian horse-drawn] Panje-wagons and cavalry can still maintain a limited degree of mobility . . . From my own experience I know that while walking on the roads one sinks to one's knees in the mud, and the water pours into one's boots from above. Fox-holes are collapsing . . . Some of the troops have been eating only cold food for many days, as the field kitchens and Panje-wagons could not get through and the number of food-carriers did not suffice.

It is no wonder that these conditions had a direct impact on the soldiers' physical health and state of mind. As the corps commander added,

> The health of men and horses is deteriorating due to the wretched housing facilities . . . The men have been lying for weeks in the rain and stand in knee-deep mud. It is impossible to change wet clothing. I have seen the soldiers and spoken with them. They are hollow-eyed, pale, many of them are ill. Frostbite incidence is high.

The situation of the German infantry formations south of Leningrad became much worse when six divisions were encircled by the Red Army in the area of Demyansk. Between February and April 1942 these 96,000 men found themselves in an extremely precarious operational and logistical predicament. Here again the failure of technology resulted in tremendous misery. As the *Luftwaffe*'s promises to airlift supplies to the besieged troops were fulfilled only to a very limited degree, the men were compelled somehow to fend for themselves with ever diminishing provisions of food, wearing tattered summer uniforms with hardly any shelter from the fierce weather, and fighting an increasingly well-equipped enemy with ineffective weapons and never enough ammunition. The demodernization of the Eastern Front was nowhere more evident than in the Demyansk 'pocket': soldiers insulated themselves from the cold with newspapers, until those too ran out; boots, gloves, caps, sweaters, and coats were all in very short supply, and hardly appropriate for Russian winter conditions in any case; the meagre food rations invariably reached the front line frozen and consequently were hardly edible. The 12th Infantry Division's doctor reported that the troops were living in dark, damp bunkers, badly ventilated and cramped, almost impossible to heat and thus offering little opportunity to rest from action out in the open. The foul air caused numerous respiratory diseases, while due to the absence of any means for washing and cleaning clothes, the men were all infested with lice and suffered from endless skin infections. The extreme cold and indifferent hygiene also led to frequent inflammations of the bladder and a high incidence of frostbite. Manpower shortage meant long hours of guard duty, and the consequent lack of sleep along with the incessant tension had a debilitating effect on the troops, making them, in the doctor's words, increasingly apathetic ('*gestig immer Stumpfer*'). There were reports of soldiers fainting from exhaustion while on guard duty, as well as of cases of nervous disorders.

. . .

When the last phase of the campaign began with the attack on Moscow, the remnants of the *Ostheer*'s modern elements were rapidly destroyed. The 18th Panzer was reduced to only fourteen tanks by 9 November, and ten days later whatever had remained of its armour was put out of action due to lack of fuel. On the eve of the Soviet counter-offensive in early December, the division had only a quarter of its original mobility. This in turn also meant severe shortages in supplies of food and clothes. The harsh living conditions naturally made for a great rise in the incidence of frostbite, disease, and exhaustion. The retreat from the attacking Red Army made things even worse, for much of what had remained of the division's matériel had to be left behind. Symptoms of mental attrition caused by fatigue, hunger, exposure, and anxiety also became increasingly prevalent. On 22 December the division's Operations Section noted: 'The physical and mental condition of the soldiers and of some of the commanders calls for issuing very detailed orders and carefully examining them, in order to avoid breakdowns.' Indeed, on Christmas Eve two young soldiers died of exhaustion. Apathy was widespread. A soldier from the 57th Infantry Division wrote at the time that due to the 'snow-storms, blizzards and the great cold reaching down to 45 degrees [Celsius] . . . there are many men who cannot find enough energy to withstand the severity of winter and escape an otherwise certain death'. The demodernization of armoured formations did not consist merely in losing their tanks and trucks, but just as much in the numerous cases of physical and psychological breakdown caused by the wretched living conditions . . .

Throughout the rest of the first winter in Russia the 18th Panzer's troops remained in essentially the same conditions as those of the 12th Infantry. This was characteristic of most *Ostheer* armoured divisions which, stripped bare of their matériel and forced into entrenched, defensive warfare, underwent a relatively far more radical process of demodernization than the regular infantry. Later on the 18th Panzer did manage to scrape together a few tanks, but their number never rose much above twenty, and was usually far lower than that. In fact, the division's material condition was even worse than that of most Great War formations, for during the second part of winter 1941–42 it never had more than thirty-two guns, and often as few as five, while due to a great shortage of motorized supply vehicles and the high mortality of horses, it was quite immobile for much of the time, relying on primitive Russian Panje-wagons and sledges for its provisions. Another indication of the decay of the front was the quality of the equipment. While even the best German tanks were inferior to their Russian equivalents, by now Panzer units were compelled to fall back on more obsolete models, quite useless against Soviet armour; similarly, the few artillery pieces left were so worn out that their barrels were in imminent danger of exploding, while anti-tank guns, as was the case in the 12th Infantry, were mostly ineffective due to their small calibre. The sense among the troops that they had been plunged into a state of extreme backwardness was enhanced by the fact that although this division, rather exceptionally, had a relatively large though still insufficient stock of winter clothes, these were far from adequate for Russian winter conditions. And, although front-line units kept reporting this to the rear, the quality of Wehrmacht winter uniforms showed little improvement well into 1943. Nor did it occur to those in charge of tank production that equipping them with heating systems might be essential for fighting in the East . . .

Badly fed and clothed, filthy and infested with lice, lacking shelter and fighting against increasing enemy pressure with diminishing manpower reserves, the troops were assailed by an array of diseases, ranging from influenza, skin infections, and frostbite, to intestinal inflammations and typhus and spotted fever epidemics. In mid-February 1942 the 18th Panzer's commander pointed out that

> due to the constant great demand of guard duty and patrols, and furthermore because of the wretched accommodation facilities, a significant deterioration in the physical and mental resistance strength [of the troops] can be observed . . . one company was pulled out of the line and quarantined owing to frequent outbreaks of spotted fever . . . The reduction of food rations is unbearable in the long run in view of the troops' condition. A full rest is advisable for replenishment, restoration of health and morale.

As rest was out of the question, it is not surprising that during the first three months of 1942 some 5,000 soldiers, or close to a third of the division's manpower, reported sick. This was of course by no means exceptional. In 1942 spotted fever reached epidemic proportions throughout the *Ostheer*, claiming no less than 36,434 victims. Indeed, in December 1941 alone the number of the sick in the East rose steeply to 90,000, along with a similarly high incidence of frostbite. By January 1942 almost two-thirds of the overall 214,000 troops lost to the *Ostheer* were victims of illness and frostbite rather than enemy action, with their numbers rising to as many as half a million by spring 1942. The wretched living conditions and the resulting deterioration in the troops' health also had a serious psychological effect. The commander of the 18th Panzer was not alone in urging his officers 'to take vigorous action against the clearly widespread fatigue and indifference among our men'. The first winter in Russia both materially demodernized the German side of the front and produced a changed mentality among the Wehrmacht's troops. Symptomatic of this metamorphosis was the complaint made by the commander of Army Group Centre, Field Marshal von Bock, that 'our troops run away whenever a Russian tank appears', an unprecedented phenomenon in an army which had only recently introduced modern armoured warfare to Europe. The man who had led this military revolution, General Heinz Guderian, now described his once invincible Panzer group as 'a lot of armed camp-followers who trudge slowly backwards', plagued by a 'serious crisis of confidence' prevalent both 'among the troops and the junior commanders'.

Yet the changing character of warfare on the Eastern Front did not merely produce fatigue and apathy, but also a new image of war. Between 1918 and 1939 men had come to accept the idea that the combination of the machine-gun and barbed wire which had caused the stalemate along the continuous Western Front of the Great War, would remain a permanent feature of modern warfare. But during the first two years of the Second World War the Wehrmacht's tanks and aircraft accelerated the pace of fighting to such a degree that the notion of a front seemed to have vanished altogether. The image of war became one of highly trained professionals wielding sophisticated fighting machines and conducting rapid and spectacular campaigns. Once 'Barbarossa' was launched, however, the striking imbalance between the *Ostheer*'s modern and obsolete elements, already evident in the Western campaign, could no longer be bridged due to the much greater spaces of Russia and the strength and determination of the Red Army. As a consequence, the *Ostheer* became stranded along an overextended front deep inside the Soviet Union. The front assumed once more the character associated with the Great War, and the *Ostkämpfer*'s war came to consist of traditional, entrenched warfare, rather than of the quick marches and decisive encounters he had learned to expect. 'To say: "Even a dog wouldn't go on living like this," means little, for hardly any animal lives in lower and more primitive conditions than us,' wrote one soldier as early as 18 August 1941. But his was a much more frustrating and demoralizing situation than that of his Great War predecessors, for unlike them he was well aware of the now lost potential of conducting war quickly, conclusively, and at a relatively low cost. Worse still, now his enemies began increasingly to inflict upon him what only a year earlier he had inflicted on them, using those technologies and tactics he could no longer employ. As one soldier wrote home, 'I didn't know what trench warfare was like, but now I have learned. Our casualties are great, more than in France.' But, as he went on to say, this was not simply a repetition of 1914–18, for now he was made to feel as the French and Poles had felt: 'I have never seen such tough dogs as the Russians, and it is impossible to tell their tactics in advance, and above all their endless matériel, tanks and so forth.' This could indeed read as a letter written by a Frenchman in May 1940. Thus for the individual *Landser*, technology was transformed from an ally to an enemy, and his animosity toward its deadly products hurled at him at the front was only further enhanced by the growing intensity and ferocity of the Western Allies' strategic bombing of civilian centres and industrial targets far in the rear. The old romantic view of war was badly shaken. One soldier complained: 'Yet why is this suffering in itself not great, but so unspeakably common and dirty?' Instead, combat troops now began to rationalize these developments by employing a sort of nihilistic, social-Darwinian argumentation, not unlike that of Ernst Jünger, according to which not only was war hell, one also had to be a beast if one wished to survive it. The chronicler of the élite Grossdeutschland Division, who had served in its ranks as an officer, succinctly described this new attitude:

> Man becomes an animal. He must destroy, in order to live. There is nothing heroic on this battlefield . . . The battle returns here to its most primeval, animal-like form; whoever does not see well, fires too slowly, fails to hear the crawling on the ground in front of him as the enemy approaches, he will be sent under . . . The battle here is no assault with 'hurrah' cries over a field of flowers.

. . . Paradoxically, the troops may have clung to each other and kept on fighting precisely because of that terrible sense of isolation and abandonment which oppressed them so heavily, for there was nowhere to flee to in the depths of Russia . . .

The demodernization of the front had several important consequences. First, it led to such heavy losses among combat units that the traditional backbone of the German army, the 'primary groups' which had hitherto assured its cohesion, were largely wiped out. Second, in order to prevent the disintegration of the army as a whole which might have resulted from the breakup of the 'primary group', the Wehrmacht introduced and ruthlessly implemented an extremely harsh disciplinary system, to which was given not merely a military, but also an ideological legitimation. Yet draconian punishment did not suffice in cases where fear of the enemy was greater than fear of one's superiors. Thus in compensation for their obedience, and as a logical conclusion of the politicization of discipline, the troops were in turn given licence to vent their anger and frustration on the enemy's soldiers and civilians. The demodernization of the front consequently greatly enhanced the brutalization of the troops, and made the soldiers more receptive to ideological indoctrination and more willing to implement the policies it advocated. This process was possible, however, only because a large proportion of the Wehrmacht's officers and men already shared some key elements of the National Socialist world-view. Confronted with a battlefield reality which no longer corresponded to their previous image of war, and with an enemy who could not be overcome by employing familiar military methods, German soldiers now accepted the Nazi vision of war as the only one applicable to their situation. It was at this point that the Wehrmacht finally became Hitler's army.

Yevtushenko's Babiy Yar

When the Wehrmacht took Kiev in 1941 a total of 33,000 Jewish men, women and children were killed in three days – taken from the city to a nearby ravine, Babiy Yar, and there machine-gunned.

Yevgeny Yevtushenko's response to this atrocity represented a significant moment in Soviet cultural history. After Khrushchev's admission in 1956 of his predecessor Stalin's criminality, censorship was, erratically, relaxed. Yevtushenko, born in 1933, a tall and charismatic public reader, stood forth as the poet of a brave new Soviet generation, and made an impact on non-Russian-speaking audiences as he travelled the world declaiming his verse. 'Babiy Yar' (1961) could be read as a rebuke to the Russian anti-Semitism which had resurfaced in the Soviet Union after the war. Dmitry Shostakovich made a setting of it part of his Thirteenth Symphony, giving it extra life as protest.

The poem's allusion to the published diary of the Dutch Jew, Anne Frank, which had made a world-wide impact in the 1950s, typifies the latently subversive internationalism of Yevtushenko's outlook.

BABIY YAR

Over Babiy Yar
there are no memorials.
The steep hillside like a rough inscription.
I am frightened.
Today I am as old as the Jewish race.
I seem to myself a Jew at this moment.
I, wandering in Egypt.
I, crucified. I perishing.
Even today the mark of the nails.
I think also of Dreyfus. I am he.
The Philistine my judge and my accuser.
Cut off by bars and cornered,
ringed round, spat at, lied about;
the screaming ladies with the Brussels lace
poke me in the face with parasols.

I am also a boy in Belostok,
the dropping blood spreads across the floor,
the public-bar heroes are rioting
in an equal stench of garlic and of drink.
I have no strength, go spinning from a boot,
shriek useless prayers that they don't listen to;
with a cackle of 'Thrash the kikes and save Russia!'
the corn-chandler is beating up my mother.
I seem to myself like Anna Frank
to be transparent as an April twig
and am in love, I have no need for words,
I need for us to look at one another.
How little we have to see or to smell
separated from foliage and the sky,
how much, how much in the dark room
gently embracing each other.
They're coming. Don't be afraid.
The booming and banging of the spring.
It's coming this way. Come to me.
Quickly, give me your lips.
They're battering in the door. Roar of the ice.

Over Babiy Yar
rustle of the wild grass.
The trees look threatening, look like judges.
And everything is one silent cry.
Taking my hat off
I feel myself slowly going grey.
And I am one silent cry
over the many thousands of the buried;
am every old man killed here,
every child killed here.
O my Russian people, I know you.
Your nature is international.
Foul hands rattle your clean name.
I know the goodness of my country.
How horrible it is that pompous title
the anti-semites calmly call themselves,
Society of the Russian Race.

No part of me can ever forget it.
When the last anti-semite on the earth
is buried for ever
let the International ring out.
No Jewish blood runs among my blood,
but I am as bitterly and hardly hated
by every anti-semite
as if I were a Jew. By this
I am a Russian.

Offensive Women

'Mother Russia' – the phrase is conventional. Typically, Soviet women were expected to function as traditional carers, while very often undertaking full-time jobs as well. Neither the Western allies nor the Germans used women in combat roles, though many had 'offensive' tasks in Resistance groups. Reina Pennington's essay, abridged here, was published in 1997 in Time to Kill: The Soldier's Experience of War in the West, 1939–1945 *(edited by Paul Addison and Angus Calder). It exposes the remarkable extent to which the Soviet Union cast women into battle.*

WOMEN IN COMBAT IN THE RED ARMY

When the Germans invaded the Soviet Union on 22 June 1941, only a few Soviet women were in military service. During the first weeks of the war tens of thousands volunteered for active duty; most were rejected. When the war began, there was no plan in place for the large-scale military mobilization of women. Only those with selected technical skills, such as medical and communications, were liable for conscription, or were even accepted as volunteers. In fact, the Soviets' first response was quite similar to that in the West: they urged women to replace men in industry and agriculture. Women would 'man' the home front so that men could go to war. This was a less radical shift in the Soviet Union than in the West, since Soviet women already comprised 40 per cent of the industrial labour force.

As the war progressed, however, female volunteers were accepted increasingly, and there were many mobilizations of women, particularly for the rear services, communications and the air defence forces. The central committee of the Komsomol handled most of the mobilizations. One veteran described the Komsomol selection process as 'stringent and thorough'. However, there were no tests of strength, endurance or physical fitness; the Soviets apparently assumed women would be able to do the job.

Some people are surprised that women could drive a tank or load an anti-aircraft gun. Yet serving as a cook or laundress with the Red Army, roles that we take for granted, also required great strength. Women cooks hauled huge cauldrons that were so heavy that many men said they feared these women would never be able to bear children. Laundresses also handled extremely heavy physical loads for long hours each day.

Women military mechanics routinely lifted heavy weights, of course. Armourers with the all-female 46th Guards Night Bomber Regiment had only a few minutes to rearm aircraft between flights; they loaded four 100-kg bombs by hand. Soviet women were accustomed to heavy physical labour before the war, and women in the Red Army were simply expected to carry ammunition, load bombs and big guns, change propellers, and so on. The Soviets seem to have taken for granted what many Westerners still see as an insurmountable obstacle.

By 1943 Soviet women had been integrated into all services and all military roles, ranging from traditional support roles like medical service, to primarily defensive work in anti-aircraft defence, to offensive combat roles in the infantry, artillery and armour, as well as the partisan movement. Many women commented on the fact that when they were accepted for duty they were given men's clothing, right down to the underwear. Oversized boots were a particular problem. No special women's uniforms were issued until half-way through the war.

Why did so many Soviet women want to go to war? Their motivations ranged from following relatives to the front, to avenging the death of a friend or relative, to simple patriotism. Quite a few women whose fathers had been arrested during the purge years hoped to redeem their families by serving at the front. Perhaps Sergeant Klara Tikhonovich, an anti-aircraft gunner, best expressed a common impulse that sent women to war. She writes,

> A young person recently told me that going off to fight was a masculine urge. No, it was a human urge . . . That was how we were brought up, to take part in everything. A war had begun and that meant that we must help in some way.

Soviet women did manage to take part in nearly every wartime duty. In addition to the 800,000 in the army, thousands of women served in so-called 'fighting battalions', which were local security units similar to the British Home Guard; not part of the regular army, but still an armed force. Around 25,000 women served with the Soviet navy, and another 30,000 in river transportation. In the Soviet air force there were three combat regiments that started the war as all-female, and numerous women pilots, mechanics, and so on, in other line units. Within the Red Army women made up 75 per cent of military drivers and communications was heavily staffed by women. Most of the Red Army's women served in positions that were considered non-combatant, but nearly all were trained to handle weapons. Even military drivers trained with rifles and bayonets.

My focus here is on the women who experienced war most directly, beginning with medical personnel. Female medical orderlies and nurses served in the Red Army down to the company level. More than 40 per cent of all Red Army doctors, surgeons, paramedics and medical orderlies, and 100 per cent of nurses, were women. Many were quite young and had minimal training, but as one veteran noted, 'When a young boy . . . has his arm or leg cut off before your very eyes, childishness quickly gets wiped out of your mind.' The primary duty of medical personnel was, of course, to tend the sick and wounded. For front-line medics, that meant rescuing the wounded from under enemy fire, and whenever possible, retrieving precious weapons together with the wounded soldiers.

Medic A. M. Strelkova describes what was required:

> I don't know how to explain this. We carried men who were twice or three times our own weight. On top of that, we carried their weapons, and the men themselves were wearing greatcoats and boots. We would hoist a man weighing 80 kilograms on our backs and carry him. Then we would throw the man off and go to get another one . . . And we did this five or six times during an attack.

This work was extremely hazardous; front-line medics had a casualty rate second only to the active infantry.

Senior Sergeant Sofia Dubniakova, a medical orderly, told an interviewer:

> There are films about the war in which one sees a nurse at the front line. There she goes, so neat and clean, wearing a skirt, not padded trousers, and with a side-cap perched on top of an attractive hairdo. It is just not true. Could we have hauled a wounded man dressed like that?

Medical orderlies dragged incredible numbers of wounded soldiers from the field of battle. Maria Smirnova, with the 333rd Division of the Fifty-sixth Army, rescued a total of 481 wounded from under fire during the war. This number seems fantastic, but Soviet sources document some women medics who rescued twenty wounded soldiers, with their weapons, in a single day, others who carried the wounded as much as fourteen kilometres from where they fell to a medical station.

Olga Omelchenko tells a terrible tale of her experience as a front-line medic with the First Company of the 118th Rifle Regiment, 37th Guards Division. After a heavy battle in 1943, she says:

> I crawled up to the last man, whose arm was completely smashed. The arm had to be amputated immediately and bandaged . . . But I didn't have a knife or scissors . . . What was I to do? I gnawed at the flesh with my teeth, gnawed it through and began to bandage the arm.

Soviet medical personnel were not, strictly speaking, non-combatants. Many medics, nurses and doctors took up weapons in battle . . . In addition, many women who started as nurses ended as soldiers. Some had applied for combat and been forced into nursing against their will, but later managed transfers. Others were trained nurses who discovered a taste for combat as the war progressed. Lieutenant-General Kilomiets, former commander of the Independent Maritime Army, wrote in his memoirs that after the death of a well-known woman machine-gunner in his unit,

> a great many of the nurses who served in the Division kept asking to be transferred to machine-gun duty. We tried to convince them that [they] were also considered combatants and heroes. All the same, during the relatively quiet periods at the front we organized training in machine-gun firing for a group of nurses, and we made an exception of those who were especially proficient by transferring them to machine-gun duty.

One last point on medical personnel is that nearly every Soviet woman who served in the Red Army, whatever her assigned position, was expected to fill in as a medic simply because she was a woman. Tens of thousands of women pulled this sort of double duty, and often they are dismissed as medics rather than combatants.

Women also served as communications operators throughout the Soviet armed forces, and constituted about 12 per cent of the total . . .

One of the first conscriptions of women was for communications work; in August 1941 10,000 women were drafted for front-line duty with the signals troops. In 1942 another 50,000 were trained. By 1943 some communications regiments at the front were 80 per cent female. In addition, more than 1,200 female radio-operators were trained for parachute drops behind the lines. N. M. Zaitseva, for example, made nineteen parachute drops behind enemy lines during her career. This work was extremely dangerous; a number of women were forced to kill themselves with hand grenades to avoid imminent capture and to destroy their equipment.

Women in communications were expected to fight; Elena Stempkovskaia was awarded the Hero of the Soviet Union after she died defending her command post from attack; she reportedly killed some twenty enemy soldiers with a machine-gun. Tatiana Baramzina had been a sniper but transferred to communications when her vision deteriorated; she was still a good enough shot to kill a number of Germans in July 1944 when her battalion was sent behind enemy lines. Of course, she had to alternate between shooting the enemy and filling in as a medic, in addition to her communications duties. She was captured and then executed with an anti-tank rifle.

More than a quarter of a million women served in the Air Defence Forces during the war. In fact, Stalin was personally involved in the integration of women into the Air Defence Forces. In 1942 there were two mobilizations to bring women into air defence. Specific goals were established: women were to replace 8 out of 10 men in instrument sections, 6 out of 10 men in machine-gun crews, 5 out of 6 men in air warning posts, 3 out of 11 men in searchlight crews, and all male privates and NCOs in the Air Defence Forces rear services. Women between the ages of 18 and 27 were subject to conscription. There were many women officers, and women served in every position on gun crews. By the end of the war, more than 121,000 women served on gun crews, and about 80,000 in Air Defence Forces aviation or in searchlight and observation.

Klavdia Konovalova served with the 784th Anti-Aircraft Artillery Regiment. She was initially assigned as a gunlayer, but sought to be a loader. She says that being a loader 'was considered purely masculine work, since you had to be able to handle 6-kilogram shells easily and maintain intensive fire at the rate of a salvo every five seconds'. Since she had worked as a blacksmith's striker before the war, she was more than capable of handling that role. She served as a loader for a year, then was appointed commander over a gun crew of two women and four men.

Women also played a role in the partisan movement. By 1944 there were a minimum of 280,000 active partisans; women filled 25 per cent of the total, and 9 per cent of operational roles, or approximately 26,000 active women partisans . . . First-hand accounts indicate that there was wide regional variation in the extent to which women were permitted to fight. We know that virtually all partisan women were armed, and many were directly involved in combat and sabotage. While there were no female detachment or brigade commanders in the partisans, some women did command companies and platoons, both all-female and mixed units.

The most famous female partisan was Zoya Kosmodemianskaia, a teenager who was caught and executed by the Germans early in the war. Many women partisans performed extraordinary acts of resistance. For example, Elena Mazanik assassinated the German governor of occupied Belorussia by planting a bomb under his bed. Partisan scout Antonina Kondrashova endured a special torture. Her mother had been captured by the Germans, and for two years she and other prisoners were made to lead the way whenever the Germans went on missions. Kondrashova says the Germans

> were afraid of partisan mines and always drove the local population in front of them . . . on more than one occasion we would be sitting in ambush and suddenly see women walking towards us, and behind them the Nazis. They would come closer and you would see that your mother was there. The most terrible thing was to wait for the commander to give orders to open fire. We all awaited this order with fear . . . [but] if the order to fire was given, you fired.

Her mother was eventually shot, along with other prisoners, by the Germans when they retreated from the area in 1943 . . .

Although comparatively few women served in Soviet armour, they filled a variety of roles, including medic, radio operator, turret gunner, driver-mechanic, tank commander and platoon commander. Most served with the T-14 medium tank, which was also the fastest Soviet tank. Others served in test functions; for example, Polina Volodina commanded an all-woman crew that tested the T-40 floating tank and later served as the head of tank salvage and repair service of the Southern Front.

Nina Vishnevskaia, who worked as a medic in a tank battalion, reports that they were reluctant to take women in tank units, even as medics. While male members of armour were issued canvas trousers with reinforced knees, the women were given cotton overalls. She recalled:

> Very soon we were . . . wearing rags, because we did not sit in tanks, but had to crawl on the ground. Tanks often caught fire and the tankmen, if they remained alive, were all covered with burns. And we also got burns, because to get hold of the burning men, we had to rush right into the flames. It's very difficult to drag out a man, especially a turret gunner, from the hatch . . . In tank units medical orderlies didn't last long. There was no place in a tank for us. We clung to the armour and thought about one thing only: how to keep our feet clear of the caterpillars so we wouldn't get dragged in. And all the time you had to watch if there were any tanks on fire. You had to run, to crawl there.

Vishnevskaia, who was at the Battle of Kursk, was the only survivor of five women medics who had enlisted together.

A number of women served on tank crews in combat positions. Irma Levchenko started the war in 1941 as a medic, eventually serving with a tank battalion in the Crimea. After recovering for the second time from battle wounds, she applied to the Commander of the Armoured Troops, General Fedorenko, to be sent for combat training in armour. She was allowed to attend the Stalingrad Tank School, and thereafter drove a T-34. She ended the war with the rank of lieutenant-colonel and a Hero of the Soviet Union medal.

Marina Lagunova was a driver-mechanic who saw combat at Kursk and on the drive to the Dnieper River. In September 1943 her tank was destroyed and she lost both her legs. She recovered from her wounds and went on to become an instructor with a tank-training brigade. Probably the most famous woman to serve in armour was Maria Oktiabrskaia. After her husband was killed, she donated her life savings to buy her own T-34. At the age of thirty-eight, she entered combat in October 1943 with the 26th Guards Tank Brigade, and fought until she was killed in battle near Vitebsk in 1944 while making a repair to her tank track.

A number of women also served in the 45-ton IS-2 tank, equipped with a 122-mm gun. Ola Parshonok first drove the T-34, and later the IS-2; she went all the way to Berlin with the 231st Tank Regiment. Only one woman became commander of a heavy tank: Junior Lieutenant Aleksandra Boiko. She and her husband volunteered for duty and donated 50,000 roubles to build a tank, on the condition that they be crewed together. They graduated from the Cheliabinsk Tank Technical School in 1943. Aleksandra was commander of the four-person crew, and her husband was driver-mechanic. They fought in the Baltic States and into Poland, Czechoslovakia and Germany. Both were wounded and decorated.

A unique role in the Red Army was that of sniper. A so-called 'sniper movement' was started in the autumn of 1941, sponsored by the Komsomol, and spread rapidly. More than 100,000 women went through sniper-training courses during the war. In May 1943 the Central Sniper Training Centre for Women began operation under the command of N. P. Chegodaeva, a graduate of the Frunze Military Academy and veteran of the Spanish Civil War; its 1,500 graduates accounted for 11,280 enemy troops killed by the end of the war.

The job of sniper was an exacting one. Snipers needed a good eye for distance and motion, the ability to handle a rifle blindfolded, the endurance to crawl long distances to get near enemy lines, then dig in and camouflage themselves, and the patience to wait nearly motionless for long hours in all kinds of weather. Snipers usually tried to get into position in the pre-dawn darkness, and only returned to their own lines after nightfall. They sought positions as close as 500 metres from the enemy lines, and might lie in snow, sit in a tree, or perch on a roof for twelve hours or more at a time. Many snipers worked in pairs in order to keep one another alert.

Some women snipers operated in all-female platoons. A platoon of 50 women snipers in the 3rd Shock Army, commanded by Nina Lobkovskaia, was credited with killing 3,112 German soldiers. Many women snipers were killed in action. The most famous woman sniper was Liudmila Pavlichenko with 309 kills to her credit, including 78 enemy snipers. She fought with the 25th Chapaev Rifle Division during the defence of Odessa and the siege of Sevastopol. After she recovered from serious wounds, she was made a master sniper instructor, and later toured the United States to urge the opening of a second front.

A number of women also served with the Red Army as machine-gunners. In 1942 alone the Komsomol Vseobuch, or Universal Military Training service, claims to have trained 4,500 women as heavy machine-gun operators, and another 7,800 on light machine-guns. Women machine-gunners served down to the platoon level, and many commanded platoons and companies. Just one example is that of Zoya Medvedeva, who served on machine-gun crews throughout the war, first as a crew member, then commanding machine-gun platoons with both air defence and rifle units, and later as a company commander.

Medvedeva describes the experience of battle at Odessa. During the enemy artillery bombardment, she says, 'I sat, my face buried in my lap . . . feeling like an ant on an anvil that a blind blacksmith was striking with all his strength; he never missed the anvil and each one of his blows narrowly avoided flattening me completely.' She graphically describes the rigours of serving on a machine-gun crew, of having repeatedly to lift the gun into place, remove it during artillery attacks, and move it from one location to another. In their first battle, only thirteen soldiers of her platoon survived; Medvedeva herself was wounded in the head. Ironically, she was not wounded while at her gun, but only after the battle, when she was helping bring in the wounded. Two months later, she returned to her division at Sevastopol. She was told there were no vacancies in the machine-gun companies and was forced to work as a medic. Only after demonstrating her skill with a gun was she allowed to return to her assigned position. Later, she was one of only seven soldiers to survive out of the entire company. They broke out of an encirclement and then fought with a naval infantry unit, where Medvedeva took over a machine-gun position. She sustained a concussion and shrapnel wounds and was evacuated. After recovering, she went on a course for machine-gun platoon commanders and returned to the front as a junior lieutenant.

No comprehensive statistics are available for women who served in combat positions in the infantry. Aside from the roles already mentioned, women served in mortar crews and as reconnaissance scouts. In 1942 more than 6,000 women were given training on mortars; more than 15,000 were trained with automatic weapons or sub-machine-guns. Women are rarely categorized simply as soldiers; women who served with infantry units are generally designated as medics, snipers, scouts or members of gun crews. However, in February 1942, the First Independent Women's Reserve Rifle Regiment, an infantry training unit, was formed; eventually nearly 10,000 women (3,900 privates, 2,500 NCOs and 3,500 officers) graduated from this group. In addition, the Voroshilov Infantry School in Ryazan included three women's battalions and sent nearly 1,400 women platoon commanders to the field in 1943: 704 took over rifle sections; 382 machine-gun sections; and 302 mortar crews. Can these women be regarded as infantry soldiers? A man who commanded a rifle platoon would be called a soldier; there is no reason why women who did the same thing should not.

Some people ask whether women had trouble killing. But there was no 'woman's' reaction to killing. Some say they never got used to it and it was always difficult. Others say it was a matter of self-defence. Still others say their anger and hatred was motivation enough. Sergeant-Major Liubov Novik says,

> Whenever I recall the past now I am seized with terror, but at that time I could do anything – say, sleep next to a dead person, and I myself fired the rifle and saw blood; I remember only too well the especially strong smell of blood in the snow . . . [but] It wasn't that bad then and I could go through anything.

Partisan Antonina Kondrashova points out that she once heard the cries of a child who was thrown by the Germans into a well. 'After that,' she says,

> when you went on a mission, your whole spirit urged you to do only one thing: to kill them as soon as possible and as many as possible, destroy them in the cruellest way.

On the other hand, one woman pilot sees killing as a military skill, and says that should not be equated with cruelty. Women's reactions to killing varied widely, depending on the role they filled and their personality . . .

The Soviets have not published precise figures on women's wartime casualties. Losses for the women's aviation regiments can be calculated based on unit histories and regimental albums; they varied from 22 per cent to 30 per cent of flying personnel, which were typical rates for aviation. Losses among women in the front-line Red Army appear to have been proportionately heavier than among men, even though most were not in designated combat jobs. The high casualty rate for front-line medics has been already noted. Women sappers undoubtedly had a casualty rate as high or higher than that of the infantry. Until hard statistical data becomes available, only a subjective conclusion is possible: women at the front appear to have taken the same risks and suffered casualty rates typical for their duties.

Boris Slutsky

Literature was an immensely important element in Russian patriotism. New poems given public exposure would be read and quoted aloud by millions. A lot of poets, predictably, projected noble pathos and sublime defiance in diffuse and uninteresting ways.

Introducing Boris Slutsky in his huge personal selection of Twentieth Century Russian Verse *(1993), Yevtushenko emphasizes his singularity. Born in 1919, he published some poetry in 1941 but did not appear in print again until after the death of Stalin in 1953. His poetry is 'deliberately coarse, prosaic, and always distinctive'.*

CLERKS

The Deed
that was done in the Beginning
was done by the private soldier,
But the Word
written in the Beginning –
that was written by clerks.
Slipping lightly through the front lines
on an operational summary
It sank into the archives
and stayed there, floating at anchor.
Archives of the Red Army:
preserved like Holy Writ
Layers and layers of documents
serried like seams of coal.
And as coal stores the sun
so in them does our brightness cool,
Collected, numbered,
and laid down there in files.
Four Ukrainian fronts
Three Belorussian fronts
Three Baltic fronts
All the other fronts

By platoons
By batteries
By battalions
By companies –
Each will receive its memorial
with its own particular beauty.
But who quarried the stones
for these statues? Why, the clerks.
Kerosene lanterns shone
with their dim and murky light
Upon the pages of notebooks
where, in plain terms,
The bases were being laid
of a literary style.
A few hundred yards from death
that was the deep rear
Where the clerk did his work
But it did not cramp his style.
In accordance with his instructions
in precise terms he set down all
That, according to his instructions,
he was supposed to set down.
If Corporal Sidorov was wounded
in the course of combat duty
And if no one witnessed
the gallant deed he had done,
Then, whipping a page from his notebook,
his imagination spurred,
The clerk wrote for him a deed
the length of a notebook page.
If a schoolgirl cried out on the scaffold
and the peasants recalled 'We'll win!'
The clerk wrote for her a speech,
a monologue based on what
He himself would have shouted
as he mounted the scaffold steps.
They wrote about everything, clerks,
in simple and vivid words

They gave us all glory; but we –
                    we do not glorify them.
Let us remedy that omission,
                    correct that error now:
And let us givc thanks to the clerks
                    with a deep, low bow.

Heinrich Böll: In the Darkness

Heinrich Böll served throughout the war as a German infantryman; he was lucky enough to transfer from the Eastern to the Western Front in the autumn of 1944. After the war he wrote fiction in a new 'German–American' style, Kurzgeschichte. *'In the Darkness' was first published in 1950.*

IN THE DARKNESS

'Light the candle,' said a voice.

There was no sound, only that exasperating, aimless rustle of someone trying to get to sleep.

'Light the candle, I say,' came the voice again, on a sharper note this time.

The sounds at last became distinguishable as someone moving, throwing aside the blanket, and sitting up; this was apparent from the breathing, which now came from above. The straw rustled too.

'Well?' said the voice.

'The lieutenant said we weren't to light the candle except on orders, in an emergency . . .' said a younger, diffident voice.

'Light the candle, I say, you little pip-squeak,' the older voice shouted back.

He sat up now too, their heads were on the same level in the dark, their breathing was parallel.

The one who had first spoken irritably followed the movements of the other, who had tucked the candle away somewhere in his pack. His breathing relaxed when he eventually heard the sound of the matchbox.

The match flared up, and there was light: a sparse yellow light.

Their eyes met. Invariably, as soon as there was enough light, their eyes met. Yet they knew one another so well, much too well. They almost hated each other, so familiar was each to each; they knew one another's very smell, the smell of every pore, so to speak, but still their eyes met, those of the older man and the younger. The younger one was pale and slight with a nondescript face, and the older one was pale and slight and unshaven with a nondescript face.

'Now listen,' said the older man, calmer now, 'when are you ever going to learn that you don't do everything the lieutenants tell you?'

'He'll . . .' the younger one tried to begin.

'He won't do a thing,' said the older one, in a sharper tone again and lighting a cigarette from the candle. 'He'll keep his trap shut, and if he doesn't, and I don't happen to be around, then tell him to wait till I get back, it was me who lit the candle, understand? Do you understand?'

'Yessir.'

'To hell with that Yessir crap, just Yes when you're talking to me. And undo your belt,' he was shouting again now, 'take that damn crappy belt off when you go to sleep.'

The younger man looked at him nervously and took off his belt, placing it beside him in the straw.

'Roll your coat up into a pillow. That's right. O.K. . . . and now go to sleep, I'll wake you when it's time for you to die . . .'

The younger man rolled onto his side and tried to sleep. All that was visible was the young brown hair, matted and untidy, a very thin neck, and the empty shoulders of his uniform tunic. The candle flickered gently, letting its meagre light swing back and forth in the dark dugout like a great yellow butterfly uncertain where to settle.

The older man stayed as he was, knees drawn up, puffing out cigarette smoke at the ground in front of him. The ground was dark brown, here and there white blade marks showed where the spade had cut through a root or, a little closer to the surface, a tuber. The roof consisted of a few planks with a ground sheet thrown over them, and in the spaces between the planks the groundsheet sagged a little because the earth lying on top of it was heavy, heavy and wet. Outside it was raining. The soft swish of steadily falling water sounded indescribably persistent, and the older man, still staring fixedly at the ground, now noticed a thin trickle of water oozing into the dugout under the roof. The tiny stream backed up slightly on encountering some loose earth, then flowed on past the obstacle until it reached the next one, which was the man's feet, and the ever-growing tide flowed all around the man's feet until his black boots lay in the water just like a peninsula. The man spat his cigarette butt into the puddle and lit another from the candle. In doing so he took the candle down from the edge of the dugout and placed it beside him on an ammunition case. The half where the younger man was lying was almost in darkness, reached now by the swaying light in brief spasms only, and these gradually subsided.

'Go to sleep, damn you,' said the older man. 'D'you hear? Go to sleep!'

'Yessir . . . yes,' came the faint voice, obviously wider awake than before, when it had been dark.

'Hold on,' said the older man, less harshly again. 'A couple more cigarettes and then I'll put it out, and at least we'll drown in the dark.'

He went on smoking, sometimes turning his head to the left, where the boy was lying, but he spat the second butt into the steadily growing puddle, lit the third, and still he could tell from the breathing beside him that the kid couldn't sleep.

He then took the spade, thrust it into the soft earth, and made a little mud wall behind the blanket forming the entrance. Behind this wall he heaped up a second layer of earth. With a spadeful of earth he covered the puddle at his feet. Outside there was no sound save the gentle swish of the rain; little by little, the earth lying on top of the groundsheet had evidently become saturated, for water was now beginning to drip from above too.

'Oh shit,' muttered the older man. 'Are you asleep?'

'No.'

The man spat the third cigarette butt over the mud wall and blew out the candle. He pulled up his blanket again, worked his feet into a comfortable position, and lay back with a sigh. It was quite silent and quite dark, and again the only sound was that aimless rustle of someone trying to get to sleep, and the swish of the rain, very gentle.

'Willi's been wounded,' the boy's voice said suddenly, after a few minutes' silence. The voice was more awake than ever, in fact not even sleepy.

'What d'you mean?' asked the man in reply.

'Just that – wounded,' came the younger voice, with something like triumph in it, pleased that it knew some important piece of news which the older voice obviously knew nothing about. 'Wounded while he was shitting.'

'You're nuts,' said the man; then he gave another sigh and went on: 'That's what I call a real break, I never heard such luck. One day you come back from leave and the next day you get wounded while you're shitting. Is it serious?'

'No,' said the boy with a laugh, 'though actually it's not minor either. A bullet fracture, but in the arm.'

'A bullet fracture in the arm! You come back from leave and while you're shitting you get wounded, a bullet fracture in the arm! What a break . . . How did it happen?'

'When they went for water last evening,' came the younger voice, quite animated now. 'When they went for water, they were going down the hill at the back, carrying their water cans, and Willi told Sergeant Schubert: "I've got to shit, Sergeant!" "Nothing doing," said the sergeant. But Willi couldn't hold on any longer so he just ran off, pulled down his pants, and bang! A grenade. And they had to actually pull up his pants for him. His left arm was wounded, and his right arm was holding it, so he ran off like that to get it bandaged, with his pants around his ankles. They all laughed, everyone laughed, even Sergeant Schubert laughed.' He added the last few words almost apologetically, as if to excuse his own laughter, because he was laughing now . . .

But the older man wasn't laughing.

'Light!' he said with an oath. 'Here, give me the matches, let's have some light!' He struck a match, cursing as it flared up. 'At least I want some light, even if I don't get wounded. At least let's have some light, the least they can do is give us enough candles if they want to play war. Light! Light!' He was shouting again as he lit another cigarette.

The younger voice had sat up again and was poking around with a spoon in a greasy can held on his knees.

And there they sat, crouching side by side, without a word, in the yellow light.

The man smoked aggressively, and the boy was already looking somewhat greasy: his childish face smeared, bread crumbs sticking to his matted hair around most of his hairline.

The boy then proceeded to scrape out the grease can with a piece of bread.

All of a sudden there was silence: the rain had stopped. Neither of them moved, they looked at each other, the man with the cigarette in his hand, the boy holding the bread in his trembling fingers. It was uncannily quiet, they took a few breaths, and then heard rain still dripping somewhere from the groundsheet.

'Hell,' said the older man, 'D'you suppose the sentry's still there? I can't hear a thing.'

The boy put the bread into his mouth and threw the can into the straw beside him.

'I don't know,' said the boy, 'they're going to let us know when it's our turn to relieve.'

The older man got up quickly. He blew out the light, jammed on his steel helmet, and thrust aside the blanket. What came through the opening was not light. Just cool damp darkness. The man snipped out his cigarette and stuck his head outside.

'Hell,' he muttered outside, 'not a thing. Hey!' he called softly. Then his dark head reappeared inside, and he asked: 'Where's the next dugout?'

The boy groped his way to his feet and stood next to the other man in the opening.

'Quiet!' said the man suddenly, in a sharp, low tone. 'Something's crawling around out there.'

They peered ahead. It was true, in the silent darkness there was a sound of someone crawling, and all of a sudden an unearthly snapping sound that made them both jump. It sounded as if someone had flung a live cat against the wall: the sound of breaking bones.

'Hell,' muttered the older man, 'there's something funny going on. Where's the sentry?' 'Over there,' said the boy groping in the dark for the other man's hand and lifting it towards the right.

'Over there,' he repeated, 'that's where the dugout is too.'

'Wait here,' said the older man, 'and better get your rifle just in case.'

Once again they heard that sickening snapping sound, then silence, and someone crawling.

The older man crept forward through the mud, occasionally halting and quietly listening, until after a few yards he finally heard a muffled voice; then he saw a faint gleam of light from the ground, felt around till he found the entrance, and called 'Hey, chum!'

The voice stopped, the light went out, a blanket was pushed aside, and a man's dark head came up out of the ground.

'What's up?'

'Where's the sentry?'

'Over there – right here.'

'Where?'

'Hey there, Neuer! . . . Hey there!'

No answer: the crawling sound had stopped, all sound had stopped, there was only darkness out there, silent darkness. 'God damn it, that's queer,' said the voice of the man who had come up out of the ground. 'Hey there! . . . That's funny, he was standing right here by the dugout, only a few feet away.' He pulled himself up over the edge and stood beside the man who had called him.

'There was someone crawling around out there,' said the man who had come across from the other dugout. 'I know there was. The bastard's quiet now.'

'Better have a look,' said the man who had come up out of the ground. 'Shall we take a look?'

'Hm, there certainly ought to be a sentry here.'

'You fellows are next.'

'I know, but . . .'

'Ssh!'

Once again they could hear someone crawling out there, perhaps twenty feet away.

'God damn it,' said the man who had come up out of the ground, 'you're right.'

'Maybe someone still alive from last night, trying to crawl away.'

'Or new ones.'

'But what about the sentry, for God's sake?'

'Shall we go?'

'Okay.'

Both men instantly dropped to the ground and started to move forward, crawling through the mud. From down there, from a worm's-eye view, everything looked different. Every minutest elevation in the soil became a mountain range behind which, far off, something strange was visible: a slightly lighter darkness, the sky. Pistol in hand, they crawled on, yard by yard through the mud.

'God damn it,' whispered the man who had come up out of the ground, 'a Russki from last night.'

His companion also soon bumped into a corpse, a mute, leaden bundle. Suddenly they were silent, holding their breath: there was that cracking sound again, quite close, as if someone had been given a terrific wallop on the jaw. Then they heard someone panting.

'Hey,' called the man who had come up out of the ground, 'who's there?'

The call silenced all sound, the very air seemed to hold its breath, until a quavering voice spoke: 'It's me . . .' 'God damn it, what the hell are you doing out there, you old arsehole, driving us all nuts?' shouted the man who had come up out of the ground. 'I'm looking for something,' came the voice again.

The two men had got to their feet and now walked over to the spot where the voice was coming from the ground.

'I'm looking for a pair of shoes,' said the voice, but now they were standing next to him. Their eyes had become accustomed to the dark, and they could see corpses lying all around, ten or a dozen, lying there like logs, black and motionless, and the sentry was squatting beside one of these logs, fumbling around its feet.

'Your job's to stick to your post,' said the man who had come up out of the ground.

The other man, the one who had summoned him out of the ground, dropped like a stone and bent over the dead man's face. The man who had been squatting suddenly covered his face with his hands and began whimpering like a cowed animal.

'Oh no,' said the man who had summoned the other out of the ground, adding in an undertone: 'I guess you need teeth too, eh? Gold teeth, eh?'

'What's that?' asked the man who had come up out of the ground, while at his feet the cringing figure whimpered louder than ever.

'Oh no,' said the first man again, and the weight of the world seemed to be lying on his breast.

'Teeth?' asked the man who had come up out of the ground, whereupon he threw himself down beside the cringing figure and ripped a cloth bag from his hand.

'Oh no!' the cringing figure cried too, and every extremity of human terror was expressed in this cry.

The man who had summoned the other out of the ground turned away, for the man who had come up out of the ground had placed his pistol against the cringing figure's head, and he pressed the trigger.

'Teeth,' he muttered, as the sound of the shot died away. 'Gold teeth.'

They walked slowly back, stepping very carefully as long as they were in the area where the dead lay.

'You fellows are on now,' said the man who had come up out of the ground, before vanishing into the ground again.

'Right,' was all the other man said, and he too crawled slowly back through the mud before vanishing into the ground again.

He could tell at once that the boy was still awake; there was that aimless rustle of someone trying to get to sleep.

'Light the candle,' he said quietly.

The yellow flame leaped up again, feebly illuminating the little hole.

'What happened?' asked the boy in alarm, catching sight of the older man's face.

'The sentry's gone, you'll have to replace him.'

'Yes,' said the youngster, 'give me the watch, will you, so I can wake the others.'

'Here.'

The older man squatted down on his straw and lit a cigarette, watching thoughtfully as the boy buckled on his belt, pulled on his coat, defused a hand grenade, and then wearily checked his machine pistol for ammunition.

'Right,' said the boy finally, 'so long now.'

'So long,' said the man, and he blew out the candle and lay in total darkness all alone in the ground . . .

Victory at Stalingrad

Vasily Grossman's Life and Fate, *smuggled out of Russia and first published in the West in the mid-eighties (q.v. above), is deliberately 'Tolstoyan', to ironic effect. Tolstoy's* War and Peace *was officially and unofficially inspirational as the Soviet Union resisted the Wehrmacht. But Grossman took other devices from Tolstoy besides a two-term abstract title and a story-line in which an army of conquest is turned back by Russian valour. Like Tolstoy he introduces real people by name – such as Lieutenant General Chuykov, Commander of the 62nd Army at Stalingrad, his chief of staff, Krylov, and the Divisional Commissar, Gurov – and attributes thoughts and feelings to them. He develops an epic with multiple protagonists, most related in, or connected by friendship to, a single family. Darensky, one of these, corresponds exactly to the type recurrent in Tolstoy's fiction of the 'conscience-stricken nobleman' – an aristocrat by birth on both sides of the family, he suffered a while in the Gulag before the war. The passages extracted here correspond partly to those in* War and Peace *where Kutuzov's Russian soldiers shoo Napoleon's* Grande Armée *over their western border, but the writing is haunted by such satire of top brass and officialdom as dominated Tolstoy's last big novel,* Resurrection.

The Cheka *was the murderous secret police force created by the Bolsheviks after their Revolution.*

The men in the bunkers and command-posts of the 62nd Army felt very strange indeed; they wanted to touch their faces, feel their clothes, wiggle their toes in their boots. The Germans weren't shooting. It was quiet.

The silence made their heads whirl. They felt as though they had grown empty, as though their hearts had gone numb, as though arms and legs moved in a different way from usual. It felt very odd, even inconceivable, to eat *kasha* in silence, to write a letter in silence, to wake up at night and hear silence. This silence then gave birth to many different sounds that seemed new and strange: the clink of a knife, the rustle of a page being turned in a book, the creak of a floorboard, the sound of bare feet, the scratching of a pen, the click of a safety-catch on a pistol, the ticking of the clock on the wall of the bunker.

Krylov, the chief of staff, entered Chuykov's bunker; Chuykov himself was sitting on a bed and Gurov was sitting opposite him at the table. He had hurried in to tell them the latest news: the Stalingrad Front had gone over to the offensive and it would be only a matter of hours before Paulus was surrounded. Instead, he looked at Chuykov and Gurov and then sat down without saying a word. What he had seen on his comrades' faces must have been very special – his news was far from unimportant.

The three men sat there in silence. The silence had already given birth to sounds that had seemed erased for ever. Soon it would give birth to new thoughts, new anxieties and passions that had been uncalled-for during the fighting itself.

But they were not yet aware of these new thoughts. Their anxieties, ambitions, resentments and jealousies had yet to emerge from under the crushing weight of the fighting. They were still unaware that their names would be forever linked with a glorious page of Russian military history.

These minutes of silence were the finest of their lives. During these minutes they felt only human feelings; none of them could understand afterwards why it was they had known such happiness and such sorrow, such love and such humility.

Is there any need to continue this story? Is there any need to describe the pitiful spectacle many of these generals then made of themselves? The constant drunkenness, the bitter disputes over the sharing-out of the glory? How a drunken Chuykov leapt on Rodimtsev and tried to strangle him at a victory celebration – merely because Nikita Khrushchev had thrown his arms round Rodimtsev and kissed him without so much as a glance at Chuykov?

Is there any need to say that Chuykov and his staff first left the right bank in order to attend the celebrations of the twenty-fifth anniversary of the Cheka? And that the following morning, blind drunk, he and his comrades nearly drowned in the Volga and had to be fished out by soldiers from a hole in the ice? Is there any need to describe the subsequent curses, reproaches and suspicions?

There is only one truth. There cannot be two truths. It's hard to live with no truth, with scraps of truth, with a half-truth. A partial truth is no truth at all. Let the wonderful silence of this night be the truth, the whole truth . . . Let us remember the good in these men; let us remember their great achievements.

Chuykov left the bunker and climbed slowly up to the top of the slope; the wooden steps creaked under his boots. It was dark. Both the east and the west were quiet. The silhouettes of factories, the ruined buildings, the trenches and dug-outs all merged into the calm, silent darkness of the earth, the sky and the Volga.

This was the true expression of the people's victory. Not the ceremonial marches and orchestras, not the fireworks and artillery salutes, but this quietness – the quietness of a damp night in the country . . .

Chuykov was very moved; he could hear his heart thumping in his breast. Then he realized the silence was not total. From Banniy Ovrag and the 'Red October' factory came the sound of men singing. Below on the banks of the Volga, he could hear quiet voices and the sound of a guitar.

He went back to the bunker. Gurov was waiting for him so they could have supper.

'What silence, Nikolay Ivanovich!' said Gurov. 'I can't believe it.'

Chuykov sniffed and didn't answer.

They sat down at table. Gurov said: 'Well, comrade, you must have had a hard time if a happy song makes you cry.'

Chuykov looked at him in astonishment.

In a dug-out on the slope leading down to the Volga, a few soldiers were sitting around a table fashioned from a few planks. The sergeant-major was pouring out mugs of vodka by the light of an oil-lamp; the soldiers watched as the precious liquid slowly mounted to the level indicated by his horny fingernail.

They drank and then reached out for some bread.

One of the soldiers finished chewing his piece of bread and said: 'Yes, he gave us a hard time. But we were too much for him in the end.'

'He's certainly quietened down now. You can't hear a sound.'

'He's had enough.'

'The epic of Stalingrad is over.'

'He's done a lot of damage, though. He's set half of Russia on fire.'

They chewed their bread very slowly. It was as though they were breaking off for a meal, after a long and difficult job of work.

Their heads grew hazy, but somehow this haziness left them clear-headed. The taste of bread, the crunch of onion, the weapons piled beside the mud wall, the Volga, this victory over a powerful enemy, a victory won by the same hands that had stroked the hair of their children, fondled their women, broken bread and rolled tobacco in scraps of newspaper – they experienced all this with extraordinary clarity.

...

Darensky felt a strange mixture of feelings as he looked at the German tanks and lorries that had been abandoned in the snow, at the frozen corpses, at the column of men being marched under escort to the East. This was retribution indeed.

He remembered stories about how the Germans had made fun of the poverty of the peasant huts, how they had gazed in surprise and disgust at the simple cradles, the crude stoves, the earthenware pots, the pictures on the walls, the wooden tubs, the painted clay cocks, at the beloved and wonderful world in which the boys then fleeing from their tanks had been born and brought up.

'Look, comrade Lieutenant-Colonel!' said his driver.

Four Germans were carrying one of their comrades on a greatcoat. You could tell from their faces, from their straining necks, that soon they too would fall to the ground. They swayed from side to side. They tripped over the tangled rags wound round their feet. The dry snow lashed their mindless eyes. Their frozen fingers gripped the corners of the greatcoat like hooks.

'So much for the Fritzes,' said the driver.

'We never asked them to come here,' said Darensky.

Suddenly he felt a wave of happiness. Straight through the steppe, in a cloud of mist and snow, Soviet tanks were making their way to the West. They looked quick and fierce, strong and muscular ...

Soldiers were standing up in the hatches. He could see their faces and shoulders, their black helmets and their black sheepskins. There they were, tearing through the ocean-like steppe, leaving behind them a foaming wake of dirty snow. Darensky caught his breath in pride and happiness.

Terrible and sombre, a steel-clad Russia had turned her face to the West.

There was a hold-up as they came to a village. Darensky got out of his jeep and walked past two rows of trucks and some tarpaulin-covered Katyushas. A group of prisoners was being herded across the road. A full colonel who had just got out of his car was watching; he was wearing a cap made from silver astrakhan fur, the kind you can only obtain if you are in command of an army or if you have a quartermaster as a close friend. The guards waved their machine-guns at the prisoners and shouted: 'Come on, come on! Look lively there!'

An invisible wall separated these prisoners from the soldiers and lorry-drivers. A cold still more extreme than the cold of the steppes prevented their eyes from meeting.

'Look at that!' said a laughing voice. 'One of them's got a tail.'

A German soldier was crawling across the road on all fours. A torn quilt trailed along behind him. The soldier was crawling as quickly as he could, moving his arms and legs like a dog, his head to the ground as though he were following a scent. He was making straight for the colonel. The driver standing beside the colonel said: 'Watch out, comrade Colonel. He's going to bite you.'

The colonel stepped to one side. As the German came up to him, he gave him a push with his boot. The feeble blow was enough to break him. He collapsed on the ground, his arms and legs splayed out on either side.

The German looked up at the man who had just kicked him. His eyes were like those of a dying sheep; there was no reproach or suffering in them, nothing at all except humility.

'A fine warrior that shit makes!' said the colonel, wiping the sole of his boot on the snow. There was a ripple of laughter among the onlookers.

Everything went dark. Darensky was no longer his own master; another man, someone who was at once very familiar to him and yet utterly alien, someone who never hesitated, was directing his actions.

'Comrade Colonel,' he said, 'Russians don't kick a man when he's down.'

'What do you think I am then?' asked the colonel. 'Do you think I'm not a Russian?'

'You're a scoundrel,' said Darensky. He saw the colonel take a step towards him. Forestalling the man's angry threats, he shouted: 'My surname's Darensky. Lieutenant-Colonel Darensky – inspector of the Operations Section of Stalingrad Front Headquarters. I'm ready to repeat what I said to you before the commander of the Front and before a military tribunal.'

In a voice full of hatred, the colonel said: 'Very well, Lieutenant-Colonel Darensky. You will be hearing from me.'

He stalked away. Some prisoners came up and dragged their comrade to one side. After that, wherever Darensky turned, he kept meeting the eyes of the prisoners. It was as though something attracted them to him.

As he walked slowly back to his jeep, he heard a mocking voice say: 'So the Fritzes have found a defender!'

Soon Darensky was on his way again. But they were held up by another column of prisoners being marched towards them, the Germans in grey uniforms, the Rumanians in green.

Darensky's fingers were trembling as he lit a cigarette. The driver noticed this out of the corner of his eye and said: 'I don't feel any pity for them. I could shoot any one of them just like that.'

'Fine,' said Darensky. 'But you should have shot them in 1941 instead of taking to your heels like I did.'

He said nothing more for the rest of the journey.

This incident, however, didn't open his heart. On the contrary, it was as though he'd quite exhausted his store of kindness.

What an abyss lay between the road he was following today and the road he had taken to Yashkul through the Kalmyk steppe. Was he really the same man who, beneath an enormous moon, had stood on what seemed to be the last corner of Russian earth? Who had watched the fleeing soldiers and the snake-like necks of the camels, tenderly making room in his heart for the poor, for the weak, for everyone whom he loved?

Mid-Twentieth-Century Portraits

In his anatomy of the Eastern European intelligentsia, The Captive Mind *(1953), Czesław Miłosz makes a case-study of a writer whom he calls 'Gamma', a man of aristocratic stock who nevertheless becomes a Communist in pre-war Poland – a stiff and mediocre poet, not rated by his more gifted acquaintances. Submission to the Stalinist line, for a Pole, involved negation of one's own nationality along with one's humanity. Gamma fled East after the Nazis invaded Soviet-held Poland in the summer of 1941. There were already hundreds of thousands of Poles in the Soviet Union, deported there as undesirables, to work as slave labourers, from 1939 onwards.*

There were two risings in Warsaw in 1943. In April the city's Jews, confined in a ghetto, whence hundreds of thousands had been transported, but only 60,000 remained alive, decided to die with dignity, in armed rebellion. Fighting went on until July. The underground Polish Home Army and left-wing People's Guard resistance fighters tried to help them, but after 14,000 Jews had been killed 7,000 were sent to Treblinka for extermination, and most of the rest were sent to Majdanek, another death camp. In August the Home Army itself rose, under orders from the Polish C-in-C in London. Its aim was to maintain Polish autonomy from the Soviet Union and rebuff propaganda that it was the Red Army alone which was freeing Poland. Successful elsewhere, the rising failed in Warsaw after sixty-three days, while the Red Army was stalled for technical reasons on the outskirts of Eastern Warsaw. Stalin had no interest in the rising, during which about a quarter of Warsaw's one million people may have perished, along with 15,000 armed insurgents.

GAMMA, THE SLAVE OF HISTORY

Many Poles who observed life in the Soviet Union at first hand underwent a change of heart. After a sojourn in prisons or labour camps, former Communists entered the army of the London government. One of those released as a result of the amnesty was the poet W. B. When the Polish army was evacuated from Russia to the Near East (later to take part in the battles in Italy), W. B. was happy to leave the country of hopes unrealized after thirty years. Yet after the end of the War, he could not bear to remain an exile. He returned to a Poland ruled by Gamma and others like him. He forgave. Today every schoolchild learns his *Ode to Stalin* by heart.

Despite any internal vacillations or moments of despair, Gamma and his comrades in the Union of Patriots persevered. They played for high stakes, and their expectations were fulfilled. The tide of victory swung in Russia's favour. A new Polish army started to form in the Soviet Union. It was to enter Poland with the Red Army and to serve as a mainstay of the new pro-Soviet Polish government. Gamma was among the first organizers of this army. Since there were no Polish officers, the higher ranks were filled by Russians. But one could not complain of a lack of soldiers. Only a small number of the deportees had managed to make their way to Persia together with the London army. For those who were left behind the only remaining chance of salvation, that is of escape outside the borders of the Soviet Union, was enlistment in the new army politically supervised by the NKVD and the Union of Patriots.

The summer of 1944 arrived. The Red Army, and with it the new Polish army, set foot on Polish soil. How the years of suffering, humiliation, and clever manoeuvring were repaid! This was what came of betting on a good horse! Gamma joyously greeted the little towns ravaged by artillery fire, and the narrow plots of land which were a relief for the eyes after the monotonous expanses of Russian collective farms. His jeep carried him over roads bordered by the twisted iron of burnt-out German tanks toward power and the practical embodiment of what had hitherto been theoretic discussions full of citations from Lenin and Stalin. This was the reward for those who knew how to think correctly, who understood the logic of History, who did not surrender to senseless sentimentality! It was they, and not those tearful fools from London, who were bringing Poland liberation from the Germans. The nation would, of course, have to undergo a major operation; Gamma felt the excitement of a good surgeon entering the operating room.

Gamma, now a political officer with the rank of major, brought with him from Russia a new wife, a Polish soldier-wife. In uniform, wearing heavy Russian boots, she looked as if she might be of any age. In reality she was very young, but she had lived through many hardships in Russia. She was barely in her teens when she, her sister, brother, and mother were arrested and deported from the centre of Europe to the Asiatic steppes. Summers there are as hot as they are in tropical countries; winters so severe that the tears that flow from the cold are instantly transformed into icicles. A loaf of bread is a small fortune; hard work breaks the strength of undernourished bodies. Police supervision and the vastness of the Asiatic continent kill all hope of escape. The young girl, a daughter of a middle-class family, was not accustomed to hard, physical toil, but she had to support her family. She succeeded after a while in entering a course on tractor driving, and after completing it she drove huge Russian tractors on the steppes of Kazakhstan. Her sympathy for the Stalinist system, after these experiences, was not great. In fact, like almost all the soldiers of the new Polish army, she had come to hate it. At last, however, she found herself in Poland, and the game for high stakes that Gamma was playing was also her game.

The Red Army reached the Vistula. The new government, which was as yet known only as the Liberation Committee, began to function in the city of Lublin. Great tasks and great difficulties faced the Union of Patriots. There was little fear that the Western allies would cause any trouble. The obstacles were of an internal nature; they sprang from the hostile attitude of the people. Once again the old conflict between two loyalties flared up. In the territories now held by the Russians large units of partisans, the so-called Home Army, affiliated with the London Government-in-Exile, had operated against the occupying Germans. Now these units were disarmed, their members drafted into the new Polish army or else arrested and deported to Russia. Gamma humorously recounted what happened in Vilna [Vilnius], the city of our youth. An uprising against the Germans broke out, and detachments of the Home Army entered the city simultaneously with the Russian troops. Then the Soviet command gave a magnificent banquet to which it invited the officers of the Home Army. This was, as Gamma said, a feast in the ancient Slavonic manner, a sumptuous repast during which, according to legend, midst friendly embraces, toasts, and song, invited kinsmen were quietly poisoned. In the course of the banquet, the officers of the Home Army were arrested.

From Lublin, Gamma observed that much the same thing, but on an incomparably larger scale, was happening in Warsaw. At that time the Red Army stood on the line of the Vistula, with Warsaw on the opposite side of the river. The radio of the Liberation Committee urged the inhabitants of the capital to revolt against the Germans. Yet once the uprising broke out, the radio, receiving new instructions, began to heap abuse on the leaders. Of course: they were acting on orders from the Soviet Union's rival in the struggle for power. A feast in the Slavonic tradition was an inadequate measure in this instance; Warsaw itself, a centre of opposition to the Russians just as much as to the Germans, had to be destroyed. The officers of the Red Army gazed through their binoculars at the street fighting on the other side of the river. Smoke obscured their field of vision more and more. Day after day, week after week, the battle went on, until at last the fires merged to form a wall of flame. Gamma and his friends listened to awkward accounts of what was happening in this hell, from the lips of insurgents who managed to swim across the river. Indeed, the price one had to pay to remain true to the logic of History was terrible. One had to behold passively the death of thousands, take on one's conscience the torture of women and children transformed into human torches. Who was guilty? The London Government-in-Exile because it wanted to use the uprising as a trump card in its play for power? The Kremlin because it refused to aid the stricken city out of its conviction that national independence is a bourgeois concept? Or no one?

Leaning over a table, Communist intellectuals dressed in heavy wool uniforms listened to the tale of a young girl, one of those who had succeeded in swimming the river. Her eyes were crazed, she was running a high fever as she spoke. 'Our unit was smashed and pushed to the river. A few succeeded in joining other units. All of those who remained on the bank were wounded. At dawn the SS would attack. That meant that all of us would be shot. What was I to do? Remain with my wounded comrades? But I couldn't help them. I decided to swim. My chances of getting across were small because the river is lit by floodlights. There are German machine-gun nests everywhere. On the shoals in the middle of the river I saw lots of corpses of people who had tried to swim across. The current carries them to the sandbanks. I was very weak. It was hard for us to find food, and I was sick. The current is very strong. They shot at me, so I tried to swim under water as much as possible.'

After two months of battle, the Germans were masters of the ruins of the city. But Communist intellectuals had too much work before them to have time to brood over the misfortunes of Warsaw. First of all, they had to set the printing presses into motion. Because Communism recognizes that rule over men's minds is the key to rule over an entire country, the word is the cornerstone of this system. Gamma became one of the chief press organizers in the city of Lublin.

In the course of these years, he became a better writer than he had been before the war. He thrived on a strict diet of the doctrine, for 'socialist realism' strengthens weak talents and undermines great ones. His primitivism, of which he had long since ceased to be ashamed, now lent the semblance of sincerity to his works. His true voice, which he had once tried to smother, now spoke in his verse, sharp and clamorous. He also wrote a number of orthodox stories about the War and Nazi atrocities, all of them modelled on the pattern that was to produce thousands of pages of Russian prose.

In January 1945, the Red Army began its offensive, crossed the Vistula and swiftly neared Berlin. Gamma also moved to the west. The Party directed him to Cracow, the city in which the greatest number of writers, scholars, and artists had sought refuge after the fall of Warsaw. There he tasted the delights of dictatorship. Strange creatures dressed in remnants of furs, belted peasant jerkins and clumsy rope-laced boots began to swarm out of holes in old houses, indeed from beneath their very floors. Among them were the intellectuals who had survived the years of German occupation. Many remembered Gamma as a young pre-war poet whose works they had ignored. Now they knew he was all-powerful. On his word depended the possibility of their obtaining a chance to publish, a house, an income, a job with a newspaper, magazine, or publishing firm. They approached him apprehensively. Neither before the war nor in their underground activity were they Communist. But the new government was a fact. Nothing could prevent events from evolving as Moscow, as well as Gamma and his friends, desired. With a broad smile of friendship, he pressed the extended hands of these people and amused himself. Some were recalcitrant; some tried not to show how much his favour meant to them; some were openly servile. In a short time, he was surrounded by a court of yes-men who frowned when he frowned or guffawed loudly whenever he deigned to tell a joke.

MID-TWENTIETH-CENTURY PORTRAIT

Hidden behind his smile of brotherly regard,
He despises the newspaper reader, the victim of the dialectic of power.
Says: 'Democracy,' with a wink.
Hates the physiological pleasures of mankind,
Full of memories of those who also ate, drank, copulated,
But in a moment had their throats cut.
Recommends dances and garden parties to defuse public anger.

Shouts: 'Culture!' and 'Art!' but means circus games really.

Utterly spent.
Mumbles in sleep or anaesthesia: 'God, oh God!'
Compares himself to a Roman in whom the Mithras cult has mixed with the cult of Jesus.
Still clings to old superstitions, sometimes believes himself to be possessed by demons.
Attacks the past, but fears that, having destroyed it,
He will have nothing on which to lay his head.
Likes most to play cards, or chess, the better to keep his own counsel.

Keeping one hand on Marx's writings, he reads the Bible in private.
His mocking eye on processions leaving burned-out churches.
His back drop: a horseflesh-coloured city in ruins.
In his hand: a memento of a boy 'fascist' killed in the Uprising.

1945
Kraków

Radnóti's Forced March

Miklós Radnóti was a Hungarian poet of Jewish extraction who had already published a number of books when the war broke out. Between 1940 and 1944 he was intermittently drafted for forced labour battalions in various parts of Eastern Europe. In 1944 he was working on a railway line at Bor in Serbia when the Axis armies arrived and began force-marching the labourers into Hungary. Radnóti was shot when he became too weak to continue. His body was exhumed from a mass grave in 1946 and a notebook full of poems was found in his greatcoat pocket.

FORCED MARCH

A fool is he who, collapsed,
rises and walks again,
Ankles and knees moving
alone, like wandering pain,
Yet he, as if wings uplifted him,
sets out on his way,
And in vain the ditch calls him
back, who dare not stay.
And if asked why not, he might answer
– without leaving his path –
That his wife was awaiting him,
and a saner, more beautiful death.
Poor fool! He's out of his mind:
now, for a long time,
Only scorched winds have whirled
over the houses at home,
The wall has been laid low,
the plum-tree is broken there,
The night of our native hearth
flutters, thick with fear.
O if only I could believe
that everything of worth

Were not just in my heart –
that I still had a home on earth;
If only I had! As before,
jam made fresh from the plum
Would cool on the old verandah,
in peace the bee would hum,
And an end-of-summer stillness
would bask in the drowsy garden,
Naked among the leaves
would sway the fruit-trees' burden,
And she would be waiting, blonde
against the russet hedgerow,
As the slow morning painted
slow shadow over shadow, –
Could it perhaps still be?
The moon tonight's so round!
Don't leave me friend, shout at me:
I'll get up off the ground!

15 September 1944

POSTCARDS

I

From Bulgaria, wild and swollen, the noise of cannon rolls;
It booms against the ridge, then hesitates, and falls.
Men, animals, carts, thoughts pile up as they fly;
The road rears back and whinnies, maned is the racing sky.
But you, in this shifting chaos, are what in me is constant:
In my soul's depth you shine forever – you are silent
And motionless, like an angel who marvels at destruction,
Or a beetle, burying, in a hollow tree's corruption.

30 August 1944
In the mountains

II

No more than six or seven miles away
Haystacks and houses flare;
There, on the meadow's verges, peasants crouch,
Pipe-smoking, dumb with fear.
Here still, where the tiny shepherdess steps in,
Ripples on the lake spread;
A flock of ruffled sheep bend over it
And drink the clouds they tread.

6 October 1944
Cservenka

III

Blood-red, the spittle drools from the oxen's mouths;
The men, stooping to urinate, pass blood;
The squad stands bunched in groups whose reek disgusts.
And loathsome death blows overhead in gusts.

24 October 1944
Mohács

IV

I fell beside him. His body – which was taut
As a cord is, when it snaps – spun as I fell.
Shot in the neck. 'This is how you will end,'
I whispered to myself; 'keep lying still.
Now, patience is flowering into death.'
'*Der springt noch auf*,' said someone over me.
Blood on my ears was drying, caked with earth.

31 October 1944
Szentkirályszabadja

8
Grief and Guilt

Rainer Maria Rilke wrote the first of ten Elegies in the winter of 1911–12 at Schloss Duino, near Trieste, from which the sequence, published in 1923, would eventually take its name. Before him lay his bitter reactions to European war and failed German revolution, of which later elegies would take account. These might be said to echo back through the conclusion of the First Elegy (as translated by J. B. Leishman and Stephen Spender), where the 'Linos' referred to was a God of ancient Greek nature-worship, sometimes associated with the origins of song and music in general:

> *They've finally no more need of us, the early-departed,*
> *one's gently weaned from terrestrial things as one mildly*
> *outgrows the breasts of a mother. But we, that have need of*
> *such mighty secrets, we, for whom sorrow's so often*
> *source of blessedest progress, could we exist without them?*
> *Is the story in vain, how once, in the mourning for Linos,*
> *venturing earliest music pierced barren numbness, and how,*
> *in the startled space an almost deified youth*
> *suddenly quitted for ever, emptiness first*
> *felt the vibration that now lifts us and comforts and helps?*

This passage might be used to interrogate the sentiments regarding Britain's Great War dead expressed in 'For the Fallen' by Laurence Binyon (1869–1943). So often recited at Armistice Day ceremonies, or used as a source for inscriptions on memorials, Binyon's verses, with their patriotic gratitude for the 'sacrifice' of young lives, imply that a rarefied species of pleasure is experienced by the living through their grief:

Solemn the drums thrill: Death august and royal
Sings sorrow up into immortal spheres.
There is music in the midst of desolation
And a glory that shines upon our tears.

They shall grow not old, as we that are left grow old:
Age shall not weary them, nor the years condemn.
At the going down of the sun and in the morning
We will remember them.

But when the English composer Arthur Bliss (1891–1975), who had served throughout the Great War, created his symphonic Morning Heroes *in 1930 as a requiem for the war dead, especially remembering his brother Francis, killed on the Somme in 1916, he could not offer an uncomplicated conflation of heroic sacrifice with moving music. He included a stark setting of Owen's 'Spring Offensive' (q.v.). Grief may involve fearful doubts and painful self-blame. Of the items included in this section, only Aragon's acclamation of a dead Resistance fighter offers the experience of grief as pleasure.*

Memorials

The complex significance of war memorials is noticed first by Martin Gilbert, followed by David Gilmour.

ARMISTICE, 1919

'What's an Armistice, mate?' one British soldier asked another. 'Time to bury the dead,' was the reply. Every area in which the war had been fought was marked with its cemeteries, every town and village from which the soldiers came has its memorial. In the summer of 1996 the author was in the small Slovak village of Skalite. Between 1914 and 1918 it had been an Austro-Hungarian village. Later it had been part of Czechoslovakia. During the Second World War, and since 1994, it was in independent Slovakia. The forty-five family names on its First World War memorial are the names of the families who live in the village today. Though their national allegiances have been changed four times since the end of the First World War, their family identity remains. Skalite's memorial encapsulates suffering and grief that knows no borders.

There are British, Australian, German and Turkish war graves in the First World War cemetery in Gaza. There is a list of Italian village youth – often of groups of brothers – in every Italian hill village. The names of the dead on the war memorials in universities and schools all attest to the loss of vital forces in every land, and in every corner of every land. In the main cemetery in Vienna a plaque records 427 soldiers buried there:

THEY DIED FOR THEIR COUNTRY
AND REST FAR AWAY FROM THEIR BELOVED HOMES IN
ETERNAL PEACE,

1 Englishman
Wilson, George Alexander

426 Italians

In 1971, when Queen Elizabeth II visited the British naval war memorial at Cape Helles, there was no Turkish monument on the Gallipoli peninsula. Twenty years later a Turkish monument overlooked the Aegean Sea. On it were carved the words of a speech made in 1934 by Mustafa Kemal (Atatürk). Addressing the Allied 'heroes' who had shed their blood and lost their lives on the peninsula twenty years earlier, he declared:

> You are now lying in the soil of a friendly country. Therefore rest in peace. There is no difference between the Johnnies and the Mehmets to us where they lie side by side here in this country of ours.
>
> You, the mothers, who sent your sons from far away countries, wipe away your tears; your sons are lying now in our bosom and are in peace. After having lost their lives on this land they have become our sons as well.

On all fronts, the machine-gun had been one of the most effective weapons of the war. It had mown down line after line of advancing infantrymen. Its devastating power was recognized on the post-war memorial to the British Machine Gun Corps at Hyde Park Corner. Below the naked figure of 'The Boy David' – a statue which, at peak traffic times in 1997, was passed by five to six thousand motorists an hour – is the inscription:

> Saul hath slain his thousands
> But David his tens of thousands.

Curzon's Memorial

George Nathaniel Curzon, Marquis Curzon of Kedleston (1859–1925), was the most brilliant man in British politics in the first quarter of the twentieth century, and one of the most unpopular, because of his social and intellectual arrogance. As Viceroy of India he had displayed an obsession with pomp and circumstance and elaborate ceremonial. When the 1914–18 war ended he was Lord President of the Council in the British Cabinet. The war had chastened him.

Curzon's experience of ceremonies made him a natural choice as an organizer of events and memorials to celebrate victory and commemorate the dead. His most tedious duty was to act as chairman of a committee to set up a House of Lords memorial for the two hundred peers or sons of peers who had been killed in the war. What should have been a straightforward task was complicated by divisions among the surviving peers over whether the structure should go in the Princes' Chamber or the Royal Gallery, and whether it merited the displacement of a statue of Queen Victoria. A month before his death Curzon was still wrestling with the problems of the memorial. For nearly six years, he complained to Lansdowne, he had 'borne the whole burden of this wretched affair, trying to carry out the wishes and instructions of the House without help from anybody'.

More rewarding was his chairmanship of a committee set up by the Cabinet to organize peace celebrations in the summer of 1919. After these had passed off successfully, he was asked to supervise the erection of a permanent cenotaph in Whitehall and to make arrangements for its unveiling. At the head of a second committee he then designed a restrained and moving ritual centred on a two minutes' silence and the haunting lament of the 'Last Post'. Determined that the ceremony should be one of poignant simplicity rather than high-ranking grandeur, he insisted that widows and ex-servicemen should be given priority on the occasion. After it had been decided that the unveiling of the Cenotaph should be accompanied by the burial of an unknown soldier in Westminster Abbey, Curzon again planned the ceremony and again stipulated that places should be given 'not to society ladies or the wives of dignitaries, but to the selected widows and mothers of those who had fallen, especially in the humbler ranks'. Conducted in an atmosphere of emotional intensity seldom matched in Britain, the events aroused such strong feelings that popular opinion demanded an annual service at the site of the Cenotaph. One final ceremony was thus given to Curzon to devise, and it has lasted as long as anything he ever did. The Remembrance Day service, still performed three-quarters of a century later, is his creation.

Kipling's Epitaphs of the War

Rudyard Kipling's only son was lost in the Great War. In 1919 he published a collection of classically inspired Epitaphs.

THE REFINED MAN

I was of delicate mind. I stepped aside for my needs,
Disdaining the common office. I was seen from afar and
killed. . . .
How is this matter for mirth? Let each man be judged by his
deeds.
*I have paid my price to live with myself on the terms that I
willed.*

BOMBED IN LONDON

On land and sea I strove with anxious care
To escape conscription. It was in the air!

THE SLEEPY SENTINEL

Faithless the watch that I kept: now I have none to keep.
I was slain because I slept: now I am slain I sleep.
Let no man reproach me again, whatever watch is unkept –
I sleep because I am slain. They slew me because I slept.

BATTERIES OUT OF AMMUNITION

If any mourn us in the workshop, say
We died because the shift kept holiday.

COMMON FORM

If any question why we died,
Tell them, because our fathers lied.

A DRIFTER OFF TARENTUM

He from the wind-bitten North with ship and companions
 descended,
Searching for eggs of death spawned by invisible hulls.
Many he found and drew forth. Of a sudden the fishery ended
In flame and a clamorous breath known to the eye-pecking
 gulls.

DESTROYERS IN COLLISION

For Fog and Fate no charm is found
To lighten or amend.
I, hurrying to my bride, was drowned –
Cut down by my best friend.

UNKNOWN FEMALE CORPSE

Headless, lacking foot and hand,
Horrible I come to land.
I beseech all women's sons
Know I was a mother once.

A Paris Street

Louis Aragon – erstwhile Surrealist, then a Communist – was regarded in 1940–44 as the leading poet of the French Resistance. Afterwards, he commemorated its commemoration. This poem appeared in Le Roman Inachevé *(The Unfinished Romance), in 1956. Erivan is the capital of Armenia, normally now spelt 'Yerevan' in English texts.*

STANZAS IN MEMORY

Poem written for the naming of a Paris street, 'Groupe Manouchian'. The Armenian poet Manouchian, a hero of our Resistance, leader of the group called 'Strangers' or 'Red Mark', was shot by the Nazis in February 1944.

You neither claimed glory nor tears
Nor the organ nor the prayer for the dying
Eleven years already how quickly eleven years pass
You had simply used your arms
Death does not dazzle the eyes of the Partisans

You had your portraits on the walls of our towns
Black of beard and of night hirsute menacing
The poster which looked like a blood stain
Because your names are difficult to pronounce
Looked for an effect of fear on the passers-by

No one seemed to see you Frenchmen by adoption
People went without eyes for you during the day
But under the curfew straying fingers
Had written under your photos DEAD FOR FRANCE
And the bleak mornings were different for it

Everything had the uniform white frost colour
At the end of February for your last moments
And then one of you said calmly

'Good luck to everyone Good luck to those who will live on
I died without hatred in me for the German people

Farewell pain and pleasure Farewell roses
Farewell life Farewell light and wind
Marry be happy and think of me often
You who will live in the loveliness of things
When it will all be over later in Erivan

A bright winter sun lights up the hill
How beautiful nature is and how it breaks my heart
Justice will follow in our triumphant footsteps
My Mélinée my love my orphan
And I tell you to live and have a child'

They were twenty-three when the rifles flowered
Twenty-three who gave their hearts before their time
Twenty-three strangers and yet our brothers
Twenty-three in love with life so much as to die for it
Twenty-three who called out 'France' in falling

Testament of Youth

Vera Brittain's Testament of Youth *(1933) tells the story of a young woman whose life is permanently blighted by the deaths of a group of young men who had entered the army as ardent volunteers – her brother's friend Roland who became her fiancé, other friends, and finally her beloved brother Edward himself. She had been serving as a VAD (Voluntary Aid Detachment) nurse in France until shortly before she received the last, worst news; she had had to return home because her mother's health had broken down.*

A friendly Life *of Vera Brittain, published in 1995 by Paul Berry and Mark Bostridge, provides a sinister footnote to her account of her grief. After* Testament of Youth *appeared, Colonel Charles Hudson, Edward's last commanding officer, aggrieved by her unpleasant account of him, got in touch with her and told her what he had withheld from her in 1918. Edward had died under the cloud of a report from the Military Police which announced that a censored letter made it 'plain' that Edward and another officer 'were involved with the men of their company in homosexuality'. Hudson had given Edward a friendly warning. He was the only officer killed in the action against the Austrians on 15 June 1918, and Hudson believed that, faced with an inquiry and possible court martial, he might have taken his own life, or deliberately courted death by sniper fire. Though Brittain had suspected Edward's homosexuality, she was very distressed by the thought of suicide. As Conrad's Marlow knew when he met Kurtz's Intended, there are some things which loving women, perhaps, should not be told . . .*

The first of July 1916 was significant as the day when the British launched the catastrophic Battle of the Somme.

I was no better reconciled to staying at home when I read in *The Times* a few weeks after my return that the persistent German raiders had at last succeeded in their intention of smashing up the Étaples hospitals, which, with the aid of the prisoner patients, had so satisfactorily protected the railway line for three years without further trouble or expense to the military authorities.

It was clear from the guarded *communiqué* that this time the bombs had dropped on the hospitals themselves, causing many casualties and far more damage than the breaking of the bridge over the Canche in the first big raid. Hope Milroy, I was thankful to remember, had been moved to Havre a fortnight earlier, but a few days later a letter from Norah filled in the gaps of the official report. The hospital next door, she told me, had suffered the worst, and several Canadian Sisters had been killed. At 24 General one of the death-dealing bombs had fallen on Ward 17, where I had nursed the pneumonias on night-duty; it had shattered the hut, together with several patients, and wounded the VAD in charge, who was in hospital with a fractured skull. The Sisters' quarters were no longer safe after dark, she concluded, and they all had to spend their nights in trenches in the woods.

More than ever, as I finished her letter, I felt myself a deserter, a coward, a traitor to my patients and the other nurses.

How could I have played with the idea – as I had, once or twice lately – of returning to Oxford before the end of the War? What did the waste of an immature intellect matter, when such things could happen to one's friends? My comrades of the push had been frightened, hurt, smashed up – and I was not there with them, skulking safely in England. Why, oh why, had I listened to home demands when my job was out there?

A brief note that came just afterwards from Edward seemed an appropriate – and fear-provoking – comment on the news from Étaples.

'*Ma chère*,' he had written just before midnight on May 12th, '*la vie est brève* – usually too short for me to write adequate letters, and likely to be shorter still.'

For some time now, my apprehensions for his safety had been lulled by the long quiescence of the Italian front, which had seemed a haven of peace in contrast to our own raging vortex. Repeatedly, during the German offensive, I had thanked God and the Italians who fled at Caporetto that Edward was out of it, and rejoiced that the worst I had to fear from this particular push was the comparatively trivial danger that threatened myself. But now I felt the familiar stirrings of the old tense fear which had been such a persistent companion throughout the War, and my alarm was increased when Edward asked me a week or two later to send him 'a funny cat from Liberty's . . . to alleviate tragedy with comedy'.

'This evening,' he added wistfully, 'I should like to hear Dr Farmer play the same Bach Prelude and Fugue which he played in Magdalen chapel on the evening of November 15th, 1914.'

We had perhaps gone to Magdalen together that evening, I thought; it had been just before he left the OTC to join the 11th Sherwood Foresters at Sandgate.

I procured the 'funny cat' and sent it off; was he in for yet another July 1st? I wondered. And because the original July 1st was so nearly approaching its second anniversary, I felt moved to write him a poem that would tell him, as I could never quite tell him in words or in letters, how greatly I esteemed him for the brave endurance which he had shown on that day and so many times since. So I wrote the poem, purchased a copy of the newly published war-poets' anthology, *The Muse in Arms*, and sent the book to Italy with my own verses inscribed on the fly-leaf:

TO MY BROTHER
(In Memory of July 1st, 1916)

Your battle-wounds are scars upon my heart,
Received when in that grand and tragic 'show'
You played your part
Two years ago,

And silver in the summer morning sun
I see the symbol of your courage glow –
That Cross you won
Two years ago.

Though now again you watch the shrapnel fly,
And hear the guns that daily louder grow,
As in July
Two years ago,

May you endure to lead the Last Advance,
And with your men pursue the flying foe,
As once in France
Two years ago.

In the meantime my sudden dread had somewhat diminished, for the newspapers, though they had plenty to say about the new German advance on the Aisne, remained persistently silent about Italy, and instead of further hints of imminent peril, a present came for me from Edward of a khaki silk scarf, and a letter, begun on May 30th and finished on June 3rd, which told me that he was again in hospital.

'Thanks awfully for sending off the cat though of course it hasn't arrived as parcels take so long now. However there isn't as much hurry for it now as there was . . . It so happens, quite unexpectedly too, that the time when I wanted it particularly is not yet . . . If the War goes on much longer nobody will go back to Oxford in spite of the concessions; I often think I am too old now to go back.'

On June 3rd he continued in pencil.

'I am now in hospital and oddly enough not so bored as before because it is rather a relief to be down in the foothills again and not to have anything to do for a change. It is just a form of PUO which everybody is having just now but fortunately not all at quite the same time. I shall be back again in a few days. I have now finished *Fortitude* and find it excellent . . . I rather think leave has been reopened while I have been away, but of course I am about 20th on the list.'

Temporarily reassured about his safety, I went on grieving for the friendly, exhausting, peril-threatened existence that I had left behind at Étaples. To my last day I shall not forget the aching bitterness, the conscience-stricken resentment, with which during that hot, weary June, when every day brought gloomier news from France, I read Press paragraphs stating that more and more VADs were wanted, or passed the challenging posters in Trafalgar Square, proclaiming that my King and Country needed me to join the WAAC, or the WRNS, or the WRAF.

And it was just then, a few days before midsummer, that the Austrians, instigated by their German masters, decided to attack the Allies on the Asiago Plateau.

On Sunday morning, June 16th, I opened the *Observer*, which appeared to be chiefly concerned with the new offensive – for the moment at a standstill – in the Noyon-Montdidier sector of the Western Front, and instantly saw at the head of a column the paragraph for which I had looked so long and so fearfully:

ITALIAN FRONT ABLAZE
GUN DUELS FROM MOUNTAIN TO SEA
BAD OPENING OF AN OFFENSIVE

> The following Italian official *communiqué* was issued yesterday:
> 'From dawn this morning the fire of the enemy's artillery, strongly countered by our own, was intensified from the Lagerina Valley to the sea. On the Asiago Plateau, to the east of the Brenta and on the middle Piave, the artillery struggle has assumed and maintains a character of extreme violence.'

There followed a quotation from the correspondent of the *Corriere della Sera*, who described 'the Austrian attack on the Italian positions in the neighbourhood of the Tonale Pass'. 'Possibly,' he suggested,

> this is the prelude of the great attack which the Austrian Army has been preparing for so long a time . . . the employment of heavy forces proves that this is not a merely isolated and local action, but the first move in a great offensive plan. The Austrian infantry and the *Feldjäger* have not passed. The Italian defenders met them in their first onslaught and immediately retook the few small positions that had been lost in the first moments of the fighting. This success on the part of the Italian defence is a good augury for the future.

'I'm afraid,' I thought, feeling suddenly cold in spite of the warm June sunlight that streamed through the dining-room window. True, the *communiqué* didn't specifically mention the British, but then there was always a polite pretence on the part of the Press that the Italians were defending the heights above Vicenza entirely on their own. The loss of a 'few small positions', however quickly recaptured, meant – as it always did in dispatches – that the defenders were taken by surprise and the enemy offensive had temporarily succeeded. Could I hope that Edward had missed it through being still in hospital? I hardly thought so; he had said as long ago as June 3rd that he expected to be 'back again in a few days'.

However, there was nothing to do in the midst of one's family but practise that concealment of fear which the long years of war had instilled, thrusting it inward until one's subconscious became a regular prison-house of apprehensions and inhibitions which were later to take their revenge. My mother had arranged to stay with my grandmother at Purley that week in order to get a few days' change from the flat; it was the first time that she had felt well enough since her breakdown to think of going away, and I did not want the news from Italy to make her change her plans. At length, though with instinctive reluctance, she allowed herself to be prevailed upon to go, but a profound depression hung over our parting at Charing Cross.

A day or two later, more details were published of the fighting in Italy, and I learnt that the Sherwood Foresters had been involved in the 'show' on the Plateau. After that I made no pretence at doing anything but wander restlessly round Kensington or up and down the flat, and, though my father retired glumly to bed every evening at nine o'clock, I gave up writing the semi-fictitious record which I had begun of my life in France. Somehow I couldn't bring myself even to wrap up the *Spectator* and *Saturday Review* that I sent every week to Italy, and they remained in my bedroom, silent yet eloquent witnesses to the dread which my father and I, determinedly conversing on commonplace topics, each refused to put into words.

By the following Saturday we had still heard nothing of Edward. The interval usually allowed for news of casualties after a battle was seldom so long as this, and I began, with an artificial sense of lightness unaccompanied by real conviction, to think that there was perhaps, after all, no news to come. I had just announced to my father, as we sat over tea in the dining-room, that I really must do up Edward's papers and take them to the post office before it closed for the week-end, when there came the sudden loud clattering at the front-door knocker that always meant a telegram.

For a moment I thought that my legs would not carry me, but they behaved quite normally as I got up and went to the door. I knew what was in the telegram – I had known for a week – but because the persistent hopefulness of the human heart refuses to allow intuitive certainty to persuade the reason of that which it knows, I opened and read it in a tearing anguish of suspense.

'Regret to inform you Captain E. H. Brittain MC killed in action Italy June 15th.'

'No answer,' I told the boy mechanically, and handed the telegram to my father, who had followed me into the hall. As we went back into the dining-room I saw, as though I had never seen them before, the bowl of blue delphiniums on the table; their intense colour, vivid, ethereal, seemed too radiant for earthly flowers.

Then I remembered that we should have to go down to Purley and tell the news to my mother.

Late that evening, my uncle brought us all back to an empty flat. Edward's death and our sudden departure had offered the maid – at that time the amateur prostitute – an agreeable opportunity for a few hours' freedom of which she had taken immediate advantage. She had not even finished the household handkerchiefs, which I had washed that morning and intended to iron after tea; when I went into the kitchen I found them still hanging, stiff as boards, over the clothes-horse near the fire where I had left them to dry.

Long after the family had gone to bed and the world had grown silent, I crept into the dining-room to be alone with Edward's portrait. Carefully closing the door, I turned on the light and looked at the pale, pictured face, so dignified, so steadfast, so tragically mature. He had been through so much – far, far more than those beloved friends who had died at an earlier stage of the interminable War, leaving him alone to mourn their loss. Fate might have allowed him the little, sorry compensation of survival, the chance to make his lovely music in honour of their memory. It seemed indeed the last irony that he should have been killed by the countrymen of Fritz Kreisler, the violinist whom of all others he had most greatly admired.

And suddenly, as I remembered all the dear afternoons and evenings when I had followed him on the piano as he played his violin, the sad, searching eyes of the portrait were more than I could bear, and falling on my knees before it I began to cry 'Edward! Oh Edward!' in dazed repetition, as though my persistent crying and calling would somehow bring him back.

[*Brittain sought out – and disliked – Edward's commanding officer, back in London, wounded himself, and awarded the VC. His stiff reticence dismayed her.*]

Before he [Hudson] went back to the front just in time for the ending of the War, the 11th Sherwood Foresters and several other British regiments had left the demoralized Austrians to the mercy of the now jubilant Italians and returned to France, where the surviving officers from Edward's company had been killed in the last great push. So whether Edward's part in the vital counter-attack on the Plateau really involved some special act of heroism, I shall now never know.

Even if I had found out, it would have made little difference at the time, for as the sudden closing-down of silence upon our four years' correspondence gradually forced on my stunned consciousness the bare fact that Edward was dead, I became progressively unable to take in other facts, or to estimate their value.

So incredible was our final separation that it made life itself seem unreal. I had never believed that I could actually go on living without that lovely companionship which had been at my service since childhood, that perfect relation which had involved no jealousy and no agitation, but only the profoundest confidence, the most devoted understanding, on either side. Yet here I was, in a world emptied of that unfailing consolation, most persistently, most unwillingly alive. I was even alive enough to unpack his possessions when they were returned to us from Italy, and to find amongst them *The Muse in Arms*, which had arrived just after the battle, with my poem inside, unopened and unread. I knew then that he had died without even being aware of my last endeavour to show him how deeply I loved and admired him.

The return of the poem began a period of isolation more bleak, more complete and far more prolonged than the desperate months in 1916 which had followed the death of Roland. My early diaries had been full of the importance of 'standing alone', 'being sufficient unto one's self', and I sometimes re-read them with sombre cynicism during the time that, for nearly two years after Edward's death, I had to be 'sufficient unto myself' whether I liked it or not. However deep our devotion may be to parents, or to children, it is our contemporaries alone with whom understanding is instinctive and entire, and from June 1918 until April 1920, I knew no one in the world to whom I could speak spontaneously, or utter one sentence completely expressive of what I really thought or felt. I 'stood alone' in very truth – and I hope profoundly that I may never repeat the experience. It lasted so long, perhaps, because I decided in the first few weeks after his loss that nothing would ever really console me for Edward's death or make his memory less poignant; and in this I was quite correct, for nothing ever has.

A Letter in Lancashire

Peter Strongman had published fiction before the Second World War, but his 'war work' was teaching maths to industrial trainees in a college in Lancashire. Here he lodged with Mrs Warren ('Bunnie'), of whom he became very fond in a filial kind of way. Her son Peter was serving in the Merchant Navy: her daughter Daphne was at home. Bad news came in 1942.

We've had a dreadful week. Last Thursday first post in the morning came a letter to say that Peter's ship was overdue, that is, presumably lost, and everything has been terrible ever since. Bunnie came in crying while I was still asleep, and has been crying ever since, off and on. The first morning, getting my breakfast in the kitchen, with Bunnie and Daphne crying, and me sitting in the dining-room, was frightful. So I said what I could, and thought it best to keep out of the way and kept out of it till supper time, and then came in to find Bunnie and Daphne, and Rhoda, the girl that Peter wanted to marry, all sitting round the fire and talking dismally and trying to keep their spirits up with stuff about ships and so on. And I ate my supper as best I could, and the girls went to bed, and I had to go through the whole thing again, and read the letter again, and talk everything over again – I suppose it's a help to talk – and then Bunnie went to bed. The whole of the morning they had been dashing about – to the police to get her husband's address and send him a message, and Bunnie is very bitter against her husband, so that it was almost a consolation to send him a telegram saying, 'Your son lost at sea'. In the afternoon she had a message from a friend that he was coming to see her, and that gave her a sour triumph, too, for he has treated her very badly, and she has a positive pleasure in speculating how badly he must be feeling now in his turn. However, that was Thursday and now it's Monday, and no sign of Warren, so perhaps the desire to do the right thing has failed. So that evening the whole day was raked over again, and as they had got all the consolation and advice from each other that they could they tried to get some out from me. Unfortunately Bunnie is well-read in sea-matters and knows that the first wireless man – which Peter was – is the most likely person on the whole ship to get left behind, because he must send out a message to the last. And she's heard so many tales about life at sea and conditions generally, and how it's each man for himself and all this heroism in the newspapers is just rot, that there's nothing she can cheer herself with. But she keeps speculating. There were three wireless officers on the *Biela*, and she's met all of them. Would they be likely to lose their heads, and what would happen? Peter was in the captain's life-boat, that had been arranged before they left Liverpool – and the captain should be the last to leave the vessel. On the other hand, if it was a U-Boat, sometimes the U-boat commander just makes them sign a document promising not to go to sea again, and sets them adrift in an open boat with supplies. But sometimes he just lets them drown. We've been all over this a dozen times by now, and her nerves are so upset that her head aches all the time and her eyes feel funny. She doesn't sleep properly since, but dreams every night that Peter is in the sea and he's lost because he forgot his glasses, and if only he had his glasses he'd be all right, and she tries to shout to him to go back for his glasses, and can't. And then she cheers up a bit, for an hour or two, and then lets go again, and is wandering round the house with a little tight mouth and red eyes. It's really dreadful, and they were so nice to me, the only one not directly concerned, that I could have broken down and howled with the rest of them . . .

Poor Bunnie is now more or less recovering from the first stress of the loss of Peter. It was dreadful while it lasted – such tears, and such valiant attempts to keep cheerful, and then sudden givings way. But she was good. It's ten days ago by now and things are about normal in outward appearances, bless her heart, though of course there's no knowing what she feels like inside. Her husband hasn't come after all, I suppose he changed his mind as soon as the first shock of the affair was over, and gave way under the idea of the shock after so many years. But everyone else has rallied round mightily, including me. When I had been out all day the Thursday that the news arrived it felt so strange and intrusive to come in in the evening and there she was in the kitchen as pale as a ghost, having lived all that day on cigarettes and cups of tea, quite unable to eat, and I hardly knew what to say, and felt dreadful, and just said something silly about having plenty of money if she wasn't all right – a great pity that in emergencies my mind runs on money, but it does, and that wasn't the right thing to say – not at all helpful. Instinct and better nature then prompted me to put one arm round her shoulder and hug her a bit, and that was right. She really is a darling, and though I say it as shouldn't, I do seriously believe that a hug was a relief and let down the general tension better than saying things – and for the first couple of days the tension was dreadful. We went over all the same ground that evening, and we've been over it again since – all about U-boat commanders and turning people adrift, and staying to the bitter end, and being picked up at sea, and all the rest of it.

So I got creditably – more by instinct than design, and chiefly by going quietly, through one of the difficult things in the world – my first encounter with someone else's bitter grief, and that someone in some ways almost a stranger. It's well to know how it feels, and how to behave, for grief must soon come nearer than that. Bunnie rather undermined me by being solicitous over what an upset it was for me – but that's just one way of bringing the inevitable subject – the one thing that everyone is thinking about and had better talk about, into the conversation, and getting the oppressive feeling cleared away for a few minutes. To grief one must pay the tribute it demands, there is no other way. Daphne and Rhoda on the first evening were washed out with tears –. Daphne looked absolutely lovely, which is a triumph of youth and complexion – and sitting dismally over the fire looking at woman's magazines. I remember how Daphne passed something across to Rhoda and said, 'What do you think of that?' and Rhoda with a mechanical flash of her brilliant manner, said, 'I think it *ter*rible!' and I pretended to be reading a book . . .

Then letters that had been written to Peter began to be returned, but Bunnie knew that they must come and they didn't feel so bad. She read one of them aloud and said how Peter complained of the punctuation, and so that was got over all right.

And so of course she began to conceal things a little better, and I – how callous one comes to be – began to feel that it was perhaps a little shallow to recover so soon, – and that's why people who are sensitive to atmospheres tend to exaggerate the manifestations of grief, of course, – they're afraid they'll be thought callous if they don't. But she had merely bottled things down a bit. On the Sunday night, instead of going to the usual cinema, they were in playing cards, and trying to be cheerful, when some friends came to take Bunnie out for a drink, just to cheer her up. She came in, and got my supper and brought me my tray, and seemed cheerful, but the drink had had a releasing effect on the restraint she had built up, and though she came in seeming cheerful, just as usual, she just put the tray on the table, sat down on a chair, made a dreadful face and began to cry, and say all the things that one does say – the obvious things that one can't invent, 'I don't know what you can think of us. It's not very nice for you to come into lodgings and find everybody upset and everything all wrong is it? I've been trying to keep cheerful for the others – you've got to pretend, but, oh Petie, he was a good boy, he didn't deserve it! Remember what he said about you, what a gentleman you were. And he was right, he'd knocked about and he knew. They're playing cards . . . Oh dear, eat your toast, it'll be cold, and your supper's late. Funny the last time he was home he did all that insurance. "I want to be sure you're looked after," he said. Well, his father knows now and I've nothing to reproach myself with. Warren'll come here, and what can he say? Well, there's one thing he can do for me, he can keep you out of the army . . .'

'But Bunnie, I . . . Oh no, he . . . Besides, it wouldn't be right to –'

'Oh, it's not because of the money – I'm going to be all right – only I keep thinking about your mother. I know what it feels like. And if you go too. Last night he was in the sea again and I was trying to shout to him that he hadn't got his glasses' – and from this gradually working our way round through the possibility of Warren's coming, and what he would feel like, which cheered her a little with the thought of his discomfiture, we talked on and on, and Rhoda and Daphne went to bed, one after the other, calling out good night from the hall, and gradually we worked our way back to cheerfulness, and she went to bed fairly calm. But didn't sleep very much, and still isn't sleeping well. On the following days things got a little better, and letters of condolence begin to arrive, including one from a woman who lost her boy for certain – a friend of Peter's, – who was definitely and finally lost, and she tells Bunnie not to give up hope, because she hasn't. A very nice tactful one came from the woman at the Hotel in the Orkneys, that Peter told her was too old for him. How we laughed at that!

Webern's Death

To see a comrade die could be traumatic. To kill a man could be traumatic. To kill a perfectly harmless man by mistake must be traumatic for anyone with any sensitivity. The accidental death of the Austrian composer Anton Webern under the US occupation of Austria in 1945 had such an effect on his killer.

Mahler *(1969) by the American poet Jonathan Williams is a sequence containing one poem for each of the forty-four movements of Mahler's ten symphonies. Hildegard Jone was a poet whose works Webern was setting at the time of his death.* Das Lied Von Der Erde *(Song of the Earth) is a work by Mahler for two singers and orchestra, of symphonic proportions – arguably, an eleventh symphony. Its last words are* 'ewig, ewig' – *'forever, forever'.*

SYMPHONY NO. 10 IN F SHARP MINOR

'Grace is courage to try to put the
world in order through love.'
– Hildegard Jone

Yea, Lord!

cowbells, cold streams, warm hills, animals
die, we

die . . . *'ewig, ewig'* . . . *Das Lied*
Von Der Erde

red red red *Der*
Erde

Anton Webern's last words were
es ist aus

Hans Moldenhauer's
book on the death

tells us about Raymond N. Bell,
American Army cook,
who fired three shots the night of September 15, 1945
and killed Webern:

Mount Olive, North Carolina
April 7, 1960

'. . . My husband's middle name was Norwood. Date of birth was August 16, 1914. We have one son who will be 21 in June. My husband's occupation was a chef in restaurants. He died from alcoholism (September 3, 1955).

I know very little about the accident. When he came home from the war he told me he killed a man in the line of duty. I know he worried greatly over it. Everytime he became intoxicated, he would say, "I wish I hadn't killed that man." I truly think it helped to bring on his sickness. He was a very kind man who loved everyone. These are the results of war. So many suffer. I do not know any of the details . . .'

Sincerely,

(Mrs) Helen S. Bell

es ist aus,
that's all she wrote,
buddy . . .

The Assault

The nature of Resistance activity was such that it could engender particularly complex and painful patterns of grief and guilt. The Dutch novelist Harry Mulisch explores such complexities in The Assault *(1982). Mulisch himself was born in Haarlem in 1927 to a Jewish mother whose family died in the camps and an Austrian father who was jailed after the war for collaborating with the Nazis.*

The Assault *begins in January 1945 with the murder by Resistance activists of a detested, collaborationist Dutch Chief Inspector of Police in a quiet street. Mr Korteweg and his daughter rush out to remove the corpse from outside their house and put it in front of the Steenwyks'. In the retaliation by German soldiers which follows, the Steenwyks' house is burnt down and the couple and their elder son are summarily executed. Only the younger son Anton, a schoolboy, survives. In complete darkness, in a police prison, he is comforted by a wounded woman whose face he cannot see. Brought up by an uncle, he becomes a successful doctor. His memory pushes the trauma aside, but meetings throughout his life revive the episode and extend his knowledge of it. His first wife's father was active in the Resistance, and at a funeral in 1966 Anton meets other Resistance fighters.*

Suddenly silence fell at the table. Only the two men sitting on Anton's left were still involved in a subdued private conversation that they had been carrying on all the time.

Anton caught the following sentence: 'I shot him first in the back, then in the shoulder, and then in the stomach as I bicycled past him.'

Far away, deep inside the tunnel of the past, Anton heard the six shots ring: first one, then two, then two more, and finally one last shot. His mother looks at his father, his father at the sliding doors. Peter lifts the lid of the carbide lamp . . .

Anton turned to the man he had been sitting next to all this time. Before he knew what he was doing, he had already asked: 'Wasn't there a fourth and a fifth shot? And then one more, a sixth?'

The other looked at him with half-closed eyes. 'How do you know?'

'Are you talking about Ploeg, Fake Ploeg in Haarlem?'

A few seconds went by before the other man asked slowly, 'Who are you? How old are you?'

'I was living there. It happened in front of our house. At least . . .'

'In front of your . . .' The man caught his breath. He had understood at once. Only on the operating table had Anton seen anyone lose all colour so rapidly. The man had had the swollen, blotchy-red complexion of someone who drinks too much. As if the light had changed, he now turned pale and waxen as old ivory. Anton began to tremble.

'Oh oh!' said the man two chairs away. 'Now you're in trouble.'

Everyone at the table noticed at once that something was wrong. The silence deepened; then confusion set in, with everyone talking at once, some standing up. De Graaff wanted to come between them, explaining that Anton was his son-in-law, but the man insisted on handling it himself. Then, to Anton, as if he wanted to fight it out, 'Come outside.'

He took his jacket from the back of his chair, grabbed Anton by the hand, and pulled him along through the crowd as if he had been a child. And that's how it felt to Anton, the hot hand of that man twenty years his senior, dragging him along – something he had never felt with his uncle, only sometimes with his father. In the other part of the café no one was aware of what was going on. Laughing, they let the two pass. 'It's been a hard day's night . . ' the Beatles were singing on the jukebox.

Outside, he was struck by the silence. The village square lay shimmering in the sun. Here and there groups of people were still standing about, but Saskia and Sandra were nowhere in sight. 'Come,' said the man, having surveyed the scene. They crossed to the cemetery and entered through the wrought-iron gate. Villagers had gathered around the open grave to read the inscriptions on the ribbons and cards that accompanied the flowers. Chickens from a neighbouring farm walked about the paths and the other graves. Near a stone bench in the shade of an oak tree the man stood still and held out his hand.

'Cor Takes,' he said. 'And your name is Steenwijk.'

'Anton Steenwijk.'

'They call me Gijs,' he said, tossing his head in the direction of the café, and sat down.

Anton sat next to him. He didn't need any of this. He had said what he did in spite of himself, as a reflex, the way a nerve reacts to the impulse of a tendon. Takes produced a pack of cigarettes, pulled one halfway out, and offered it to him. Anton shook his head and faced him. 'Listen,' he said. 'Let's get up and walk out of here and never mention it again. There's nothing to discuss, really. What happened, happened. It doesn't bother me, believe me. It happened over twenty years ago. I have a wife and child and a good job. Everything is fine. I should have kept my mouth shut.'

Takes lit a cigarette, inhaled deeply, and gave him a grim look. 'But you didn't keep your mouth shut.' And after a pause, 'So now it happened.' Only at the second sentence did the smoke accompany his words.

Anton nodded. 'Right,' he said. He couldn't evade the sombre, dark-brown eyes staring at him. The left one was different from the right, the eyelid somewhat heavier, its piercing glance leaving him defenceless. Takes must have been about fifty, but his lank, darkish-blond hair was greying only slightly at the sideburns. Under his armpits were large sweat marks. It occurred to Anton as in a fairy tale that this was the man who, that evening in the winter of starvation, had killed Ploeg.

'I was saying something you shouldn't have heard,' said Takes. 'But you did hear, and then you said something you didn't mean to say. Those are the facts, and that's why we're sitting here. I knew of your existence. How old were you then?'

'Twelve.'

'Did you know him, that pig?'

'Only by sight,' said Anton, but the word pig in connection with Ploeg did sound familiar.

'I should think so; he came by your house regularly.'

'And I was in the same class as his son.' As he said this he didn't remember that boy of long ago, but the big fellow who had thrown a stone into his mirror ten years before.

'Wasn't his name also Fake?'

'Yes.'

'There were two other daughters besides. The youngest was four then?'

'The same age mine is now.'

'So you see, those are not attenuating circumstances.' Anton realized he was shivering. He felt in the presence of a nameless violence such as he had never known in anyone, except possibly in that man with the scar under his cheek-bone. Should he say so? He didn't. He didn't want to give the impression that he was attacking Takes. Besides, it would be nothing new to Takes; clearly he had put such considerations behind him long ago.

'Do you want me to tell you what sort of man this Ploeg was?'

'Not for my sake.'

'But for mine. He had a whip with barbed wire braided into it that ripped the skin off your bare ass, which he then shoved against the blazing stove. He put a garden hose up your ass and let it run till you vomited your own shit. He killed God knows how many people, and sent many more to their deaths in Germany and Poland. Very well. So he had to be got rid of . . . Do you agree?' And as Anton kept silent, 'Yes, or yes?'

'Yes,' said Anton.

'Okay. But on the other hand, it was clear to us that there were certain to be reprisals.'

'Mr Takes,' Anton interrupted him. 'Am I right to assume . . .'

'Call me Gijs.'

'. . . that you are sitting here justifying yourself for my sake? I'm not criticizing you, after all.'

'I'm not justifying myself to you.'

'To whom, then?'

'I don't know,' he answered impatiently. 'Certainly not to myself, or to God, or some such nonsense. God doesn't exist, and perhaps I don't either.' With the same index finger that had pulled the trigger, he now flicked away the cigarette butt and looked out over the cemetery. 'Do you know who exists? The dead. The friends who have died.'

As if to announce that someone was in command after all, a small cloud crept over the sun, making the flowers on the new grave look bleached, as if they were repenting, while the grey of the gravestones became dominant. But the next moment, everything was once more bathed in light. Anton wondered whether the sympathy he felt for the man sitting next to him had an ambiguous source. Through him, Anton was no longer simply a victim; now he was vicariously taking part in the violence of the assault. A victim? Of course he had been a victim, even though he was still alive. Yet at the same time, he felt as if it had all happened to someone else.

Takes had lit another cigarette.

'Good. So we knew there would be reprisals, right? That one of the houses would be set on fire, and that some of the hostages would be shot. Is that a reason for not doing it?'

When he kept silent, Anton looked up.

'Do you expect *me* to give you an answer?'

'Sure.'

'I can't do that. I don't know about that.'

'Then I'll tell you: the answer is no. If you should tell me that your family would still be alive if we hadn't liquidated Ploeg, you'd be right. That's the truth, but no more. If someone were to say that your family would still be alive if your father had rented another house in another street, that too would be the truth. Then I might be sitting here with someone else . . . although it might have happened in that other street, because maybe Ploeg too might have lived somewhere else. Those are the kinds of truths that don't do us any good. The only truth that's useful is that everyone gets killed by whoever kills them, and by no one else. Ploeg by us, your family by the Germans. If you believe we shouldn't have done it, then you also believe that, in the light of history, the human race shouldn't have existed. Because then all the love and happiness and goodness in this world can't outweigh the life of a single child. Yours, for instance. Is that what you believe?'

Anton, confused, looked at the ground. He didn't quite understand it; he had never really thought about these things. But perhaps Takes never thought about anything else.

'So we did it. We knew . . .'

'You mean that it *does* outweigh it?' Anton asked suddenly.

Takes threw the cigarette at his feet and crushed it with his shoe so thoroughly that only a few shreds remained. These he covered with gravel. He did not answer the question.

'We knew that probably at least one of those houses would get it. The Fascist gentlemen were rather consistent as far as that goes. But we didn't know which house. We had chosen that spot because it was the most secluded and the easiest to get away from. And we had to get away, for we had a few more scum like that on our list.'

Anton said slowly, 'If your parents had lived in one of those houses, would you have shot him there?'

Takes stood up, took two steps in his sloppy pants, and turned to him. 'No, dammit,' he said. 'Of course not. What do you mean? Not if it might as well have been done somewhere else. But that same night, you know, my youngest brother happened to be among those hostages, and I knew this. And would you like to know what Mother thought of that? She agreed that I was right to do it. She's still alive; you can ask her. Would you like her address?'

Anton tried to avoid looking at his left eye. 'You keep at me as if it were my fault. I was twelve years old and reading a book when it happened, for goodness' sake.'

Takes sat down again and lit another cigarette. 'It's just a stupid coincidence that it happened in front of your house?'

Anton eyed him sideways. 'It didn't happen in front of our house,' he said.

Slowly Takes turned to face him. 'I beg your pardon?'

'It happened in front of a neighbour's house. They put him in front of our house.'

Takes stretched his legs, crossed his feet, and put one hand in his pocket. Nodding, he surveyed the cemetery. 'Better a good neighbour than a distant friend,' he said after a while. He was shaking with something, perhaps laughter. 'What kind of people were they?'

'A widower and his daughter. A seaman.' Takes once more nodded his head.

'Well, I must say . . . I hadn't thought of that possibility: one can always help fate along a bit.'

'And is that morally justifiable?' asked Anton, realizing instantly that it was a childish question.

'Justifiable . . .' repeated Takes. 'You'll have to ask the clergyman about that. I believe he's still wandering around here somewhere. Some people simply take justice into their own hands. Go tell them they're wrong to do it. Three seconds later it would have happened in front of your door.'

'I'm only asking,' said Anton, 'because my brother then tried to move him up one house further, or to put him back where he was . . . I'm not sure, because the police arrived next.'

'Jesus, now I'm beginning to understand!' cried Takes. 'That's why he was outside. But how did he get hold of that gun?'

Anton looked up at him in surprise. 'How do you know about the gun?'

'Because I looked it up after the War, of course.'

'It was Ploeg's gun.'

'What an *instructive* afternoon,' Takes said slowly. He puffed on his cigarette and blew the smoke out of the corners of his mouth. 'Who was living in the next house further down?'

'Two old people.' The trembling hand reaching for him. Pickles are just like crocodiles, Mr Beumer had said. Anton had repeated this once to Sandra, but she didn't laugh; she just agreed.

'Yes,' said Takes. 'Of course, if he'd put the body back, there would have been a fight.' And then right away, 'My, my, my, what a clumsy mess. A bunch of fools, all of you, traipsing up and down with that body.'

'What else should we have done?'

'Taken it in, of course!' snarled Takes. 'You should have dragged him into the house at once.'

Anton looked at him, perplexed. Of course! Columbus's egg! Before he had time to say another word, Takes continued, 'Just think: they'd heard shots somewhere in the neighbourhood. What could they possibly have done about it if they hadn't seen anything on the street? It wouldn't occur to them that a man had been rubbed out, would it? They'd think that one of the militia had taken a shot at someone, maybe. Or were your neighbours collaborators who might have given you away?'

'No. But what would we have done with the body?'

'How should I know? Hidden it. Under the floorboards, or buried in the garden. Or better yet, eaten it up right away – cooked it and shared it with the neighbours. After all, it was the winter of starvation. War criminals don't count as far as cannibalism is concerned.'

Now laughter shook Anton. His father the clerk baking a police inspector and eating him for dinner! *De gustibus non est disputandum.*

'Or were you under the impression that such things never happened? Forget it; everything has happened. The weirdest things you can think of have happened, and weirder yet.'

The people strolling back and forth to the grave eyed them in passing, two men on a stone bench under a tree (one younger than the other), still mourning their lost friend while the others were sitting in the bar, exchanging memories: do you remember the time that he . . . As they walked by, they fell thoughtfully silent.

'It's easy for you to say,' said Anton. 'You thought of nothing else but this sort of thing – and it seems to me you still do – whereas we were sitting at home, reading, around the dining-room table, and then suddenly we heard those shots.'

'I still would have thought of it at once.'

'Maybe, but then you were part of a gang. My father was a clerk who never took action; he just wrote down the actions of others. We wouldn't have had time, anyway. Although . . .' he said, looking up suddenly into the leaves overhead, 'we had a kind of quarrel . . .'

In spite of the brilliance of the day, a scene flashed through his mind.

Some obscure activity taking place in total darkness, in a hall; an exclamation, as if Peter were stumbling over some branches, something about a key. It disappeared like the shred of a dream briefly remembered the next morning.

He was brought back to reality by Takes, who drew four squares in the gravel with his heel, making this design in the bare earth:

□ □ □ □

'Listen,' he said. 'There were four houses, weren't there?'

'Yes.'

'You've got a good memory.'

'I go back there now and then. Heroes always return to the scene, it's a well-known fact. Although . . . quite probably I'm the only one, at least as far as that quay of yours is concerned. Now, as far as I knew he was lying here, in front of your house. At which neighbour's was he shot – this one, or this one?'

'This one,' said Anton, and pointed with his shoe to the second house from the right.

Takes nodded and looked at the stripes.

'Excuse me, but in that case there's a mystery. Why did the seaman deposit him at your doorstep and not here, at his other neighbour's?'

Anton too looked at the stripes. 'No idea. I've never wondered about it.'

'There must be a reason. Did he dislike you?'

'Not as far as I know. I used to go there sometimes. I should think they would have been more inclined to dislike the people on the other side, who ignored everybody else on the street.'

'And you never tried to find out?' asked Takes, surprised. 'Don't you care at all?'

'Care, care . . . I told you, I don't feel any need to go over all that again. What happened happened, and that's all there is to it. It can't be changed now, even if I understood it. It was wartime, one big disaster, my family was murdered, and I stayed alive. I was adopted by an aunt and uncle, and everything turned out all right for me. You were right to kill the bastard, really; I have no complaints about that. You just convince his son! With me that's not necessary, but why in God's name do you want to make it all logical? That's impossible, and who cares? It's history, ancient history. How many times has the same sort of thing happened since? It may be happening right now somewhere, while we're sitting here talking. Could you swear, your hand in the fire, that at this very moment someone's house somewhere isn't being set on fire by a flamethrower? In Vietnam, for instance? What are you talking about? When you took me outside just now, I thought maybe you were concerned about my peace of mind, but that doesn't seem to be the case – at least, not altogether. You're more upset than I am. It seems to me that you can't leave the War alone, but time goes on. Or do you regret what you did?'

He had spoken fast but calmly, yet with the vague feeling that he must be careful, that he must control himself so as not to hit the other.

'I'd do it again tomorrow, if necessary,' said Takes without hesitation. 'And maybe I will do it again tomorrow. I've rubbed out a whole rat's nest of that scum, and the fact still gives me great satisfaction. But the incident on that quay of yours . . . there was more to it. Something happened there.' He clasped the edge of the bench and shifted his position. 'Let's just say that I wish we hadn't gone through with it.'

'Because my parents were killed as well?'

'No,' said Takes roughly. 'I'm sorry to say that's not the reason. That couldn't have been foreseen or expected. It probably happened because they caught your brother with a gun, or because of something else, or for no reason; I don't know.'

'It probably happened,' said Anton without looking up, 'because my mother flew at the leader of those Germans.'

Takes was silent and stared straight ahead. At last he turned to Anton and said, 'I'm really not torturing you just to satisfy my nostalgia for the War, in case you're wondering. I know people like that, but I'm not one of them. Those people spend all their holidays in Berlin and would just love to hang a portrait of Hitler over their beds. No, the problem is that something else happened over there in Haarlem.' A light went on in his eyes. Anton saw his Adam's apple bob up and down a couple of times. 'Your parents and your brother and those hostages were not the only ones who lost their lives. The fact is that I wasn't alone when I shot Ploeg; there were two of us. Someone was with me – someone who . . . Let's just say she was my girl-friend. But never mind, leave it at that.'

Anton stared at him, and suddenly all the pent-up emotion washed over him. Putting his face in his hands, he turned away and began to sob. She was dying. For him she died at this very moment, as if twenty-one years were nothing. Yet at the same time she was resurrected together with all she had meant to him, hidden there in the darkness. *If* he had ever thought about her in these twenty-one years, he would have wondered whether she were still alive. But just now, he realized, he had been looking for her, in the church and later in the café – and in fact it was the reason why he had come to this funeral where he had no need to be.

He felt Takes's hand on his shoulder. 'What's this about?' He dropped his hands. His eyes were dry.

'How did she die?'

'They shot her in the dunes, three weeks before Liberation. She's buried there in the memorial cemetery. But why should you care so much?'

'Because I know her,' Anton said softly. 'Because I talked to her. I spent that night with her in the cell.'

Takes looked at him in disbelief. 'How do you know it was her? What's her name? Surely she didn't tell you who she was.'

'No, but I'm quite sure.'

'Did she tell you that she was involved in the assault?'

Anton shook his head. 'No, not even that. But I'm quite certain.'

'How can you be, for God's sake,' Takes said crossly. 'What did she look like?'

'I don't know. It was pitch-dark.'

Takes thought for a while. 'Would you recognize her if you saw a picture?'

'I never really saw her, Takes. But . . . I'd very much like to see her picture.'

'But what did she say? You must know *something*!'

Anton shrugged. 'I wish I did. It was so long ago . . . She had been wounded.'

'Where?'

'I don't know.'

Tears came to Takes's eyes. 'It must have been her,' he said. 'If she didn't even mention her name . . . Ploeg took a final shot at her, just as we were about to turn the corner.'

When Anton saw Takes's tears he began to weep himself.

'What was her name?' he asked.

'Truus. Truus Coster.' Now the people around the grave were watching them, discreetly but steadily. They must have been surprised to see two grown men so much affected by the death of a friend. Some may have wondered if they were showing off.

'There they are, the silly fools.' His mother-in-law's voice. She entered the gate, Saskia and Sandra in her wake – two figures in black and a child in white against the blinding gravel. Sandra called 'Papa!' dropped her doll, and ran toward Anton. He picked her up and held her in his arms. From Saskia's wide-eyed look he could tell that she was worried about him, and he nodded to her reassuringly. But her mother, leaning on her shiny black cane with the silver handle, would not be fobbed off that easily.

'Good Lord, are they actually crying?' she asked angrily, at which Sandra looked up at Anton. Mrs De Graaff pretended to gag. 'You two make me positively ill. Can't you stop carrying on about that rotten War? Tell me, Gijs, do you enjoy torturing my son-in-law? Yes, of course, you would.' She gave a strange, mocking laugh and her wobbly cheeks shook. 'This is impossible, the way you two stand there like two exposed necrophiliacs, and in the cemetery, of all places. Stop it at once. Come along, all of you.'

She turned about and walked away, pointing at the doll that lay on the gravel, not doubting for a minute that she would be obeyed. And so she was.

9

Reckonings

This final section includes writing which in one way or another transmutes particular wartime circumstances into very powerful literary statements. Just as Anna Karenina *does not merely document an early phase of Russian industrialization (though Tolstoy's novel says and implies a great deal about that), so such fictional creations as Švejk, Yossarian, Billy Pilgrim and Mother Courage range beyond the wars in Europe which gave rise to their creation. Marguerite Duras eerily counterpoints Conrad's* Heart of Darkness. *Sorley Maclean, Paul Celan, Yeats and Auden – and Jacques Brel – invest temporal accidents with the timelessness of achieved poetic form. Finally, Wilfred Owen goes as far as any very young soldier could in giving pattern to devastation and mortal combat.*

Below the Ruweisat Ridge

The Scottish Gaelic poet Sorley Maclean responded to the war in the North African Desert (1940–43) with the vision of an internationalist from a small community on the very edge of Europe. The English translation, again, is his own.

DEATH VALLEY

Some Nazi or other has said that the Fuehrer had restored to German manhood the 'right and joy of dying in battle'.

Sitting dead in 'Death Valley'
below the Ruweisat Ridge
a boy with his forelock down about his cheek
and his face slate-grey;

I thought of the right and the joy
that he got from his Fuehrer,
of falling in the field of slaughter
to rise no more;

of the pomp and the fame
that he had, not alone,
though he was the most piteous to see
in a valley gone to seed

with flies about grey corpses
on a dun sand
dirty yellow and full of the rubbish
and fragments of battle.

Was the boy of the band
who abused the Jews
and Communists, or of the greater
band of those

led, from the beginning of generations,
unwillingly to the trial
and mad delirium of every war
for the sake of rulers?

Whatever his desire or mishap,
his innocence or malignity,
he showed no pleasure in his death
below the Ruweisat Ridge.

The Good Soldier Švejk

Jaroslav Hašek – anarchist, communist, drinker, trickster – created Švejk to help himself out of financial difficulties in 1921. Within two years he was dead, not yet forty, with the fourth volume of his huge book still incomplete. But it was always episodic, anyway, and Švejk marched away from its pages as a byword. Up to a point, his is the same world as Kafka's. The ludicrous and incompetent civil and military bureaucracy of the Austro-Hungarian Empire at its point of collapse is his target. Hašek's Czech anti-hero takes no moral stances. Discharged from peacetime military service for patent idiocy, he is nevertheless conscripted again in wartime. He is not 'anti-war', but he wants to eat, drink and survive. Typically, he is complaisant with whatever is put to him, especially by officers and bureaucrats, however insane they are. Since he is in fact a clever man, this produces ringing irony. The episode which follows occurs at Budapest railway station as his regiment is proceeding towards the Galician front.

In the staff carriage Captain Ságner announced that according to schedule they should now actually be already at the Galician frontier. At Eger they were due to draw a three days' ration of bread and tins for the men, but Eger was still ten hours away. It was in fact so full of trains with wounded after the offensive at Lwów that according to a telegram there was not a single loaf of army bread or tin left there. He had received orders to pay out 6 crowns 72 hellers per man instead of bread and tins. This was to be issued with their pay in nine days' time, that is to say if they got the money from brigade by that time. There was only a little more than twelve thousand crowns in the till.

'It's a bloody rotten trick of the regiment to send us out into the world in such a wretched state,' said Lieutenant Lukáš.

A whispered colloquy began between Ensign Wolf and Lieutenant Kolář to the effect that Colonel Schröder in the last three weeks had paid sixteen thousand crowns into his account in the Wiener Bank.

Then Lieutenant Kolář explained how economies are made. You filch six thousand crowns from the regiment and put them in your pocket.

With inescapable logic you then order all kitchens to deduct three grammes of peas from every man's ration in every kitchen.

In a month that makes ninety grammes per man so that in the kitchen and in every company a store of at least sixteen kilos of peas should have been saved and the cook has to show this.

Lieutenant Kolář talked with Wolf only in general terms about certain cases which he had noticed.

But it was certainly true that the whole military administration was bursting at the seams with cases like this. It started with the quartermaster sergeant-major in some unfortunate company and ended with the hamster in general's epaulettes who was salting something away for himself for a rainy day when the war was over.

War demanded valour even in pilfering.

The controllers of supplies looked at each other affectionately, as if to say: 'We are one body and soul, we steal, old chap, we cheat, brother, but what can you do? It's hard to swim against the tide. If you don't salt it away someone else will, and people will say that the only reason why you've not salted anything away is that you've already salted enough.'

A gentleman with red and gold stripes on his trousers came into the carriage. It was again one of those generals travelling on inspection over all railway routes.

'Sit down, gentlemen,' he nodded affably, pleased that he had again surprised a train which he had not expected to find there.

When Captain Ságner wanted to make a report to him, he only waved his hand. 'Your transport is not in proper order. Your transport is not sleeping. Your transport should already be asleep. When transports stand at a station the men in them have to be asleep at 9 p.m. as in barracks.'

He spoke curtly: 'Before nine o'clock the men have to be taken out to the latrines behind the station. After that they have to go to bed. If not they commit a nuisance on the track during the night. Do you understand me, captain? Repeat that to me. Or rather, don't repeat it to me. Just do what I ask. Sound the alarm, drive the men to the latrines, sound the retreat and lights out, control who is not sleeping and punish them! Yes. Is that all? Issue supper at six o'clock.'

He was speaking now of something which belonged to the past, something which no longer happened, which was, as it were, round some other corner. He stood there like a phantom from the world of the fourth dimension.

'Issue supper at six o'clock,' he continued, looking at his watch which showed ten minutes past eleven at night. 'At half past eight alarm, latrine shitting, then bed. For supper at six o'clock – goulash with potatoes instead of fifteen dekas of Emmentaler cheese.'

Then he gave the order 'stand to'. Again Captain Ságner had the alarm sounded and the inspecting general, watching the battalion falling in, strolled with the officers and talked to them all the time as though they were idiots and couldn't immediately understand. As he did so he pointed at the hands of his watch: 'Very well, now, look! At half past eight shitting and half an hour later bed. That's quite sufficient. In this time of transition the men have a thin stool anyhow. But I put the main stress on sleep. It fortifies them for further marches. As long as the men are in the train they must rest. If there's not enough space in the vans they must sleep *in shifts*. A third of the men can lie comfortably in the vans and sleep from nine to midnight and the others can stand and look at them. Then the first shift who have slept can give up their places to the next shift who will sleep from midnight to three o'clock in the morning. The third shift sleeps from three to six and then there's reveille and the men wash. No jumping out of the vans when – they're – in – motion! Station patrols along the train so that no one jumps out when – it's – in – motion! If the enemy breaks a soldier's leg . . .' The general tapped himself on the leg: '. . . that's something praiseworthy, but crippling yourself by uselessly jumping out of a van when the train is in full motion is a penal offence.

'So this is your battalion?' he asked Captain Ságner, looking at the sleepy figures of the men, many of whom could not control themselves and having been whipped out of sleep were yawning in the fresh night air. 'It's a yawning battalion, captain. The men must go to bed at nine.'

The general took up a position in front of the 11th company, where Švejk stood on the left flank and yawned terribly, but while he was doing it he was good-mannered enough to hold his hand before his mouth. But from underneath his hand there resounded such a roar that Lieutenant Lukáš trembled all over in case the general should pay closer attention to it. It struck him that Švejk was yawning on purpose.

And the general, as though he knew it, turned round to Švejk and went up to him: 'Czech or German?'

'Czech, humbly report, sir,' Švejk replied in German.

'Goot,' said the general, who was a Pole and knew a little Czech, although he pronounced it as though it were Polish and used Polish expressions. 'You roars like a cow doess for hiss hay. Shot op! Shot your mog! Dawn't moo! Haf you already been to ze latrines?'

'Humbly report, I haven't, sir.'

'Vy didn't you go and sheet wiz ze ozer mens?'

'Humbly report, sir, Colonel Wachtl always used to tell us on manoeuvres at Písek, when during the rest period the men crept in among the corn, that a soldier mustn't think all the time only about shitting. A soldier must think about fighting. Besides, humbly report, what would we do in those latrines? There would be nothing to squeeze out of us. According to our march schedule we ought to have got supper at several stations, but instead we got nothing at all. It's not good going to the latrines on an empty stomach!'

Švejk, explaining the situation to the general in simple words, looked at him somehow so trustingly that the general sensed a wish on their part that he should help them. If the order was given that they should go to the latrines in march formation, then that order should have some internal build-up.

'Send them all back to the vans,' said the general to Captain Ságner. 'How did it come that they didn't get any supper? All the transports going through this station must get supper. This is a provisioning station. It's not possible otherwise. There is a definite plan.'

The general said this with an assurance which meant that although it was already approaching eleven o'clock at night, supper should have been served at six o'clock, as he had already previously observed, so that there was nothing to be done but to keep the train another night and day until six o'clock in the evening, so that the men could have goulash and potatoes.

'When you are transporting an army in wartime,' he said with enormous gravity, 'there's nothing worse than to forget about its provisioning. It's my duty to find out the truth and to see how it looks in the station commander's office, for you know, gentlemen, sometimes it is the transport commanders themselves who fail in their duties. When I inspected the station of Subotiště on the Bosnian southern railway I discovered that six transports had not got supper because the transport commanders had forgotten to ask for it. Six times they cooked goulash and potatoes at the station and no one asked for it. And so they poured it away in masses. Gentlemen, there was a pit full of potatoes and goulash there, and three stations further on the soldiers from the transports which had just gone by those masses and mountains of goulash in Subotiště were begging on the station for a piece of bread. In this case, as you see, it was not the fault of the military administration.'

He made an impetuous gesture with his hand: 'The transport commanders were not up to their duties. Let's go into the office.'

They followed him, wondering why it was that all generals went off their heads.

At the station command it turned out that really nothing was known about the goulash. It was true that today meals should have been cooked for all transports passing through, but then the order had come to subtract from the army catering accounts 72 hellers for every soldier, so that every detachment which passed through would have a credit of 72 hellers per man, which they would get paid out by the supply office on the next pay-day. As far as bread was concerned the men would get half a loaf at Watian.

The commander of the provisioning point was not afraid. He told the general straight out that orders changed every hour. It often happened that he had messing prepared for the transports and then an ambulance train would arrive, refer to higher orders and that was the end of it. The transport was then confronted with the problem of empty cauldrons.

The general nodded his head in agreement and observed that conditions were definitely improving and that at the beginning of the war it had been much worse. One could not expect everything to go right all at once. Experience and practice were of course required. In fact theory stood in the way of practice. The longer the war lasted the more things would be put into order.

'I can give you a practical example,' he said with obvious delight that he had hit upon something outstanding. 'Two days ago transports passing through the station of Hatvan got no bread at all, whereas you will be able to draw your rations of it there tomorrow. Let's go now to the station restaurant.'

In the station restaurant the general began to speak again about the latrines and to say how ugly it looked when there were cactuses everywhere on the track. Meanwhile he ate beef steak and all of them imagined that he had a cactus in his mouth.

He laid so much stress on latrines that you would think that the victory of the Monarchy depended on them.

As for the new situation with Italy he asserted that it was in our army's latrines that our undeniable superiority in the Italian campaign lay.

Austria's victory crawled out of her latrines.

To the general everything was so simple. The road to military glory ran according to the recipe: at 6 p.m. the soldiers get goulash and potatoes, at half past eight the troops defecate it in the latrines and at nine they go to bed. In the face of such an army the enemy flees in panic.

The general grew meditative, lit a cigar and looked for a very long time at the ceiling. He was trying to think what else he could say now he was here and how he could further educate the officers of the transport.

'The core of your battalion is sound,' he said suddenly, when everyone was expecting that he would continue to look at the ceiling and say nothing. 'Your complement's in perfect order. That man I was talking to, with his frankness and military bearing, offers the best hope that the whole battalion will fight to the last drop of blood.'

He paused and looked once more at the ceiling, leaning against the back of his chair and continuing in his position, while only Lieutenant Dub, obedient to the slavish instincts of his soul, looked at the ceiling too. 'But your battalion requires that its good deeds should not be buried in oblivion. Your brigade's battalions already have their history and yours must continue with it. But what you need is a man to keep exact records and write up the history of the battalion. All the strands of what every company in the battalion has done must go to him. He must be an intelligent fellow, not a mule or a cow. Captain, you must appoint a battalion historian in your battalion.'

Then he looked at the clock on the wall, the hands of which reminded the whole sleepy company that it was time to go.

The general had his inspection train on the track and asked the gentlemen to accompany him to his sleeping-car.

The station commander sighed. The general had forgotten to pay for his beef steak and bottle of wine, and the commander had to pay for it himself again. Every day there were several visits like this. They had already cost him two wagons of hay which he had had to shunt on to a side line and sell to the firm of Löwenstein, the army corn suppliers, as standing corn is sold. The army had bought these two wagons back again and he had left them standing there for all eventualities. Perhaps he would sometime have to sell them back to the firm of Löwenstein again.

But all the army inspectors who passed through this main station of

Budapest used to tell each other that the station commander there always had good food and drink.

In the morning the transport was still standing at the station, the reveille was sounded and the soldiers washed out of their mess-tins at the pump. The general and his train had not yet left and he went personally to inspect the latrines, where according to Captain Ságner's order of the day to the battalion the men went 'by sections under the command of the section commanders' to give the major-general pleasure. To give Lieutenant Dub some pleasure too, Captain Ságner informed him that he would be the inspecting officer that day.

And so Lieutenant Dub supervised the latrines.

The extensive long latrines with their two rows accommodated two sections of one company. So now the soldiers sat neatly on their haunches, one beside the other over the dug-up pits, like swallows on telephone wires when they prepare for their autumn flight to Africa.

Every one of them had his trousers down and his knees showing, every one had his belt round his neck as though he was going to hang himself any moment and was just waiting for the order.

The whole procedure was manifestly characterized by iron military discipline and efficient organization.

On the left flank sat Švejk, who had got there by mistake and was reading with interest a scrap of paper torn from some novel or other by Růžena Jesenská:

> . . . ensive finishing school, young ladies unfortunately . . .
> . . . ontent not quite certain, but perhaps more rea . . .
> who were mostly reticent, and uncommunicative, lo . . .
> . . . ived lunch in their apartments, or perhaps would ha . . .
> devoted themselves to those doubtful delights. And if . . .
> . . . ed a man and only grief and sorrow for her hon . . .
> . . . ently she was getting better, but she did not want . . .
> as they themselves would have wished. Successfully
> . . . othing was more welcome to young Křička than . . .

When he managed to tear his eyes away from the scrap of paper he looked involuntarily at the exit from the latrines and was astounded. There stood the major-general of the night before in his full glory. He was accompanied by his adjutant and beside them stood Lieutenant Dub who was eagerly explaining something to them.

Švejk looked around him. All the men went on sitting calmly over the latrines and only the NCOs were somehow rigid and motionless.

Švejk sensed the gravity of the situation.

He jumped up just as he was, with his trousers down and belt round his neck, and, having used the scrap of paper in the very last moment, he roared out: 'Halt! Up! Attention! Eyes right!' and saluted. Two sections with their trousers down and their belts round their necks rose over the latrines.

The major-general smiled affably and said: 'At ease! Carry on!' Lance-Corporal Málek was the first to give an example to his section and resume his original posture. Only Švejk continued to stand and salute, because from one side he was being approached menacingly by Lieutenant Dub and from the other by the major-general with his smile.

'I seess you last night,' the major-general said on observing Švejk's strange posture; whereupon the infuriated Lieutenant Dub turned to the major-general and said in German: 'Humbly report, sir, the fellow is feeble-minded and a well-known idiot. He is an unparalleled imbecile.'

'What are you saying, lieutenant?' the major-general roared suddenly at Lieutenant Dub and let fly at him, saying that the very opposite was true. It was a case of a man who knew his duties when he saw his superior officer, and of an officer who did not see him and ignored him. It was just like in the field. The ordinary soldier assumes command in time of danger. And it was Lieutenant Dub himself who should have given the order that soldier gave: 'Halt! Up! Attention! Eyes right!'

'Haf you viped your arsch?' the major-general asked Švejk.

'Humbly report, sir, everything is in order.'

'Von't you sheet no more?'

'Humbly report, sir, I've finished.'

'Vell, now pull your hoses op and shtand at attention again!' Because the major-general pronounced the word 'attention' rather louder, the men who were nearest started getting up over the latrine.

The major-general waved to them affably and said in a gentle, fatherly voice: 'No, no! At eess! At eess! Jost go on!'

Švejk in his full splendour was already standing in front of the major-general, who delivered a short address to him in German: 'Respect for superiors, knowledge of service regulations and presence of mind mean everything in wartime. And if added to that we have courage, there is no enemy we need fear.' Turning to Lieutenant Dub, he prodded Švejk's belly with his finger and said: 'Make a note of this: when you get to the front this man must be promoted at once and at the next opportunity his name should be put forward for the Bronze Medal for meticulous execution of duties and perfect knowledge of . . . But you know what I mean . . . Dismiss!'

The major-general went away from the latrines, while Lieutenant Dub gave orders in a loud voice so that the major-general could hear: 'First section up! Form fours! . . . Second section . . .'

Meanwhile Švejk went away and when he passed Lieutenant Dub he saluted as was right and proper, but Lieutenant Dub said all the same, 'As you were!' and Švejk had to salute again and hear once more: 'Do you know me? You don't know me! You know me from my good side, but wait till you get to know me from my bad side! I'll make you cry!'

Catch-22

Set in a USAAF base on the fictionalized island of Pianosa, eight miles south of Elba in the Mediterranean, Joseph Heller's Catch-22, *originally published in 1961, caught the anti-war mood of the 1960s, yet has not dated at all. Its protagonist, Yossarian, is a Švejk with compassion, confronted, like Švejk, by an extraordinary range of officer-crooks and officer-buffoons. Like Hašek's Austro-Hungarian officers, such men wage war for profit. But their military-bureaucratic tricks do have one consistent underlying principle. When he asks Doc Daneeka to ground him after he has flown more than the regulation number of missions, Yossarian learns that this is called Catch-22.*

Doc Daneeka lived in a splotched gray tent with Chief White Halfoat, whom he feared and despised.

. . .

Chief White Halfoat thought he was crazy. 'I don't know what's the matter with that guy,' he observed reproachfully. 'He's got no brains, that's what's the matter with him. If he had any brains he'd grab a shovel and start digging. Right here in the tent, he'd start digging, right under my cot. He'd strike oil in no time. Don't he know how that enlisted man struck oil with a shovel back in the States? Didn't he ever hear what happened to that kid – what was the name of that rotten rat bastard pimp of a snotnose back in Colorado?'

'Wintergreen.'

'Wintergreen.'

'He's afraid,' Yossarian explained.

'Oh, no. Not Wintergreen.' Chief White Halfoat shook his head with undisguised admiration. 'That stinking little punk wise-guy son of a bitch ain't afraid of nobody.'

'Doc Daneeka's afraid. That's what's the matter with him.'

'What's he afraid of?'

'He's afraid of you,' Yossarian said. 'He's afraid you're going to die of pneumonia.'

'He'd *better* be afraid,' Chief White Halfoat said. A deep, low laugh rumbled through his massive chest. 'I will, too, the first chance I get. You just wait and see.'

Chief White Halfoat was a handsome, swarthy Indian from Oklahoma with a heavy, hard-boned face and tousled black hair, a half-blooded Creek from Enid who, for occult reasons of his own, had made up his mind to die of pneumonia. He was a glowering, vengeful, disillusioned Indian who hated foreigners with names like Cathcart, Korn, Black and Havermeyer and wished they'd all go back to where their lousy ancestors had come from.

'You wouldn't believe it, Yossarian,' he ruminated, raising his voice deliberately to bait Doc Daneeka, 'but this used to be a pretty good country to live in before they loused it up with their goddam piety.'

Chief White Halfoat was out to revenge himself upon the white man. He could barely read or write and had been assigned to Captain Black as assistant intelligence officer.

'How could I learn to read or write?' Chief White Halfoat demanded with simulated belligerence, raising his voice again so that Doc Daneeka would hear. 'Every place we pitched our tent, they sank an oil well. Every time they sank a well, they hit oil. And every time they hit oil, they made us pack up our tent and go someplace else. We were human divining rods. Our whole family had a natural affinity for petroleum deposits, and soon every oil company in the world had technicians chasing us around. We were always on the move. It was one hell of a way to bring a child up, I can tell you. I don't think I ever spent more than a week in one place.'

His earliest memory was of a geologist.

'Every time another White Halfoat was born,' he continued, 'the stock market turned bullish. Soon whole drilling crews were following us around with all their equipment just to get the jump on each other. Companies began to merge just so they could cut down on the number of people they had to assign to us. But the crowd in back of us kept growing. We never got a good night's sleep. When we stopped, they stopped. When we moved, they moved, chuckwagons, bulldozers, derricks, generators. We were a walking business boom, and we began to receive invitations from some of the best hotels just for the amount of business we would drag into town with us. Some of those invitations were mighty generous, but we couldn't accept any because we were Indians and all the best hotels that were inviting us wouldn't accept Indians as guests. Racial prejudice is a terrible thing, Yossarian. It really is. It's a terrible thing to treat a decent, loyal Indian like a nigger, kike, wop or spic.' Chief White Halfoat nodded slowly with conviction.

'Then, Yossarian, it finally happened – the beginning of the end. They began to follow us around from in front. They would try to guess where we were going to stop next and would begin drilling before we even got there, so we couldn't stop. As soon as we'd begin to unroll our blankets, they would kick us off. They had confidence in us. They wouldn't even wait to strike oil before they kicked us off. We were so tired we almost didn't care the day our time ran out. One morning we found ourselves completely surrounded by oilmen waiting for us to come their way so they could kick us off. Everywhere you looked there was an oilman on a ridge, waiting there like Indians getting ready to attack. It was the end. We couldn't stay where we were because we had just been kicked off. And there was no place left for us to go. Only the Army saved me. Luckily, the war broke out just in the nick of time, and a draft board picked me right up out of the middle and put me down safely in Lowery Field, Colorado. I was the only survivor.'

Yossarian knew he was lying, but did not interrupt as Chief White Halfoat went on to claim that he had never heard from his parents again. That didn't bother him too much, though, for he had only their word for it that they were his parents, and since they had lied to him about so many other things, they could just as well have been lying to him about that too. He was much better acquainted with the fate of a tribe of first cousins who had wandered away north in a diversionary movement and pushed inadvertently into Canada. When they tried to return, they were stopped at the border by American immigration authorities who would not let them back into the country. They could not come back in because they were red.

It was a horrible joke, but Doc Daneeka didn't laugh until Yossarian came to him one mission later and pleaded again, without any real expectation of success, to be grounded. Doc Daneeka snickered once and was soon immersed in problems of his own, which included Chief White Halfoat, who had been challenging him all morning to Indian wrestle, and Yossarian, who decided right then and there to go crazy.

'You're wasting your time,' Doc Daneeka was forced to tell him.

'Can't you ground someone who's crazy?'

'Oh, sure. I have to. There's a rule saying I have to ground anyone who's crazy.'

'Then why don't you ground me? I'm crazy. Ask Clevinger.'

'Clevinger? Where *is* Clevinger? You find Clevinger and I'll ask him.'

'Then ask any of the others. They'll tell you how crazy I am.'

'They're crazy.'

'Then why don't you ground them?'

'Why don't they ask me to ground them?'

'Because they're crazy, that's why.'

'Of course they're crazy,' Doc Daneeka replied. 'I just told you they're crazy, didn't I? And you can't let crazy people decide whether you're crazy or not, can you?'

Yossarian looked at him soberly and tried another approach. 'Is Orr crazy?'

'He sure is,' Doc Daneeka said.

'Can you ground him?'

'I sure can. But first he has to ask me to. That's part of the rule.'

'Then why doesn't he ask you to?'

'Because he's crazy,' Doc Daneeka said. 'He has to be crazy to keep flying combat missions after all the close calls he's had. Sure, I can ground Orr. But first he has to ask me to.'

'That's all he has to do to be grounded?'

'That's all. Let him ask me.'

'And then you can ground him?' Yossarian asked.

'No. Then I can't ground him.'

'You mean there's a catch?'

'Sure there's a catch,' Doc Daneeka replied. 'Catch-22. Anyone who wants to get out of combat duty isn't really crazy.'

There was only one catch and that was Catch-22, which specified that a concern for one's own safety in the face of dangers that were real and immediate was the process of a rational mind. Orr was crazy and could be grounded. All he had to do was ask; and as soon as he did, he would no longer be crazy and would have to fly more missions. Orr would be crazy to fly more missions and sane if he didn't, but if he was sane he had to fly them. If he flew them he was crazy and didn't have to; but if he didn't want to he was sane and had to. Yossarian was moved very deeply by the absolute simplicity of this clause of Catch-22 and let out a respectful whistle.

'That's some catch, that Catch-22,' he observed.

'It's the best there is,' Doc Daneeka agreed.

Yossarian saw it clearly in all its spinning reasonableness. There was an elliptical precision about its perfect pairs of parts that was graceful and shocking, like good modern art, and at times Yossarian wasn't quite sure that he saw it all, just the way he was never quite sure about good modern art or about the flies Orr saw in Appleby's eyes. He had Orr's word to take for the flies in Appleby's eyes.

'Oh, they're there, all right,' Orr had assured him about the flies in Appleby's eyes after Yossarian's fist fight with Appleby in the officers' club, 'although he probably doesn't even know it. That's why he can't see things as they really are.'

'How come he doesn't know it?' inquired Yossarian.

'Because he's got flies in his eyes,' Orr explained with exaggerated patience. 'How can he see he's got flies in his eyes if he's got flies in his eyes?'

. . .

Like all the other officers at Group Headquarters except Major Danby, Colonel Cathcart was infused with the democratic spirit: he believed that all men were created equal, and he therefore spurned all men outside Group Headquarters with equal fervor. Nevertheless, he believed in his men. As he told them frequently in the briefing room, he believed they were at least ten missions better than any other outfit and felt that any who did not share this confidence he had placed in them could get the hell out. The only way they could get the hell out, though, as Yossarian learned when he flew to visit ex-PFC Wintergreen, was by flying the extra ten missions.

'I still don't get it,' Yossarian protested. 'Is Doc Daneeka right or isn't he?'

'How many did he say?'

'Forty.'

'Daneeka was telling the truth,' ex-PFC Wintergreen admitted. 'Forty missions is all you have to fly as far as Twenty-seventh Air Force Headquarters is concerned.'

Yossarian was jubilant. 'Then I can go home, right? I've got forty-eight.'

'No, you can't go home,' ex-PFC Wintergreen corrected him. 'Are you crazy or something?'

'Why not?'

'Catch-22.'

'Catch-22?' Yossarian was stunned. 'What the hell has Catch-22 got to do with it?'

'Catch-22,' Doc Daneeka answered patiently, when Hungry Joe had flown Yossarian back to Pianosa, 'says you've always got to do what your commanding officer tells you to.'

'But Twenty-seventh Air Force says I can go home with forty missions.'

'But they don't say you have to go home. And regulations do say you have to obey every order. That's the catch. Even if the colonel were disobeying a Twenty-seventh Air Force order by making you fly more missions, you'd still have to fly them, or you'd be guilty of disobeying an order of his. And then Twenty-seventh Air Force Headquarters would really jump on you.'

Yossarian slumped with disappointment. 'Then I really have to fly the fifty missions, don't I?' he grieved.

'The fifty-five,' Doc Daneeka corrected him.

'What fifty-five?'

'The fifty-five missions the colonel now wants all of you to fly.'

Hungry Joe heaved a huge sigh of relief when he heard Doc Daneeka and broke into a grin. Yossarian grabbed Hungry Joe by the neck and made him fly them both right back to ex-PFC Wintergreen.

'What would they do to me,' he asked in confidential tones, 'if I refused to fly them?'

'We'd probably shoot you,' ex-PFC Wintergreen replied.

'*We*?' Yossarian cried in surprise. 'What do you mean, *we*? Since when are you on their side?'

'If you're going to be shot, whose side do you expect me to be on?' ex-PFC Wintergreen retorted.

Yossarian winced. Colonel Cathcart had raised him again.

Mother Courage and Her Children

Bertolt Brecht's play, probably now his most famous, was written in exile in the late thirties as the Second World War loomed, and first performed in Zurich in 1941. Brecht's general view, exemplified here, is that wars could not be fought if ordinary people were not so short-sighted. If they saw that wars are essentially against their own interests (and banded together to overthrow the rulers and businessmen who make war for their own selfish reasons), wars would cease.

Mother Courage herself can be played in many different ways. She owns a travelling canteen wagon and is seen following the armies round Europe between 1624 and 1636, in the first phase of the Thirty Years War. Her two sons go into the Protestant army. When the Catholics overrun her wagon, she changes side. Her son Swiss Cheese is captured and executed as she haggles over the bribe needed to save his life. When peace briefly breaks out, her son Eilif suffers a similar fate for looting from the peasantry – a skill which had made him a 'hero' in his commander's eyes. Eventually her dumb daughter, Kattrin, is shot as she beats a drum to warn a Protestant town of a surprise Catholic attack, saving the lives of children such as she loves and can never herself have. At last Courage drags her wagon alone, still determined to make her living the only way she can. Each actor playing her must strike her own balance between cynicism and good-heartedness. The chaplain who takes refuge with her and helps drag her wagon for a time is another ambivalent character.

Scene Five

TWO YEARS HAVE PASSED. THE WAR COVERS WIDER AND WIDER TERRITORY. FOREVER ON THE MOVE, THE LITTLE WAGON CROSSES POLAND, MORAVIA, BAVARIA, ITALY, AND AGAIN BAVARIA. 1631. TILLY'S VICTORY AT MAGDEBURG COSTS MOTHER COURAGE FOUR OFFICERS' SHIRTS.

The Wagon stands in a War-ruined Village

Faint military music from the distance. Two soldiers are being served at a counter by Kattrin and Mother Courage. One of them has a woman's fur coat about his shoulders.

MOTHER COURAGE: What, you can't pay? No money, no brandy! They can play victory marches, they should pay their men.

THE FIRST SOLDIER: I want my brandy! I arrived too late for plunder. The Chief allowed one hour to plunder the town, it's a swindle. He's not inhuman, he says. So I suppose they bought him off.

THE CHAPLAIN (*staggering in*): There are more in the farmhouse. A family of peasants. Help me someone. I need linen!

The second soldier goes with him. Kattrin is getting very excited. She tries to get her mother to bring linen out.

MOTHER COURAGE: I have none. I sold all my bandages to the regiment. I'm not tearing up my officers' shirts for these people.

THE CHAPLAIN (*calling over his shoulder*): I said I need linen!

MOTHER COURAGE (*stopping Kattrin from entering the wagon*): Not a thing! They have nothing and they pay nothing!

THE CHAPLAIN (*to a woman he is carrying in*): Why did you stay out there in the line of fire?

THE WOMAN: Our farm –

MOTHER COURAGE: Think they'd ever let go of *anything*? And now I'm supposed to pay. Well, I won't!

THE FIRST SOLDIER: They're Protestants, why should they be Protestants?

MOTHER COURAGE: Protestant, Catholic, what do *they* care? Their farm's gone, that's what.

THE SECOND SOLDIER: They're not Protestants anyway, they're Catholics.

THE FIRST SOLDIER: In a bombardment we can't pick and choose.

A PEASANT (*brought on by the chaplain*): Where's that linen?

All look at Mother Courage, who does not budge.

MOTHER COURAGE: I can't give you any. With all I have to pay out – taxes, duties, bribes . . . (*Kattrin takes up a board and threatens her mother with it, emitting gurgling sounds.*) Are you out of your mind? Put that board down or I'll fetch you one, you lunatic! I'm giving nothing, I daren't, I have myself to think of. (*The chaplain lifts her bodily off the steps of the wagon and sets her down on the ground. He takes out shirts from the wagon and tears them in strips.*) My shirts, my officers' shirts! (*From the house comes the cry of a child in pain.*)

THE PEASANT: The child's still in there! (*Kattrin runs in.*)

THE CHAPLAIN (*to the woman*): Stay where you are. She's getting it for you.

MOTHER COURAGE: Hold her back, the roof may fall in!

THE CHAPLAIN: I'm not going back in there!

MOTHER COURAGE (*pulled in both directions*): Go easy on my expensive linen.

The second soldier holds her back. Kattrin brings a baby out of the ruins.

MOTHER COURAGE: Another baby to drag around, you must be pleased with yourself. Give it to its mother this minute! Or do I have to fight you again for hours till I get it from you? Are you deaf? (*To the second soldier:*) Don't stand about gawking, go back there and tell 'em to stop that music, I can see their victory without it. I have nothing but losses from your victory!

THE CHAPLAIN (*bandaging*): The blood's coming through.

Kattrin is rocking the child and half humming a lullaby.

MOTHER COURAGE: There she sits, happy as a lark in all this misery. Give the baby back, the mother is coming to! (*She sees the first soldier. He had been handling the drinks, and is now trying to make off with the bottle.*) God's truth! You beast! You want another victory, do you? Then pay for it!

THE FIRST SOLDIER: I have nothing.

MOTHER COURAGE (*snatching the fur coat back*): Then leave this coat, it's stolen goods anyhow.

THE CHAPLAIN: There's still someone in there.

Scene Six

BEFORE THE CITY OF INGOLSTADT IN BAVARIA MOTHER COURAGE IS PRESENT AT THE FUNERAL OF THE FALLEN COMMANDER, TILLY. CONVERSATIONS TAKE PLACE ABOUT WAR HEROES AND THE DURATION OF THE WAR. THE CHAPLAIN COMPLAINS THAT HIS TALENTS ARE LYING FALLOW AND KATTRIN GETS THE RED BOOTS. THE YEAR IS 1632.

The inside of a Canteen Tent

The inner side of a counter at the rear. Rain. In the distance, drums and funeral music. The chaplain and the regimental scrivener are playing draughts. Mother Courage and her daughter are taking an inventory.

THE CHAPLAIN: The funeral procession is just starting out.

MOTHER COURAGE: Pity about the Chief – twenty-two pairs of socks – getting killed that way. They say it was an accident. There was a fog over the fields that morning, and the fog was to blame. The Chief called up another regiment, told 'em to fight to the death, rode back again, missed his way in the fog, went forward instead of back, and ran smack into a bullet in the thick of the battle – only four lanterns left. (*A whistle from the rear. She goes to the counter. To a soldier:*) It's a disgrace the way you're all skipping your Commander's funeral! (*She pours a drink.*)

THE SCRIVENER: They shouldn't have handed the money out before the funeral. Now the men are all getting drunk instead of going to it.

THE CHAPLAIN (*to the scrivener*): Don't you have to be there?

THE SCRIVENER: I stayed away because of the rain.

MOTHER COURAGE: It's different for you, the rain might spoil your uniform. I hear they wanted to ring the bells for his funeral, which is natural, but it came out that the churches had been shot up by his orders, so the poor Commander won't be hearing any bells when they lower him in his grave. Instead, they'll fire off three shots so the occasion won't be too sober – sixteen leather belts.

A VOICE FROM THE COUNTER: Service! One brandy!

MOTHER COURAGE: Your money first. No, you *can't* come inside the tent, not with those boots on. You can drink outside, rain or no rain. I only let officers in here. (*To the scrivener:*) The Chief had his troubles lately, I hear. There was unrest in the Second Regiment because he didn't pay 'em but he said it was a war of religion and they must fight it free of charge.

Funeral March. All look towards the rear.

THE CHAPLAIN: Now they're filing past the body.

MOTHER COURAGE: I feel sorry for a commander or an emperor like that – when he might have had something special in mind, something they'd talk about in times to come, something they'd raise a statue to him for. The conquest of the world now, *that's* a goal for a commander, he wouldn't know any better . . . Lord, worms have got into the biscuits . . . In short, he works his hands to the bone and then it's all spoiled by the common riffraff that only wants a jug of beer or a bit of company, not the higher things in life. The finest plans have always been spoiled by the littleness of them that should carry them out. Even emperors can't do it all by themselves. They count on support from their soldiers and the people round about. Am I right?

THE CHAPLAIN (*laughing*): You're right, Mother Courage, till you come to the soldiers. They do what they can. Those chaps outside, for example, drinking their brandy in the rain, I'd trust 'em to fight a hundred years, one war after another, two at a time if necessary. And I wasn't trained as a commander.

MOTHER COURAGE: . . . Seventeen leather belts . . . Then you don't think the war might end?

THE CHAPLAIN: Because a commander's dead? Don't be childish, they're sixpence a dozen. There are always heroes.

MOTHER COURAGE: Well, I wasn't asking for the sake of argument. I was wondering if I should buy up a lot of supplies. They happen to be cheap just now. But if the war ended, I might just as well throw them away.

THE CHAPLAIN: I realize you are serious, Mother Courage. Well, there've always been people going round saying some day the war will end. I say, you can't be sure the war will *ever* end. Of course it may have to pause occasionally – for breath, as it were – it can even meet with an accident – nothing on this earth is perfect – a war of which we could say it left nothing to be desired will probably never exist. A war can come to a sudden halt – from unforeseen causes – you can't think of everything – a little oversight, and the war's in the hole, and someone's got to pull it out again! The someone is the Emperor or the King or the Pope. They're such friends in need, the war has really nothing to worry about, it can look forward to a prosperous future.

A SOLDIER (*sings at the counter*):

> One schnapps, mine host, be quick, make haste!
> A soldier's got no time to waste:
> He must be shooting, shooting, shooting
> His Kaiser's enemies uprooting!

Make it a double. This is a holiday.

MOTHER COURAGE: If I was sure you're right . . .

THE CHAPLAIN: Think it out for yourself: how *could* the war end?

THE SOLDIER (*offstage*):

> Two breasts, my girl, be quick, make haste!
> A soldier's got no time to waste:
> He must be hating, hating, hating
> He cannot keep his Kaiser waiting!

THE SCRIVENER (*suddenly*): What about peace? Yes, peace. I'm from Bohemia. I'd like to get home once in a while.

THE CHAPLAIN: Oh, you would, would you? Dear old peace! What happens to the hole when the cheese is gone?

THE SOLDIER (*offstage*):

> Your blessing, priest, be quick, make haste!
> A soldier's got no time to waste:
> He must be dying, dying, dying
> His Kaiser's greatness glorifying!

THE SCRIVENER: In the long run you can't live without peace!

THE CHAPLAIN: Well, I'd say there's peace even in war, war has its islands of peace. For war satisfies *all* needs, even those of peace, yes, they're provided for, or the war couldn't keep going. In war – as in the very thick of peace – you can take a crap, and between one battle and the next there's always a beer, and even on the march you can snatch a nap – on your elbow maybe, in a gutter – something can always be managed. Of course you can't play cards during an attack, but neither can you while ploughing the fields in peace-time; it's when the victory's won that there are possibilities. You have your leg shot off, and at first you raise quite an outcry as if it *was* something, but soon you calm down or take a swig of brandy, and you end up hopping about, and the war is none the worse for your little misadventure. And can't you be fruitful and multiply in the thick of slaughter – behind a barn or somewhere? Nothing can keep you from it very long in any event. And so the war has your offspring and can carry on. War is like love, it always finds a way. Why *should* it end?

Kattrin has stopped working. She stares at the chaplain.

MOTHER COURAGE: Then I will buy those supplies, I'll rely on you. (*Kattrin suddenly bangs a basket of glasses down on the ground and runs out. Mother Courage laughs.*) Kattrin! Lord, Kattrin's still going to wait for peace. I promised her she'll get a husband – when it's peace. (*She runs after her.*)

THE SCRIVENER (*standing up*): I win. You were talking. You pay.

MOTHER COURAGE (*returning with Kattrin*): Be sensible, the war'll go on a bit longer, and we'll make a bit more money, then peace'll be all the nicer. Now you go into the town, it's not ten minutes' walk, and brings the things from the Golden Lion, just the dearer ones, we can get the rest later in the wagon. It's all arranged, the clerk will go with you, most of the soldiers are at the Commander's funeral, nothing can happen to you. Do a good job, don't lose anything, Kattrin, think of your trousseau!

Kattrin ties a cloth round her head and leaves with the scrivener.

THE CHAPLAIN: You don't mind her going with the scrivener?

MOTHER COURAGE: She's not so pretty anyone would want to ruin her.

THE CHAPLAIN: The way you run your business and always come through is highly commendable, Mother Courage – I see how you got your name.

MOTHER COURAGE: The poor need courage. They're lost, that's why. That they even get up in the morning is something – in *their* plight. Or that they plough a field – in war time. Even their bringing children into the world shows they have courage, for they have no prospects. They have to hang each other one by one and slaughter each other in the lump, so if they want to look each other in the face once in a while, well, it takes courage. That they put up with an Emperor and a Pope, that takes an unnatural amount of courage, for they cost you your life . . .

[*The Chaplain and Mother Courage bicker as she sets him to chop wood. He proposes to her, or at least propositions her* . . .]

MOTHER COURAGE: Dear Chaplain, be a sensible fellow. I like you, and I don't want to heap coals of fire on your head. All I'm after is to bring me and my children through in that wagon. It isn't just mine, the wagon, and anyway I've no mind to start having a private life. At the moment I'm taking quite a risk buying these things when the Commander's fallen and there's all this talk of peace. Where would you go, if I was ruined? See? You don't even know. Now chop some firewood and it'll be warm of an evening, which is quite a lot in times like these. What was that? (*She stands up. Kattrin enters, breathless, with a wound across the eye and forehead. She is dragging all sorts of articles, parcels, leather goods, a drum, etc.*) What is it, were you attacked? On the way back? She was attacked on the way back! I'll bet it was that soldier who got drunk on my liquor. I should never have let you go. Dump all that stuff! It's not bad, the wound is only a flesh wound. I'll bandage it for you, it'll be all healed up in a week. They're worse than animals. (*She bandages the wound.*)

THE CHAPLAIN: I reproach them with nothing. At home they never did these shameful things. The men who start the wars are responsible, they bring out the worst in people.

MOTHER COURAGE: Didn't the scrivener walk you back home? That's because you're a respectable girl, he thought they'd leave you alone. The wound's not at all deep, it will never show. There: all bandaged up. Now, I've got something for you, rest easy. A secret. I've been holding it, you'll see. (*She digs Yvette's red boots out of a bag.*) Well, what do you see? You always wanted them. Now you have them. (*She helps her to put the boots on.*) Put them on quick, before I'm sorry I let you have them. It will never show, though it wouldn't bother *me* if it did. The fate of the ones they like is the worst. They drag them round with them till they're finished. A girl they don't care for they leave alone. I've seen so many girls, pretty as they come in the beginning, then all of a sudden they looked a fright – enough to scare a wolf. They can't even go behind a tree on the street without having something to fear from it. They lead a frightful life. Like with trees: the tall, straight ones are cut down for roof timber, and the crooked ones can enjoy life. So this wound here is really a piece of luck. The boots have kept well. I gave them a good clean before I put them away.

Kattrin leaves the boots and creeps into the wagon.

THE CHAPLAIN (*when she's gone*): I hope she won't be disfigured?

MOTHER COURAGE: There'll be a scar. She needn't wait for peace now.

THE CHAPLAIN: She didn't let them get any of the stuff away from her.

MOTHER COURAGE: Maybe I shouldn't have made such a point of it. If only I ever knew what went on inside her head. Once she stayed out all night, once in all the years. I could never get out of her what happened. I racked my brains for quite a while. (*She picks up the things Kattrin spilled and sorts them angrily.*) This is war. A nice source of income, I must say!

Cannon shots.

THE CHAPLAIN: Now they're lowering the Commander into his grave! A historic moment.

MOTHER COURAGE: It's a historic moment to me when they hit my daughter over the eye. She's all but finished now, she'll never get a husband, and she's so mad about children! Even her dumbness comes from the war. A soldier stuck something in her mouth when she was little. I'll not see Swiss Cheese again, and where my Eilif is the Good Lord knows. Curse the war!

Celan's Death Fugue

*Paul Celan, born Paul Antschel in 1920 to Jewish parents in Bukovina, a German enclave in Romania, escaped the Holocaust though both his parents were transported to a camp in Transnistria where his father died of typhus and his mother was shot. From 1948 till his suicide in 1970 he lived in Paris where he became a lecturer on German literature. Though his writing showed cosmopolitan affinities – with French, Romanian, Russian and English poetry – he was quickly recognized as a major German poet. His early 'Death Fugue', a direct response to the Holocaust, is described by Omer Bartov (q.v.) as 'one of the greatest single poems of the century'. Bartov adds: 'Perhaps only those who have heard Celan reading this poem aloud can perceive the extent to which its relentless rhythm and stark imagery seem to recapture the whole experience of the death camp, the crazy logic of the extermination, the horrifying irony of installing the 'chosen people' as smoke in the sky, this insane world of music and bloodhounds, of beauty and ashes, of total, endless, unremitting despair' (*Murder in Our Midst, *p. 129). Yet, as Celan's translator Michael Hamburger observes, the poem 'celebrates beauty and energy while commemorating their destruction'. Celan himself was disturbed by the success of 'Todesfuge' – it was set to music and used in schools to demonstrate the art of poetic fugue. He came to believe that it was too explicit, and forbade its reprinting in yet more anthologies. However, I have no compunction over placing this masterpiece here, three decades after his death. His later poetry was more cryptic.*

DEATH FUGUE

Black milk of daybreak we drink it at sundown
we drink it at noon in the morning we drink it at night
we drink and we drink it
we dig a grave in the breezes there one lies unconfined
A man lives in the house he plays with the serpents he writes
he writes when dusk falls to Germany your golden hair
  Margarete

he writes it and steps out of doors and the stars are flashing he
whistles his pack out
he whistles his Jews out in earth has them dig for a grave
he commands us strike up for the dance

Black milk of daybreak we drink you at night
we drink in the morning at noon we drink you at sundown
we drink and we drink you
A man lives in the house he plays with the serpents he writes
he writes when dusk falls to Germany your golden hair
Margarete
your ashen hair Shulamith we dig a grave in the breezes there
one lies unconfined

He calls out jab deeper into the earth you lot you others sing
now and play
he grabs at the iron in his belt he waves it his eyes are blue
jab deeper you lot with your spades you others play on for the
dance

Black milk of daybreak we drink you at night
we drink you at noon in the morning we drink you at sundown
we drink and we drink you
a man lives in the house your golden hair Margarete
your ashen hair Shulamith he plays with the serpents

He calls out more sweetly play death death is a master from
Germany
he calls out more darkly now stroke your strings then as smoke
you will rise into air
then a grave you will have in the clouds there one lies
unconfined

Black milk of daybreak we drink you at night
we drink you at noon death is a master from Germany
we drink you at sundown and in the morning we drink and we
drink you
death is a master from Germany his eyes are blue
he strikes you with leaden bullets his aim is true

a man lives in the house your golden hair Margarete
he sets his pack on to us he grants us a grave in the air
he plays with the serpents and daydreams death is a master
from Germany

your golden hair Margarete
your ashen hair Shulamith

Jacques Brel's 'Next' ('Au Suivant')

Wars have had deeply corrupting effects on the sexuality of young men (a major theme in, for instance, Heller's Catch-22*). The Belgian singer-songwriter Jacques Brel attacks one source of corruption, the army brothel, with great power. The version of 'Au Suivant' in English, first heard in a New York show,* Jacques Brel is Alive and Well and Living in Paris *(1968), is powerful in itself – there is a notable recording by Scott Walker – but misses subtleties in the original: the full grim emphasis on forms of the verb 'suivre', for instance, and the point when the anonymous soldier-singer ironically compares himself with Napoleon, triumphant at Arcola, defeated at Waterloo. Hence the French text is also given.*

AU SUIVANT

Tout nu dans ma serviette qui me servait de pagne
J'avais le rouge au front et le savon à la main
Au suivant au suivant
J'avais juste vingt ans et nous étions cent vingt
A être le suivant de celui qu'on suivait
Au suivant au suivant
J'avais juste vingt ans et je me déniaisais
Au bordel ambulant d'une armée en campagne
Au suivant au suivant

Moi j'aurais bien aimé un peu plus de tendresse
Ou alors un sourire ou bien avoir le temps
Mais au suivant au suivant
Ce ne fut pas Waterloo mais ce ne fut pas Arcole
Ce fut l'heure où l'on regrette d'avoir manqué l'école
Au suivant au suivant
Mais je jure que d'entendre cet adjudant de mes fesses
C'est des coups à vous faire des armées d'impuissants
Au suivant au suivant

Je jure sur la tête de ma première vérole
Que cette voix depuis je l'entends tout le temps
Au suivant au suivant
Cette voix qui sentait l'ail et le mauvais alcool
C'est la voix des nations et c'est la voix du sang
Au suivant au suivant
Et depuis chaque femme à l'heure de succomber
Entre mes bras trop maigres semble me murmurer
Au suivant au suivant

Tous les suivants de monde devraient se donner la main
Voilà ce que la nuit je crie dans mon délire
Au suivant au suivant
Et quand je ne délire pas j'en arrive à me dire
Qu'il est plus humiliant d'être suivi que suivant
Au suivant au suivant
Un jour je me ferai cul-de-jatte ou bonne soeur ou pendu
Enfin un de ces machins ou je ne serai jamais plus
Le suivant le suivant.

NEXT

Naked as sin, an army towel
Covering my belly,
Some of us blush, some howl,
Knees turning to jelly.
Next! Next!

I was still just a kid,
There were a hundred like me,
I followed a naked body
A naked body followed me.
Next! Next!

I was still just a kid,
When my innocence was lost
In a mobile army whorehouse,

Gift of the army, free of cost.
Next! Next!

Me I really would have liked
But a little touch of tenderness,
Maybe a word, a smile,
An hour's happiness,
But next! Next!

Oh, it wasn't so tragic,
The high heavens didn't fall,
But how much at that time
I hated being there at all.
Next! Next!

Now I will always recall
The brothel truck, the flying flags
The queer lieutenant who slapped
Our asses as if we were fags.
Next! Next!

I swear on the wet head
Of my first case of gonorrhea,
It is his ugly voice
That I forever hear,
Next! Next!

The voice that stinks of whisky,
Of corpses and of mud,
It is the voice of nations,
It is the thick voice of blood.
Next! Next!

And since then each woman
I have taken to bed
Seems to laugh in my arms;
To whisper through my head.
Next! Next!

All the naked and the dead
Should hold each other's hands,
As they watch me scream at night,
In a dream no one understands.
Next! Next!

And when I am not screaming,
In a voice grown dry and hollow,
I stand on endless naked lines
Of the following and the followed.
Next! Next!

One day I'll cut my legs off
Or burn myself alive,
Anything, I'll do anything
To get out of line to survive.
Not ever to be next, not ever to be next.

Slaughterhouse 5

The bombing of Dresden in 1945 shocked numerous people on the Allied side at the time. Even Churchill was soon suggesting privately that it might have been a mistake. The historic capital of Saxony was a beautiful old city, famous for architecture, for music and for the production of fine china. Its strategic significance had been judged so slight that up to early 1945 it had received only one small raid. In January 1945 the British Air Ministry drew up a plan, code-named THUNDERCLAP, to attack Berlin and other population centres in eastern Germany, thus abetting Soviet advance westward. Dresden's turn came on February 13. Over 800 British planes that night dropped 1,478 tons of explosives and 1,182 tons of incendiaries. The latter started a firestorm in the city centre. Next day over 3,000 USAAF bombers added to the destruction.

When this episode surfaced again in British and American consciousness in the 1960s, it was widely credited, on the basis of a book by the tendentious historian David Irving, that 135,000 people had died in one night – far more than in Hiroshima from the first A-Bomb. Some scholars now believe that the number was less than 50,000. However, the city was packed with refugees. The exact number of deaths will never be known.

There were also numerous Russian, British and American prisoners of war encamped on the outskirts. One of them was Kurt Vonnegut, a young US soldier captured during the recent German thrust in the Ardennes. When the USA was fully committed to a huge and hideous new war in Vietnam Vonnegut made the bombing of Dresden central to his most famous novel, Slaughterhouse 5 *(1969).*

His protagonist Billy Pilgrim is a college student from New York State, who after the war becomes a successful optometrist. In the 1960s he is captured by aliens from Tralfamadore who take him to their distant planet and exhibit him in a zoo, where he is joined by an abducted film star, Montana Wildhack. Their copulation attracts great local interest, but the Tralfamadorians are unimpressed with the human conception of time as serial. They see all time as always present, so that the moment of death is no more decisive than days of jubilation. Billy, simultaneously resident on earth, can now travel in time.

Vonnegut's novel is 'about' many things. It comments obliquely on the Vietnam War, it satirizes the crassness of American social relation-

ships, and it conveys serious philosophical insights. But Vonnegut's first-person introduction and coda make it clear that it must be seen primarily as the book in which he struggles to come to terms with the horror of Dresden, nearly a quarter of a century after the firestorm. Suppression of memory by those who have killed and suffered in war now interests historians greatly. Survivors find it hard to speak about traumatic events. Trauma and guilt combine with the real or supposed indifference of families, friends and colleagues to tie their tongues.

Billy Pilgrim's time-travelling means that in the past he foresees the future – Edgar Derby, elected leader of the American POWs, is 'poor' because the Germans will shortly execute him. But it also provides a metaphorical aid to Vonnegut's own dives into the terrible past. Pilgrim, issued by the Germans with a silly little coat when other POWs get serious coats, is an innocent – naïve, shy, apolitical, a futile clown – who makes it possible for Vonnegut to write in bitter earnest about the destruction of his own innocence.

The Americans began to feel much better. They were able to hold their food. And then it was time to go to Dresden. The Americans marched fairly stylishly out of the British compound. Billy Pilgrim again led the parade. He had silver boots now, and a muff, and a piece of azure curtain which he wore like a toga. Billy still had a beard. So did poor old Edgar Derby, who was beside him. Derby was imagining letters to home, his lips working tremulously:

Dear Margaret – We are leaving for Dresden today. Don't worry. It will never be bombed. It is an open city. There was an election at noon, and guess what? And so on . . .

The trip to Dresden was a lark. It took only two hours. Shriveled little bellies were full. Sunlight and mild air came in through the ventilators. There were plenty of smokes from the Englishmen.

The Americans arrived in Dresden at five in the afternoon. The boxcar doors were opened, and the doorways framed the loveliest city that most of the Americans had ever seen. The skyline was intricate and voluptuous and enchanted and absurd. It looked like a Sunday school picture of Heaven to Billy Pilgrim.

Somebody behind him in the boxcar said, 'Oz.' That was I. That was me. The only other city I'd ever seen was Indianapolis, Indiana.

Every other big city in Germany had been bombed and burned ferociously. Dresden had not suffered so much as a cracked windowpane. Sirens went off every day, screamed like hell, and people went down into cellars and listened to radios there. The planes were always bound for someplace else – Leipzig, Chemnitz, Plauen, places like that. So it goes.

Steam radiators still whistled cheerily in Dresden. Street-cars clanged. Telephones rang and were answered. Lights went on and off when switches were clicked. There were theaters and restaurants. There was a zoo. The principal enterprises of the city were medicine and food-processing and the making of cigarettes.

People were going home from work now in the late afternoon. They were tired.

Eight Dresdeners crossed the steel spaghetti of the railroad yard. They were wearing new uniforms. They had been sworn into the army the day before. They were boys and men past middle age, and two veterans who had been shot to pieces in Russia. Their assignment was to guard one hundred American prisoners of war, who would work as contract labor. A grandfather and his grandson were in the squad. The grandfather was an architect.

The eight were grim as they approached the boxcars containing their wards. They knew what sick and foolish soldiers they themselves appeared to be. One of them actually had an artificial leg, and carried not only a loaded rifle but a cane. Still – they were expected to earn obedience and respect from tall, cocky, murderous American infantrymen who had just come from all the killing at the front.

And then they saw bearded Billy Pilgrim in his blue toga and silver shoes, with his hands in a muff. He looked at least sixty years old. Next to Billy was little Paul Lazzaro with a broken arm. He was fizzing with rabies. Next to Lazzaro was the poor old high school teacher, Edgar Derby, mournfully pregnant with patriotism and middle age and imaginary wisdom. And so on.

The eight ridiculous Dresdeners ascertained that these hundred ridiculous creatures really *were* American fighting men fresh from the front. They smiled, and then they laughed. Their terror evaporated.

There was nothing to be afraid of. Here were more crippled human beings, more fools like themselves. Here was light opera.

So out of the gate of the railroad yard and into the streets of Dresden marched the light opera. Billy Pilgrim was the star. He led the parade. Thousands of people were on the sidewalks, going home from work. They were watery and putty-colored, having eaten most potatoes during the past two years. They had expected no blessings beyond the mildness of the day. Suddenly – here was fun.

Billy did not meet many of the eyes that found him so entertaining. He was enchanted by the architecture of the city. Merry amoretti wove garlands above windows. Roguish fauns and naked nymphs peeked down at Billy from festooned cornices. Stone monkeys frisked among scrolls and seashells and bamboo.

Billy, with his memories of the future, knew that the city would be smashed to smithereens and then burned – in about thirty more days. He knew, too, that most of the people watching him would soon be dead. So it goes.

And Billy worked his hands in his muff as he marched. His fingertips, working there in the hot darkness of the muff, wanted to know what the two lumps in the lining of the little impresario's coat were. The fingertips got inside the lining. They palpated the lumps, the pea-shaped thing and the horseshoe-shaped thing. The parade had to halt by a busy corner. The traffic light was red.

There at the corner, in the front rank of pedestrians, was a surgeon who had been operating all day. He was a civilian, but his posture was military. He had served in two world wars. The sight of Billy offended him, especially after he learned from the guards that Billy was an American. It seemed to him that Billy was in abominable taste, supposed that Billy had gone to a lot of silly trouble to costume himself just so.

The surgeon spoke English, and he said to Billy, 'I take it you find war a very comical thing.'

Billy looked at him vaguely. Billy had lost track momentarily of where he was or how he had gotten there. He had no idea that people thought he was clowning. It was Fate, of course, which had costumed him – Fate, and a feeble will to survive.

'Did you expect us to *laugh*?' the surgeon asked him.

The surgeon was demanding some sort of satisfaction. Billy was mystified. Billy wanted to be friendly, to help, if he could, but his resources were meager. His fingers now held the two objects from the lining of the coat. Billy decided to show the surgeon what they were.

'You thought we would enjoy being *mocked*?' the surgeon said. 'And do you feel *proud* to represent America as you do?'

Billy withdrew a hand from his muff, held it under the surgeon's nose. On his palm rested a two-carat diamond and a partial denture. The denture was an obscene little artifact – silver and pearl and tangerine. Billy smiled.

The parade pranced, staggered and reeled to the gate of the Dresden slaughterhouse, and then it went inside. The slaughterhouse wasn't a busy place any more. Almost all the hooved animals in Germany had been killed and eaten and excreted by human beings, mostly soldiers. So it goes.

The Americans were taken to the fifth building inside the gate. It was a one-story cement-block cube with sliding doors in front and back. It had been built as a shelter for pigs about to be butchered. Now it was going to serve as a home away from home for one hundred American prisoners of war. There were bunks in there, and two potbellied stoves and a water tap. Behind it was a latrine, which was a one-rail fence with buckets under it.

There was a big number over the door of the building. The number was *five*. Before the Americans could go inside, their only English-speaking guard told them to memorize their simple address, in case they got lost in the big city. Their address was this: 'Schlachthof-fünf.' *Schlachthof* meant *slaughterhouse*. *Fünf* was good old *five*.

Billy Pilgrim got onto a chartered airplane in Ilium twenty-five years after that. He knew it was going to crash, but he didn't want to make a fool of himself by saying so. It was supposed to carry Billy and twenty-eight other optometrists to a convention in Montreal.

His wife, Valencia, was outside, and his father-in-law, Lionel Merble, was strapped to the seat beside him.

Lionel Merble was a machine. Tralfamadorians, of course, say that every creature and plant in the Universe is a machine. It amuses them that so many Earthlings are offended by the idea of being machines.

Outside the plane, the machine named Valencia Merble Pilgrim was eating a Peter Paul Mound Bar and waving bye-bye.

*

The plane took off without incident. The moment was structured that way. There was a barbershop quartet on board. They were optometrists, too. They called themselves 'The Febs', which was an acronym for 'Four-eyed Bastards'.

When the plane was safely aloft, the machine that was Billy's father-in-law asked the quartet to sing his favorite song. They knew what song he meant, and they sang it, and it went like this:

In my prison cell I sit,
With my britches full of shit,
And my balls are bouncing gently on the floor.
And I see the bloody snag
When she bit me in the bag.
Oh, I'll never fuck a Polack any more.

Billy's father-in-law laughed and laughed at that, and he begged the quartet to sing the other Polish song he liked so much. So they sang a song from the Pennsylvania coal mines that began:

Me and Mike, ve vork in mine.
Holy shit, ve have good time.
Vunce a veek ve get our pay.
Holy shit, no vork next day.

Speaking of people from Poland: Billy Pilgrim accidentally saw a Pole hanged in public, about three days after Billy got to Dresden. Billy just happened to be walking to work with some others shortly after sunrise, and they came to a gallows and a small crowd in front of a soccer stadium. The Pole was a farm laborer who was being hanged for having had sexual intercourse with a German woman. So it goes.

Billy, knowing the plane was going to crash pretty soon, closed his eyes, traveled in time back to 1944. He was back in the forest in Luxembourg again – with the Three Musketeers. Roland Weary was shaking him, bonking his head against a tree. 'You guys go on without me,' said Billy Pilgrim.

The barbershop quartet on the airplane was singing 'Wait Till the Sun Shines, Nelly', when the plane smacked into the top of Sugarbush Mountain in Vermont. Everybody was killed but Billy and the co-pilot. So it goes.

The people who first got to the crash scene were young Austrian ski instructors from the famous ski resort below. They spoke to each other in German as they went from body to body. They wore black wind masks with two holes for their eyes and a red topknot. They looked like golliwogs, like white people pretending to be black for the laughs they could get.

Billy had a fractured skull, but he was still conscious. He didn't know where he was. His lips were working, and one of the golliwogs put his ear close to them to hear what might be his dying words.

Billy thought the golliwog had something to do with World War Two, and he whispered to him his address: 'Schlachthof-fünf.'

Billy was brought down Sugarbush Mountain on a tobaggan. The golliwogs controlled it with ropes and yodeled melodiously for right-of-way. Near the bottom, the trail swooped around the pylons of a chair lift. Billy looked up at all the young people in bright elastic clothing and enormous boots and goggles, bombed out of their skulls with snow, swinging through the sky in yellow chairs. He supposed that they were part of an amazing new phase of World War Two. It was all right with him. Everything was pretty much all right with Billy.

He was taken to a small private hospital. A famous brain surgeon came up from Boston and operated on him for three hours. Billy was unconscious for two days after that, and he dreamed millions of things, some of them true. The true things were time-travel.

One of the true things was his first evening in the slaughterhouse. He and poor old Edgar Derby were pushing an empty two-wheeled cart down a dirt lane between empty pens for animals. They were going to a communal kitchen for supper for all. They were guarded by a sixteen-year-old German named Werner Gluck. The axles of the cart were greased with the fat of dead animals. So it goes.

The sun had just gone down, and its afterglow was backlighting the city, which formed low cliffs around the bucolic void to the idle stockyards. The city was blacked out because bombers might come, so Billy didn't get to see Dresden do one of the most cheerful things a city is capable of doing when the sun goes down, which is to wink its lights on one by one.

There was a broad river to reflect those lights, which would have made their nighttime winkings very pretty indeed. It was the Elbe.

Werner Gluck, the young guard, was a Dresden boy. He had never been in the slaughterhouse before, so he wasn't sure where the kitchen was. He was tall and weak like Billy, might have been a younger brother of his. They were, in fact, distant cousins, something they never found out. Gluck was armed with an incredibly heavy musket, a single-shot museum piece with an octagonal barrel and a smooth bore. He had fixed his bayonet. It was like a long knitting needle. It had no blood gutters.

Gluck led the way to a building that he thought might contain the kitchen, and he opened the sliding door in its side. There wasn't a kitchen in there, though. There was a dressing room adjacent to a communal shower, and there was a lot of steam. In the steam were about thirty teen-age girls with no clothes on. They were German refugees from Breslau, which had been tremendously bombed. They had just arrived in Dresden, too. Dresden was jammed with refugees.

There those girls were with all their private parts bare, for anybody to see. And there in the doorway were Gluck and Derby and Pilgrim – the childish soldier and the poor old high school teacher and the clown in his toga and silver shoes – staring. The girls screamed. They covered themselves with their hands and turned their backs and so on, and made themselves utterly beautiful.

Werner Gluck, who had never seen a naked woman before, closed the door. Billy had never seen one, either. It was nothing new to Derby.

When the three fools found the communal kitchen, whose main job was to make lunch for workers in the slaughterhouse, everybody had gone home but one woman who had been waiting for them impatiently. She was a war widow. So it goes. She had her hat and coat on. She wanted to go home too, even though there wasn't anybody there. Her white gloves were laid out side by side on the zinc counter top.

She had two big cans of soup for the Americans. It was simmering over low fires on the gas range. She had stacks of loaves of black bread, too.

She asked Gluck if he wasn't awfully young to be in the army. He admitted that he was.

She asked Edgar Derby if he wasn't awfully old to be in the army. He said he was.

She asked Billy Pilgrim what he was supposed to be. Billy said he didn't know. He was just trying to keep warm.

'All the real soldiers are dead,' she said. It was true. So it goes.

Another true thing that Billy saw while he was unconscious in Vermont was the work that he and the others had to do in Dresden during the month before the city was destroyed. They washed windows and swept floors and cleaned lavatories and put jars into boxes and sealed cardboard boxes in a factory that made malt syrup. The syrup was enriched with vitamins and minerals. The syrup was for pregnant women.

The syrup tasted like thin honey laced with hickory smoke, and everybody who worked in the factory secretly spooned it all day long. They weren't pregnant, but they needed vitamins and minerals, too. Billy didn't spoon syrup on his first day at work, but lots of other Americans did.

Billy spooned it on his second day. There were spoons hidden all over the factory, on rafters, in drawers, behind radiators, and so on. They had been hidden in haste by persons who had been spooning syrup, who had heard somebody else coming. Spooning was a crime.

On his second day, Billy was cleaning behind a radiator, and he found a spoon. To his back was a vat of syrup that was cooling. The only other person who could see Billy and his spoon was poor old Edgar Derby, who was washing a window outside. The spoon was a tablespoon. Billy thrust it into the vat, turned it around and around, making a gooey lollipop. He thrust it into his mouth.

A moment went by, and then every cell in Billy's body shook him with ravenous gratitude and applause.

There were diffident raps on the factory window. Derby was out there, having seen all. He wanted some syrup, too.

So Billy made a lollipop for him. He opened the window. He stuck the lollipop into poor old Derby's gaping mouth. A moment passed, and then Derby burst into tears. Billy closed the window and hid the sticky spoon. Somebody was coming.

The Americans in the slaughterhouse had a very interesting visitor two days before Dresden was destroyed. He was Howard W. Campbell, Jr, an American who had become a Nazi. Campbell was the one who had written the monograph about the shabby behavior of American prisoners of war. He wasn't doing more research about prisoners now. He had come to the slaughterhouse to recruit men for a German military unit called 'The Free American Corps'. Campbell was the inventor and commander of the unit, which was supposed to fight only on the Russian front.

Campbell was an ordinary-looking man, but he was extravagantly costumed in a uniform of his own design. He wore a white ten-gallon hat and black cowboy boots decorated with swastikas and stars. He was sheathed in a blue body stocking which had yellow stripes running from his armpits to his ankles. His shoulder patch was a silhouette of Abraham Lincoln's profile on a field of pale green. He had a broad armband which was red, with a blue swastika in a circle of white.

He was explaining this armband now in the cement-block hog barn.

Billy Pilgrim had a boiling case of heartburn, since he had been spooning malt syrup all day long at work. The heartburn brought tears to his eyes, so that his image of Campbell was distorted by jiggling lenses of salt water.

'Blue is for the American sky,' Campbell was saying. 'White is for the race that pioneered the continent, drained the swamps and cleared the forests and built the roads and bridges. Red is for the blood of American patriots which was shed so gladly in years gone by.'

Campbell's audience was sleepy. It had worked hard at the syrup factory, and then it had marched a long way home in the cold. It was skinny and hollow-eyed. Its skins were beginning to blossom with small sores. So were its mouths and throats and intestines. The malt syrup it spooned at the factory contained only a few of the vitamins and minerals every Earthling needs.

Campbell offered the Americans food now, steaks and mashed potatoes and gravy and mince pie, if they would join the Free American Corps. 'Once the Russians are defeated,' he went on, 'you will be repatriated through Switzerland.'

There was no response.

'You're going to have to fight the Communists sooner or later,' said Campbell. 'Why not get it over with now?'

And then it developed that Campbell was not going to go unanswered after all. Poor old Derby, the doomed high school teacher, lumbered to his feet for what was probably the finest moment in his life. There are almost no characters in this story, and almost no dramatic confrontations, because most of the people in it are so sick and so much the listless playthings of enormous forces. One of the main effects of war, after all, is that people are discouraged from being characters. But old Derby was a character now.

His stance was that of a punch-drunk fighter. His head was down. His fists were out front, waiting for information and battle plan. Derby raised his head, called Campbell a snake. He corrected that. He said that snakes couldn't help being snakes, and that Campbell, who *could* help being what he was, was something much lower than a snake or a rat – or even a blood-filled tick.

Campbell smiled.

Derby spoke movingly of the American form of government, with freedom and justice and opportunities and fair play for all. He said there wasn't a man there who wouldn't gladly die for those ideals.

He spoke of the brotherhood between the American and the Russian people, and how those two nations were going to crush the disease of Nazism, which wanted to infect the whole world.

The air-raid sirens of Dresden howled mournfully.

The Americans and their guards and Campbell took shelter in an echoing meat locker which was hollowed in living rock under the slaughterhouse. There was an iron staircase with iron doors at the top and bottom.

Down in the locker were a few cattle and sheep and pigs and horses hanging from iron hooks. So it goes. The locker had empty hooks for thousands more. It was naturally cool. There was no refrigeration. There was candlelight. The locker was whitewashed and smelled of carbolic acid. There were benches along a wall. The Americans went to these, brushing away flakes of whitewash before they sat down.

Howard W. Campbell, Jr, remained standing, like the guards. He talked to the guards in excellent German. He had written many popular German plays and poems in his time, and had married a famous German actress named Resi North. She was dead now, had been killed while entertaining troops in the Crimea. So it goes.

Nothing happened that night. It was the next night that about one hundred and thirty thousand people in Dresden would die. So it goes . . .

[*Billy Pilgrim's memories of that night are triggered at a party in 1964, by when he is a successful optometrist back in the USA.*]

Now an optometrist called for attention. He proposed a toast to Billy and Valencia, whose anniversary it was. According to plan, the barbershop quartet of optometrists, 'The Febs', sang while people drank and Billy and Valencia put their arms around each other, just glowed. Everybody's eyes were shining. The song was 'That Old Gang of Mine'.

Gee, that song went, *but I'd give the world to see that old gang of mine*. And so on. A little later it said, *So long forever, old fellows and gals, so long forever old sweethearts and pals – God bless 'em* – And so on.

Unexpectedly, Billy Pilgrim found himself upset by the song and the occasion. He had never had an old gang, old sweethearts and pals, but he missed one anyway, as the quartet made slow, agonized experiments with chords – chords intentionally sour, sourer still, unbearably sour, and then a chord that was suffocatingly sweet, and then some sour ones again. Billy had powerful psychosomatic responses to the changing chords. His mouth filled with the taste of lemonade, and his face became grotesque, as though he really were being stretched on the torture engine called the *rack*.

He looked so peculiar that several people commented on it solicitously when the song was done. They thought he might have been having a heart attack, and Billy seemed to confirm this by going to a chair and sitting down haggardly . . .

. . .

The barbershop quartet sang again. Billy was emotionally racked again. The experience was *definitely* associated with those four men and not what they sang.

Here is what they sang, while Billy was pulled apart inside:

'Leven cent cotton, forty cent meat,
How in the world can a poor man eat?
Pray for the sunshine, 'cause it will rain.
Things gettin' worse, drivin' all insane;
Built a nice bar, painted it brown;

Lightnin' came along and burnt it down:
No use talkin', any man's beat,
With 'leven cent cotton and forty cent meat.
'Leven cent cotton, a car-load of tax,
The load's too heavy for our poor backs . . .

And so on.

Billy fled upstairs in his nice white home . . .

Billy went into his bedroom, even though there were guests to be entertained downstairs. He lay down on his bed, turned on the Magic Fingers. The mattress trembled, drove a dog out from under the bed. The dog was Spot. Good old Spot was still alive in those days. Spot lay down again in a corner.

Billy thought hard about the effect the quartet had had on him, and then found an association with an experience he had had long ago. He did not travel in time to the experience. He remembered it shimmeringly – as follows:

He was down in the meat locker on the night that Dresden was destroyed. There were sounds like giant footsteps above. Those were sticks of high-explosive bombs. The giants walked and walked. The meat locker was a very safe shelter. All that happened down there was an occasional shower of calcimine. The Americans and four of their guards and a few dressed carcasses were down there, and nobody else. The rest of the guards had, before the raid began, gone to the comforts of their own homes in Dresden. They were all being killed with their families.

So it goes.

The girls that Billy had seen naked were all being killed, too, in a much shallower shelter in another part of the stockyards.

So it goes.

A guard would go to the head of the stairs every so often to see what it was like outside, then he would come down and whisper to the other guards. There was a fire-storm out there. Dresden was one big flame. The one flame ate everything organic, everything that would burn.

It wasn't safe to come out of the shelter until noon the next day. When the Americans and their guards did come out, the sky was black with smoke. The sun was an angry little pinhead. Dresden was like the moon now, nothing but minerals. The stones were hot. Everybody else in the neighborhood was dead.

So it goes.

The guards drew together instinctively, rolled their eyes. They experimented with one expression and then another, said nothing, though their mouths were often open. They looked like a silent film of a barbershop quartet.

'So long forever,' they might have been singing, 'old fellows and pals; So long forever, old sweethearts and gals – God bless 'em –'

'Tell me a story,' Montana Wildhack said to Billy Pilgrim in the Tralfamadorian zoo one time. They were in bed side by side. They had privacy. The canopy covered the dome. Montana was six months pregnant now, big and rosy, lazily demanding small favors from Billy from time to time. She couldn't send Billy out for ice cream or strawberries, since the atmosphere outside the dome was cyanide, and the nearest strawberries and ice cream were millions of light years away.

She could send him to the refrigerator, which was decorated with the blank couple on the bicycle built for two – or, as now, she could wheedle, 'Tell me a story, Billy boy.'

'Dresden was destroyed on the night of February 13, 1945,' Billy Pilgrim began. 'We came out of our shelter the next day.' He told Montana about the four guards who, in their astonishment and grief, resembled a barbershop quartet. He told her about the stockyards with all the fenceposts gone, with roofs and windows gone – told her about seeing little logs lying around. These were people who had been caught in the fire-storm. So it goes.

Billy told her what had happened to the buildings that used to form cliffs around the stockyards. They had collapsed. Their wood had been consumed, and their stones had crashed down, had tumbled against one another until they locked at last in low and graceful curves.

'It was like the moon,' said Billy Pilgrim.

The guards told the Americans to form in ranks of four, which they did. Then they had them march back to the hog barn which had been their home. Its walls still stood, but its windows and roofs were gone, and there was nothing inside but ashes and dollops of melted glass. It was realized then that there was no food or water, and that the survivors, if they were going to continue to survive, were going to have to climb over curve after curve on the face of the moon.

Which they did.

The curves were smooth only when seen from a distance. The people climbing them learned that they were treacherous, jagged things – hot to the touch, often unstable – eager, should certain important rocks be disturbed, to tumble some more, to form lower, more solid curves.

Nobody talked much as the expedition crossed the moon. There was nothing appropriate to say. One thing was clear: Absolutely everybody in the city was supposed to be dead, regardless of what they were, and that anybody that moved in it represented a flaw in the design. There were to be no moon men at all.

American fighter planes came in under the smoke to see if anything was moving. They saw Billy and the rest moving down there. The planes sprayed them with machine-gun bullets, but the bullets missed. Then they saw some other people moving down by the riverside and they shot at them. They hit some of them. So it goes.

The idea was to hasten the end of the war.

Billy's story ended very curiously in a suburb untouched by fire and explosion. The guards and the Americans came at nightfall to an inn which was open for business. There was candlelight. There were fires in three fireplaces downstairs. There were empty tables and chairs waiting for anyone who might come, and empty beds with covers turned down upstairs.

There was a blind innkeeper and his sighted wife, who was the cook, and their two young daughters, who worked as waitresses and maids. This family knew that Dresden was gone. Those with eyes had seen it burn and burn, understood that they were on the edge of a desert now. Still – they had opened for business, had polished the glasses and wound the clocks and stirred the fires, and waited and waited to see who would come.

There was no great flow of refugees from Dresden, clocks ticked on, the fires crackled, the translucent candles dripped. And then there was a knock on the door, and in came four guards and one hundred American prisoners of war.

The innkeeper asked the guards if they had come from the city.

'Yes.'

'Are there more people coming?'

And the guards said that, on the difficult route they had chosen, they had not seen another living soul.

The blind innkeeper said that the Americans could sleep in his stable that night, and he gave them soup and ersatz coffee and a little beer. Then he came out to the stable to listen to them bedding down in the straw.

'Good night, Americans,' he said in German. 'Sleep well.'

Meditations in Time of Civil War

The Anglo-Irish Treaty of 1921, narrowly accepted by the Dail (Parliament) in January 1922, split the Irish Nationalist movement, since six counties in the north remained part of the United Kingdom and Eire had 'Dominion' status under the British crown. After the pro-Treaty faction won the June 1922 election, civil war broke out. The Republicans led by De Valera were crushed by government forces by May 1923.

W. B. Yeats was by this time living with his wife and children in a converted medieval tower, Thor Ballylee, deep in the countryside. His sequence of 'Meditations' (dated 1923), of which two follow, is controlled by inner calmness. 'Stare', in the sixth, means 'starling' – but also 'stare'.

V

The Road at My Door

An affable Irregular,
A heavily-built Falstaffian man,
Comes cracking jokes of civil war
As though to die by gunshot were
The finest play under the sun.

A brown Lieutenant and his men,
Half dressed in national uniform,
Stand at my door, and I complain
Of the foul weather, hail and rain,
A pear-tree broken by the storm.

I count those feathered balls of soot,
The moor-hen guides upon the stream,
To silence the envy in my thought;
And turn towards my chamber, caught
In the cold snows of a dream.

VI
The Stare's Nest by My Window

The bees build in the crevices
Of loosening masonry, and there
The mother birds bring grubs and flies.
My wall is loosening; honey-bees,
Come build in the empty house of the stare.

We are closed in, and the key is turned
On our uncertainty; somewhere
A man is killed, or a house burned,
Yet no clear fact to be discerned:
Come build in the empty house of the stare.

A barricade of stone or of wood;
Some fourteen days of civil war;
Last night they trundled down the road
That dead young soldier in his blood:
Come build in the empty house of the stare.

We had fed the heart on fantasies,
The heart's grown brutal from the fare;
More substance in our enmities
Than in our love; O honey-bees,
Come build in the empty house of the stare.

La Douleur

Marguerite Duras's La Douleur, *translated into English with that original French title, is a short work published in 1985, in which the author handles memories of France in 1944 and 1945. She participated in the Resistance. She writes candidly, though in the third person, about her leading part in torturing a Gestapo spy. She describes in the first person a non-physical 'affair' with a Gestapo official, strangely attracted to her, from whom she is instructed to glean information about Resistance workers in German hands. Chronologically these episodes precede the first section of the book, from which the excerpt here is taken, purportedly based on a 'diary' of months of agony without news of her husband Robert L. who was captured by the Nazis not long before the Liberation of Paris by the Allies, and entrained to Germany. She is helped through them by her lover D., Resistance name 'Masse'. 'Morland' is the Resistance name of François Mitterrand, later President of the French Republic. By the point where this excerpt begins the 'diary' format has been dropped.*

The sick and emaciated Robert, talking hectically in his fever, is like a benevolent version of Conrad's delirious Kurtz – a man who has seen 'the horror, the horror' but has responded with compassion for the Germans who have caused it.

I can't remember what day it was, whether it was in April, no, it was a day in May when one morning at eleven o'clock the phone rang. It was from Germany, it was François Morland. He doesn't say hello, he's almost rough, but clear as always. 'Listen carefully. Robert is alive. Now keep calm. He's in Dachau. Listen very, very carefully. Robert is very weak, so weak you can't imagine. I have to tell you – it's a question of hours. He may live for another three days like that, but no more. D. and Beauchamp must start out today, this morning, for Dachau. Tell them this: they're to go straight to my office – the people there will be expecting them. They'll be given French officers' uniforms, passports, mission orders, gasoline coupons, maps, and permits. Tell them to go right away. It's the only way. If they tried to do it officially they'd arrive too late.'

François Morland and Rodin were part of a mission organized by Father Riquet. They had gone to Dachau, and that was where they'd found Robert L. They had gone into the prohibited area of the camp, where the dead and the hopeless cases were kept. And there, one of the latter had distinctly uttered a name: 'François.' 'François,' and then his eyes had closed again. It took Rodin and Morland an hour to recognize Robert L. Rodin finally identified him by his teeth. They wrapped him up in a sheet, as people wrap up a dead body, and took him out of the prohibited part of the camp and laid him down by a hut in the survivors' part of the camp. They were able to do so because there were no American soldiers around. They were all in the guardroom, scared of the typhus.

Beauchamp and D. left Paris the same day, early in the afternoon. It was May 12, the day of the peace. Beauchamp was wearing a colonel's uniform belonging to François Morland. D. was dressed as a lieutenant in the French army and carried his papers as a member of the Resistance, made out in the name of D. Masse. They drove all night and arrived at Dachau the next morning. They spent several hours looking for Robert L., then, as they were going past a body, they heard someone say D.'s name. It's my opinion they didn't recognize him; but Morland had warned us he was unrecognizable. They took him. And it was only afterward they must have recognized him. Under their clothes they had a third French officer's uniform. They had to hold him upright, he could no longer stand alone, but they managed to dress him. They had to prevent him from saluting outside the SS huts, get him through the guard posts, see that he wasn't given any of the vaccinations that would have killed him. The American soldiers, blacks for the most part, wore gas masks against typhus, the fear was so great. Their orders were such that if they'd suspected the state Robert L. was really in, they'd have put him back immediately in the part of the camp where people were left to die. Once they got Robert L. out, the other two had to get him to walk to the Citroën II. As soon as they'd stretched him out on the back seat, he fainted. They thought it was all over, but no. The journey was very difficult, very slow. They had to stop every half hour because of the dysentery. As soon as they'd left Dachau behind, Robert L. spoke. He said he knew he wouldn't reach Paris alive. So he began to talk, so it should be told before he died. He didn't accuse any person, any race, any people. He accused man. Emerging from the horror, dying, delirious, Robert L. was still able not to accuse anyone except the governments that come and go in the history of nations. He wanted D. and Beauchamp to tell me after his death what he had said. They reached the French frontier that night, near Wissemburg. D. phoned me: 'We've reached France. We've just crossed the frontier. We'll be back tomorrow by the end of the morning. Expect the worst. You won't recognize him.' They had dinner in an officers' mess. Robert L. was still talking and telling his story. When he entered the mess all the officers stood up and saluted him. He didn't see. He never had seen that sort of thing. He spoke of the German martyrdom, of the martyrdom common to all men. He told what it was like. That evening he said he'd like to eat a trout before he died. In deserted Wissemburg they found a trout for Robert L. He ate a few mouthfuls. Then he started talking again. He spoke of charity. He'd heard some rhetorical phrases of Father Riquet's, and he started to say these very obscure words: 'When anyone talks to me of Christian charity, I shall say Dachau.' But he didn't finish. That night they slept somewhere near Bar-sur-Aube. Robert L. slept for a few hours. They reached Paris at the end of the morning. Just before they came to the rue Saint-Benoît, D. stopped to phone me again: 'I'm ringing to warn you that it's more terrible than anything we've imagined . . . He's happy.'

I heard stifled cries on the stairs, a stir, a clatter of feet. Then doors banging and shouts. It was them. It was them, back from Germany.

I couldn't stop myself – I started to run downstairs, to escape into the street. Beauchamp and D. were supporting him under the arms. They'd stopped on the first-floor landing. He was looking up.

I can't remember exactly what happened. He must have looked at me and recognized me and smiled. I shrieked no, that I didn't want to see. I started to run again, up the stairs this time. I was shrieking, I remember that. The war emerged in my shrieks. Six years without uttering a cry. I found myself in some neighbours' apartment. They forced me to drink some rum, they poured it into my mouth. Into the shrieks.

I can't remember when I found myself back with him again, with him, Robert L. I remember hearing sobs all over the house; that the tenants stayed for a long while out on the stairs; that the doors were left open. I was told later that the concierge had put decorations up in the hall to welcome him, and that as soon as he'd gone by she tore them all down and shut herself up alone in her lodge to weep.

°

In my memory, at a certain moment, the sounds stop and I see him. Huge. There before me. I don't recognize him. He looks at me. He smiles. Lets himself be looked at. There's a supernatural weariness in his smile, weariness from having managed to live till this moment. It's from this smile that I suddenly recognize him, but from a great distance, as if I were seeing him at the other end of a tunnel. It's a smile of embarrassment. He's apologizing for being here, reduced to such a wreck. And then the smile fades, and he becomes a stranger again. But the knowledge is still there, that this stranger is he, Robert L., totally.

He wanted to see around the apartment again. We supported him, and he toured the rooms. His cheeks creased, but didn't release his lips; it was in his eyes that we'd seen his smile. In the kitchen he saw the clafoutis we'd made for him. He stopped smiling. 'What is it?' We told him. What was it made with? Cherries – it was the height of the season. 'May I have some?' 'We don't know, we'll have to ask the doctor.' He came back into the sitting room and lay down on the divan. 'So I can't have any?' 'Not yet.' 'Why?' 'There have been accidents in Paris already from letting deportees eat too soon after they got back from the camps.'

He stopped asking questions about what had happened while he was away. He stopped seeing us. A great, silent pain spread over his face because he was still being refused food, because it was still as it had been in the concentration camp. And, as in the camp, he accepted it in silence. He didn't see that we were weeping. Nor did he see that we could scarcely look at him or respond to what he said.

The doctor came. He stopped short with his hand on the door handle, very pale. He looked at us, and then at the form on the divan. He didn't understand. And then he realized: the form wasn't dead yet, it was hovering between life and death, and he, the doctor, had been called in to try to keep it alive. The doctor came into the room. He went over to the form and the form smiled at him. The doctor was to come several times a day for three weeks, at all hours of the day and night. Whenever we were too afraid we called him and he came. He saved Robert L. He too was caught up in the passionate desire to save Robert L. from death. He succeeded.

We smuggled the clafoutis out of the house while he slept. The next day he was feverish and didn't talk about food any more.

*

If he had eaten when he got back from the camp his stomach would have been lacerated by the weight of the food, or else the weight would have pressed on the heart, which had grown enormous in the cave of his emaciation. It was beating so fast you couldn't have counted its beats, you couldn't really say it was beating – it was trembling, rather, as if from terror. No, he couldn't eat without dying. But he couldn't go on not eating without dying. That was the problem.

The fight with death started very soon. We had to be careful with it, use care, tact, skill. It surrounded him on all sides. And yet there was still a way of reaching him. It wasn't very big, this opening through which to communicate with him, but there was still life in him, scarcely more than a splinter, but a splinter just the same. Death unleashed its attack. His temperature was 104.5° the first day. Then 105°. Then 106°. Death was doing all it could. 106°: his heart vibrated like a violin string. Still 106°, but vibrating. The heart, we thought – it's going to stop. Still 106°. Death deals cruel knocks, but the heart is deaf. This can't go on, the heart will stop. But no.

Gruel, said the doctor, a teaspoonful at a time. Six or seven times a day we gave him gruel. Just a teaspoonful nearly choked him, he clung to our hands, gasped for air, and fell back on the bed. But he swallowed some. Six or seven times a day, too, he asked to go to the toilet. We lifted him up, supported him under the arms and knees. He must have weighed between eighty-two and eighty-four pounds: bone, skin, liver, intestines, brain, lungs, everything – eighty-four pounds for a body five feet ten inches tall. We sat him on the edge of the sanitary pail, on which we'd put a small cushion: the skin was raw where there was no flesh between it and the joints. (*The elbows of the little Jewish girl of seventeen from the Faubourg du Temple stick through the skin on her arms. Probably because she's so young and her skin so fragile, the joint is outside instead of in, sticking out naked and clean. She suffers no pain either from her joints or from her belly, from which all her genital organs have been taken out one by one at regular intervals.*) Once he was sitting on his pail he excreted in one go, in one enormous, astonishing gurgle. What the heart held back the anus couldn't: it let out all that was in it. Everything, or almost everything, did the same, even the fingers, which no longer kept their nails, but let them go too. But the heart went on holding back what it contained. The heart. And then there was the head. Gaunt but sublime, it emerged alone from that bag of bones, remembering, relating, recognizing, asking for things. And talking. Talking. The head was connected to the body by the neck, as heads usually are, but the neck was so withered and shrunken – you could circle it with one hand – that you wondered how life could pass through it; a spoonful of gruel almost blocked it. At first the neck was at right angles to the shoulders. Higher up, the neck was right inside the skeleton, joined on at the top of the jaws and winding around the ligaments like ivy. You could see the vertebrae through it, the carotid arteries, the nerves, the pharynx, and the blood passing through: the skin had become like cigarette paper. So, he excreted this dark green, slimy, gushing thing, a turd such as no one had ever seen before. When he'd finished we put him back to bed. He lay for a long time with his eyes half shut, prostrated.

For seventeen days the turd looked the same. It was inhuman. It separated him from us more than the fever, the thinness, the nailless fingers, the marks of SS blows. We gave him gruel that was golden yellow, gruel for infants, and it came out of him dark green like slime from a swamp. After the sanitary pail was closed you could hear the bubbles bursting as they rose to the surface inside. Viscous and slimy, it was almost like a great gob of spit. When it emerged the room filled with a smell, not of putrefaction or corpses – did his body still have the wherewithal to make a corpse – but rather of humus, of dead leaves, of dense undergrowth. It was a sombre smell, dark reflection of the dark night from which he was emerging and which we would never know. (*I leaned against the shutters, the street went by below, and as they didn't know what was going on in the room I wanted to tell them that here, in this room above them, a man had come back from the German camps, alive.*)

Of course he'd rummaged in trashcans for food, he'd eaten wild plants, drunk water from engines. But that didn't explain it. Faced with this strange phenomenon we tried to find explanations. We thought that perhaps there, under our very eyes, he was consuming his own liver or spleen. How were we to know? How were we to know what strangeness that belly still contained, what pain?

For seventeen whole days that turd still looks the same. For seventeen days it's unlike anything ever known. Every one of the seven times he excretes each day, we smell it, look at it, but can't recognize it. For seventeen days we hide from him that which comes out of him, just as we hide from him his own legs and feet and whole unbelievable body.

We ourselves never got used to seeing them. You couldn't get used to it. The incredible thing was that he was still alive. Whenever anyone came into the room and saw that shape under the sheets, they couldn't bear the sight and averted their eyes. Many went away and never came back. He never noticed our horror, not once. He was happy, he wasn't afraid any more. The fever bore him up. For seventeen days.

One day his temperature drops.

After seventeen days, death grows weary. In the pail his excretion doesn't bubble any more, it becomes liquid. It's still green, but it smells more human, it smells human. And one day his temperature drops – he's been given twelve litres of serum, and one morning his temperature drops. He's lying on his nine cushions, one for the head, two for the forearms, two for the arms, two for the hands, and two for the feet. For no part of his body could bear its own weight; the weight had to be swathed in down and immobilized.

And then, one morning, the fever leaves him. It comes back, but abates again. Comes back again, not quite so high, and falls again. And then one morning he says, 'I'm hungry.'

Hunger had gone as his temperature rose. It came back when the fever abated. One day the doctor said, 'Let's try – let's try giving him something to eat. We can begin with meat extract. If he can take that, keep on giving it, but at the same time give him all kinds of other food, just small amounts at first, increasing the quantity just a little every three days.'

I spend the morning going around to all the restaurants in Saint-Germain-des-Prés trying to find a meat-juice extractor. I find one in a fashionable restaurant. They say they can't lend it. I say it's for a political deportee who's very ill, it's a matter of life and death. The woman thinks for a minute and says, 'I can't lend it to you, but I can rent it to you for a thousand francs a day.' I leave my name and address and a deposit. The Saint-Benoît restaurant sells me the meat at cost price.

He digested the meat extract without any difficulty, so after three days he began to take solid food.

His hunger grew from what it fed on. It grew greater and greater, became insatiable.

It took on terrifying proportions.

We didn't serve him food. We put the dishes in front of him and left him and he ate. Methodically, as if performing a duty, he was doing what he had to do to live. He ate. It was an occupation that took up all his time. He would wait for food for hours. He would swallow without knowing what he was eating. Then we'd take the food away and he'd wait for it to come again.

He has gone and hunger has taken his place. Emptiness has taken his place. He is giving to the void, filling what was emptied: those wasted bowels. That's what he's doing. Obeying, serving, ministering to a mysterious duty. How does he know what to do about hunger? How does he perceive that this is what he has to do? He knows with a knowledge that has no parallel.

He eats a mutton chop. Then he gnaws the bone, eyes lowered, concentrating on not missing a morsel of meat. Then he takes a second chop. Then a third. Without looking up.

He's sitting in the shade in the sitting room near a half open window, in an armchair, surrounded by his cushions, his stick beside him. His legs look like crutches inside his trousers. When the sun shines you can see through his hands.

Yesterday he made enormous efforts to gather up the breadcrumbs that had fallen on his trousers and on the floor. Today he lets a few lie.

We leave him alone in the room while he's eating. We don't have to help him now. His strength has come back enough for him to hold a spoon or a fork. But we still cut up the meat for him. We leave him alone with the food. We try not to talk in the adjoining rooms. We walk on tiptoe. We watch him from a distance. He's performing a duty. He has no special preference for one dish over another. He cares less and less. He crams everything down. If the dishes don't come fast enough, he sobs and says we don't understand.

Yesterday afternoon he stole some bread out of the refrigerator. He steals. We tell him to be careful, not to eat too much. Then he weeps.

I used to watch him from the sitting-room door. I didn't go in. For two weeks, three, I watched him eat with unremitting pleasure. I couldn't get used to it either. Sometimes his pleasure made me weep too. He didn't see me. He'd forgotten me.

*

Strength is coming back.

I start to eat again too, and to sleep. I put on some weight. We're going to live. Like him I haven't been able to eat for seventeen days. Like him I haven't slept for seventeen days, or at least that's what I think. In fact, I've slept for two or three hours a day. I fall asleep anywhere. And wake in terror. It's awful, every time I think he's died while I was asleep. I still have that slight fever at night. The doctor who comes to see him is worried about me, too. He prescribes injections. The needle breaks in the muscle in my thigh, my muscles are knotted, as if tetanized. The nurse won't give me any more injections. Lack of sleep gives me eye trouble. I have to hold on to the furniture when I walk, the ground seems to slope away from me, I'm afraid of falling. We eat the meat from which we extracted the juice. It's like paper or cotton wool. I don't cook any more, except coffee. I feel very close to the death I wished for. It's a matter of indifference to me; I don't even think about it's being a matter of indifference. My identity has gone. I'm just she who is afraid when she wakes. She who wills in his stead, for him. I exist in that will, that desire, and even when Robert L. is at death's door it's inexpressibly strong because he is still alive. When I lost my younger brother and my baby I lost pain too. It was without an object, so to speak: it was built on the past. But now there is hope, and pain is implanted in hope. Sometimes I'm amazed I don't die; a cold blade plunged deep into the living flesh, night and day, and you survive.

Strength is coming back.

We were informed by telephone. For a month we kept the news from him. It was only after he'd got some of his strength back, while he was staying at Verrières-le-Buisson at a convalescent home for deportees, that we told him of the death of his younger sister, Marie-Louise L. It was at night. His youngest sister and I were there. We said, 'There's something we've been keeping from you.' He said, 'Marie-Louise is dead.' We stayed together in the room till daylight, without speaking about her, without speaking. I vomited. I think we all did. He kept saying, 'Twenty-four years old.' Sitting on the bed, his hands on his stick, not weeping.

More strength came back. Another day I told him we had to get a divorce, that I wanted a child by D., that it was because of the name the child would bear. He asked if one day we might get together again.

I said no, that I hadn't changed my mind since two years ago, since I'd met D. I said that even if D. hadn't existed I wouldn't have lived with him again. He didn't ask me my reasons for leaving. I didn't tell him what they were.

One time we're at Saint-Jorioz on Lake Annecy, in a rest home for deportees. It's a roadside hotel with a restaurant attached. It's in August 1945. It's there we hear about Hiroshima. He's got some of his weight back. But he hasn't the strength to carry it. He walks with that stick: I can see it now, a thick stick, made of some dark wood. Sometimes it's as if he'd like to lash out with it, hit walls, furniture, doors – not people, no, but all the things he meets. D. is there by Lake Annecy too. We haven't any money to go to hotels where we'd have to pay.

I don't see him as near to us during that trip to Savoy. He's surrounded by strangers, he's still alone, he doesn't say what he's thinking. He's hidden. He's dark. Then by the side of the road one morning that huge headline: Hiroshima.

It's as if he'd like to lash out, as if he's blinded by a rage through which he has to pass before he can live again. After Hiroshima I think he talks to D. D. is his best friend Hiroshima is perhaps the first thing outside his own life that he sees or reads about.

Another time, it was before Savoy, he was standing among the tables outside the Café Flore. It was very sunny. He wanted to go to the Flore 'to see', he said. The waiters came up and greeted him. And it's at that moment that I see him now, shouting, banging on the ground with his stick. I'm afraid he's going to smash the windows. The waiters look at him in consternation, almost in tears, speechless. And then I see him sit down, and sit there for a long while in silence.

Then more time went by.

It was the first summer of the peace – 1946.

It was a beach in Italy, between Leghorn and La Spezia.

A year and four months have gone by since he came back from the camps. He's known about his sister, he's known about our separation, for many months.

He's there, on the beach, he's watching some people approach. I don't know who. The way he looked at things, his way of seeing – that was what died first in the German image of his death I had while I was waiting for him in Paris. Sometimes he stays a long while without saying anything, looking at the ground. He still can't get used to the death of his younger sister: twenty-four years old, blind, her feet frostbitten, in the last stages of consumption, flown from Ravensbrück to Copenhagen and dead on the day she arrived, the day of the armistice. He never mentions her, never utters her name.

He wrote a book on what he thought he had experienced in Germany. It was called *The Human Race*. Once the book was written, finished, published, he never spoke of the German concentration camps again. Never uttered the words again. Never again. Nor the title of the book.

Auden's Shield of Achilles

W. H. Auden never fought as a soldier, yet came close to three wars. In January 1937 he went to Spain hoping to serve as an ambulance driver on the Republican side, but the government refused his services and employed him only for futile propaganda broadcasting. A year later he went to China with his friend Christopher Isherwood, experienced air-raids on Chinese cities and met generals on the other side in Japanese-occupied Shanghai. His much-execrated departure with Isherwood for America in 1939 when war was imminent could not fairly be attributed to cowardice – its motives were complex. After the end of hostilities in Europe in 1945, Auden, by now an American citizen, went to Germany, in the implausible uniform of an honorary major, to participate in the research of the US Strategic Bombing Survey. He saw at its rawest the damage inflicted by Allied bombers on German cities, the desperate lives of the surviving population – and the recently cleared death camps. 'The Shield of Achilles', written in 1952 as the Cold War threatened yet more devastation, was therefore deeply informed by first-hand experience of war's effects.

In Greek legend, Thetis, the mother of the hero Achilles, fearful for his life in the siege of Troy, prevailed on the god Hephaestos to make him a suit of armour, proof against all weapons. The first item which the Olympian smith fashions is a shield decorated with many scenes, allegorical or representative of everyday life. Auden imagines Thetis overlooking the work of a modern Hephaestos.

THE SHIELD OF ACHILLES

She looked over his shoulder
   For vines and olive trees,
Marble well-governed cities
   And ships upon untamed seas,
But there on the shining metal
   His hands had put instead
An artificial wilderness
   And a sky like lead.

A plain without a feature, bare and brown,
   No blade of grass, no sign of neighborhood,
Nothing to eat and nowhere to sit down,
   Yet, congregated on its blankness, stood
   An unintelligible multitude,
A million eyes, a million boots in line,
Without expression, waiting for a sign.

Out of the air a voice without a face
   Proved by statistics that some cause was just
In tones as dry and level as the place:
   No one was cheered and nothing was discussed;
   Column by column in a cloud of dust
They marched away enduring a belief
Whose logic brought them, somewhere else, to grief.

She looked over his shoulder
   For ritual pieties,
White flower-garlanded heifers,
   Libation and sacrifice,
But there on the shining metal
   Where the altar should have been,
She saw by his flickering forge-light
   Quite another scene.

Barbed wire enclosed an arbitrary spot
   Where bored officials lounged (one cracked a joke)
And sentries sweated for the day was hot:
   A crowd of ordinary decent folk
   Watched from without and neither moved nor spoke
As three pale figures were led forth and bound
To three posts driven upright in the ground.

The mass and majesty of this world, all
   That carries weight and always weighs the same
Lay in the hands of others; they were small
   And could not hope for help and no help came:
   What their foes liked to do was done, their shame

Was all the worst could wish; they lost their pride
And died as men before their bodies died.

She looked over his shoulder
For athletes at their games,
Men and women in a dance
Moving their sweet limbs
Quick, quick, to music,
But there on the shining shield
His hands had set no dancing-floor
But a weed-choked field.

A ragged urchin, aimless and alone,
Loitered about that vacancy; a bird
Flew up to safety from his well-aimed stone:
That girls are raped, that two boys knife a third,
Were axioms to him, who'd never heard
Of any world where promises were kept,
Or one could weep because another wept.

The thin-lipped armorer,
Hephaestos, hobbled away,
Thetis of the shining breasts
Cried out in dismay
At what the god had wrought
To please her son, the strong
Iron-hearted man-slaying Achilles
Who would not live long.

I am the Enemy You Killed, My Friend

A setting of Wilfred Owen's most famous poem, 'Strange Meeting', fittingly concludes Benjamin Britten's War Requiem *(1961). In the first recording, at the height of the Cold War, the soloists were a Russian soprano, Galina Vishnevskaya, an English tenor, Peter Pears, and the great German baritone, Dietrich Fischer-Dieskau, exemplifying the pacifist composer's hunger for reconciliation.*

STRANGE MEETING

It seemed that out of battle I escaped
Down some profound dull tunnel, long since scooped
Through granites which titanic wars had groined.
Yet also there encumbered sleepers groaned,
Too fast in thought or death to be bestirred.
Then, as I probed them, one sprang up, and stared
With piteous recognition in fixed eyes,
Lifting distressful hands as if to bless.
And by his smile, I knew that sullen hall,
By his dead smile I knew we stood in Hell.
With a thousand pains that vision's face was grained;
Yet no blood reached there from the upper ground,
And no guns thumped, or down the flues made moan.
'Strange friend,' I said, 'here is no cause to mourn.'
'None,' said that other, 'save the undone years,
The hopelessness. Whatever hope is yours,
Was my life also; I went hunting wild
After the wildest beauty in the world,
Which lies not calm in eyes, or braided hair,
But mocks the steady running of the hour,
And if it grieves, grieves richlier than here.
For of my glee might many men have laughed,
And of my weeping something had been left,
Which must die now. I mean the truth untold,
The pity of war, the pity war distilled.

Now men will go content with what we spoiled,
Or, discontent, boil bloody, and be spilled.
They will be swift with swiftness of the tigress.
None will break ranks, though nations trek from progress.
Courage was mine, and I had mystery,
Wisdom was mine, and I had mastery:
To miss the march of this retreating world
Into vain citadels that are not walled.
Then, when much blood had clogged their chariot-wheels,
I would go up and wash them from sweet wells,
Even with truths that lie too deep for taint.
I would have poured my spirit without stint
But not through wounds; not on the cess of war.
Foreheads of men have bled where no wounds were.
I am the enemy you killed, my friend.
I knew you in this dark: for so you frowned
Yesterday through me as you jabbed and killed.
I parried; but my hands were loath and cold.
Let us sleep now. . . .'

Coda

The Encyclopedia of the Dead

Danilo Kiš (1935–89) was born in Vojvodina, a province within the former Yugoslavia, to Hungarian Jewish parents who died in Auschwitz. Under Serbian domination, Vojvodina is a microcosm of Eastern Europe, with people of Croat, Magyar, Ruthene, Slovak, German and Romanian stock – altogether twenty-four recognizable ethnicities. Under the rule of Hungarian Fascists, during the second world war, 2,000 Jews and Serbs were slaughtered in Novi Sad, the provincial capital, and their corpses were pushed through the ice on the frozen Danube.

Kiš's story 'The Encyclopedia of the Dead', originally published in 1983, is not specifically 'about war'. But its detail illustrates the dominance, indirect and direct, of war on European life throughout the first half of the twentieth century – a dominance revived in Yugoslavia after Kiš's death.

Last year, as you know, I went to Sweden at the invitation of the Institute for Theater Research. A Mrs. Johansson, Kristina Johansson, served as my guide and mentor. I saw five or six productions, among which a successful *Godot* – for prisoners – was most worthy of note. When I returned home ten days later, I was still living in that far-off world as if in a dream.

Mrs. Johansson was a forceful woman, and she intended to use those ten days to show me everything there was to see in Sweden, everything that might interest me "as a woman". She even included the famous *Wasa*, the sailing ship that had been hauled out of the sludge after several hundred years, preserved like a pharaoh's mummy. One evening, after a performance of *Ghost Sonata* at the Dramaten, my hostess took me to the Royal Library. I barely had time to wolf down a sandwich at a stand.

It was about eleven by then, and the building was closed. But Mrs. Johansson showed a pass to the man at the door, and he grudgingly let us in. He held a large ring of keys in his hand, like the guard who had let us into the Central Prison the day before to see *Godot*. My hostess, having delivered me into the hands of this Cerberus, said she would call for me in the morning at the hotel; she told me to look through the library in peace, the gentleman would call me a cab, he was at my disposal . . . What could I do but accept her kind offer? The guard escorted me to an enormous door, which he unlocked, and then switched on a dim light and left me alone. I heard the key turn in the lock behind me; there I was, in a library like a dungeon.

A draft blew in from somewhere, rippling the cobwebs, which, like dirty scraps of gauze, hung from the bookshelves as over select bottles of old wine in a cellar. All the rooms were alike, connected by a narrow passageway, and the draft, whose source I could not identify, penetrated everywhere.

It was at that point, even before I had had a good look at the books (and just after noticing the letter *C* on one of the volumes in the third room), that I caught on: each room housed one letter of the alphabet. This was the third. And, indeed, in the next section all the books were marked with the letter *D*. Suddenly, driven by some vague premonition, I broke into a run. I heard my steps reverberating, a multiple echo that faded away in the darkness. Agitated and out of breath, I arrived at the letter *M* and *with a perfectly clear goal in mind* opened one of the books. I had realized – perhaps I had read about it somewhere – that this was the celebrated *Encyclopedia of the Dead*. Everything had come clear in a flash, even before I opened the massive tome.

The first thing I saw was his picture, the only illustration, set into the double-column text in roughly the middle of the page. It was the photograph you saw on my desk. It was taken in 1936, on November 12, in Maribor, just after his discharge. Under the picture were his name and, in parentheses, the years 1910–79.

You know that my father died recently and that I had been very close to him from my earliest years. But I don't want to talk about that here. What concerns me now is that he died less than two months before my trip to Sweden. One of the main reasons I decided to take the trip was to escape my grief. I thought, as people in adversity are wont to think, that a change of scene would help me escape the pain, as if we did not bear our grief *within* ourselves.

Cradling the book in my arms and leaning against the rickety wooden shelves, I read his biography completely oblivious of time. As in medieval libraries, the books were fastened by thick chains to iron rings on the shelves. I did not realize this until I tried to move the heavy volume closer to the light.

I was suddenly overcome with anguish; I felt I had overstayed my welcome and Mr. Cerberus (as I called him) might come and ask me to halt my reading. I therefore started skimming through the paragraphs, turning the open book, insofar as the chain would allow, in the direction of the pale light shed by the lamp. The thick layer of dust that had gathered along their edges and the dangling scraps of cobwebs bore clear witness to the fact that no one had handled the volumes in a long time. They were fettered to one another like galley slaves, but their chains had no locks.

So this is the famous *Encyclopedia of the Dead*, I thought to myself. I had pictured it as an ancient book, a "venerable" book, something like the Tibetan Book of the Dead or the Cabbala or the *Lives of the Saints* – one of those esoteric creations of the human spirit that only hermits, rabbis, and monks can enjoy. When I saw that I might go on reading until dawn and be left without any concrete trace of what I had read for either me or my mother, I decided to copy out several of the most important passages and make a kind of summary of father's life.

The facts I have recorded here, in this notebook, are ordinary, encyclopedia facts, unimportant to anyone but my mother and me: names, places, dates. They were all I managed to jot down, in haste, at dawn. What makes the *Encyclopedia* unique (apart from its being the only existing copy) is the way it depicts human relationships, encounters, landscapes – the multitude of details that make up a human life. The reference (for example) to my father's place of birth is not only complete and accurate ("Kraljevčani, Glina township, Sisak district, Banija province") but is accompanied by both geographical and historical details. Because *it* records everything. Everything. The countryside of the native region is rendered so vividly that as I read, or rather flew over the lines and paragraphs, I felt I was in the heart of it: the snow on distant mountain peaks, the bare trees, the frozen river with children skating past as in a Brueghel landscape. And among those children I saw him clearly, my father, although he was not yet my father, only he who would become my father, who *had been* my father. Then the countryside suddenly turned green and buds blossomed on the trees, pink and white, hawthorn bushes flowered before my eyes, the sun arched over the village of Kraljevčani, the village church bells chimed, cows mooed in their barns, and the scarlet reflection of the morning sun glistened on the cottage windows and melted the icicles hanging from the gutters.

Then, as if it were all unfolding before my eyes, I saw a funeral procession headed in the direction of the village cemetery. Four men, hatless, were carrying a fir casket on their shoulders, and at the head of the procession walked a man, hat in hand, whom I knew to be – for that is what the book said – my paternal grandfather Marko, the hunsband of the deceased, whom they were laying to rest. The book tells everything about her as well: date of birth, cause of illness and death, progression of disease. It also indicates what garments she was buried in, who bathed her, who placed the coins on her eyes, who bound her chin, who carved the casket, where the timber was felled. That may give yu an idea – some idea, at least – of the copiousness of the information included in *The Encyclopedia of the Dead* by those who undertake the difficult and praiseworthy task of recording – in what is doubtless an objective and impartial manner – everything that can be recorded concerning those who have completed their earthly journey and set off on the eternal one. (For they believe in the miracle of biblical resurrection, and they compile their vast catalogue in preparation for that moment. So that everyone will be able to find not only his fellow men but also – and more important – his own forgotten past. When the time comes, this compendium will serve as a great treasury of memories and a unique proof of resurrection.) Cleraly, they make no distinction, where a life is concerned, between a provincial merchant and his wife, between a village priest (which is what my great-grandfather was) and a village bell ringer called Ćuk, whose name also figures in the book.

The only condition – something I grasped at once, it seems to have come to me even before I could confirm it – for inclusion in *The Encyclopedia of the Dead* is that no one whose name is recorded here may appear in any other encyclopedia. I was struck from the first, as I leafed through the book – one of the thousands of *M* volumes – by the absence of famous people. (I received immediate confirmation as I turned the pages with my frozen fingers, looking for my father's name.) The *Encyclopedia* did not include separate listings for Mažuranić or Meyerhold or Malmberg or Maretić, who wrote the grammar my father used in school, or Meštrović, whom my father had once seen in the street, or Dragoslav Maksimović, a lathe operator and Socialist deputy whom my grandfather had known, or Tasa Milojević, Kautsky's translator, with whom my father had once conversed at the Russian Tsar Café. It is the work of a religious organization or sect whose democratic program stresses an egalitarian vision of the world of the dead, a vision that is doubtless inspired by some biblical precept and aims at redressing human injustices and granting all God's creatures an equal place in eternity. I was also quick to grasp that the *Encyclopedia* did not delve into the dark distance of history and time, that it came into being shortly after 1789. The odd caste of erudites must have members all over the world digging tirelessly and discreetly through obituaries and biographies, processing their data, and delivering them to headquarters in Stockholm. (Couldn't Mrs. Johansson be one of them? I wondered for a moment. Couldn't she have brought me to the library, after I had confided my grief to her, so that I might discover *The Encyclopedia of the Dead* and find a modicum of consolation in it?) That is all I can surmise, all I infer about their work. The reason for their secrecy resides, I believe, in the Church's long history of persecution, though work on an encyclopedia such as this understandably requires a certain discretion if the pressures of human vanity are to be avoided and attempts at corruption thwarted.

No less amazing than their secret activities, however, was their style, an unlikely amalgam of encyclopedic conciseness and biblical eloquence. Take, for example, the meagre bit of information I was able to get down in my notebook: *there* it is condensed into a few lines of such intensity that suddenly, as if by magic, the reader's spirit is overwhelmed by the radiant landscape and swift succession of images. We find a three-year-old boy being carried up a mountain path to see his maternal grandfather on a sweltering sunny day, while in the background – the second or third plane, if that is what it is called – there are soldiers, revenue officers, and police, distant cannon thunder and muffled barking. We find a pithy chronology of World War I: trains clanking past a market town, a brass band playing, water gurgling in the neck of a canteen, glass shattering, kerchiefs fluttering . . . Each item has its own paragraph, each period its own poetic essence and metaphor – not always in chronological order but in a strange symbiosis of past, present, and future. How else can we explain the plaintive comment in the text – the 'picture album' covering his first five years, which he spent with his grandfather in Komogovina – the comment that goes, if I remember correctly, "Those *would* be the finest years of his life"? Then come condensed images of childhood, reduced, so to speak, to ideographs: names of teachers and friends, the boy's "finest years" against a backdrop of changing seasons, rain splashing off a happy face, swims in the river, a toboggan speeding down a snow-swept hill, trout fishing, and then – or, if possible, simultaneously – soldiers returning from the battlefields of Europe, a canteen in the boy's hands, a shattered gas mask abandoned on an embankment. And names, life stories. The widower Marko meeting his future wife, Sofija Rebrača, a native of Komogovina, the wedding celebration, the toasts, the village horse race, pennants and ribbons flapping, the exchange-of-rings ceremony, singing and kolo-dancing outside the church doors, the boy dressed up in a white shirt, a sprig of rosemary in his lapel.

[*After reading about her father's childhood and adolescence, the narrator finds him in Belgrade. As events in the 1990s would show, his chosen career as surveyor had acute political significance.*]

In that distant year of 1929, one approached Belgrade via the Sava Bridge, probably with the same joy of arrival as one feels today. The train wheels clatter as they pass over the metal trestles, the Sava flows mud-green, a locomotive blows its whistle and loses speed, and my father appears at a second-class window, peering out at the distant view of an unfamiliar city. The morning is fresh, the fog slowly lifts off the horizon, black smoke puffs from the stack of the steamer *Smederevo*, a muffled horn hoots the imminent departure of the boat for Novi Sad.

With brief interruptions, my father spent approximately fifty years in Belgrade, and the sum of his experiences – the total of some eighteen thousand days and nights (432,000 hours) is covered here, in this book of the dead, in a mere five or six pages! And yet, at least in broad outline, chronology is respected: the days flow like the river of time, toward the mouth, toward death.

In September of that year, 1929, my father enrolled in a school that taught surveying, and the *Encyclopedia* chronicles the creation of the Belgrade School of Surveying and gives the text of the inaugural lecture by its director, Professor Stojković (who enjoined the future surveyors to serve king and country loyally, for on their shoulders lay the heavy burden of mapping the new borders of their motherland). The names of the glorious campaigns and no less glorious defeats of World War I – Kajmakčalan, Mojkovac, Cer, Kolubara, Drina – alternate with the names of professors and students who fell in battle, with my father's grades in trigonometry, draftsmanship, history, religion, and calligraphy. We find also the name Roksanda-Rosa, a flower girl with whom D.M. "trifled," as they said in those days, along with the names of Borivoj-Bora Ilić, who ran a café; Milenko Azanja, a tailor; Kosta Stavroski, at whose place he stopped every morning for a hot *burek*; and a man named Krtinić, who fleeced him once at cards. Next comes a list of films and soccer matches he saw, the dates of his excursions to Avala and Kosmaj, the weddings and funerals he attended, the names of the streets where he lived (Cetinjska, Empress Milica, Gavrilo Princip, King Peter I, Prince Miloš, Požeška, Kamenička, Kosmajska, Brankova), the names of the authors of his geography, geometry, and planimetry texts, titles of the books he enjoyed (*King of the Mountain*, *Stanko the Bandit*, *The Peasant Revolt*), church services, circus performances, gymnastics demonstrations, school functions, art exhibits (where a watercolor done by my father was commended by the jury). We also find mention of the day he smoked his first cigarette, in the school lavatory, at the instigation of one Ivan Gerasimov, the son of a Russian émigré who took him one week later to a then-celebrated Belgrade café with a Gypsy orchestra and Russian counts and officers weeping to guitars and balalaikas . . . Nothing is omitted: the ceremonial unveiling of the Kalemegdan monument, food poisoning from ice cream bought on the corner of Macedonia Street, the shiny pointed shoes purchased with the money his father gave him for passing his examinations.

. . .

As for my father's military service, the book traces the marches he took with the Fifth Infantry stationed in Maribor, and specifies the names and ranks of the officers and N.C.O.s and the names of the men in his barracks, the quality of the food in the mess, a knee injury sustained on a night march, a reprimand received for losing a glove, the name of the café at which he celebrated his transfer to Požarevac.

At first glance it may seem quite the same as any military service, any transfer, but from the standpoint of the *Encyclopedia* both Požarevac and my father's seven months in the barracks there were unique: never again, never, would a certain D.M., surveyor, in the autumn of 1935, draw maps near the stove of the Požarevac barracks and think of how, two or three months before, on a night march, he had caught a glimpse of the sea.

The sea he glimpsed, for the first time, at twenty-five, from the slopes of the Velebit on April 28, 1935, would reside within him – a revelation, a dream sustained for some forty years with undiminished intensity, a secret, a vision never put into words. After all those years he was not quite sure himself whether what he had seen was the open sea or merely the horizon, and the only true sea for him remained the aquamarine of maps, where depths are designated by a darker shade of blue, shallows by a lighter shade.

That, I think, was why for years he refused to go away on holiday, even at a time when union organizations and tourist agencies sent people flocking to seaside resorts. His opposition betrayed an odd anxiety, a fear of being disillusioned, as if a closer encounter with the sea might destroy the distant vision that had dazzled him on April 28, 1935, when for the first time in his life he glimpsed, from afar, at daybreak, the glorious blue of the Adriatic.

All the excuses he invented to postpone that encounter with the sea were somehow unconvincing: he didn't want to spend his summers like a vulgar tourist, he couldn't spare the money (which was not far from the truth), he had a low tolerance for the sun (though he had spent his life in the most blistering heat), and would we please leave him in peace, he was just fine in Belgrade behind closed blinds. This chapter in *The Encyclopedia of the Dead* goes into his romance with the sea in great detail, from that first lyric sighting, in 1935, to the actual encounter, face to face, some forty years later.

It took place – his first true encounter with the sea – in 1975, when at last, after an all-out family offensive, he agreed to go to Rovinj with my mother and stay at the house of some friends who were away for the summer.

He came back early, dissatisfied with the climate, dissatisfied with the restaurant service, dissatisfied with the television programs, put out by the crowds, the polluted water, the jellyfish, the prices and general "highway robbery". Of the sea itself, apart from complaints about pollution ("The tourists use it as a public toilet") and jellyfish ("They're attracted by human stench, like lice"), he said nothing, not a word. He dismissed it with a wave of the hand. Only now do I realize what he meant: his age-old dream of the Adriatic, that distant vision, was finer and keener, purer and stronger than the filthy water where fat men paddled about with oil-slathered, "black as pitch" women.

That was the last time he went to the seaside for his summer holiday. Now I know that something died in him then, like a dear friend – a distant dream, a distant illusion (if it was an illusion) that he had borne within him for forty years.

°

As you can see, I've just made a forty-year leap forward in his life, but chronologically speaking we are still back in 1937, 1938, by which time D.M. had two daughters, myself and my sister (the son was yet to come), conceived in the depths of the Serbian hinterland, villages like Petrovac-on-the-Mlava or Despotovac, Stepojevac, Bukovac, Ćuprija, Jelašica, Matejevica, Ćečina, Vlasina, Knjaževac, or Podvis. Draw a map of the region in your mind, enlarging every one of the dots on the map or military chart (1:50,000) to their actual dimensions; mark the streets and houses he lived in; then walk into a courtyard, a house; sketch the layout of the rooms; inventory the furniture and the orchard; and don't forget the names of the flowers growing in the garden behind the house or the news in the papers he reads, news of the Ribbentrop–Molotov pact, of the desertion of the Yugoslav royal government, of the prices of lard and of coal, of the feats of the flying ace Aleksić . . . That is how the master encyclopedists go about it.

As I've said before, each event connected with his personal destiny, every bombing of Belgrade, every advance of German troops to the east, and their every retreat, is considered from his point of view and in accordance with how it affects his life. There is mention of a Palmotićeva Street house, with all the essentials of the building and its inhabitants noted, because it was in the cellar of that house that he – and all of us – sat out the bombing of Belgrade; by the same token, there is a description of the country house in Stepojevac (name of owner, layout, etc., included) where Father sheltered us for the rest of the war, as well as the prices of bread, meat, lard, poultry, and brandy. You will find my father's talk with the Knjaževac chief of police and a document, dated 1942, relieving him of his duties, and if you read carefully you will see him gathering leaves in the Botanical Gardens or along Palmotićeva Street, pressing them and pasting them into his daughter's herbarium, writing out "Dandelion (*Taraxacum officinale*)" or "Linden (*Tilia*)" in the calligraphic hand he used when entering "Adriatic Sea" or "Vlasina" on maps.

The vast river of his life, that family novel, branches off into many tributaries, and parallel to the account of his stint in the sugar refinery in 1943–44 runs a kind of digest or chronicle of the fate of my mother and of us his children – whole volumes condensed into a few cogent paragraphs. Thus, his early rising is linked to my mother's (she is off to one village or another to barter an old wall clock, part of her dowry, for a hen or a side of bacon) and to our, the children's, departure for school.

This morning ritual (the strains of "Lilli Marlene" in the background come from a radio somewhere in the neighbourhood) is meant to convey the family atmosphere in the sacked surveyor's home during the years of occupation (meagre breakfasts of chicory and zwieback) and to give an idea of the "fashions" of the time, when people wore earmuffs, wooden-soled shoes, and army-blanket overcoats.

The fact that, while working at the Milišić Refinery as a day labourer, my father brought home molasses under his coat, at great risk, has the same significance for *The Encyclopedia of the Dead* as the raid on the eye clinic in our immediate vicinity or the exploits of my Uncle Cveja Karakašević, a native of Ruma, who would filch what he could from the German Officers' Club at 7 French Street, where he was employed as a "purveyor". The curious circumstance, also Cveja Karakašević's doing, that several times during the German occupation we dined on fattened carp (which would spend the night in the large enamel tub in our bathroom) and washed it down with French champagne from the same Officers' Club, the Drei Husaren, did not, of course, escape the attention of the *Encyclopedia*'s compilers. By the same token, and in keeping with the logic of their programme (that there is nothing insignificant in a human life, no hierarchy of events), they entered all our childhood illnesses – mumps, tonsillitis, whooping cough, rashes – as well as a bout of lice and my father's lung trouble (their diagnosis tallies with Dr Djurović's: emphysema, due to heavy smoking). But you will also find a bulletin on the Bajlonova Marketplace notice board with a list of executed hostages that includes close friends and acquaintances of my father's; the names of patriots whose bodies swung from telegraph poles on Terazije, in the very centre of Belgrade; the words of a German officer demanding to see his *Ausweis* at the station restaurant in Nil; the description of a Četnik wedding in Vlasotinci, with rifles going off all through the night.

The Belgrade street battles in October 1944 are described from his point of view and from the perspective of Palmotićeva Street: the artillery rolling by, a dead horse lying on the corner. The deafening roar of the caterpillar treads momentarily drowns out the interrogation of a *Volksdeutscher* named Franjo Hermann, whose supplications pass easily through the thin wall of a neighbouring building where an OZNA security officer metes out the people's justice and revenge. The burst of machine-gun fire in the courtyard next door reverberating harshly in the abrupt silence that follows the passing of a Soviet tank, a splash of blood on the wall that my father would see from the bathroom window, and the corpse of the unfortunate Hermann, in foetal position – they are all recorded in *The Encyclopedia of the Dead*, accompanied by the commentary of a hidden observer.

For *The Encyclopedia of the Dead*, history is the sum of human destinies, the totality of ephemeral happenings. That is why it records every action, every thought, every creative breath, every spot height in the survey, every shovelful of mud, every motion that cleared a brick from the ruins.

. . .

READ MORE IN PENGUIN

In every corner of the world, on every subject under the sun, Penguin represents quality and variety – the very best in publishing today.

For complete information about books available from Penguin – including Puffins, Penguin Classics and Arkana – and how to order them, write to us at the appropriate address below. Please note that for copyright reasons the selection of books varies from country to country.

In the United Kingdom: Please write to *Dept. EP, Penguin Books Ltd, Bath Road, Harmondsworth, West Drayton, Middlesex UB7 ODA*

In the United States: Please write to *Consumer Sales, Penguin Putnam Inc., P.O. Box 12289 Dept. B, Newark, New Jersey 07101-5289.* VISA and MasterCard holders call 1-800-788-6262 to order Penguin titles

In Canada: Please write to *Penguin Books Canada Ltd, 10 Alcorn Avenue, Suite 300, Toronto, Ontario M4V 3B2*

In Australia: Please write to *Penguin Books Australia Ltd, P.O. Box 257, Ringwood, Victoria 3134*

In New Zealand: Please write to *Penguin Books (NZ) Ltd, Private Bag 102902, North Shore Mail Centre, Auckland 10*

In India: Please write to *Penguin Books India Pvt Ltd, 11 Community Centre, Panchsheel Park, New Delhi 110017*

In the Netherlands: Please write to *Penguin Books Netherlands bv, Postbus 3507, NL-1001 AH Amsterdam*

In Germany: Please write to *Penguin Books Deutschland GmbH, Metzlerstrasse 26, 60594 Frankfurt am Main*

In Spain: Please write to *Penguin Books S. A., Bravo Murillo 19, 1º B, 28015 Madrid*

In Italy: Please write to *Penguin Italia s.r.l., Via Benedetto Croce 2, 20094 Corsico, Milano*

In France: Please write to *Penguin France, Le Carré Wilson, 62 rue Benjamin Baillaud, 31500 Toulouse*

In Japan: Please write to *Penguin Books Japan Ltd, Kaneko Building, 2-3-25 Koraku, Bunkyo-Ku, Tokyo 112*

In South Africa: Please write to *Penguin Books South Africa (Pty) Ltd, Private Bag X14, Parkview, 2122 Johannesburg*

READ MORE IN PENGUIN

Publish

1900 Edited by Mike Jay and Michael Neve

At the turn of the century, just as today, many people were terrified – or thrilled – by the seemingly unstoppable progress of science, wrestling with questions of sexual identity, turning away from traditional religions or taking refuge in spiritualism, the paranormal and 'new age' philosophies.

From poetry to pulp fiction, scientific polemic to sexological speculation, *1900* brings together a fascinating collage of writings which encompass the amazing range of beliefs, ideas and obsessions current at the turn of the century.

'*1900* offers a striking vision of the fin-de-siècle shock of the new no less than the fatigue of the old, regeneration no less than degeneration, the viewpoints of scientists and futurists as well as decadent poets' Roy Porter

'*1900* is a splendid starting-point for analysis of fin-de-siècle thought and for understanding the millennium' Elaine Showalter